ABOUT THIS BOOK

Every year, summer in Havenwood Falls starts with Midsummer's Night Terrors and ends with Founders Day, and this year is no different. Or is it?

Summer in the mountains offers the perfect setting for summer love and fun. As temperatures climb, relationships heat up. Enemies become lovers. Long-time mates reignite passion. College students and kids of all ages make the most of summer break, discovering true love, making unexpected friends, and awakening to new powers. But when a young oracle comes into her gifts, she brings news that changes everything for the people of Havenwood Falls.

The threat that's been hanging over the town for years, since the first battle with the Collector, has become very real. A solution is proposed that should keep everyone safe—but it's a heart wrenching one that will split families apart. Not to mention the risks that it could potentially destroy not only the town, but the rest of the world with it. But if the Court of the Sun and the Moon decide not to go through with it, all will be lost anyway.

So plans are made. The town prepares. Final moments are enjoyed with loved ones before goodbyes are said. And when the sun goes down on Autumn Equinox, it not only marks the conclusion of summer—but this could very well be the final sunset on Havenwood Falls. For even in this charming fairy-tale town, nothing lasts forever.

Enjoy these 14 short stories that conclude the town's saga, brought to you by *USA Today* and bestselling and award-winning authors in the Havenwood Falls Collective.

Authors in this anthology include:
Kristie Cook
Tish Thawer
Morgan Wylie
Rose Garcia
Belinda Boring
E.J. Fechenda

Susan Burdorf
Amy Richie
S.F. Benson
T.V. Hahn

DON'T MISS OUT!

Stay up to date at www.HavenwoodFalls.com

Subscribe to our reader group and receive free stories and more!

HAVENWOOD FALLS SUNSET ANTHOLOGY 2022

HAVENWOOD FALLS COLLECTIVE

Published by

Ang'dora Productions, LLC

5621 Strand Blvd, Ste 210

Naples, FL 34110

Havenwood Falls and Ang'dora Productions and their associated logos are trademarks and/or registered trademarks of Ang'dora Productions, LLC

Cover design by Regina Wamba at MaeIDesign.com

To the Fans of Havenwood Falls:
You, too, are Family

SUNRISES, SECRETS AND SEXY SURPRISES

KRISTIE COOK

CHAPTER 1

*H*avenwood Falls may have been the epitome of a Winter Wonderland in January, but as I sat on a boulder toward the top of Mt. Alexa gazing across town toward Mount Mae, even this snow-bunny could admit that June wasn't so bad either. Grayish-purple storm clouds gathered over the peaks to the south, and the rising sun's pinkish-golden glow from the east transformed the falling rain into a rainbow waterfall flowing to the mountains below. Grass and pine trees blanketed the slopes surrounding town, wildflowers dotting the emerald- and deep-forest-green with periwinkle, fuchsia, amber, and violet. Mother Gaia and the sky gods seemed to be in competition for who was the master artist, and this early in the morning, I felt like I was the sole beneficiary to their divine co-creation.

As the sun peaked over the top of Mount Sousa, golden light poured down her slopes and flooded the town below, gilding the rooftops and trees. The inhabitants began to stir, and I hadn't even been to bed yet.

Skywalker, my raven familiar, landed on my shoulder, clicking and grumbling in my ear. I sensed Chewie, the wolf, pacing nearby in the forest.

"I know. I'm sorry. We'll go soon," I promised, knowing the other two familiars were likely going crazy since we hadn't come home yet. Kylo Ren and Princess Leia always held down the fort at home. Leia because she was a miniature dragon and couldn't be seen by human eyes, and I liked to think Kylo stayed in to keep her company. But more probable, the tuxedo cat was simply being his cat self—a lazy fat ass.

A twinge of guilt jabbed at my heart for being gone all night, but Quin, my new roommate and ward, was there to keep them company. I'd needed to catch up on some work at the academy last night and fell asleep at my desk. With all but a handful of the college's students and most of the professors gone for summer break, it'd been nice and quiet. Nobody there to interrupt me, which I couldn't say for anywhere else in town. I'd awoken with a start, and as soon as I realized the time, a few expletives spewed from my mouth as I rushed out of my office and down the steps of Halstein Hall, where I promptly crashed right into Dr. Sam Frazer.

"Easy there, lass," said the sexy Scotsman, who was our professor of time and inter-dimensional travel, steadying me with large, strong hands. He studied my face with piercing blue eyes, as though making sure I was okay. He arched an eyebrow, as though to ask, and when I nodded, another drawn-out moment passed before he finally released me. "I, uh, I'm surprised to see ya here, Addie," he stammered, which was out of character. So was his disheveled strawberry-blond hair, looking as though he'd been anxiously running his hands through the curls.

"Yeah, um, same," I said, missing the weight of his hands on my shoulders. Which was weird. Yes, Dr. Frazer was wickedly hot. More than half the student body and the faculty obsessed over him (particularly what was under that kilt). But I'd never considered him as anything more than a colleague. Human touch—I just missed human touch. That must be it. I didn't get a lot of that these days. "I thought you'd be in a different country…or different time by now."

"Aye," he said with a nod. "I have much travel planned for the summer, but I forgot my trusty wuwu."

I couldn't help the weird noise that escaped my lips. "I'm sorry—you're what?"

His hand moved to his waist, and my eyes widened until I realized he was reaching for the little satchel hanging on his belt.

His face flushing, he held his hand up for me to see, and my breath caught for a moment when I eyed the device he cradled in his palm. It reminded me of the Eye of Valerian, a dark artifact that had wreaked all kinds of havoc in my life a few years ago. Like the artifact, this object looked somewhat like an old-fashioned pocket watch at first glance, and when Dr. Frazer clicked it open, several layers of gears and parts lifted out of it, just like the Eye of Valerian. But these were different, marked with unfamiliar symbols and runes, and it didn't pulse with that dark energy that made my spine crawl.

"Nothing to be afraid of, lass," Dr. Frazer said. "It's called a Wuwometer. It's a mouthful, so I tend to call it my wuwu." He paused, his eyes taking a faraway look for a moment. "Guess that could sound, uh...inappropriate." He chuckled, his face reddening again, and I gave my own awkward laugh. "So, yes, anyway...it was invented by our own Tang Wu's great-great-great-times-a-hundred-or-so descendent."

"Ah, okay," I said, as though I understood when I really did not. Tang Wu was Teeny Weeny's new husband, a time traveler himself, so that part registered, at least.

"It aids with time and dimension travel. Also tells me when someone else has crossed the dimensions into the current timeline." Staring at the device, his eyebrows pinched together, and his other hand rubbed at the scruff on his square jaw. He lifted those blue eyes to lock on mine. "The Court's not expecting a special visitor, are they?"

"A special visitor?"

"From another time or dimension?"

My brows lifted. "I don't think so. Why?"

He closed his fist around the device, snapping it closed. "It's probably nothing."

"Dr. Frazer, did someone just pass into our timeline?" If so, I'd need to alert the Court of the Sun and the Moon immediately.

He hesitated before finally answering. "Not just now, but maybe earlier. It wasn't a strong signal, though. I tried to trace it and couldn't find a culprit."

"Would someone coming through the portal from Faerie set it off? Because Chase MacElvoy often goes back and forth." Willow's husband worked for the Seelie Queen herself in Faerie. Time moved differently there, so it could involve time travel. "Elsmed, too."

"Aye, I did have to adjust it for that when I first came here, because they kept setting it off. Teeny Weeny, as well, with her stipple in the ripple, as she calls it. That's probably all it is—just one of them. I must need to recalibrate it." He gave a warm, reassuring smile. "Nothing for you to worry about, lass. I better let you go to wherever you were rushing off to."

He started to turn back toward the faculty's tower.

"Make sure you recalibrate before you leave," I said. "We don't want you to miss the beginning of next semester because your timing is off."

He chuckled. "No worries. I'll be back in plenty of time."

"Good. And I'd love to hear about your adventures."

His eyes lit up. "I'd love to share with you." He paused, uncertainty flashing through those baby blues. "Maybe over coffee…or dinner?"

I nearly choked on my own spit. I wasn't quite expecting that. "Uh…well…okay. Yeah, sure."

Biting my lip, I forced myself to shut up. What the hell was wrong with me?

"Good. See you then." He turned and walked away, and for the first time, I wondered if I just might find out what was under that kilt.

I'd left campus to find the sky lightening in the east, so I'd hiked up here to watch the sunrise before starting another hectic day. Now standing from my perch on the boulder, I snorted at myself for being all flustered about a possible date with the smoking hot Dr. Frazer, which I knew in my right mind should never happen. At the end of last fall semester, I'd been promoted to Provost of the Sun & Moon Academy College of Supernatural Guardians, which pretty much made me his boss.

That appointment had been one of several new responsibilities my grandmother, Saundra Beaumont, had dumped on me when she'd divulged to me that she'd soon be stepping down from all of her leadership positions. She'd told me that last year before Yule and six months later, she still hadn't announced it or began the official transfer of power. Thank the goddess because with everything that had been going on around town, I just didn't have the time or energy to be a Court member and High Priestess, too.

As I approached my home from the forest bordering my backyard, Quin's singing and the smell of frying bacon filtered from the back screened door of my home. I focused on the witch-turned-vampire's incredible singing voice, trying not to think about how Michaela and I had found her body a month ago, even as I passed the spot this very moment. And just a few paces down was the place where Michaela and I had knocked out Travis Mullins, FBI agent. I could still hear the clang of the shovel smacking his skull. What a mess that had turned out to be.

Quin couldn't remember who had murdered her and turned her into a vampire, but the last face she'd seen before that she'd described as that of Travis Mullins. So when Michaela and I found him lurking just beyond my backyard, we naturally took him out with a shovel to the head. Later, when Quin went to the sheriff's office to identify her attacker, she swore Mullins' energy was not the same as the man she remembered—literally made a sworn statement in front of Elsmed Fairchild, who was reading her mind to detect any lies.

Mullins, or Dimples McCocky Pants as Kales and I had dubbed him, was a piece of work. Cute, yes, especially with all those dimples and twinkling brown eyes, but arrogant as hell. He claimed to not know how he'd come to Havenwood Falls or who Quin was, although he'd felt drawn to her in a way he couldn't explain. He only said he needed to protect her.

First of all, bullshit—that was my job. My inner hellhound had been adamant that Quin was *my* ward, which was why she still lived with me. Second of all, the Court had Tasha Young, our local FBI agent and liaison, check on him, and her department said Travis Mullins had gone missing in Europe over a year ago. Elsmed questioned him but couldn't pick a single piece of insight out of his brain regarding who he really was, how he found our town, or what he was doing here. His story was all kinds of suspicious, so of course the Court banished him. I'd escorted him to our ward's borders myself and ensured his memories had been wiped clean—of our town and of Quin. *So long, Dimples McCocky Pants, glad I'll never have to see your smug face again.* Even if my traitorous body quite appreciated that face…and body…oh, that body. I shook my head, snapping myself out of it.

Quin's song cut off before I even climbed the steps to the back door.

"Oh, good, you're okay," she said, turning toward me as I strode into the kitchen, Chewie and Skywalker right behind me. She couldn't actually see me—her eyes had been gouged out, presumably by the same evil asshat who had turned her. All of her other senses, though, including her witchy ones, were ten times stronger than even a normal vamp. Because of this, she probably didn't need protection, but try telling that to my inner hellhound. "I was worried. There was a breach in the wards—"

7

"A breach?" I stopped in my tracks, staring at the young woman, her long, black curls piled on top of her head under a scarf, her body still clad in a tank top and sleep shorts, exposing smooth, dark taupe skin. The image of a calathea plant, symbolizing turning over a new leaf, that I'd given as her permanent resident tattoo, decorated her left shoulder. "When?"

"You didn't feel it?" she asked as she dumped eggs on a plate, moving expertly around the kitchen, though blind. "About an hour or so ago? Right before sunrise."

"Shit. I was on campus, under the mountain." I'd been Keeper of the Wards for not even six months, and this was the second time I hadn't noticed a breach. Although… "That's probably what woke me up, but I didn't realize it."

"Makes sense. It wasn't like normal, how I usually feel it." Because Quin was so energetically sensitive, we'd thought it only made sense to make her part of the ward guard after she'd been initiated into the Luna Coven just last week. All of the coven members were connected to the wards, but a handful were charged with actively monitoring it. "I almost wasn't sure that's what it was."

Double shit. That's how it had been when Quin had arrived—the Lunas weren't sure what had happened. When Quin had breached the ward right behind my house, it had been like she'd fallen from the sky rather than crossed in at the border's edge. We still hadn't figured it out.

I'd barely dug into my breakfast when my phone rang from my pocket. Pulling it out, I frowned at the number on the screen.

"We found another not-quite-dead witch in the forest," Sheriff Kasun barked into my ear.

CHAPTER 2

"*O*kay…but why did you call me?" I asked the sheriff, although my intuition already knew the answer.

"Her eyes," is all he said in reply, and my heart sank.

"Fuck," I breathed as I disconnected the call after he told me where to find them. If Quin had eyes, I could feel them boring into me. Rather, it was her witch senses digging into mine. I turned to her. "Did you hear that?"

She nodded, her bottom lip slipping between her teeth as her chin trembled. "Another one," she whispered. "Like me. I'm going with you."

"Quin—" I began without knowing how to finish. It's not like I had to worry about the gruesome sight and how seeing it would affect her.

"I might find answers," she said. "Besides, if anyone can help this girl, I can. If nothing else, as someone who understands what it's like to have your eyes ripped out of your fucking head and changed into the very thing you've always been taught to hate."

Before I could reply—Kasun never said this one had been turned into a vampire—she was already headed toward her room to dress.

Within five minutes, we were on the slope of Mt. Sousa behind the Rocas' family home, not twenty yards from the cave where we used to sneak off to as children. Where more recently I'd been sneaking off to and creating a portal to see Tase and Carter. Only to check on them, to make sure they were still safe. My hellhound had insisted—that was my story anyway, the one I told to nobody but Michaela. And now I would tell nobody because those visits were over.

"Your scent is quite strong here, Adelaide," Sheriff Kasun said as soon as I arrived. I lifted a brow at the wolf shifter. "Not recent, but in the past few weeks. Rusty noticed it a few months ago, too, on his forest runs."

He let that hang in the air for a moment. No accusation, but close enough.

"Are you suggesting something, Sheriff?" I finally asked. "Why exactly did you call me here?"

His gaze slid over me and then behind me, where Quin stood, before coming back to my face. "Follow me."

My gut clenched as we neared the mouth of the cave, but we didn't enter it. A few yards outside it, a small group crowded around a prone body. Scottlin Glover, a nurse practitioner at the medical center, was one of them, her red hair curtaining her face as she knelt over her patient and victim. Deputy Conall, Kasun's oldest son, stood next to her, speaking with Adrian Roca...and Sindi, another vampire and Michaela's other bestie, holding Adrian's hand. Shit. This wasn't good. The Kasuns inherently hated the Rocas, the whole vampire-wolf thing, so they were always prime suspects when vampires were involved.

But also—when did Adrian and Sindi become a thing?

Quin rushed past me and pushed through the group to investigate the victim herself. Conall, Adrian, and Sindi stepped aside, Sindi's full red lips frowning as I passed. Quin dropped to the unconscious young woman's side, placing her hands over her solar plexus, sensing her energy.

"Is she familiar?" I asked Quin as I squatted next to Scottlin and studied the victim myself.

"No," Quin whispered. "Not exactly."

"What does that mean?" I asked, but she didn't answer. My gaze traveled over the body, the narrow chest rising and falling in shallow breaths. Her eyes had been gouged out, just like Quin's, but the similarities stopped there. She was blond, Caucasian, and quite thin. And she didn't lie in a pool of blood like Quin had. "Has she been turned, too?" I asked Scottlin.

The healer, half human and half witch, turned her bright blue eyes on me. "Hard to say. There are bite marks, but not vampire. They look like a wolf's bite. And not a run-of-the-mill wolf, either."

She pointed to the wound, and it was definitely not a vampire's signature two-hole puncture. Definitely a shifter's mark.

"But you don't know if she'll turn?"

"She will," Quin said, rocking back on her heels. "I sense the wolf magic in her."

I placed my own hands on the woman, replacing Quin's, and sensed for myself. Yep. Witch and wolf energies both ran through her veins. At least that should let the Rocas off the hook this time. The situation was bizarre, though. It was rare for a shifter of any kind to turn someone else. Most weren't even capable. As far as I knew, not any of our residents could, including the Kasun pack.

"Addie," Sheriff Kasun said, "come with me."

He turned toward the cave, and my stomach clenched again. Any more of this and I'd puke up the two bites of egg I'd had before our breakfast had been interrupted.

"Looks like there was one heck of a scuffle in here," he said, taking in the scene. "And conveniently right behind the Roca house."

"A vampire didn't do this," I said, staring at his back because I didn't want to see the mess. I already knew what happened here.

"A vampire may not have bit her, but that doesn't mean one wasn't behind it all. Heard from Atanase lately?" he asked as he squatted next to a break in the salt circle, his head cocking to the side as he took in the broken glass, the burn marks on the walls and ceiling, the shattered amazonite that had once formed Ganesha. "Maybe brought him back?"

"Are you *kidding* me?" I nearly shouted. "He has nothing to do with this!"

He looked over his shoulder at me, a brow raised, probably not liking my tone. "Then you tell me what happened here. Your scent is all over it. I smell a trace of Michaela, too, and other Rocas. This woman was dumped behind their property, right in front of a cave where you've obviously been practicing magic. Quin was dumped behind your own home, attacked by a vampire. You can't deny the connection."

No, I couldn't. But— "I had nothing to do with this."

"Then what *were* you doing here? I'd say about two or three weeks ago?"

11

His sniffer was spot on—it had been three weeks since I'd been here, right after sending Travis Mullins away. I'd needed to check on Tase and Carter to ensure the supposed FBI agent and Quin hadn't been a distraction from something even worse. They were fine. Perfectly. Fucking. Fine.

I pressed the heels of my palms against my eyes, pushing back the tears that threatened, guarding against the images trying to shove their way in.

"Adelaide?"

Without removing my hands from my eyes, I twisted the truth and said quietly, "I was doing a locator spell. That's all. Tase is far, far away, in the suburbs of Chicago."

"Is that all?" Kasun asked.

"That's. All," I said through gritted teeth.

"You're not supposed to be checking on him."

"I know." I dropped my hands and looked him directly in the eyes. "It won't happen again." And that was the goddess honest truth.

"A locator spell isn't supposed to work on them, either," he pointed out. That had been part of the security for both them and the town when the Court had agreed to help ensure their safety as long as they left. Then Kasun caught on. "But you're the one who did the spell. I should have known." Pushing his hand through his dark hair, he let out a sigh, and I knew there would be consequences for this.

"As I just said, it won't happen again. They're safe. I have no need to check on them anymore. My hellhound is satisfied."

He watched me for another moment, and I noticed his nostrils flare as he sniffed my way. One shifter checking another. He was fully aware of what it meant when a hellhound claimed a ward to protect, so it was a reasonable excuse. Plausible enough. He must have believed me, because he stood and strode past me, toward the mouth of the cave.

With a deep inhale, I forced myself to look around and see my destruction, to remind myself that I really was telling the truth. I'd made my decision that day that Tase was in the past. We had no future anymore. My heart stuttered as my mind insisted on showing those memories of that day, the images so clear…

Tase and Carter must have liked Chicago because it'd been less than two weeks since I'd seen them there at the coffee shop, the same day Michaela and I had returned to find Quin's body, and already, they stood in front of a typical suburban home with a "Sold" sign in the yard. A woman, whose face was on the sign, and a girl about five or six years old stood with them. The memories came in quick succession: Tase unlocking the front door. Tase turning toward the woman…leaning over as she lifted on her toes, their mouths meeting in a lovers' kiss. The woman squealing as Tase lifted her in his arms and carried her inside.

My heart pounding, I'd blindly ran for the copse of trees nearby to reopen the portal, a car blaring its horn as it almost hit me. I could barely breathe when I'd returned to the cave, my heart feeling like a vice squeezed it, pulverized it. I kicked at the candles within my ritual circle, the glass holders shattering against the stone wall. My familiars still sat in their designated spots to hold the magic, and one of the candles almost hit Kylo. Princess Leia hissed fire over my head in warning, singeing a black mark on the cave's ceiling. Skywalker flew circles around my head, cawing loudly, as though *that* could settle me down. Chewie, though… the silver wolf only pressed his large body against my legs, and that was enough.

"Get Micheala," I told Skywalker as I sank to my ass in the middle of the circle, the salt line broken during my antics, and buried my face in my hands. My bestie arrived only moments later, swallowed me in her arms, and let me cry it out.

"He's happy, though?" she'd asked when the tears had dried up and I'd been able to explain.

I stared at the amazonite Ganesha in my hands, the talisman that had protected Tase and Carter when they'd left, had returned to me to signal they were safe, and had been my only link to them. The only way to find them. No, a typical locator spell wouldn't have worked, but the talisman had been my secret key to the spell's lock. The only connection we had left.

"He is," I whispered. "Both of them. Happy and safe."

"And that's all we wanted," she replied quietly. "It'll be enough for Xandru. Is it enough for you?"

Nodding, I wiped the remaining dampness from my face.

I knew what I had to do. Swallowing the lump in my throat, I closed my eyes and whispered the spell as I squeezed the amazonite. I knew it was done, once and for all, when it shattered in my hand.

Even if I wanted to check on Tase and Carter again, I couldn't.

And to my surprise, once it was done and I walked out of the cave arm-in-arm with Michaela, I was…okay. My heart didn't hurt anymore.

That hole in my soul that felt like something had been missing since the day he left was healed. My time with Tase, with all of our ups and downs, had become fond memories to be cherished…but in the past.

I had a feeling my grandmother or someone equally as powerful had woven another secret spell into that talisman. Someone who knew I would eventually be okay but that I would need to reach this place in my own time.

Although…if I were being completely honest with myself, there would always be a tiny little crack in my heart that might never heal. Tase had been too big a part of my life since I was a teen.

Still, I'd been so okay that I'd had a fleeting thought to chase after Dimples McCocky Pants just for a roll in the hay. Very fleeting, as I'd quickly remembered what an arrogant bastard he was. There were plenty of hot men in Havenwood Falls who'd be happy for the chance, although I hadn't pursued anything yet. At least, not until Dr. Frazer this morning…

"I need to get her to the med center," Scottlin was saying as I exited the cave. "We'll need to examine her for any other injuries, probably keep her overnight."

"I'm here," Nicholas Jordan, mountain lion shifter and EMT, said as he came onto the scene with a stretcher in hand.

They already had the woman loaded and were carrying her off when Michaela showed up.

"Sorry, I got hung up," she said to Kasun.

"Not much you can do now," he quipped. "Adelaide will suffice as the Court's representative here. Elsmed and Saundra are meeting me at the medical center."

He barked some instructions to his men who were investigating the scene before he and Conall headed down the mountain.

Michaela and I waited until they were far ahead before following. She fell into step next to me and whispered quiet enough that only I could hear, "You're never going to believe who showed up at the inn."

CHAPTER 3

"*Y*ou've got to be kidding me," I groaned as I walked into the interrogation room at the sheriff's office ten minutes later. There was nothing we could do at the medical center for the unconscious girl, so Michaela and I dropped Quin at my house, then stopped here, where the inn's most recent check-in had been brought.

Elsmed actually did not meet anyone at the med center, either, because he and Gabriel Doyle, a vampire who could also read minds, had been here, interrogating someone named Kyle Mason.

Except…he was not Kyle Mason.

Dark eyes lifted to my face, and dimples popped as full lips curved into a grin. "Well, hello, there, gorgeous. About time they sent someone in worth looking at."

"Seriously?" I asked, dropping my hands to my hips. He gave me a blank look. "After all the BS last time you were here, you're going to act like this?"

His brows pulled together for a moment before understanding dawned in his eyes. "Ah, I see. You, like those idiots—" He flicked a hand toward the door where Elsmed and Gabriel were out in the corridor speaking with Rusty Higgins, the forest ranger, and Michaela and Xandru "—think I've been to this quaint yet unhospitable town before. I assure you, I have not."

I noticed a slight accent he hadn't had before—before, when he'd been posing as FBI Agent Travis Mullins. It brought back memories of my time in Norway, where my grandmother Saundra had sent me one summer for my witchcraft studies. I wondered which was real—the American accent or the Norwegian one—then decided it really didn't matter.

His grin returned as he added, "Trust me. I would never forget a face like yours."

I suppressed a snort. Regardless of the name he gave everyone else— either time—he would forever be Dimples McCocky Pants. I also suppressed the thoughts of how easily the supposed love of my life had completely forgotten my face and everything else about me and his hometown.

"How did you get here this time?" I asked.

He rolled his eyes. Were they lighter than they'd been last time? They seemed almost hazel in this lighting. "Like I told them, I don't remember."

"You don't remember?" I echoed with dripping sarcasm.

He shook his head and shrugged. "I woke up on a bus stopped in front of Whisper Falls Inn. I remember nothing before that. The bus driver was nowhere in sight, so I went inside the inn, and the next thing I know, that arsehole with the strange eyes grabs me and hauls me over here. I should be at the hospital, not jail."

That arsehole with the strange eyes had been Xandru. He'd been behind the desk with Michaela when McCocky wandered into the inn. Michaela had said he'd looked disoriented, giving no indication she or the inn were familiar to him, although he had stayed there last time he was in town. Xandru had brought him straight to the sheriff's office while Michaela had gone to the crime scene. And the bus driver? Claimed he never saw this guy get on the bus in the first place.

"Are you injured or sick?" I asked, though I didn't care. I already knew. His story had been nearly identical last time. Of course, then, by the time anyone interrogated him, he *had* been injured, thanks to Michaela swinging my shovel to the back of his head. But he'd claimed to have already lost his memory before that, when he'd suddenly found himself in our town with no idea of how he'd arrived.

"It doesn't take a brain surgeon to know something is wrong, considering I have no recollection of my life before!" he snapped. The flirting had come to an abrupt halt, the cockiness gone. I almost felt sorry for him...if I could believe a word he said.

"Let's see if I can find anything out."

His eyes watched me closely—I didn't miss them traveling over my chest and ass—as I moved around the table and to his back. He flinched when I lifted my hands around the back of his head.

"Are *you* a doctor?" he demanded, and I realized he really didn't remember me. It was easily explainable why he didn't remember being here before. That would be our protective wards at work. People regained their memories when they returned to town, but magic affected everyone differently, so the recollections could come immediately and all at once or they might trickle in over days or even weeks, or somewhere in between. It was possible his hadn't returned—yet.

"No, not a doctor but a witch who has put a spell on you." I figured it would do no harm to tell him since we'd have to wipe his memories again before he even left this room and once more before sending him out of town. Again.

"Yeah, I can see how easy that would be for you. Under any other circumstances, I probably would fall right under your spell, but—"

"Just shut up for a minute, will you?" I snarled, tired of his antics, but also picking up on the magical trace inside his head. Closing my eyes, I focused on sending my energy into his mind and following that thread. "Hmm…"

"What?"

"Shh!"

The previous spell remained. There was no reason he *should* remember being here before. I sensed no other magic, either, except… that one annoying little knot deep within. It'd been there last time, the energy threads impossible to untangle. Now it felt even tighter, the protection around it stronger. He was definitely hiding something. I'd thought that before. But now I wondered if someone else was. If maybe someone had done this *to* him.

"Well?" he asked when I stepped around him and the table and turned back toward him.

"I believe that you believe you've never been here before. And that's exactly how it should be."

He blinked, as though trying to process that. "So what does that mean? Hey, where are you going?" he shouted after me as I slipped out the door. "Are you going to let me go now? By the gods, at least call a doctor!"

Leaning against the door, I paused, my head cocking as I contemplated that last sentence. *Gods*. He had used the plural. Interesting, considering he was supposedly a mundane human. Was that what the knot hid—a protection of his magical blood? If so, then he, or whoever did that to him, knew more about Havenwood Falls than I liked.

The next hour consisted of a debate of what to do with and about him among the sheriff and the Court members, followed by another debate regarding the wolf-witch-girl, who'd regained consciousness with no memory of what had happened to her. Her name was Arya, and like Quin, she'd been abducted and sold into the same magic-trafficking ring, though they'd never met each other. Also like Quin, she may have lost her eyesight, but her other senses were incredibly heightened.

"He showed up at the same time as both Quin and Arya—they're definitely connected," Sheriff Kasun said to the Court in an emergency meeting after lunch.

Tonight was Midsummer Night's Terrors, when the humans were put into a deep sleep so the supernaturals could come out to play as themselves—their true, authentic selves. The Court and the sheriff's department couldn't be tied up in a meeting when that was going on, so here we were in a rare daytime gathering.

"Is he dangerous, though?" Mathilde Augustine asked. "That is the question."

"If he's doing this to the witches, certainly," Saundra said, "but we don't know that he is, do we?"

"Unfortunately, none of them remember anything to help us connect the dots, outside of the trafficking ring," Elsmed said from his seat behind the table on the dais, his silver head cocking from side to side as his frosty blue eyes swept over the other Court members. "Mr. Doyle and I both sense some form of blockage on their minds."

"Some kind of protection," I agreed, and all eyes turned on me. "I noticed it last time with Mullins and again today when I tested to make sure *our* memory spell was still in place." I inhaled a breath, not really wanting to admit this, but knew that I needed to. "To be honest, as much as I don't like the arrogant jerk, I don't think he did this to the girls. As heightened as their senses are, I would think one of them would have sensed him on some level as a threat, and neither have done that.

He might know who did it, though, or at least who's protected their minds."

"I say we threaten him with the sirens," Lawrence Mills said. "Then he'll talk!"

"Or we could offer him for tonight's chase in the woods," I muttered, only half joking. "The shifters would love it."

"Adelaide," my grandmother admonished before glaring at Old Man Mills. "We will not torture him if he's not dangerous."

"We need to know who's behind this," Kasun said, "since they keep sending injured people into our town. But while Addie's idea is outrageous, she makes a good point that tonight is not a good night to risk him out on the streets. My pack knows better than to be vigilantes, but others who get wind that he has anything to do with Quin and now the newest victim, they might try to take things into their own claws. We'll keep him locked up for his own safety for a couple of days."

It was long past midnight by the time I finally stumbled home after Midsummer's Night Terrors, exhausted from the long day and night after only a couple of hours of sleep at my desk at SMA. Goddess, was that really only this morning? Unfortunately, I couldn't go to bed until I checked on the ward breach by Arya. As expected, the break was similar to Quin's—right in the middle of the wards, rather than at the edge. Again, as though she'd been dropped from the sky.

I eventually drifted off to blissful sleep, but whether an hour or four later, I sat up with a gasp.

"Not from the sky. From a damn portal!"

Glancing at the window, I noticed the sun had risen high above the mountains. I checked my phone: 8:06. Four hours of sleep would have to do because there wasn't a chance in hell I could sleep now.

Rather, I immediately began to make a list of who could create portals into town from somewhere else. Some fae could create portals, but only between Faerie and here. There were only a handful of witches capable of creating them, and as far as I knew, all of them were here. Except maybe the Bishops. I couldn't keep track of their comings and goings, and frankly didn't try. This didn't seem like something they'd do, although...Roman hadn't been around yesterday. That was something to note down. I'd taught some SMA students, too, but I didn't think any of them capable of producing a portal that could breach our wards. Outsiders definitely could not portal straight into town—they were the whole reason for our wards. Except maybe powerful deities. That was how Zandra, a Vanir-turned-Asgardian goddess, also known as the Collector (and also known as Kialah), had been able to come to town, although she was usually stealthier than this.

But this was totally something she'd do.

She claimed to have our best interests at heart and only wanted to protect our town and this world from some asshole Asgardian god named Hermod, who wanted to end all magic in our world...which would include ending the existence of all supernatural creatures. Her tactics, though, were always pretty messed up, nearly destroying the SMA campus and our town more than once. She didn't care about collateral damage. To her, the ends always justified the means.

Yep, this had Zandra's name written all over it.

But how could I prove it? Dimples McCocky Pants was the only way.

CHAPTER 4

a week passed, and the dude spilled nothing. His memory never returned, not about being here before or anything prior. But he did seem to know something about his rights because he demanded to be charged or let go. The sheriff couldn't hold him much longer.

"I have a plan," Kasun said at another Court meeting the Thursday evening before the beer festival and 4ᵗʰ of July weekend, and as soon as he finished outlining it, the Court agreed.

A couple of hours later, Kyle or Travis or whatever the hell his name was sat in a CDI delivery truck driven by hellhound Tychon Savage, my bio father, and surrounded by several rumbling motorcycles. The SIN MC was going to escort McCocky not just out of town this time, but all the way to Colorado Springs. Savage and a few others would then follow him to see if he connected with the trafficking ring—or someone else. The Court convinced him that he did indeed need medical attention, after all, but our small town didn't have the kind he needed. They would ensure he was taken to a bigger hospital for proper care.

It was after midnight before I fell into bed, and sometime later I awoke with a start, once again thinking about portals. My windows were still dark, which meant I could go back to sleep, but my phone said it was 6:00 a.m., which meant I should probably begin my day. I'd had a decent night's sleep and much to do. Besides, I wanted to know if Kasun had any kind of update yet. As I turned for the kitchen to start coffee, a familiar surge ran down my spine.

A breach in the wards.

Pausing only long enough to grab onto the energetic thread, I threw some jeans over my sleep shorts, shoved my feet into boots, and rushed out the door as quietly as possible, trying not to wake Quin. I wanted to see if I was right about the portal, so time was of the essence. Chewie beat me to my jeep and jumped in as soon as I opened the door without me having to call for him.

The sky was barely a shade lighter of blue in the east behind me as I drove west, headed to Alverson Road. Turning right, we climbed up Mount Alexa, stars still twinkling beyond its peaks. Chewie sat in the passenger seat, his head crouched down as he watched the road and the surrounding woods ahead of us. Pulling onto a gravel parking area for a trailhead, I jumped out, the wolf right behind me. To the east was the great falls, but we weren't headed that way. We turned to the west, following the direction of the breach.

Since I'd been awake and alert already, I'd been able to latch onto the energetic thread and kept hold of it. I thanked the goddess for giving me the nudge to throw on hiking boots rather than my usual All-Stars or heeled knee-high boots because this was going to be quite the hike. Calling on my inner hellhound, I moved as quickly as I could, keeping my senses open for the scent of blood, sound of a faint heartbeat, the smell of fear...anything to help. Because I feared I'd soon be finding another dead or nearly dead witch.

Chewie snarled at the same time I felt the magical force. We ran through the forest, but I felt the energetic whoosh of a closing portal just moments before we came into the clearing.

"Zandra!" I shouted, although I knew there wasn't a chance in hell she could hear me. "I know that's you. Cut this shit out!"

I spun around, looking for a prone body, but Chewie found it first. It was a lot larger than the average woman, slumped against a boulder near the edge of Peacock Lake. An arm moved, a hand rubbing the head. Chewie crouched and growled.

"Holy shit," the body snapped, the voice deep. And familiar. And annoyingly sexy, especially with that accent. "Whoa, whoa, whoa. It's okay, big guy. Keep those fangs to yourself, if you don't mind. I won't hurt you."

"What in the actual fuck?" I muttered as I stomped toward the man who was slowly trying to rise to his knees, his hands held out in front of him as his and Chewie's eyes stayed locked on each other. "How are you even here? What the hell happened!"

His gaze remained on Chewie. "Is this guy yours? Can you call him off?"

Stopping behind the wolf, I crossed my arms over my chest. "Not until you explain yourself."

"I'm sorry?" He slowly pulled his hazel eyes from the wolf toward me, squinting at first, then widening as he drank me in. That sexy smirk curled one side of his mouth, one dimple popping. "I will tell you anything you want to know."

"Tell me what the fuck you're doing here!"

"Uh…" His face went blank. "I don't know."

"You should be pulling into Colorado Springs right now. Surrounded by a gods-damned motorcycle gang!"

"I should? Why?" He glanced around, taking in his surroundings for the first time. "Where *am* I? And how did I get here?" His head cocked to the side. "More importantly, *who* am I?"

Shit. Not again.

"Where's the witch?" I demanded.

"The *what*?"

"Your traveling companion?"

The guy—no name this time, apparently—shook his head, bewilderment filling his face.

I blew out a sigh. "Chewie, search. I'll take care of this asshole."

The wolf pulled back and began trotting around the clearing, his nose to the ground. Dimples rose to his feet, brushing off his very perfect backside.

"What do you remember?" I asked.

He shook his light brown head slowly, his brows pinching together. "Nothing. At all. I can't remember a damn thing about my life. What happened to me?"

I wished I knew. If this was Zandra's doing, why did she keep sending him back here? There had to be a reason, and it must have been something other than his connection to what happened to Quin and Arya—if there even was a connection. He was a human, after all, so his involvement couldn't be that deep. Unless…

Zandra wouldn't bother sending some human to our town, repeatedly, regardless of his involvement. There had to be something more about him. Something she wanted from him or thought we could use for our defense? *Or maybe...* No, I scratched that theory before even thinking it through. There was no way she would send Hermod himself to us. Would she?

Shoving my hands through my hair, I stared past him at the triple falls on the far side of Peacock Lake. And I had an idea.

Shooting my hand out, I grabbed his wrist before he could stop me and clamped tightly, dragging him to the edge of the lake.

"You see those waterfalls?" I asked him, the faint light of the rising sun barely hitting them but just enough for him to hopefully see. "They're stunning, right?"

"Uh...yeah," he said, trying to pull loose from my grip, though it was a half-ass attempt, his attention more focused on the water in front of us. "Looks like the lake is hanging in the air. Kind of magical."

"Not just *kind of*," I said. "These aren't the great falls, though, the ones our town is named after. This is Smalls Falls. But they're not named that because they're quite a bit smaller than the big ones. See, they're named after the first man who discovered the hanging lake—and died from it. Because this water...it's magical in a different way than the great falls. It has a special effect on magic, but more importantly, this water doesn't like humans. In fact, it kills them." And with that, I gave him a shove, throwing him into the lake, his surprised shriek drowned out when he went under.

"Goddess, I hope I'm right," I murmured, clapping my hands over my mouth as I watched him sink. As if in answer, my phone dinged with a text message. Pulling it out of my pocket, I glanced at the screen, hoping it was the sheriff. Nope, it was from Rhian, an SMA student who also happened to be Rhiannon, a moon goddess of magic and one-time friend of Zandra, shouting at me in all caps:

STOP SENDING MY SURPRISE BACK! HE'S IMPORTANT FOR THE TOWN!

My heart might have stopped beating for a moment as my gaze returned to the perfectly still lake.

"Oh, no!" I lurched toward the edge, trying to kick off my shoes, forgetting I wore the hiking boots. "Fuck it." I swung my arms up to dive in, clothes, boots, and all, but a large dark shape rose from the depths.

Jumping back just as it broke through the surface and soared into the air, I fell on my ass and stared at the sky above the lake with my mouth hanging open. Well, then. At least I'd been right and hadn't killed the guy. I had hoped the lake's water would strip the magical protection on him, but the last thing I'd expected for it to reveal was this.

He was a gods-damned dragon.

CHAPTER 5

J'd seen Jetta Mills, Simon, and others in their dragon forms before, and this one was every bit as jaw-dropping. Iridescent scales gradated from light blue on its belly to a deep sapphire blue over its back, shimmering like rainbows where the faint sunlight hit them. Although larger than a semi-truck or maybe even two, he glided gracefully through the air, circling the lake before turning in my direction. He landed softly in the clearing, the ground barely tremoring under my feet.

And if that wasn't enough of a surprise, when he shifted back...

My throat went dry, my knees weakened, and my uterus tightened as though trying to keep my ovaries from exploding.

At least six-foot-four of bare naked, hard-muscled flesh stood in front of me. Thick, broad shoulders. An expanse of lickable pecs at my eye level. And when my eyes traveled downward over the eight-pack and to the V...

That is...dragon worthy.

My breath locking in my lungs, I snapped my eyes up to his face. And I nearly tripped over my own feet and into the lake myself as I backed up a step.

"Who...who the hell are you?" I croaked out, my mouth like sandpaper.

Travis Mullins did not stand in front of me in this naked gloriousness. Neither did Kyle Mason or Dimples McCocky Pants at all.

Well…the face was the same, with those twinkling dark eyes, although they looked to be a dark blue, not brown or hazel, but that was about it. And not even quite the same—a scar slashed across his forehead and curved down around his right eye, and he wore a mustache and beard, the darker brown facial hair cut close to his jaw line but long at his chin, nearly reaching his chest. His head was shaved on the sides, the top of his sandy brown hair pulled back in a ponytail that hung past his shoulders, some of it in braids. He looked like he'd stepped right off the set of a show about the Vikings.

"Now that's more like the reaction I'd expected for my surprise for you," a familiar female said from the side of the clearing. My gaze swung over to find Rhian standing there with a strange woman and a child next to her. A moment too late, I noticed the zing along my spine from the breach in the wards.

"Rhian?" I asked stupidly, gawking at her. My mind was apparently scrambled from the massive naked Viking sex god in front of me. "This has all been you?"

"Didn't you get my messages?" she asked, her head cocking to the side, making me wonder how she didn't topple over from being so top-heavy. In her normal, everyday form, she was a thin little thing who looked like she belonged in high school, with blue eyes too large for her face and tilted like a fae's and a mass of blond dreadlocks piled on top of her head. Sometimes she dressed like a boho beach bum, but today she wore her other favorite style—tight black pants, a black leather jacket, and combat boots. She rolled those big blue eyes. "Of course—this is Havenwood Falls with its crappy signals. Guess I better catch you up."

"Rune?" the young woman at Rhian's side cried out, her hands held out in front of her, as though feeling for something, and I realized her eyelids were sealed shut by old scar tissue. "Rune, is that you?"

"Liv?" The naked Viking took three steps toward her, then dropped to one knee, bowing his head. "I have been searching through time and realms for you, sister."

Rhian blew out a sigh of relief and grinned at me. "I was right."

"Right about what?" I asked, thoroughly confused.

"Let's get the others, and I'll explain."

Thirty minutes later, we pulled in front of my house, and Quin nearly ran out the door.

"Rune?" she cried out. "You're...you're here?" Although she didn't have tear ducts to cry, I could hear the sobs in her voice.

Arya's reaction was nearly the same when Michaela pulled up with her in the car, bringing her over from the inn.

As soon as the three witches came together, some kind of magical lock broke, and they clung to each other as though they'd been reunited after lifetimes time apart. When Rune, now clothed in jeans by Rhian's magic, joined them, they all fell to the ground in a mixture of laughter and sobs.

"I'm still waiting for an explanation," I said to Rhian, who stood with me and watched, the child clinging to her other side.

"Where do I begin..."

"How about with the Viking dragon shifter dude? He seems to be at the middle of all this."

"Not really, but okay. He really is a Viking warrior. Actually, he's even older than that, but I pulled him from the Viking age."

"You did what?"

"Yeah, that's not the best place to start."

She dropped onto my front steps, the child pulling away to sit next to Chewie, leaning her head against the wolf's side.

"So," Rhian continued, "we'll start with Zandra learning that Rune has been traveling through time and across realms, searching for his sisters. They are singers for a powerful seeress, an oracle from Asgard, and he is their protectors. Their song weaves the magic that allows the oracle to *see* through time and space. We're hoping the oracle might have a solution for us to defeat Hermod when he comes. But when Zandra went to Asgard to talk to them, she found out they'd been separated long ago and sent to various timelines over and over again, finally coming to the same one right here and now. Except for Rune. He's been searching for them ever since. When Zandra discovered this, she convinced me to retrieve Rune first, then the girls. Like I said, I found him in the Viking age, a great warrior who raided villages all on the hope of finding his sisters. I'd hoped by bringing him here first, the sisters would recognize him and make the connection. But you kept sending him away. I mean, how can you send *that* fine specimen away?"

I snorted. "Did you *meet* him before? And what was with all the identities? It was all too suspicious. Of course, we sent him away."

"Guess I should have pinned a note to his shirt," Rhian quipped. "All of this wasn't easy, you know. It was quite the feat, actually."

"What happened to the sisters? Quin's a vampire, Arya's a wolf shifter, and I can sense the bear energy in Liv's blood. And they've all lost their eyes."

Rhian sighed sadly. "I don't really know. The seeress's singers have their own kind of vision, but their eyes can't physically see. That's always been their thing. I guess their eyesight *had* to be taken, but I don't know how it was done or who did it. I'm not the only one who was looking for them, Addie, and I'm guessing whoever else is has different motives. I didn't get to them in time to save them from the vampire and wolf attacks, but at least I got them here in time to save their lives."

"And this one?" I asked, tilting my head toward the child whose arm was now wrapped around Chewie.

"She's another victim of the trafficking ring. She was with Liv when I was able to rescue her. I couldn't exactly leave the child behind. Not in that situation."

"Of course not."

"I can take her somewhere else—"

"We'll take her to the Court first. If she has nowhere else to go, I'm sure we can figure out something for her here."

Rune helped his sisters to their feet, and they all turned to face us.

My eyes locked with his, and something about them now…about him…a jolt of electricity shot through my gut. In a good way. A very, very good way.

I cleared my throat. "So, uh, you brought them to Havenwood Falls because…?"

"To reunite with the oracle," Rhian answered simply.

"And where is the oracle?"

"The seeress is near," Rune proclaimed. "She has been hidden and well protected, but now that I am restored to my true self, I can sense her, right here in your town. If you want to save this world and the magic within it, we must find her quickly."

To be continued…

MIDSUMMER'S NIGHT

TISH THAWER

CHAPTER 1

"*H*appy Litha!" I jumped on my roommate's bed and threw my arms around her neck, thrilled that mid-summer had finally arrived.

"Wow. You're up early. Big plans with Caleb today?" Tempest rolled out of bed and headed straight for our altar. With the strike of a match, the pungent aroma of burning sage filled the room. I closed my eyes as she waved the cleansing smoke around us both and our shared space.

Inhaling deeply, I immediately relaxed. Though my answer to Tempest's question was bound to bring on another bout of stress. "I'm not sure. After our fall-out, he probably doesn't want anything to do with me."

"Oh, yeah. I forgot." Tempest cringed. "Sorry I asked."

I flopped down onto my bed. "It's okay. I think we just started things off at a bad time. Dating in the middle of one of our crazy-ass school projects that nearly got us killed doesn't exactly do wonders for a relationship."

Tempest raised a brow. "Yeah, I imagine not."

"I'll probably just hang around campus and chill by myself," I concluded.

With sad eyes, Tempest ground out the burning embers of the smudge stick.

"It's okay, Temp. I could use some downtime. Litha is all about the fresh start of summer, and I, for one, am ready to start anew."

She smiled sweetly. "So, Natalie 2.0?"

"You got it."

"Well, don't change too much. I love you just the way you are."

I smiled back but thought to myself … *But do* I *like me the way I am?* I wasn't sure. The last couple of years had been hard, but I'd finally processed my mother's death the best way I knew how. And after Caleb and I became close, I thought I'd opened myself up to love again. But seeing how things had ended, I wasn't sure. Needless to say, a little alone time sounded pretty good. I thought it was time I worked on *me*.

Shifting focus, I asked, "Are you sticking around campus? Or do you have plans with Eryx?"

Tempest met my gaze, looking sullen. "After our shift at the park today, I'm meeting him at Napoli's. He's arranged a romantic dinner for us before he leaves for the summer."

"Are he and his brother going back to Greece again?"

She nodded, her gaze dropping to the ground.

"What? You don't want him to go?" I asked.

"It's not that. I mean, I'm glad they've been getting answers from Athena, and I know they owe her since she freed Calix from the stone. And I *am* happy they've been able to build a relationship and grow closer after everything. I just wish… Well, dammit, I wish he'd take me with him." She practically stomped her foot.

I laughed. "Ahh, I see."

"Yeah. Well, since that's not possible, I'll be staying in Havenwood Falls but will most likely be chilling at Micah's with Holly and Sedona. You can come hang out there too, ya know. They'd love to have you."

Her offer was generous, and I did love spending time with them all, but there was a pull in my gut for the need to be alone. "Actually, since Mystic and Malyki have moved into the teacher's tower, I think I'll stay in their old room next door."

Tempest stiffened. "Are you saying you want to *move* next door? As in, no longer be my roommate?"

"No. No way, Temp. I just want to treat this like a mini vacation… or what do the old people call them…a *stay-cation*?" I joked. "I think a change of scenery, or at least a change of rooms, will help with that."

"Gotcha." Tempest relaxed. "I'm gonna jump in the shower and head to the park. See you there in a bit."

I smiled, but was dreading my shift today. I loved Litha—or

Midsummer as the humans referred to it—and during the day the entire town square was filled with people in costumes, enjoying the revelry like a Shakespeare's play had come to life. But in Danzan Park, where we'd be working, the space turned into a mini renaissance faire, with artists' booths selling goods and food, while jugglers and musicians entertained the guests throughout the day. SMA had a booth there this year, and my shift started in an hour, but it was the events later that night that put me on edge, when a Midsummer's Dream turned into Midsummer's Night Terrors.

At night, everything changed. Almost all of the humans would be put into a deep magical sleep so all of the supes could come out and really play. Magic, mayhem, and dancing ensued, along with games and competitions. But unlike Founders Day, this night could become quite sinister, and for some reason, my witch's intuition had me on high alert.

CHAPTER 2

*S*tanding in our school's booth, I adjusted the sunflower circlet on my head for the hundredth time, handing one to match to the next girl in line. Tempest and I spent last week weaving the flowers into the headpieces we wanted to give away. Between those and the honey we had available to sell, we'd seen a steady flow of customers throughout the morning.

Pink and blue ribbons blew loosely in the wind from the bottom of the little girl's braids. "Here you go, sweetie. Happy Litha!" I smiled and waved as she bounced away.

"How long do we have to stay here?" Tempest asked, less cheerful than she'd been back in our dorm tower.

"Our shift ends at five-thirty. So…another two hours, I think."

"Good. Because as much as I love this Sabbat, I really need to get off my feet."

I looked down at my best friend's choice of shoes and rolled my eyes. "Maybe if you didn't wear five-inch heels to a school-sponsored event, you wouldn't be in so much pain."

Tempest stuck out her tongue. "Come on, Nat. You know I *looove* me some fashion. Plus, I wanted to look good for Eryx. Remind him what he'll be missing while he's in Greece."

I shook my head. "Girl, there's no way anyone could forget you." Smiling wide, I nodded to the stool behind our makeshift counter.

"Why don't you relax for a bit. Kick off those shoes, and I'll handle the rest of the customers for today."

Tempest sank down onto the wooden seat, crossing her leg over a knee and easing off her red stiletto. "Thanks, but I should be good to go again here in a few."

I turned back to the park and regretted my offer immediately. Coming face to face with Caleb, all I wanted to do was duck behind the decorative scarves hanging behind me. Instead, I lifted the flower wreath in my hand, offering him the girly circlet. "Hi. Happy Litha."

Caleb laughed and took the crown, placing it cock-eyed on his head. "Thanks. This rounds out my outfit perfectly, don't you think?"

God, I missed him. His smile, his light sense of humor…his caring ways. "Indeed it does."

He shifted on his feet, then said, "I actually came to buy a couple jars of honey, if that's okay."

My smile grew. Of course the bear-shifter was here for the honey.

"Sure. Let me grab them." I walked to the back of the booth, lifting out two glass jars of the honey our horticulture class had gathered this past season.

"Here you go. That'll be twenty-four dollars."

Caleb counted out the bills, laying them on the counter instead of placing them in my hand. "Thanks. Um, see ya later, I guess."

"Sure. I guess." I shrugged, my chest tightening as he walked away.

"Wow. That was…*awkward*," Tempest teased.

"Yeah, well. It is what it is." I grabbed another flower circle and thrust it toward the next girl in line. "Here you go, kid."

"*Okay*…time to switch back. I've got this. You go relax or something."

I wiped my eyes before turning around. "You sure?"

Tempest nodded, a knowing smile plastered on her face. "I'm sure. I'll close things out here. You just go. Take some time, and I'll see you at the party later tonight."

"Thanks, Temp. You're the best."

I felt bad leaving her alone, but smiled as she slipped off her other shoe, standing barefoot in the grass with sunflowers in her hair. She was the epitome of a summer goddess. And even though water was her strongest element, she glowed as if filled by the fire magic of Midsummer's Day. I was lucky to call her my friend.

37

Easing out the back of the booth, I looked left and right, deciding where to go. I didn't want to return to campus just yet, but I also wasn't in the mood to meander through the crowds currently filling Danzan Park. I started walking west, enjoying the fresh air and letting my feet lead the way.

I passed multiple couples with kids in tow, teenagers laughing and rushing to join in on the festivities behind me, but I kept walking until the streets thinned. Looking up, I found myself in another park on the opposite side of town. Cook's Corner Park was empty, and I couldn't be more grateful.

The green space was perfectly manicured and had small walled gardens scattered throughout with beautiful stone paths leading to sitting areas that contained benches here and there. A bronze fountain marked the center of the park. Three mermaids carved into the bottom appeared as if they were holding up each of the three tiers. Water fell softly down each layer, as wildflowers, butterflies, and vine-covered arches wavered gently in the wind.

This place was so charming. Quiet. And somewhere I felt safe enough to let my tears finally flow.

CHAPTER 3

*a*fter a good cry—or four—I pushed off the bench and retraced my steps back down the stone path. Turning left, I ducked beneath the hanging wisteria and emerged on a completely different side of the park.

Across the street stood the town's rebuilt library, it's gothic-Victorian design framing two large front doors. I'd only been inside once and remembered loving the carved wooden gargoyles that flanked the balcony on the second floor. Apparently, it was an ode to the architect, Everett Weston.

While the library was closed for the festival, my feet continued forward, leading me around the side and to the back of the building. Grassy walkways continued to encircle the grounds, blooming with planted beds of phlox, poppies, lilies, and columbines in a variety of colors.

Walking on, I crossed First Street then meandered past the high school. Classes had ended almost a month ago, so the campus was quiet besides the birds chirping and fluttering around the green space that extended from the back of the building toward the cemetery and then the edge of the woods. Crossing the open space and Blackstone Road, I tiptoed under the canopy of trees, staring up into the intermixed branches of evergreens, birch, and aspens, then continued forward into the wild beyond.

I'd never ventured to this part of the woods before, and the deeper I walked, everything seemed to grow denser, darker, and more intense—including the pull of magic guiding my feet.

Stopping, I closed my eyes to concentrate, letting the hum of it call to my witch's soul.

A tingle crept up my body, starting at my toes and rising like tiny ants were marching toward my heart. It didn't feel evil, but there was definitely a strange tint to it...like nothing I'd experienced in all our training at SMA—which was a lot.

Taking a deep breath, I reinforced my bubble of protection, casting out the invisible barrier that never failed to keep me safe. But the next thing I knew, I was waking up with my back propped against a tree, sitting deeper inside the forest than I'd ever been. *How the hell did I get out here?* I pushed to stand, wiping my hands on the front of my jeans. The snap of a twig drew my attention to a cluster of ferns about ten feet away.

"Hello? Is someone there?"

The ferns shook with a tinkle of laughter, and I wondered if perhaps some of Madame Tahini's forest friends were playing a trick on me.

"Okay, you can come out now. Stop messing around." I headed back to the path, looking left and right. "Which way leads back to town?" The path here was no more than a barely-worn foot trail, and despite peering down its length in both directions, I still couldn't get my bearings.

Another trill of laughter floated from the woods behind me. I spun to see a tiny creature, dressed in tan baggy pants and a green felt vest emerge from the overgrowth. This was *not* one of Teeny Weeny's pixie friends.

"Who the hell are you?" I demanded, my hands dramatically going to my hips.

A tiny squeak was the only response I heard, though I somehow *knew* I'd been given his name...Berg.

"Well, Berg. I'd like to know how I got here, but more importantly...how do I get home?"

He shuffled closer, his tiny feet barely moving an inch. I knelt down for a closer look and noticed a thick plait of dark brown hair braided down his back, lying perfectly in the middle of a pair of almost transparent wings.

"Are you a fairy?" I asked, genuinely curious.

A shrill squeak, then he crossed his arms.

"Sorry. My apologies…a *Folk of the Forest*." I tilted my head, noticing the silver threads weaving a design around the side of his vest. Peering over his head and around his back, I recognized the design stitched in the center—a Nordic cross.

My mind spun, worried this was somehow a message from our classmate and goddess, Rhian, or worse, a messenger from Zandra herself.

"How did you get all the way out here?" I stood up straight, scanning the forest for any signs of a threat.

The sound of bells, or perhaps wind chimes, drifted to my ears, coming from even deeper in the forest somewhere behind Berg.

I nodded in that direction. "Is that where you live?"

Berg squeaked again, the sound tickling my ears, then he was off—skipping and hopping over plants and broken logs. I followed him with ease, my strides eating up large distances compared to his.

The trees were different here. Thicker. Maybe oak or ash, I thought. I forced myself to remain calm and smiled as I watched them sway gently above our heads in the warm summer breeze.

"Are we almost there?" I asked Berg.

The bells grew louder, answering for him instead.

After hopping a few more logs, I looked up and froze.

Caleb, Bale, Cade, and another guy whose name I'd forgotten all stood in front of the tiniest house I'd ever seen. Each clutching a bouquet of flowers in their hands.

"What the hell is this?" I stepped forward, demanding answers from any of the guys before me. All of whom I'd either liked, or at least thought was cute, at one point or another over the last three years at school.

More squeaking came from behind me.

"What do you mean they can't answer me? What's really going on here?"

Berg traipsed to the front porch of his fairy house, and with a tiny hand and an ornery smirk, batted the wind chimes above his head. Music filled the forest, blaring as if a band was hiding out in the trees.

All four guys stepped forward methodically, extending their flowers and intoning at the same time, "I love you, Natalie."

What the fuck?

CHAPTER 4

*A*t this point, I looked around in earnest, pulling on my magic to find out where we were.

"Caleb. Can you hear me?" I took a step toward my recent ex, hoping I could at least break through to *him*.

His brown eyes were still warm and inviting, but somehow carried a far-off gleam. I waved my hand in front of his face, looking for any hint of his presence at all.

Berg squawked something from his front porch, then disappeared inside his tiny wee-folk house.

"What? No way am I dating all these guys at once." I pushed through their line of muscle, kneeling to knock on the tiny front door. "Get back out here and fix this, Berg!" I demanded. "I have no interest in love right now."

A grumble sounded behind me, the energy shifting in the air.

I turned around and gasped. Caleb was mid-shift, his bear claw destroying the bouquet in his hand. Bale's dragon wings were stretching into the air from over his shoulders, and Cade's eyes burned red behind his sunglasses as his hellhound rose to the surface. The other guy, whose name I couldn't remember, stood there still as a statue until he muttered one word.

"Run."

Shit!

Breaking for the thickest part of the forest behind me, I pushed my legs, running as fast as I could. I was in pretty good shape from all the training we did at the Academy, but there was no way I could outrun a bear, a dragon, and a hellhound without a little magical help.

I pushed my hand out in front of me and hoped like hell this would work. I hadn't been formally trained in creating portals yet, but I'd seen Addie create a couple of them recently—actually, that wasn't true. I'd *felt* the residual magic of the portals Addie had created recently when I was hiking up on Mt. Sousa. Luckily, I was pretty sure of the energy signature she used…*maybe*.

Branches, and what sounded like entire trees, snapped behind me, pushing me farther into the unknown. I'd never attempted anything like this before, but there was nothing else I could do. With a quick look over my shoulder revealing the press of fangs and claws, I spouted my spell and ran through the resulting split in the air, hoping for the best.

I hit the ground with a thud, silence falling in waves. The oppressive unnaturalness of it pushed my back down into the dirt. A hazy sky wavered above me, like a watercolor painting not quite complete. The tips of the trees still looked the same, but everything felt different. Felt…*off*.

I sat up and started to panic. Sparkling plants covered the forest floor, shimmering proudly in a strange oddness. I was definitely no longer in Havenwood Falls and was beginning to think I hadn't been since first waking up and meeting Berg.

Moving into a crouch, I scanned the surrounding area for threats and luckily found myself alone. I stood up and looked deeper into the trees, making out a clearing at the bottom of the next hill. From this distance, the location appeared normal, but as my feet shuffled through the glittering plants, I knew this place was anything but. The haziness of the air made me feel as if I was wading through one of Addie's imaginary tests, but I knew that wasn't the case. With each step I took, the more unsafe I felt.

Pulling my magic to the surface, I kept my head on a swivel and marched forward in search of answers. As far as I could tell, none of the guys had followed me here, but I wasn't about to let my guard down. The only thing running through my head was finding Berg. I somehow knew this was entirely his fault.

"Berg," I whisper-yelled, hoping the fairy would appear out of thin air like I totally knew he could.

Multiple voices hit my ears, carried on the wind from the clearing down below. I crept to the top of the small hill then lay flat on my stomach, peering over its crest.

A green area about the size of a football field was full of tables and chairs, decorated with fine china, vases of flowers, and candelabras lining the center of them all. I suddenly worried I might be walking into an Alice-type situation.

"Have you come to join us for tea?"

I jerked away from a tiny voice practically shouting into my ear. Peering down into the grass, I spotted another fairy similar to Berg's size, but the beauty before me had long blond hair and a tiny floral belt cinching the waist of her gossamer gown.

Yep. This is some Wonderland fuckery for sure.

CHAPTER 5

"*H*i! Could you possibly tell me where I am?" I asked.

The tiny fairy cocked her head, looking around like she couldn't believe how stupid I was.

"You're in the Faerie realm, of course," her tiny voice squeaked out in reply.

Of course.

I knew multiple people from school who'd ventured between Faerie and Havenwood Falls, but I'd never actually been here myself. And honestly, I had no idea how I'd ended up here now.

"Come, come. Join us. My husband will be so happy you made it." She waved me forward.

"Your husband?" I asked, falling in step behind her.

"Yes. Berg. He always sends me the most interesting guests."

I stopped short.

"Wait. Berg is your husband? And you're saying *he's* the one who brought me here?"

She nodded her head. "Yes, and just in time for my afternoon tea."

I gawked around the forest again, completely confused how my day had been hijacked by the tiny fae.

"Do you mind if I ask what type of fairies you and your husband are? I've never met anyone like you before," I rushed on.

"We are the Landvaettir. Norse land spirits. We heard the call and settled near your mountains here, as is our nature. Now, please come, come. Before the tea gets cold."

What in the world? Norse fairies, here?

This could not be good.

"What's your name?" I asked, following along again.

"Ingrid."

"Well, Ingrid, I have to admit, I'm surprised to be here and would love to talk to Berg about it. Will he be joining us?"

A loud roar pierced the air.

"Of course. He and your suitors are already here."

My head snapped to the tables below, and there, caught between their human bodies and a full shift, were all four guys, each sitting at the head of a different table.

"Okay, seriously…what the hell is going on?"

Ingrid's tiny brow creased, and her entire body started to tremble. An explosion of energy, petals, and leaves burst before me, settling to reveal a beautiful full-sized fae queen. With antlers in her hair and her floral belt still in place, she waved me on. "I thought, perhaps, I'd be better suited to help you like this."

I eyed her up and down, awed by her wild beauty and delicate violet eyes. "Help me, how?"

"To choose your mate, of course."

My mouth dropped open. "I don't understand. I'm just a witch. And witches don't choose mates," I stammered.

She ticked her foot. "Hmm, maybe mate is the wrong word. Come, let's see what Berg has to say."

Yes, I thought, *let's see what the little bastard has to say.*

Following Ingrid down the hill, I stared at Berg while keeping the other guys in my periphery.

"Darling, our guest seems to be a little confused as to why she's here. Do you care to explain?"

Squeak. Berg sat back in his chair, crossing his arms.

"What do you mean, no?" I leaned down, bracing both hands on the edge of the table.

Ingrid laid a gentle hand on my shoulder. "I think what he means is…*No*, he doesn't care to explain."

I barked a laugh. "Thanks. I got that. I just don't understand why."

"Let's have a seat, and perhaps all will be revealed."

I huffed but took a seat beside her, not seeing much of a choice. Berg sat at the head of the table with Ingrid and me placed to his left. Across the plates and vases, I stared at the other tables, each with a friend in the midst of their own personal struggle. "Why are you holding them like that? Between their shifts?"

The gruff fairy looked to his wife, frowning and emotive, as if they were having a private conversation.

Ingrid dipped her head then explained. "From our experience, once a full shift is made, they are too much animal to consider their hearts. But held between, they can use all their natural instincts *and* decide for themselves where their human hearts truly lie."

My brow creased. "Wait. I thought I was the one picking my 'mate'. Are you saying they also have a choice of whether they want to be with me?" All my insecurities rose to the surface, choking me where I sat.

Squeak. Berg shook his head.

"I'm not sure *choice* is the right word." Ingrid continued, "The entire purpose of this is to follow your hearts...your wild, youthful, uninhibited hearts. Only then will fate step in and reveal what's meant to be. We're just trying to help you along the way."

I looked between the two fairies, suddenly wondering why Ingrid could speak to me in plain English but Berg could not. Even though I understood most of what he said, all I could hear was his squawking replies.

"How is it that you can speak plainly to me, but Berg cannot?"

Ingrid smiled. "Because I am the queen of our people, and Berg is simply *my* mate."

47

CHAPTER 6

Seated next to a fairy queen in the realm of the fae was not how I saw my solstice going. Berg picked up a tiny bell from next to his plate and rang it three times.

"It's time," Ingrid announced. "All you need to do is have a meal with each of your suitors and let fate take its course."

I glanced at the other tables. All the guys seemed to have settled a bit, but it was still hard to see them in their current state. Caleb reminded me of the beast from *Beauty and the Beast*—half bear, half man. While Bale looked like a gothic prince out of a fantasy movie—his hardened dragon wings twitching in the air while his face remained as beautiful as ever. Cade, on the other hand, just looked pissed. He'd tracked me from the moment I entered the field, the intense glow of his red eyes continuing to flare behind his sunglasses. And then there was the human guy I still couldn't remember. He had to be a shifter of some kind if he was attending SMA with me, but as hard as I tried, I couldn't pinpoint his name or what tower he was from.

"Do you know who the fourth guy is?" I asked Ingrid, embarrassed as I nodded in his direction.

"We know nothing of your heart's choices."

My heart's choices? I stared at Caleb and was rooted in place. He and the other unknown guy were my only true *options*, seeing as Bale and Cade were already spoken for. And while I may have had a crush on each of them at one time or another, I could never imagine being with them for real.

My head snapped to Ingrid. "Can I send two of them home now, if I choose?"

I didn't see the point of carrying on with such a charade.

She looked to Berg, who simply nodded.

I didn't understand why he seemed more in charge than her—the queen—but was grateful he agreed. In the next moment, Bale and Cade disappeared, without me even voicing my selections.

"How did you know?" I asked.

Squeak. Berg shrugged.

"Your heart is open, Natalie. Ready for love and easy to read."

My cheeks flushed. I didn't think I'd ever been a very "open" person, especially when it came to love. But hearing Ingrid's words made me... proud, I guess. Maybe I really was starting to grow.

Excusing myself from the elaborate main table, I made my way over to the human-looking guy first.

Caleb's growl rattled the trees around us.

I met my ex's honeyed eyes and held up a finger. "I'll be with you in just a bit."

It felt so silly to go along with all of this, but glancing back, I knew I didn't have a choice. The sneer on Berg's little face made me shiver, like he was ready to transform and devour us all. Ingrid remained seated next to him, still full-sized, and with the kind smile of a queen in place.

"How are you handling all this?" the guy asked, pulling my attention back to the table.

Meeting his dark eyes, I took in his sandy brown hair hanging longer in the front and gauged him to be in his early twenties. But you could never really tell in Havenwood Falls.

"Honestly, I don't even know what *this* really is?"

"Isn't it obvious?" He smirked and tipped his chin toward the fairy pair. "We're at the mercy of another version of Puck."

I gasped. "What? Puck from Shakespeare's *Midsummer's Night Dream*? You've got to be kidding me." I snapped my gaze around to the main table again, giving both of them a sneer of my own. "Do you mean this is some messed-up fairy trick to make us all fall in love with each other until the spell wears off?"

"I don't know the specifics, but after putting two-and-two together since being magically dumped outside a tiny house with a bouquet of flowers in my hand, that made the most sense. Needless to say, you looked even more surprised to be there than I was." He laughed, his deep voice ringing gently through the trees.

I smiled, nodding in agreement, then rallied my courage. "I'm sorry, but I don't remember your name or what type of supe you are. I'm only asking, because you're not shifting like the others," I rushed on.

Rolling up the sleeves of his button-down shirt, he took a moment to answer. "I'm Jadiel. A watcher angel."

Oh my God! I did remember him. "Mr. Brauner?"

He dipped his head.

This gorgeous, twenty-something-looking man was actually the principal at the elementary school, and the subject of my "hot for teacher" phase when I first moved here.

"I'm surprised your wings aren't fighting to get free," I blurted awkwardly, not knowing what else to say.

He shifted in his chair. "I was exiled from Heaven for loving a human woman. It was only platonic, but it was enough to get me in trouble. But that was a long time ago."

I assumed him not having wings was part of his punishment, but there was no way I was going to ask that question. "Well, I'm so sorry you've been pulled into this. I have no idea why this is happening to me."

He cocked his head, and in a very teacherly voice asked, "Why do you think that is? That *you* were targeted by their spell?"

I thought back to my cry-session in the Cook's Corner Park and wondered if they'd heard or felt my despair in some way. I remembered Ingrid saying something about *"We heard the call...",* but I still didn't understand what that meant.

"I think they probably felt my sadness when I was alone in the park. Easy pickins, I guess."

He squinted, giving me a look like he didn't buy it. And honestly, neither did I.

CHAPTER 7

"*W*ell, whatever the reason is, I'd follow this through to its end. Messing with a fairy spell isn't for the faint of heart," Mr. Brauner shared.

I completely agreed with him and knew it was time to move to the next table... Time to move on to Caleb. "Thanks for the advice, and again...I'm sorry you got mixed up in all this."

He reached for my hand. "If you don't mind me asking, do you know why *I* got pulled into this?"

Oh, God. This was going to be mortifying.

"Um...I think because I had a crush on you at one point." I shrugged. "When I first moved here," I clarified, hoping he didn't think I still liked him now.

"Ah! Well, I'm flattered." He stood from the table. "Good luck, Natalie. Maybe I'll see you around."

I dipped my head, thankful he disappeared—sent home by the spell —before noticing my reddening cheeks.

I inhaled deeply, taking a moment to center myself before moving on. Glancing back at Berg and Ingrid, I found their eyes were still plastered to me, curious and expecting. Obviously, I was meant to choose Caleb as my "mate" in this f-upped game, but why in the world did it matter to them? What was their take away from all this?

A low grumble pulled my attention to my ex. Caleb sat as still as he could, looking incredibly uncomfortable as he attempted to manage his claws.

I sat down, leaning back in my chair.

"Fancy meeting you here," I teased, hoping to lighten the mood.

"I...don't...understand," he mumbled-growled.

I shot Berg a dirty look, then shouted, "Can't you at least let him change back?"

Berg shook his head, and Ingrid looked away, occupying herself with the tiny fairy now serving them food.

"This is bullshit." I crossed my arms.

Huffing, I looked up at Caleb. His warm sweet eyes held mine, and all my anger melted away. I missed him, in any form, and I wondered if he missed me too.

"I'm sorry you got pulled into this spell, or whatever it is, but I'm sure glad you're here."

His eyes brightened, a small smile pulling at his lips.

"I've missed you," I admitted, not seeing any other way through this but to face it head on.

Caleb's arm crashed down on the table, rattling the dishes.

"Sorry," he grumbled. Working to manage his strength, he turned his claw upright and reached for my hand.

I leaned forward and ran my fingers across his furry paw. I wasn't scared of his bear when we were together, but in the Faerie realm and in his current state, I wasn't quite sure what to expect.

A low vibration rattled his chest, almost like a cat's purr. "I've missed you too." His voice was deeper than usual, but the words he shared set my heart alight.

"Look, I know this year's been crazy, but if you want to try things again, I'd really like that." I shrugged and smiled up at him, not sure if us getting back together was enough to break Berg's spell. But that's not why I was doing it...I really did want us to try again.

Caleb slid his paw out from under my hand and pushed himself up out of the chair. Fur rolled across his skin, his body twitching and aching to complete his shift. His nose elongated into a snout, and his bear finally let out a mighty roar.

I started to rise and back away, but Ingrid's shout held me in place.

"Do not move," she instructed. And so I didn't.

Caleb lumbered around the table on all fours until his teeth were barely inches from my neck. Sniffing and rooting through my hair, the cold press of his nose sent chills down my spine as I waited for his animal to make its choice.

Before his shift, I could see it in his human eyes…Caleb had already decided we were meant to be. But according to Berg and Ingrid, his shifter side had to lay claim as well…deeming me his mate.

As a witch, I still didn't understand the concept, but as I sat in the middle of a field at a tea party in the Faerie realm, I peered into my ex-boyfriend's eyes and knew he truly was the one for me.

With one last sniff, Caleb nipped my shoulder, marking me as his. I knew bears weren't monogamous in the real world, but in Havenwood Falls, reality was what we made it. And oddly enough, I liked the idea of being the newest mated witch in town.

CHAPTER 8

*W*ith a gust of wind, the field and tables disappeared, dissolving like paint being washed from a canvas. Evergreens and aspens now surrounded us, a familiar footpath lying just up ahead.

"Guess we're back." Returned to his normal self, Caleb reached for my hand, his words carrying a double meaning.

"I guess so." I smiled and stretched up on my tippy-toes, giving him a light peck on the cheek.

Cheers and music sounded in the distance, Caleb and I following its call.

Emerging back onto the edge of Danzan Park, the town's Midsummer's Night party was just getting started. I spotted Tempest as she waved at me through the crowd, draped across Eryx's lap with a wicked smile plastered on her face...like she somehow knew what we'd just gone through.

We started in their direction, but I was pulled up short by a pair of violet eyes. Ingrid, in her human form, stood at the edge of the park with her antler crown and gossamer gown, looking down her regal nose at me. I instinctively knew I wouldn't be able to tell anyone what happened, not even Tempest. The Landvaettir wanted to remain just as hidden as we were here in Havenwood Falls, and I, for one, wouldn't dare share their secret.

As if reading my thoughts, she dipped her head then disappeared into the crowd, her voice barely a whisper on the wind. *"Natalie, you are a powerful and caring witch. Keep your heart open and trust your mate in the days to come, and all will be okay."*

I looked into Caleb's eyes and realized this little game had sparked exactly the growth I needed.

Cheer rose again as the sun made its final descent. Litha was the longest day of the year, and as the horizon flared with the dying light, so did the magic of the night. It was time for the supes to come out and play, and after what I'd just experienced, I was ready to have some fun as well.

"You ready for all this craziness?" I asked, squeezing Caleb's hand.

Sliding behind me, his arms encircled my waist. "I'm ready for anything as long as I'm with you."

His warm breath feathered behind my ear, sending a shiver down my spine. Spinning in his arms, I threw my hands around his neck and placed my lips against his. Kissing him deeply, I finally felt free, unabashed, and ready to create a little magic of my own.

This was going to be the best Midsummer's Night I'd ever experienced...whether it was all a dream or not.

DULCE PERICULUM

BELINDA BORING

CHAPTER 1

"*I*'ll be back later," I hollered as I swiped another slice of toast off the counter. Today was going to be a big day, and knowing me, I'd probably forget to eat later. "I love you!"

It was just Sedona and me this morning. Micah had already left at the crack of dawn to go for a hike or something insane like that. He had grumbled last night about not being able to sleep in even though classes up at the Academy had finished for the semester. I swore the guy functioned on coffee alone. Me? I needed sleep and *lots* of it.

"You forgetting something, Holly?" Sedona called out before she appeared in the doorway. She leaned against the frame, arms crossed, a knowing expression on her face. I snorted. I'd been a scatterbrain lately so I wouldn't be surprised if I was about to leave without my head.

I looked down at my hands.

Phone—check.

Wallet—check.

Bag full of disgusting, stinky, rotting stuff—check.

"Nope. Looks like I got it all. Marcus pretty much gives me everything I need to stay alive," I quipped. That wasn't an understatement either. While I didn't know many vampires like my new friend, it surprised me how well stocked his pantry was. I had a sneaking suspicion that was because of me. It was basically him and his brother-from-another-mother, Professor Phineas Knox, who lived in the massive mansion up in the Heights, and there was no way the food was solely for them. The fact that a lot of it consisted of some of my favorite foods to snack on was also a huge giveaway.

Sedona cleared her throat. She didn't say a word, and instead, raised a piece of paper in the air, waving it. Damn. I *had* forgotten something. Her errands list.

Sedona and Micah were a serious couple, and she ran the town's bookstore called Shelf Indulgence. Usually, I spent a lot of my time there helping out and studying for school. It was my happy place—somewhere I could curl up on one of the comfy armchairs and escape into a book. Knowledge was my jam. I lived for learning.

Now that I was spending most of my free time with Marcus in his private greenhouse learning herbology, I wasn't around much to help. Guilt was a powerful thing, so I'd agreed to be her errand girl this afternoon.

I'd been in such a rush to get to today's excitement that it had totally slipped my mind.

I snatched the list from her hand.

"I'm soooo sorry," I blurted, trying to look at least a little repentant. "Thank goodness one of us has their act together!" I quickly kissed her cheek.

Her nose crinkled in disgust, shoving me a little in jest. "Get that thing out of the house!" she complained, wafting her hand in front of her nose. "Maybe you can keep your stinky experiments over with Mr. St. James in the future." She eyed the gallon baggie I was holding. "Remind me again how that's part of herbology."

I rolled my eyes, backing away toward the door. "Trust me. It's vital! I'll let you know if it works."

Pocketing her list, I shut the front door with an unintentional slam, heading down the street.

Today's lesson made my heart race in anticipation, and for a moment, I wished I had the power to teleport myself straight to the greenhouse because no matter how hard I tried, it felt like I was moving in slow motion—unbelievably . . . aggravatingly slow.

Marcus had introduced me to a rare fae flower a month ago, and I'd painstakingly been nurturing it, tending to the seed's every need. It wasn't long before I became obsessed, wanting to learn everything I could about that special kind of magic Knox had brought back with him from Faerie. He didn't talk much about his time there, and I'd learned not to pry.

We all had our secrets.

It usually took me about fifteen to twenty minutes to walk from our home to Havenwood Heights, but this morning felt like each step I took was through gallons of sticky molasses. My sole focus was getting to the mansion, and I didn't pay attention to my surroundings until I power walked into someone—knocking them over.

"Oh my gosh," I gasped in horror, my eyes dropping to the ground where the person lay sprawled. Embarrassment filled me, and I could feel my cheeks heat. I was such an idiot. With my free hand, I offered my help, and the stranger accepted it, although I could hear them muttering something below their breath. "I am sooo sorry!" I exclaimed, my words coming out in a jumble.

She didn't look up at me straight away. Instead, she took a few moments to dust themselves off, straightening their clothes before finally turning her face toward me.

Her eyes. Holy shit, her eyes were sealed behind scar tissues.

Something I couldn't quite describe—not unpleasant . . . more familiar than anything... passed between us. It was on the tip of my tongue to say something, anything to break the awkward silence because the young woman hadn't uttered a word either. She just stood there as if she was expecting me to make the first move.

The sensation that I somehow knew her spooked me more than I wanted to admit—the need to run as fast as I could surging through me.

"You okay?" I asked, my shaking hand instinctively reaching out to her arm. I ignored the warning bells ringing in my ears and convinced myself that the young woman wasn't a threat. How much danger could she impose if she couldn't see? Plus, I was the one in the wrong here.

"I wasn't paying attention to where I was going and didn't see you until it was too late." I all but gasped when I realized the slip of tongue. She couldn't have avoided the collision either. Stepping back, I waited for her to respond. She wet her lips but nothing. Impatience began tugging at me. I didn't have all day to stand here having a one-sided conversation. I had a date with a fascinating flower.

Clearing my throat, I looked about to see if there was anyone with her. She was alone, which baffled me because who would let a blind person wander around the streets by themselves? Maybe whoever helped care for the woman didn't know she was missing, and it was up to me to make sure she got home okay.

My conscience was split right down the middle. On the one hand, I liked to think I'd always do the right thing in any situation, but I still couldn't shake away the eerie feeling that all but encircled me, pressing down over my body with a sense of foreboding. Her eyes were sealed shut, yet the way her face turned to me as if she could somehow still *see* me behind her eyelids shook me to my core. The hairs at the back of my neck prickled.

The fear in my gut won. I'd stopped long enough to check on the stranger, and surely if she'd been hurt by my barging into her, she'd have said something immediately.

"Well, seeing you're fine and I'm late, I'll be on my way." I kinda stammered my farewell and turned around, refusing to feel like a jerk fleeing the scene of a crime. I'd apologized and tried to at least exchange a few sentences with her. Against my better judgement, I cast a quick glance over my shoulder and found her still standing there, her arm slowly rising as if she wanted to stop me.

"Weird," I uttered. I was used to strange things happening—it came from having to be on the run for most of my life, but since living in Havenwood Falls, I'd gotten used to life being more normal than odd.

Or as ordinary as my life could be.

I was a girl who couldn't use her powerful magic because her psycho father wanted to control it and use it for whatever nefarious reasons. He was the reason I didn't know my mother. He was the reason the only father-figure I'd ever known was my literal guardian angel, Micah.

Part of me was terrified of the day I came face to face with my sperm-donor (could I really call him anything else?) but there was something else—the part that had to be kept buried deep within me, that wanted to throw every ounce of suppressed rage and indignation at him because instead of loving me, he chose to be a threat.

He chose to disrupt what might've been a perfect life and leave me constantly looking over my shoulder and second-guessing things.

I shuddered. Hard.

This was a spiral I refused to indulge in—not now, not again. I'd finally come to peace that this was how my life was meant to be, and that whatever the Universe held in store, nothing would prevent it from unfolding.

No abusive father.

No absent mother.

No amount of running and hiding.

Havenwood Falls had become my home—a sanctuary—and I was done fixating on the what-ifs. Life wasn't perfect, but I was happy, and that's what mattered.

My phone buzzed with an alarm notification.

Damn.

I was also late.

CHAPTER 2

"You're cutting it a little fine, Miss Westbrook," Marcus chided as he looked up from the workbench. Although he wore a concerned expression, his dark brows arched high on his forehead, I knew beneath his comment lay an equal amount of excitement for this morning's task. He might be good at hiding his emotions from most people, but I'd like to think I'd figured the vampire out.

My mouth gaped open to explain the craziness I'd just encountered, but I struggled to find the words. Something whispered that if I did today's lesson would be immediately cancelled, and Marcus would march my reluctant self back to Sedona and Micah.

If I thought Micah was over the top protective, it was simply because I hadn't met Marcus St. James yet. He was both incredibly quaint in his view of the world and equally frustrating in his opinions regarding my safety. Old fashioned wasn't even the proper way to describe him. It often felt like both him and my guardian tag-teamed against me, making it near impossible to do anything without their ever-watchful eyes studying my every move. Thankfully, Knox had a little more chill than the other two.

It made having any form of privacy nonexistent. Between the two of them, I was always having to account for every single second of my day —all in the name of love and their need to keep me safe.

I tried not to complain too much. It meant a lot to be loved that much and cherished. I just wished that they didn't hold me so tightly.

"You know me," I began, plopping the plastic baggie onto my own personal workbench counter, grimacing a little as I caught a whiff of the potent contents. My gosh, it really was disgusting. "I have the mind of a squirrel . . . forever distracted." I plastered on the cheesiest grin I could, hoping that Marcus wouldn't push. While the woman I'd bumped into hadn't posed any real threat, I wasn't a hundred percent certain he wouldn't brush off the weirdness of the encounter. The last thing I wanted to do was ruin the day.

His gaze narrowed. He was suspicious, and I held my breath as I waited for him to reply.

"I thought you were excited to watch the *Dulce Periculum* blossom this morning?" There it was. He knew I wasn't being truthful. This flower had been all I'd talked about this summer. I'd practically lived and breathed everything about the fae magic that gave it the unique characteristics. Marcus knew, just as I did, that this was not a morning where I'd have my head in the clouds. "Am I wrong?"

He wiped his hands down the front of his gardening apron, his small metal shovel abandoned by his own herbology project. He'd told me when we first started working side by side in his fabulous greenhouse that he liked to tinker with soil and different seedlings, but I'd soon uncovered the truth.

He was lonely.

I chewed the inside of my cheek, and his gaze narrowed again. Crap. For the billionth time I wished that I spent time with boring humans and not supernaturals with their quirks and abilities. Keeping things from an empath witch, a guardian angel, and now a vampire was exhausting.

I held my hands up in surrender. "Fine, you caught me." I reached for the closest lie in my head. A more believable one. "I slept in. After all the anticipation, I, Holly Westbrook, forgot to set her alarm clock." I let out an exasperated sigh that was extra heavy on the dramatics. "I do declare I won't ever endure the shame of it, Marcus," I continued, in my best Scarlett O'Hara voice. I peeked at him, hoping that my theatrics was lightening the mood.

It was.

He rolled his dark eyes and finally smiled. "Sometimes I forget you're a teenager." There was a chuckle beneath his words.

I reached for my own apron and quickly tied the two straps around my waist. Usually, I didn't bother with the green leather material Marcus provided to protect my clothes, but this morning I wasn't taking any chances. I may have been wearing a pair of my oldest, grungiest jeans and T-shirt, but I didn't want any of the possible gunk this flower may throw at me, hitting me.

"Now who's not being truthful, hmm?" I fired back. "Don't bother denying it, Marcus. You find me positively charming." I cast him a sidelong glance before turning toward today's lesson.

Dulce Periculum.

Translated to *Sweet Danger.*

Knox had given us little information on the seedling he'd brought back with him from Faerie, other than it was vital within the first ten minutes of blossoming that we find the food and nourishment acceptable to the flower. Fail to do that, and the plant would turn savage and attempt to feast on whatever was closest. Succeed, and the most exquisite scent would flow from the petals—intoxicating and magical.

I was just glad my unexpected adventure earlier hadn't kept me from witnessing this. All my hard work and diligence was about to pay off. There was very little written down about the flower, which had made my job learning about it difficult. Instead of wasting my entire summer trying to figure out what the *Dulce Periculum* would eat, my studies quickly turned to researching the fae in general.

Hence, my baggie of food scraps and grossness. Something in my gut told me that my flower would have a taste for the macabre, and not the expectant sweetness Marcus assured me.

We'd instantly placed a bet on who was right.

The winner not only had bragging rights but could choose anything they wanted from the crystal store in town. I had my eye on a gorgeous piece of larimar. The gem looked like a piece of the ocean solidified and called to me.

I sat on my wooden stool and stared at the plant. It resembled a small bulbous cactus now, nestled in rich, dark soil, inside a bright yellow pot that I'd found on one of the greenhouse's shelves. I'd painted a rune on the front to encourage growth on a whim.

A second stool scraped across the ground. Marcus took the seat beside me, his own baggie in his hand. Sure enough, he'd gathered freshly cut strawberries, watermelon, banana, a rose from the bushes out front, but there was one item that made me chuckle.

"Are you seriously going to feed our flower a *Hershey's* bar?" I snorted, pointing at the chocolate. My mouth watered a little. Once this was over, I'd go hunt down the package this one came from and swipe a few.

The vampire snorted louder, this time in disgust. "As if I'd use such second-rate chocolate!" Reaching into the pocket of his apron, Marcus removed the empty wrapper of a popular Swiss brand. "Only the best for our experiment." I couldn't argue with his logic either. *Lindt* chocolate really was the more superior of the two.

As carefully as I could, I poured my own offerings into the ceramic bowl I'd gathered when preparing for today, desperately trying not to gag over the stench. I was torn between boasting at my luck in not spilling a single drop of the slimy refuse and keeping my mouth clamped shut. It was bad enough I had to smell this stuff. I sure as hell didn't want to taste it.

I placed Marcus's bowl in front of him—envious that his own choice for food didn't elicit the same visceral revulsion as mine.

"You know it's not too late for you to change your mind?" Marcus nudged, checking his watch before turning his focus to the potted plant. "Let me throw that . . ." He paused, trying to find the right words. Instead, he simply pointed at my bowl. ". . .*that* out."

Man, I was tempted. He had no idea how badly I wanted to cave, but I stood by my intuition. The fae were never as they seemed and reveled in being able to trick others. My gut was adamant I'd made the right selection.

"You ready to become plant food if you're wrong?" I teased. "How do you know our flower won't look at you and decide vampire sushi is what they most desire?" That was the risk right there. If we were both wrong, there was a strong chance the *Dulce Periculum* would turn on us and attack.

Marcus nodded his head, gesturing behind him. "That's why I came up with a Plan B." There on one of the other shelves lay a fire extinguisher, a large sledgehammer, and flame thrower.

I cocked my eyebrow. "Yep. I'd say that was a solid alternative."

Our banter died down as we returned to staring at the cactus-looking plant.

Moments ticked by.

Still nothing.

"Do you think we calculated the date wrong?" Marcus whispered, leaning in a little to peer closer. "Perhaps this is merely a cactus, and there is nothing magical whatsoever." He lifted his hand, pointer finger extended, ready to prod our experiment into action. "I wouldn't put it past my brother to play a prank on us."

I felt a pulse of something before I saw it—an electrical current appearing in the air around our plant.

"Wait!" I exclaimed, snatching back Marcus's hand at the precise moment the pot exploded, sending shards of yellow ceramic pieces everywhere. A shimmering fog hovered over the counter, obscuring our view.

"Step back, Holly!" Marcus shouted, grabbing my arm and tugging me off my stool.

I knew I should've listened, but my curiosity got the better of me. I tentatively leaned forward, my eyes squinting to see what was happening. Then, with a loud, disgusting belch, the fog dissipated, revealing the strangest looking flower-plant I'd ever seen.

With a stem that looked like three or four vines had entwined together, and large green leaves to act like makeshift feet, the *Dulce Periculum* stood on the counter, trembling as the last of its magic shivered outward. Opaque petals unfurled—reminding me of faerie wings and how they practically gleamed beneath the sunlight. That's not what drew my attention, though. The center of the flower held a protruding green lump that slowly opened to reveal fangs.

Scratch that . . . lots and lots of sharp teeth.

CHAPTER 3

"Shit!" I gasped as I finally leapt backward.

"Shit!" Marcus parroted.

Gone were all the plans we'd made beforehand for this moment.

The clock was ticking to feed this thing, and all Marcus and I could do was stand there and stare with horror.

"Feed it!" I yelped. I elbowed Marcus for him to make the first move. He cleared his throat, still rooted to where he stood. I jabbed him again. "Quick. You're the adult here!"

I could almost hear him audibly gulp. Instead of pushing his bowl forward cautiously, testing his own theory that the flower would crave sweet things, Marcus reached behind him—for the flame thrower.

The thought of destroying the newly blossomed plant triggered a stronger reaction in me, and I knocked him to the side with my hip. Any fear still coursing through my veins was nothing compared to my overwhelming need to protect my project.

With nerves of steel, I stretched my arm out, but not before the pair of leafy *feet* moved the flower toward me. Fangs chomped with hunger.

"Holly!"

It happened in the blink of an eye.

One second teeth were flashing and a howl of hunger pierced the air, and next the most ravenous sounds of gorging followed.

We didn't need to feed her at all—she'd instinctively known what she needed and helped herself . . . to my bowl of nastiness.

Marcus stepped up beside me and slowly gripped me around my shoulders, easing me back to a safer distance. Both our gazes were rivetted to the countertop where the flower was grunting and slobbering, busily devouring the contents of my offering.

"That . . ."

I interrupted him. ". . . is so freaking cool!" All I could wonder was what it would feel like to have such an intense hunger.

My friend grunted. "I was going to say that's disgusting, but okay." I looked over to him and saw that he still wasn't sure how to respond. Sure enough, Marcus held the flame thrower loosely in his hand.

Soon the bowl was empty, and the *Dulce Periculum* stopped its frenetic feasting, straightening up as its petals glimmered and swayed in place. It had grown in the last few minutes and now stood two feet tall.

The greenhouse stilled.

Marcus and I both held our breaths.

It started off subtlety—like a barely whispered note in a melody. Magic built and swirled about the stem, sparkles catching the sunbeams filtering in from outside. Then the most glorious scent filled every inch of the room, inundating us with memories from the past—the scent of cinnamon rolls Sedona liked to bake for Micah, that first hint of floral you get when you walk into the florist at Springtime, the smell of approaching rain in the air, and on and on, the intoxicating scent enveloped us—evolving with each inhale into something richer.

"Holy cow," I murmured, turning to Marcus. "Can you smell that? It's exactly like the peppermint hot chocolate from Coffee Haven!" My mouth watered instantly.

I expected Marcus to agree, but instead, he wore the softest, most reverent smile on his face, his eyes filling with tears. "I smell lavender . . . the kind that Catriona would place in the water whenever she bathed." He took in another deep breath. Tears rolled down over his cheek. "Wait. Now I smell the same daisies my daughter used to pick so I could make a crown of them for her hair."

The meaning behind the fae name for the plant hit me.

Sweet Danger.

After the threat of feeding and the uncertainty of knowing how the flower would act, came the sweetness of memories—the scent specific to those experiencing its blooming. Although Marcus and I were both here together, the flower had conjured recollections solely for us alone.

I squeezed Marcus's hand, my own eyes threatening to fill with tears. "I'm glad we did this."

"Me too," he replied, slowly wiping his face with the hem of his sleeve. "It's nice to be given such an unexpectant gift."

I nodded. "Can we keep her?" I turned back to the flower only to find that the magic had exhausted itself, and the plant had returned to its former appearance.

"Her?" With the moment over, and his emotions back under control, Marcus gathered up the abandoned bowls, careful not to get any of the remaining goo on his hands. As an afterthought, he offered me the unwanted piece of chocolate. "Have I ever told you how weird you are, Holly?"

"Every day," I countered, popping the candy into my mouth. My mind was still buzzing over what had just happened. "Mind if I take a bit to record everything in my journal?" I carried the growing book back and forth from my place to here—scribbling notes, adding thoughts, and doodling pictures. "Then we can figure out what we'll do next."

With a nod, Marcus left me to my task.

I couldn't wait to tell Knox how the seedling turned out.

Thoughts of earlier this morning surfaced briefly.

I should probably talk to Micah as well.

Or, maybe, I should just quit overthinking and being paranoid, I considered silently.

I rolled my eyes, picked up my pen, and began to write.

CHAPTER 4

"*A*re you both alive still?"

The voice of Knox startled me from the silence we'd been enjoying in the greenhouse.

I'd totally been in the zone, frantically scribbling down every thought I'd had about this morning's experiment with the *Dulce Periculum*, so it didn't surprise me to see that hours had passed and it was now midafternoon.

Glimpsing over at Marcus who was nose-deep in some old book from one of his libraries, rocking on the large wooden chair he'd dragged in beside my workbench, I could see he'd totally lost track of time as well. I loved how we could enjoy each other's company without filling every single second with conversation and noise.

It was probably why I was quickly beginning to see him as the uncle I'd never had but thank the goddess she'd blessed me with. Same with Knox.

"We're in here," Marcus chimed, after clearing his throat. Carefully placing a leather bookmark to keep the page he was on, he looked at me with a grin. "And I believe we survived yet another one of your Fae souvenirs."

The large door swung open, giving me a peek at the outside. Yep, the day didn't seem as bright as before, and a twinge of guilt tugged at my thoughts. While Sedona was used to me becoming consumed without whatever project I was involved with over here, I still tried to make it a point to let her know I was doing okay and where I was. I'd also forgotten about her errand list—the fourth time in the last two weeks.

I reached to my phone and quickly typed out a short text letting her know I hadn't had a chance to grab the things on her list, but that I had so much to tell her about the magical flower and reassured her I'd return once my notes were finished—without the baggie of putrefied waste. A short minute later, she replied with a smiley face and a capitalized 'PRAISE GAIA!!'.

Resting my pen in the crease of my notebook, I swung fully around so I could catch up on all the latest with Knox and fill him in on our success.

"You could've at least warned us about all the fangs," I said, trying to look stern, my brows furrowed. I jabbed my finger at him. "For a second there, I thought the flower had a craving for vampire."

His brows shot up as he sent a questioning glance toward Marcus. "Please tell me if he was bit, you at least captured it on your phone." When his friend snorted hard, Knox had the decency to correct himself. "I mean, strictly for research. I'm sure the students up at the academy would be interested in hearing about it."

I rolled my eyes and laughed. "Check her out for yourself."

Knox looked to Marcus. "Her?"

The vampire shrugged. "Ask Holly what she named her."

I was used to them teasing me over my quirks of naming things. It just seemed weird not to give something that had grown legs and run across the workbench surface a name. I figured the plant had at least earned that.

"Bertha," I answered, not waiting for Knox to ask. "And don't ask me why. It was the first thing that popped into my head, so I took it as a sign from Demeter." I shrugged, hoping that I hadn't offended the Greek goddess of plants.

Knox had crossed the greenhouse and now stood beside us. He peered closer to Bertha, studying her intently. While I worked a lot with Marcus in their glorious hot house, I shared a fascination for learning with Knox. He was part of the reason I took such elaborate and precise notes because we'd later discuss at length everything that happened. I also thought it was a way for him to talk a little about his time in Faerie.

Or at least the snippets he was willing to share.

Marcus slapped his hand down suddenly on Knox's shoulder. "Watch out, brother. Don't let Bertha fool you into thinking her magic is gone. Perhaps she has a hankering for academia now."

I stifled a giggle behind my hand. Knox had all but jumped out of his shoes at the surprise. That didn't stop him, however, from taking a tentative step back for his own safety. Bertha hadn't moved an inch after her last burst of magic and was pretty much dormant.

"You, my friend, are an arse. Was that truly necessary?" He shot Marcus a dirty look, but that didn't keep the wide grin from filling his face. "And now you've made me use unbecoming language in front of Holly."

It was my turn to snort out loud. "Because I'm just so impressionable." I didn't add that I'd heard much worse. It cracked me up at how despite living for over a century and being immersed into the modern world—at least for Knox—they still held on to a lot of their deep-rooted principles they'd grown up with.

"Hush," Knox fired back, lifting his hand to gesture for me to be quiet. "I'm trying to safeguard your innocence here. I can't have Micah kicking down our front door and demanding to know why you're learning such things here." He smirked. He was definitely teasing me again.

"If anyone's going to complain about the improper use of language here, it's me." Marcus had stood up from his chair, his book closed on the side table. He brushed off his pants and started heading toward the door to lead us back to the main house.

My stomach growled, and Knox laughed.

"Let me guess, no one's fed you either today."

We passed through the outside garden, along the stone pathway, and slipped into the cool room inside—Marcus in front. I knew where he was headed . . . where we always ended up when I spent any length of time here.

The massive chef's kitchen.

My second favorite place in their home.

"Need I remind you that Holly is quite capable of fending for herself. She's family and has an open invitation to anything she needs here." He glared pointedly at Knox, a slight smirk curling his mouth. "She isn't a child."

I perched myself on top of one of the barstools that lined the large marble topped island, watching them start to banter back and forth.

"True, but we both know that once she's fixated on something, she loses track of time. Sedona had strict instructions that part of the conditions for her visiting was that we made sure she was okay."

Wait—what?

I leaned forward to interrupt, but Marcus beat me to it. "Holly, have you been neglected?" One of his dark brows arched high over his darker eyes. I loved seeing this side of him—I was getting a glimpse behind the seriousness to his softer, funnier side.

"Well, now that you mention it, I'm quite famished." I let out a dramatic sigh, which was quickly followed by an even louder growl from my stomach. "I'm pretty sure I'm about this close . . ." I held up my fingers spaced only half an inch apart. ". . . from wasting away into the nothing. It's a good thing Knox came home to remind you about your host duties!"

Knox burst into laughter, followed by Marcus. They looked so relaxed here in their home . . . comfortable and with their guards lowered. Marcus even had the top TWO buttons undone and his shirt sleeves rolled up to his elbows!

"Okay, kiddo, what would you like for lunch?" Blond hair fell slightly across Knox' forehead as he brushed it away with the back of his hand. He stood in front of the opened refrigerator, the other hand on his hip. "Your choice today."

Usually I enjoyed cooking with him, but it looked like he was content with me watching.

"Hmmmm," I murmured, trying to think of something. We liked to explore different cuisines and recipes he and Marcus had tried in their travels. Sometimes I'd spend time scrolling through Pinterest for ideas, but today I went with a theme. "Surprise me. Maybe something in honor of Bertha."

Knox clapped his hands, but Marcus quickly chimed in. "That's not code for Faerie food." He placed his hand on the stainless-steel fridge door, pushing on it so it started to close. "And it must be edible. You should've seen the nastiness Holly brought with her." He gagged a little.

Knox glanced at me. "That bad, huh?"

Shrugging, I answered. "I had a hunch that maybe Bertha would enjoy some rotting garbage." When his eyes widened like saucers, I quickly added, "And Marcus is overexaggerating. It wasn't that bad."

Marcus whipped about to confront me full on. "Should I fetch the baggie you brought it in? Perhaps we need Knox to judge who is telling the tallest tale here." He paused long enough for me to argue with him or perhaps plead my case. "I didn't think so." His wink revealed his humor.

"Okay, so here's the plan . . . I'll make us a nice salad using the abundance we just harvested from the garden. Marcus, you'll set the table, making sure you bring out the pitcher of fresh blackberry lemonade, and Holly?"

Knox was already over at the countertop, perusing through the vegetables. He glanced over his shoulder.

"Yeah?"

"It's time for you to choose your next project."

Excitement exploded inside me. A new project meant one thing . . .

"Time to go grab your journal?"

He nodded.

I wasn't the only one who kept painstakingly detailed notes. Knox had volumes of journals filled with his writings from Faerie. It was where we decided what was next for me to learn.

"I'm on it!"

Scurrying out of the kitchen and toward his study on the second level of the house, my mind was already racing over the choices I had.

Perhaps we could grow Bertha a friend.

CHAPTER 5

"*M*mmgussssh!" I exclaimed noisily with my mouth full of food.

I knew I was about to get scolded for not swallowing before speaking, but I couldn't get over how incredible the salad was. Licking my lips so I didn't miss a single drop of the homemade dressing, I continued, "You are a freaking genius, Knox. A culinary prodigy. A cuisine virtuoso." I figured if I layered it on thick, I'd avoid a kind-hearted lecture. Despite my constant reminder, they both felt it was their duty to make me a lady.

It worked.

"It's all in the ingredients. The garden blessed us with an abundance of fare this summer, so it was easy to create something delicious." Knox all but beamed with pride. What he said was true, but it didn't change the fact that it also helped *a lot* if you knew how to pair ingredients together to make them edible. Poor Micah had endured many a kitchen failure over the years whenever I felt like experimenting with our meals. I'd lost count how many times his eyes had watered, his Adam's apple bobbing as he desperately tried to swallow my food without once complaining.

Marcus pointed his fork toward me. "Layering it on a bit thick there with the praise, Holly. We'll have to expand the door frames if we give Knox a big head." He played about with the salad on his plate. He didn't always eat with us, but he liked to keep up the pretense of enjoying a meal together. He was good about not drinking what he truly needed to survive in front of me for whatever reason. It didn't bother me that he drank blood. I loved him, and it was a part of him.

His lack of eating didn't stop me from shoveling another heaped forkful of lettuce covered with vinaigrette, cut tomatoes, onion, and feta cheese speared on the prongs. So. Freaking. Good.

"How else am I supposed to practice with your words of the week? If I'm going to learn it, I might as well slip it into daily conversation." I caught myself before wiping my mouth with the back of my hand, and instead used the linen serviette Marcus had laid on the table. He nodded his approval.

Knox leaned back in his chair, his fork resting on top of his emptied plate. Unlike me, he hadn't gone for a second helping. "What's this week's word?

"Dyspeptic." Marcus and I answered simultaneously.

"It means someone who is cranky due to indigestion," I added. "For example, if Marcus was to eat as much of this salad as I have, he'd become dyspeptic." These two weren't the only ones who had fun teasing.

It had quickly become a tradition between us where Marcus would teach me some old fashioned words he'd grown up using, and in exchange, I would teach him something more modern. I put a lot of thought into it each week because it was hilarious to hear him try to use slang. So far, I'd learned words like curmudgeon, flummoxed, and blithering.

I'd confided that to Knox as our little secret, and there were times where he'd volunteer something just so we could watch Marcus squirm.

"And what delightful word are you working with this week?" He turned to the vampire expectantly. This was one of those occasions, so he knew full well the answer.

Marcus rolled his eyes. "Perhaps we should focus on the next item of business." He pointed to the journal I'd brought to the table earlier. "After today's mini fiasco, could I suggest we try something a little more . . . subtle than Bertha?"

"Not until we hear your word."

I thought his head was going to explode. Slowly clearing his throat, and in barely a whisper, Marcus answered.

Knox was relentless. "I couldn't quite catch that. Can you speak a little louder, please?"

Finally, he blurted it out in his version of an American accent. "Bussin'. As in really, really good, as in if I was actually able to eat this salad Holly is singing your praises over, I would say, man, this food is bussin'."

Laughter exploded in the kitchen as Knox doubled over, his hands wrapped around his sides. "That was exactly how I imagined it!" The lines around his eyes deepened as well as his chuckling.

Marcus abruptly stood up from the table and began gathering the dirtied plates and utensils. "I should've known that you were somehow involved. Now that you've had your fun, I'm going to get the dishwasher started. Try not to plot my next utter humiliation while I'm gone."

There was that wink again that showed me he wasn't truly offended. In the beginning, it had been a huge learning curve understanding both of their personalities and the way they were with each other. They'd had the luxury of spending over a century together, and I'd worried that somehow, I'd say or do something wrong. After a quick heartfelt conversation with Marcus, we'd agreed on a secret of our own—he'd wink to let me know that no feelings were hurt. He also knew that I struggled holding eye contact when he'd misspoken.

"So, have you chosen what you'd like to learn next from the journal?" Now that our appetites were satisfied, it was time to talk and ask questions.

The problem was, there was one thing that kept screaming in my head, demanding for me to ask. It wasn't that I was nosey, but because it kinda confused me.

"You know I love you, Knox," I started, lowering my gaze so I was staring at my fingers fidgeting with his journal. I'd had countless hours to study each page and a very extensive list of projects I wanted to explore. But that wasn't the question burning at the tip of my tongue.

He stooped a little so he could catch my gaze. "That doesn't sound good, kiddo. Something else on your mind?" He placed his own warm hand on top of my mine. His touch helped comfort the nerves fluttering in my stomach. "You know you can ask me anything, right?"

I nodded and swallowed the lump in my throat.

Here goes . . .

CHAPTER 6

"So, I know you don't talk about it much and Micah told me I wasn't allowed to pry and be a nuisance about it, but well . . ." My fingertips brushed alongside the journal, softly flickering over the worn papers. "I've done a lot of research online and through some of the books Micah had shown me from the Academy when it comes to Faerie because that's where a lot of our experiments have come from. It's helped me know exactly what to prepare for and what to expect."

Knox watched me intently, remaining quiet. I drew in a breath for bravery.

"One thing that's blatantly obvious is that humans don't easily escape Faerie especially when they make a deal with a Fae themselves. There's always a trick. Marcus shared a tiny bit . . ." My eyes widened and my mouth dried when I realized I'd possibly gotten him into trouble. "Please don't be mad. I think I caught him off guard with my constant chatter and he'd slipped that you'd made a deal to got to Faerie to find a way to cure his curse."

Again, Knox sat quietly listening. The only movement he made was to softly nod his head.

"Well, Marcus is still who he is, and you're back from wherever you were taken . . ." Goddess, I was all but stammering out my question, dragging it out so painfully.

"You want to know how I was able to return." He stated it rather than answering my question with his own. "You want to know why I don't talk about my time there."

A rush of air escaped through my lips. I studied his face, trying to catch any glimpse of annoyance or anger at my prying. The lump that had lodged itself in my throat plummeted to my stomach, and I felt instantly ill. In fact, there was a good chance I'd need to run to the bathroom based on the way the acid in my gut was churning.

Knox reached over and cupped the side of my face tenderly. There was no condemnation in his eyes. All I saw was a returning of love and understanding as if he was silently telling me he knew I wasn't being malicious or wanting to gossip about him.

"I choose not to discuss my time there because it was not only unfruitful in finding a cure for Marcus, but it holds some of the most painful memories I own. I went there foolishly . . . naively believing that I could uncover some magical remedy and bring salvation to my beloved brother. I arrogantly thought that I had bewitched the Fae I'd struck the deal with and that given time, I'd find the answers I needed from her."

There was so much sorrow in his voice that I instantly regretted asking him. All I wanted to do now was open his journal and show him a few of the pages I'd memorized. Anything to help remove the regret blazing in his eyes.

"Knox," I interrupted, heartsick.

Instead, he moved the journal away as though he'd sensed my intentions.

"It's okay, Holly. While I won't tell you everything, simply because they're not memories I wish to relive, I will answer your question this one time about how I escaped my imprisonment."

Imprisonment. The word hung heavily between us, and in my own small view of the world, I earned a glimpse of some of that pain he mentioned. He hadn't been free to pursue his quest in Faerie. If the stories were correct, if you were being kept under guard by the Fae, you were lucky to survive the torture. That was something I'd learned in my research—don't be fooled by the beauty and enchantments of the Fae. They could be devastatingly cruel as they could be generous.

"Did they hurt you?" I whispered low.

I didn't like the way he hesitated as though he didn't know how to respond. "I could've suffered much worse, I'm sure. There were others there whose screams echoed through the halls and constantly filled the airs. Over time, I learned to tune their cries out. But there's more than one way to hurt someone." Knox pursed his lips together, and he laid his hand back over mine. "But I'm sure you're familiar with that too."

He knew about my father and how Micah and I had come to Havenwood Falls to hide.

I nodded.

"I'd fallen in love with someone who was also captured by the Fae and together we devised a plan to find a way back to this realm. It felt like a bitter pill to swallow once I realized that I'd failed and sacrificed everything for the pure entertainment of the Fae. She'd known that I was on a fool's errand but had tricked me anyway. The only benefit from making the deal was that my time in Faerie had granted me an extended life. It paved the way for me to remain by Marcus's side should I succeed."

All the questions I thought I'd have if ever we'd have this conversation had evaporated. I knew this for the gift that it was. There was no way I'd interrupt him now that he'd started. Marcus had popped his head out from the kitchen only to disappear again. I'm sure he'd heard this story too.

"Our plan relied heavily on our captor's vanity. We would wait for Midsummer Night's Eve and when the veil between realms thinned, we would make our move. We would shower the Fae with praise and create an elaborate feast that would result in hours of decadence and debauchery." Knox paused the second he uttered that last part. "Please don't tell Micah that I said that word, and for heaven's sake, don't look it up in the dictionary. Just know it means the Fae partied."

I didn't have the heart to tell him I already knew what it meant. I felt my cheeks heat remembering what I'd read. I didn't need any further details.

"The time came when the Fae guests were drunk and gluttonous on party favors. My lover and I waited a few moments longer and made our move . . . we slipped out into the neighboring woods with two stolen journals and a few pages that I'd swiped from our captor."

My gaze dropped to the book on the table in front of me. Was this the one?

Knox nodded. "This is one. It contained an incantation that could open a portal and bring us home. There was always this light glittery feel in Faerie from all the magic that infused the life there. I'd assumed that using just a small portion of it to say the spell wouldn't create a disturbance. Again, I was a fool, because no sooner had the portal shimmered into existence, than Fae guards stormed the small circle of trees we hid within and attacked. My lover . . ." His voice cracked with emotion, and it was my turn to comfort him as I squeezed his hand.

Marcus appeared from behind him and rested his hand lightly on Knox's shoulder. He'd been listening and known.

"My lover . . . he'd valiantly tried to fight against the guards, shouting for me to jump through the portal and that he'd follow. I knew in my heart that he was ready to sacrifice himself so I could leave, but there was no chance I wanted to leave him behind. I couldn't. He'd saved me from myself when I'd given into despair, risking his own safety as he brought me back to my right mind. He'd been my constant companion through the hell we'd both endured . . . how could I possibly abandon him to the same fate?" Fat tears broke away from his lashes and fell over his cheeks. So much pain and heartache filled his words, and I threw my arms around him.

"I'm so sorry, Knox. Oh, I'm so sorry." I held him tightly as he quietly sobbed, grieving for the love I now knew he'd lost. This was why he never spoke about his time in Faerie and why I should've listened when told not to pry. He hadn't mentioned when he'd returned, but just by the way his body shuddered with the depth of his anguish, to him his wounds and heartache were still very much fresh. "We don't have to talk about it anymore. I'm so sorry I asked."

Marcus reached around and squeezed my arm, trying to comfort my own remorse. I didn't need it though. My entire focus was on Knox and helping him.

We sat like that—the three of us with our arms around each other—for what felt like forever. Eventually Knox stirred as he wiped away his tears, his hitched breath finally returning to normal.

"I doubt I will ever love another as much as I loved Alexander."

With a slight tremble in his hand, Knox reached over to the journal and opened it to a page toward the back, revealing a simple pencil drawing.

The man was handsome, his dark hair curling about his face until it fell just above his collarbone. He had a strong jawline with well-defined cheekbones, his mouth curved ever so slightly into a smile. That wasn't what drew me in, however. I assumed that it was Knox who had drawn him, but he'd captured a sense of wit and life and intelligence in the man's eyes. He looked kind, and I could tell that he loved the one capturing his likeness.

"Alexander," I murmured.

"My Alexander." Knox tenderly traced his fingertip over the image, and a softness filled his face. "He gave his life so I could return home. I was turning back to help him fight the guards, and breaking out of the Fae's grip, he charged at me before shoving me through the portal. The last thing I saw was him mouthing that he loved me. Next thing I knew, I woke up beside the falls where I'd been taken."

We didn't say a word. There wasn't anything that could make the sacrifices made feel better. Each of us had given up something that left footprints of trauma through our hearts. Maybe that was why I felt close to Marcus and Knox. They both knew and understood major loss.

"I know it doesn't help," I finally said, breaking the silence. "But I'm glad you were able to return home. I can't imagine my life without you. You're part of my family."

Knox answered with a teary smile. "I feel the same way, kiddo While I wish I'd returned with Alexander, I know Havenwood Falls is my home, and I'm where I'm meant to be."

Maybe he realized that we needed a chance to breathe and recover from the intensity of what we were now feeling, but Marcus was the one to break the ice.

"I love you, brother," he whispered before stepping back, his hands now by his side. "Perhaps the next project we choose from your journal can be in Alexander's memory."

That sounded like the perfect idea, and I nodded eagerly. The air seemed to lighten about us. "In fact, I think I have a few ideas." I reached for the book, but Knox stopped me.

"Actually, before we dive back in, how about we take a break and have some dessert. I believe there's a strawberry cheesecake in the icebox that's just begging to be devoured. You think you can handle that?" His question was leveled at me. I'd pretty much stuffed my face with salad and bread rolls.

"Pfft, is that a challenge?" I cocked my brow.

They both barked out a laugh. "How about we grab a slice and go eat it outside before you head home. I'm sure Micah and Sedona won't let us keep you forever."

Smiling, I threw my arms around them again, hugging them tight before pushing them back.

"Race you to the kitchen!"

Forever.

That's who these two were to me.

Part of my forever family.

Maybe that was the silver lining to heartache. You endured the pain so that once it passed, you could enjoy the sweetness.

Dulce Periculum.

To be continued . . .

A NEW HOME

AMY RICHIE

CHAPTER 1

I sucked in a deep breath and let it out slowly, letting it hang in the cool air of our new home. Destiny, a good friend of mine from years ago, went to school here, and she was the one who brought us here to this perfect little town. After hearing our situation, she'd been given special permission to invite us.

Now that I was half responsible for a child, I needed a safe place to raise her. Havenwood Falls came to us like a miracle when things looked pretty bleak.

"Abram?"

I turned at the sound of my name. Vince, a vampire like me, who had agreed to help raise the child, was standing at the back door. His eyebrows lowered when they spotted me. Ugh, he was always pissed about something, and most of the time it had to do with the kid.

"What's wrong?" I asked lazily.

"It's your turn," he informed me with a click of his tongue. "Are you hiding out here?"

I really didn't think things all the way through when Beth asked me to help Vince with her baby daughter. We had been away from home when the hunters attacked us. She gave her life so we could get back to the nest and grab her baby. She had no chance to get away, and she knew that. We were the only ones who survived the attack, the only two left of our nest. Only now was I starting to realize how big our promise had been.

"I'm not hiding." I sighed. "And I just had her. It's definitely still your turn."

"Oh, no." His frown became more pronounced. "You're just out here enjoying the sun now that you can." He tapped the tattoo on his wrist, given to him by Addie Beaumont when we first got to town.

It was true that the tattoo allowed us to go into the sun without burning up, but it was still uncomfortable enough that I wasn't able to spend long periods outside.

"Since it's your turn with her," I sneered, "I can be out enjoying anything I please."

"Five more minutes." Vince held up five long fingers, then stalked back inside.

The moment was ruined now, though. This had been a rash decision, very unlike me. Vince and I only got along half the time; the other half was spent in disgruntled silence. When Beth made her request, I had reasoned with myself that it was only eighteen years and the child would be on her own. That would go by in the blink of an eye for someone with such a long lifespan like me. I really, really didn't think things through.

"What does she need?" I asked, pushing open the back door.

Vince was standing in the kitchen, and the baby was in her crib several feet away. Her breathing was slow and steady. Had he just made me come in here to watch a sleeping baby? What the hell?

"She doesn't need anything." He sniffed. "But I need a coffee. I'm going to that cute little cafe in town. What was it called?"

"Coffee Haven." I pressed my lips tightly together, unimpressed. "You're going now?"

"I'll be back in a few hours." With a final glare thrown my way, he left the house and me alone with the baby.

At least she was sleeping. The baby, who we had not given a name yet, always seemed to cry. She must have missed the mother that she barely got to know. She was only a few months old when Beth was killed by the hunters.

Beth was desperate so I had made the foolish promise to keep her daughter safe until she got old enough to take care of herself. But the reality was, I knew nothing about babies. I didn't even know what Beth called her. Mostly it was "my little princess."

If she was human, I could have looked things up online or in a book.

Hell, I probably could have asked other humans how to care for her. This baby was a vampire, though, a Belladonna vampire, to be exact. She was changed in her human mother's womb and then Beth took her after she was born.

Vince and I only knew the basics. She needed milk for now, but blood would have to be introduced later. How much later? No idea.

A sudden knock on the door took me out of my dismal musings.

There was a small flurry of fear that tried to tell me the person on the other side of the door meant us harm, but I pushed it aside. We were in a safe town now. The hunters couldn't get us here.

After a quick breath that didn't calm me down very well, I opened the front door. Destiny stood there, grinning wide at me. Next to her was a pretty little girl with deep red hair.

"Abram," Destiny gushed. She didn't hug me, which I was grateful for. "We passed Vince on the way here."

"He's going for coffee." I moved back to allow the two girls to come in. "But the baby is sleeping right now so I guess it's okay." Like it would matter to him even if it wasn't okay.

"This is my girlfriend," Destiny explained as they made their way to the long couch in the living room. "Linnie."

"Hi, Linnie." I waved one hand in her direction.

"I'm a Bella." Linnie let out a small giggle that might have been cute if the words weren't so serious.

My eyes widened. "You are?"

"I thought she might be able to help with…the baby." Destiny's eyes shifted to the crib that we had shoved into one corner of the room.

Linnie was already nodding her head. "What's her name? How old is she?"

"I'm…" I dragged my hand over my top lip and down over my chin. It was a little embarrassing to admit how little I knew. "I don't know either one of those things."

Her wide eyes shifted briefly to Destiny then back to me. "You don't know how old she is?"

"Never asked." Was that weird? I assumed she would age, and we'd be able to tell later how old she was. She was still pretty small, so her exact age couldn't matter that much—not really.

"She looks to be just a few months old," Destiny offered awkwardly. Linnie looked horrified.

"And her name?" she prompted. "If you don't know her name, what have you been calling her?"

"The baby." Obviously. "It doesn't talk yet. We'll think of something to call her later." There were more important things for now. "When will she need blood?"

"Not every Bella is the same as far as that goes," she explained slowly. "It'll be a few years still. I'll help you."

"We'll both help." Destiny moved to the edge of the couch.

That was great and all to offer help but these two could leave any time they wanted. A fifteen-minute visit every now and then wasn't a lot of help when you really thought about it.

"Thanks." I smiled tightly and held in my negative thoughts.

Linnie was a Bella. That was a huge resource right there.

The cute little house we had scored had three bedrooms, one for each of the people who would be living here for the next eighteen years. It was Vince's idea that we all three stay in the same room for now, just in case. I agreed with his idea, for the most part.

Now, though, when I was smashed back-to-back with Vince, I was cursing our inability to let our guards down.

"Can you scoot over a little bit?" he hissed, squirming his body against mine.

"No," I hissed back. Although irritated, neither of us were willing to raise our voices. The baby was sleeping for now, and the single thing we agreed on was that she was the easiest to care for when she was sleeping.

"There is no way in hell you only have half the bed."

"I'm practically hanging off."

Moving fast, he whirled around and wrapped his arm over top of me to check exactly how far I was to the edge. "You have at least four inches." His hot breath washed over the side of my face.

"Four inches isn't that much."

"Yeah," he snorted. "But it's enough to scoot over some. I'm pressed against the wall over here."

So what if he was pressed against the wall? It wasn't like he would fall off the bed. I was one wet dream from being unbalanced and thrown on the floor. Honestly, it would probably be more comfortable but at this point it was a matter of pride. Why should I have to sleep on the floor?

When Vince pushed his hand into my back, it was the last straw. Irritated, I flung my body over so that I was facing him. I meant to yell in his face, but my words got stuck in my throat. He was so close, I could count all the little hairs in his eyelashes. The moonlight through the window lit up the side of his face.

My heart stuttered. I never realized how beautiful Vince was.

The two of us were always lumped together by the rest of our nest since we both preferred men over women, but I had never looked at him like that before. He wasn't my type—at all. He whined too much, and he never thought things through.

Honestly, most days, I could barely stand him. Here we were, though, forced to stay in the same house because of a promise to a desperate woman, and I was having some strange thoughts for him. This was not good.

"I'm going to sleep on the couch," I growled out. I needed some space.

"We agreed to sleep in the same room." His pale eyes widened. "You said..."

"Fine." I clenched my teeth tight together. "Stop bitching then."

CHAPTER 2

*M*y eyes popped open. Sweat formed on my forehead. It was still dark, but the baby was screaming like someone had just hit it. My hearing was excellent, so I knew no one had come in our bedroom and abused her.

"What the fuck?" I whispered, jumping out of bed and darting to the crib. "Why isn't Vince here?"

"I'm getting her a bottle," a groggy voice called lightly from the kitchen.

A quick glance at the bed showed that Vince's side was indeed empty. Okay, the better question was how did he wake up and get out of bed with me fast asleep beside him? How did I not hear this thing crying like this?

"Pick her up," Vince said angrily. "A crying baby is a red light for predators."

"There's no one in this town who would eat her." They weren't allowed. Despite knowing this, I slid my hands under the tiny body and pulled her close to my chest.

It had been a month, and I still felt nervous when I picked her up. I didn't want to break her on accident. Linnie assured me that Bellas were sturdier than they looked. Staring down at that face scrunched in anger and her little fists balled up, she didn't seem like she could fight her way out of a paper bag.

"Here." Vince was suddenly next to me, thrusting a bottle into my hand. "Feed her this."

"Is it milk?" I shook the white liquid hard enough to make it foam on the top. It looked innocent enough.

"Of course," Vince snapped out. He crossed the room and plopped onto the edge of the bed; his head fell into his cupped hands. "I am too tired for this bullshit," he groaned.

"She's just hungry." Normally when you plugged a bottle into her, she stopped crying. This time was no different. I sat down next to Vince, cradling the baby with one arm. "Destiny came to visit today."

"I saw her," he commented without looking up. "What did she want?"

"She brought Linnie over. She's a Bella."

This made him look up at me. "What did she say about the baby?"

"She wanted to know her name and how old she is. They thought it was weird that I didn't know." I bit lightly on the side of my cheek. "Do you know?"

"She was born on March 24th," he recited quickly. "So she's like three months old, almost."

My eyes widened. He knew her birthday? "And her name?"

"I only ever heard Beth call her Princess."

"Me too."

For a moment, only the sounds of the baby drinking her milk filled the room. Then Vince asked the question we were both thinking. "Should we give her a name?"

His head turned to look at me. We were close enough that I saw him swallow.

"We'll need to eventually." I shrugged.

"Did you have something in mind?"

"Umm…" There were so many names available, how were we supposed to pick just one? She would keep it with her forever. It seemed like an important decision. "What about…Lisa?"

His nose scrunched in distaste. "No, I don't like that."

I didn't like it much either, but I did know a woman named Lisa once, and she was really nice. "Melody?"

"No. What if she hates music?"

"No one hates music."

"She might."

"What do you think it should be?"

"Nothing too fancy." He pushed one finger into his chin and began rubbing out tiny circles as he thought it through. "Her mom's name was Beth, and that's pretty plain. Plus, she's already different enough since she's a Bella. She won't want to stand out any more than that."

"But it has to mean something special."

We both fell silent.

"Let's just think about it for a while," he finally suggested. "I'm sure we'll think of something perfect."

"She fell asleep again," I pointed out the obvious. Her soft snores sounded loud in the silent room. "We better sleep while we can."

At my words, he hopped off the bed and took the baby from my arms so he could lay her back in her bed. Since it was his turn for night duty, I crawled across the bed to press myself close to the wall. Vince grumbled under his breath as he lay down beside me.

He hated night duty; the baby seemed to cry a lot more during the night. People were all afraid of the nights, even when they were too young to understand the dangers that might be hidden in the darkness. It must be an instinct we were all born with.

"I can take the rest of the night," I heard myself offering.

"It's my turn," he grunted. "I got her."

"You said you were tired."

"You're not?" He shifted his body so he could face me. "I thought this would be easy," he whispered. "She's so small. I didn't think it would be hard to keep her alive."

My lips turned up into a half smile. "I'm sure it'll be easier when she can actually wipe her own butt."

Vince's laughter started small but soon shook his whole body. The sound went through me like a jolt of electricity. It was strange, but not unwelcome.

"Get some sleep," he said when he finally sobered up.

"Thanks."

I woke up slowly, surprised to see the sunlight streaming through the bedroom window. I didn't think I would be able to sleep at all after we got up with the baby the previous night. Here it was—daylight—and I was just waking up.

Where was Vince?

I stretched my arms high over my head, relishing in the feeling of my bones popping all into place again. Since I had been changed into a vampire, many years ago, I had been tense. I was always looking over my shoulder for danger, always searching for my next meal that wouldn't raise alarm bells, always on alert for hunters.

In Havenwood Falls, I didn't have to worry so much. Before moving here, I never got to wake up whenever I felt like it and enjoy a good stretch. Even with the baby and Vince, moving here was a good idea.

"Where are you?" I called out to Vince, knowing he would hear me.

"We're out back," he immediately responded. "Enjoying a little sunshine."

Sunshine? Even though we could go out in the sun here, it still burned a bit. He better not be overdoing it.

I got up and pulled on a pair of jeans and a white T-shirt. Maybe I had slept too long. I still felt groggy.

Groaning as I walked, I made my way to the backyard where Vince and the baby were. She was laying on a blue blanket that was laid on the ground while he sat under a large umbrella that protected him from most of the sun.

"What about her?" I asked, sitting next to him. "She'll get burnt."

"I don't think the sun has any effect on her."

I mentally tucked away that question to ask Linnie later. I really didn't feel like arguing with Vince when I just woke up. "How long have you been out here?"

"About twenty minutes." He shrugged. "We took a walk earlier to get some blood. It's in the fridge."

Yet another perk of the town.

"I got some steaks from Pyntz Butcher Shoppe, too," he continued. "I thought maybe we could cook outside tonight."

"Okay."

"What about Shelia?"

"Who's Shelia?"

"I mean for the bay—a name for her."

"No." That was a stupid name for a small baby. Only middle-aged women with frizzy blonde hair were named Shelia. "Her human host was from Mexican descent. Maybe we should think of a Latino kind of Spanish name."

"It's not like she will know any Spanish," he immediately shot me down. "I thought we agreed on simple."

As if she sensed a fight about to break out, the baby started kicking her feet and blowing bubbles with her spit. If an adult tried that it would be disgusting, but somehow the baby was kind of cute.

Despite having just gotten outside, my temples were starting to burn. It was probably because I just woke up and hadn't eaten anything yet.

"Is it just us tonight?" I asked Vince.

"Yeah. Unless you think we should invite Destiny and Linnie."

"They're out of town for a few days."

"Do you have any other friends here that I should know about?" He swung his gaze to my face, making my chest clench briefly.

What the fuck was happening to me?

"Just us then," I croaked, swallowing hard past my dry throat. "I'm going inside."

CHAPTER 3

*H*alf running, I made my way into the kitchen and leaned against the fridge. I rubbed at my aching chest, my confusion mounting. Something was definitely wrong with me. I was actually having a hard time breathing.

Was this all because of Vince? I mean, it felt like I was having a heart attack so maybe.

Did I like Vince?

My eyes widened and tried to pop out of my head as the thought came to fruition. There was no way in hell I liked Vince; he wasn't my type.

He was annoying, and he whined about everything.

And yet...the way his hair stood up in odd places after he woke up was kind of cute. And he was here in a new town just to take care of someone else's kid.

He wasn't all bad.

The back door opened softly, then banged closed again. I could tell by the smell that it was Vince. He didn't have the baby with him.

"Hey." He put his hand on my shoulder to make me look at him. "Are you all right?"

"Don't touch me," I snarled, pushing him away from me. I didn't mean to be so rough, but that single touch made my senses reel.

"Wh—?"

"Where's the baby?" My wild eyes shot past him and darted to the back door. "Did you leave her out there alone?"

"Just for a second." Scowling, he pushed past me. "I came in to get a drink. She's fine. I'll be able to hear if someone comes."

I knew I was being unreasonable, so why couldn't I stop myself?

"I don't know why you're being so pissy." Vince sighed, striding to the fridge and pulling it open. "You think someone will come and take her?"

"No." I didn't think that.

Vince yanked the lemonade out and poured a tall glass full. He was still scowling when he turned back to me.

Outside, on her little blue blanket, the baby squirmed and giggled softly. "What could she be laughing about?" I wondered out loud. "She's alone out there."

"Why don't you go check?" Vince drank from his cup. His Adam's apple bobbed seductively.

What would it feel like to nibble on that neck?

What the actual fuck?

"I'm going to shower," I abruptly declared. "I need...I need a shower."

"Okay." His eyebrows dipped low. "Well, hurry up. It's your turn with her."

"My turn?"

Vince paused in front of me on his way back outside. "What's wrong with you?"

"The sun...must be getting...to me." I shifted my eyes away from him.

"You weren't even out there long." His nose wrinkled. "Go shower."

"That was...that was my plan," I stammered. This was weird. I needed to get ahold of myself before Vince found out and things got awkward.

With one last roll of his eyes, Vince walked past me and went back outside with the baby. I didn't want to notice but it was impossible not to see how good his ass looked in those jeans.

The hot water cascaded down my skin. Vince and I both liked the water pressure hard so it felt like it was stabbing our skin. It was nice that we were on the same page for that one thing.

Now that we were living together, I was starting to see more good things than I had before. He always smelled delicious—like he just came from a bakery.

And when he smiled...

I closed my eyes and raised my face into the water. My shoulders relaxed. Honestly, I did like Vince—I liked him a lot. There was no point in denying the truth while it was just me in the shower. I didn't like him very much when we first took the kid, but now it was all different.

I ran my hand over my smooth chest and down my well-maintained body. I would have rather been touching his body but mine would have to do for now.

"Oh, Vince, what are you doing to me," I mumbled under the water stream.

My nostrils flared with pleasure, and my mouth fell open. I kept my face in the water as much as possible so he wouldn't hear anything and get suspicious.

It wasn't like he was listening or anything; he was busy with the baby.

I bit back my moans as my body jerked with pleasure. "Uh," I hissed, unable to hold it back.

The big question I had to ask myself after my breathing calmed down some, was if I should tell Vince how I felt.

No, I can't.

We still had a long time together with the baby—I couldn't go and make things weird.

The meat sizzled on the grill in front of me, creating a pleasant aroma that made my mouth water. Since Vince was busy with baby duty, I gladly took over the cooking.

The sun was still in the sky where it usually was in the daytime, but it was starting to sink behind the mountain. Sunset wasn't far off. That was my favorite part of the day. It always had been.

A few feet away, the baby was laying in the grass while Vince sat next to her. For such a small human, she didn't need us as much as I had anticipated. As long as we fed her and changed her diaper at regular intervals, she was content enough.

A small squeal from the kid made me look over at where my makeshift family was hanging out. She was fine. Vince wasn't even looking at her. He was staring straight at me.

My small intake of breath could have been mistaken for a gasp, but it definitely wasn't that. But why was he staring at me like that? His eyes were trying to pierce right through me to discover all my secrets.

Fuck.

I hurried to look back down at the grill, anywhere but at him. If I stared back, it would be too easy to tell where my thoughts had strayed to lately.

Although I wasn't looking at him, it was easy to hear when Vince got up and walked over to me. He wasn't trying to hide his footsteps; he was just walking carelessly.

Not that he needed too.

My ears felt hot, along with the rest of my body. What did he want? Why did he have to come clear over here just to hover over my shoulder? Damn it!

"You're awfully tense," he said in a slow voice that had no business being so husky when it was still daylight and we had a baby two feet away. "What's wrong?"

"What?" I glanced quickly between him and the grill. "I'm not tense. Why do you think that?"

Vince repositioned so I had no choice but to see him from my peripheral vision. "Do you need me to help you with something over here?"

My forehead wrinkled dramatically, almost as dramatic as my words. "No way, I'm fine. You can go sit back down. I got this. It's just meat. I can handle meat."

"I know how well you can handle meat." He grinned.

"What?" My hands stilled.

"I heard you earlier. In the shower."

Oh fuck. Of course he heard me. "What are you...what are you talking about? It was just a normal shower. We both take them. All the time."

"No." His eyes narrowed. "I heard it all. Every last moan."

"Every last..." My face drained of what little blood was left in it. My breath was coming out too hard and fast. I could hear the way it echoed inside my ears. He was standing too close to me, but I refused to make eye contact.

"All of it," he breathed out with a faint smile. He was so close that I could feel his hot breath fan out across my face.

"Why the fuck did you listen? No one said you had to listen to me while I took a shower. What kind of creep are you?" I pushed him back but made sure it was just a light shove; not like the way I had done it in the kitchen earlier.

Vince covered his mouth with one closed fist to hide the laughter that had jumped up to his lips. "My hearing is really good." He pointed one finger into my chest. "It's not my fault I could hear you."

Shit, I might as well be a teenager again with this inability to control myself. I knew his hearing was as good as mine. How could I be so impulsive?

"Just go sit down," I grumbled. "You're supposed to be over there with the baby while I cook, remember?"

"Why do you want me to leave so bad?"

"Maybe I just want to be alone."

There went his stupid eyebrow again. "Oh," he sang, his eyes going bright. "You want to be alone?"

"I just meant…you know…for you to go over there."

"You need to be alone so you can jerk off again?"

My eyes rolled. "You think I'm just going to whip it out right here?"

"You weren't so shy earlier."

"I was in the shower." My top lip flipped up off my teeth. "Am I not allowed to enjoy myself when I'm alone?"

"Umm…being alone in this house is just an illusion." He tapped lightly on his own ears.

"Well, then, I guess you're just going to have to get used to hearing things you don't want to."

I still didn't get why he had to hear it all and even worse, why he felt the need to tell me he heard. I had good hearing too, but I didn't listen to everything just because I could.

Was nothing sacred in this house?

CHAPTER 4

"Who said I didn't want to hear?" Vince asked.

"What?"

"You said I was going to have to get used to hearing things I didn't want to hear," he prompted my memory. "But I never said that I didn't like it."

I swallowed quickly. It had been a really long time since someone had me feeling shy like this. I didn't even know what to say to him. "Well…"

"Can I ask you something?"

My eyes narrowed. "Yeah…?"

"Did it feel good?"

"Fuck," I hissed out. "Don't say things like that. She'll hear you." I tilted my chin in the direction of the baby.

"I don't think she can understand English yet."

"Go back over there." I sucked in a quick breath. "Leave me alone while I cook."

"You know…" He pursed his lips thoughtfully. I knew before he said another word that I didn't want to know what he was going to say. "I heard something else that was kind of interesting while you were in the shower."

"Oh, yeah?" I made absolutely sure to keep my face blank.

"Yeah." He nodded slowly.

"Was it the water? 'Cause I'm pretty sure there was a lot of water going on."

Vince took a partial step closer; he was already close enough before. "I heard my name." His eyes stayed locked on my face, not giving me an inch of comfort. "You were thinking about me in there."

One incredibly long and awkward moment passed between us. My lungs collapsed in my chest and couldn't get air to my brain. What the hell was I supposed to say to that?

"What?" I heard myself squeak as if it was coming from someone else. "I never said your name. You must have heard wrong. I mean... with the water and everything else...going on..."

Clamping my lips tight over any unsaid ramblings, I hurried to turn my attention back to the grill. Neither of us liked our steaks well done so I didn't want to burn them.

Vince laughed. He laughed hard enough to crinkle his eyes and shake his shoulders. If I wasn't dying of humiliation, I might have been able to take a moment to appreciate that sound.

Honestly, it was lovely.

Vince moved up behind me, so close that I felt the contours of his body molding into mine.

"Do you think of me often when you're...in the shower?" He whispered the question against the back of my neck.

Something warm moved its way up my spine, making me shudder. Not wanting him to guess what was causing my shivers, I winced away from him and whirled around.

The biggest problem now was how close he was. He didn't move away so when I turned to face him, our faces were incredibly close together. If I stuck my tongue out, I would be able to trace the soft crevices of his lips.

"I don't even know why you have to ask." I shrugged my shoulders wildly. "You can hear every sound I make so you know who I think about and how many times and..."

Vince bit down on his bottom lip, effectively cutting off all my thoughts and taking the wind from my brief outburst. He was absolutely doing that on purpose.

Excitement threatened to embarrass me again.

"Do you want to know a secret?" His soft voice went husky.

"Uh…"

"I think of you, too." His eyes bore into mine so intently that I couldn't even try to look away.

"You think of me when…?" My eyes traveled down his body suggestively.

"Yep." His grin was soft, and he looked slightly embarrassed, but he didn't look away. "More than once, actually."

"But I've never heard anything." We lived in the same house, a house that wasn't even very big. I had excellent hearing; I could hear everything inside and most things outside. I had never heard anything like *that* from him.

"Well," he chuckled, "I'm more discreet than you are. I'm not some horny teenager who jerks off without a care in the world."

"I…" I clicked my tongue against my teeth. "I wasn't being that loud." I was in the shower with the water running. He only heard me because he was listening. And this was the first time…in a month.

Vince moved without warning; he was too close to my face for me to react or move out of the way. Not that I would have wanted to.

His lips crushed against my own, moving with expertise and a gentleness I wouldn't have expected from him. When he pushed his tongue into my mouth, I responded quickly and let my tongue dance with his.

He pulled away, licking his bottom lip. "I think staying here with you might not be so bad after all."

"Oh?" I raised one eyebrow. "Did you think it was bad before?"

"I saw the potential." He laughed. "Obviously. But I didn't realize you would be so…enthusiastic."

"Whatever." Despite my eye roll, I wrapped my hand around the back of his head and pulled him back in for another kiss.

Vince's hands trailed down my body and rested at my hips where he began to lightly massage. Small noises of pleasure came from him, almost making me lose my mind. There was one thing though that brought us back to our senses.

The baby squealed from her blanket. It wasn't a sound of distress, but it very effectively broke us apart before things could go too far right here in the backyard.

"The baby is crying," Vince rasped. His chest heaved, and his face was flushed.

"You are so hot," I mumbled.

"Bonnie," he said loudly. "She's crying."

I peeked around him. "She's not crying, she just…" I ran my tongue over the name he had just called her. "Bonnie?"

Vince shrugged his shoulders. "I was thinking about it, and you said we should name her something Spanish."

"Bonnie is not Spanish."

"Yeah," he agreed. "But Bonita is Spanish for pretty. So I thought we could call her Bonnie for short."

"What if she turns out to be ugly?"

His eyes instantly narrowed. "She won't be ugly."

"You never know." I shrugged.

"We can't call her Feo," he snapped irritably.

My half-hidden grin exploded into full laughter.

"I like Bonnie. It's a cute name for her. Simple but with a hidden meaning." Vince pursed his lips in a fake pout. Not able to resist myself, I quickly kissed those lips.

I watched him walk back to Bonnie and drop down on the ground next to her. Wanting to join them, I hurried to finish the steaks then made the short walk myself.

"These smell good," Vince commented, sticking his face close to the freshly grilled meat. "We can count this as a sort of birthday celebration."

"Is it your birthday?" Honestly, I didn't know much about Vince. Now I had eighteen years to learn all I wanted to know. *Not a bad way to spend my time.*

"Did you forget the date? It's June 24th. Bonnie is three months old today."

Running one finger over her cheek, I smiled down at the small baby. I had been responsible for her for a month now, and I could already feel the strong bond between us.

"I'm glad we came here." I glanced out at the sun that was making its decent back into the earth. "Destiny was right about this town."

"Bonnie will have a safe life here. She won't live like we did."

In fairness, Vince and I hadn't been born vampires, so we were going into this a bit blind. At least here, she would have Linnie, and she'd be safe from hunters.

I shifted my body so I could wrap my arm around Vince and watch the sun go down. Sunset was our favorite time of day, even before coming to Havenwood Falls. But here, now, with Bonnie—it was that much better.

We were a family.

RECONNECTION

E.J. FECHENDA

CHAPTER 1

The moment the front door clicks closed, I lean back against it and let out a deep breath. Exhaustion eats away at my very bones, and I just want to curl up on the sofa to take a nap. A cry from the other room snuffs out any thoughts of having a moment of peace and quiet to myself. In response to the cry, my breasts begin to ache. I didn't have time to pump before I left for Coffee Haven earlier this morning, and it's a miracle I'm not leaking breastmilk all over the place. After setting my bag on the counter, I start walking down the hall toward the downstairs guest room, which has been converted into a playroom for the girls, unbuttoning my shirt along the way. My mom looks up from where she is sitting on the floor playing with Arabella and Chanell. She gives me a knowing look when she sees my half-dressed state and stands up, scooping Chanell into her arms to pass the infant off to me.

It takes just seconds for my baby girl to latch onto a nipple, and the pressure in my breast begins to ease. I sink down into the rocking chair in the corner, running my fingers through Chanell's white-blonde curls.

"Mommy, look what I made!" Arabella calls out, pointing at the lopsided castle she has constructed out of blocks.

"Very nice, sweetheart," I croon, and she beams at me before going back to playing with a couple of dolls who are defending the castle.

"Ready for your hot date tonight, Willow?" my mom asks, which causes me to close my eyes and groan as I lean my head back against the chair. My response causes her to chuckle.

"I remember those days, but it's important for you to celebrate your anniversary and have quality couple time."

Chase and I always make an effort to celebrate the first day we met as our true anniversary. I mean, it was basically love at first sight. Two children later, we're still committed to each other, but with my business and his role as liaison between Faerie and Havenwood Falls, it seems as though our time together as a couple has been limited. When there is time for each other, one of us, or both, are usually exhausted.

Case in point, just the very the idea of getting ready for our date tonight is exhausting. I can use a glamour for my hair and makeup, even for some grooming of the lady bits, which have just been cleared for active duty after giving birth to Chanell. But that would require moving —actually getting up from the chair. I switch the baby over to my other breast, and she hungrily latches on without complaint. At least the threat of leaking like a water balloon with holes in it has been taken care of.

Coffee Haven had been busy today, and I had a bunch of paperwork to slog through after we closed. The last thing I want to do is go out on a date. I briefly wonder if Chase would be happy with staying home. We could order takeout and hang in our pajamas. Not sexy, but low energy. As if she can read my mind like my great-grandfather, my mom shakes her head at me and reaches out for Chanell, who has fallen into a milk coma against my bare chest.

"Willow, go have a long bath. I'm taking the girls with me for their sleepover. Get pretty for your man and enjoy your night on the town. It will be worth it."

Gross. Is my mom giving me romance advice? I button up my blouse before heaving out of the rocking chair with a sigh. After kissing Arabella and Chanell, I heed my mom and go upstairs to the master bedroom. A basket full of unfolded laundry sits in on the bed, but I ignore it as the large stone jacuzzi tub in the ensuite bathroom calls my name. As I soak in a cloud of jasmine scented bubbles, I let go of the stress of the day. I let go of the exhaustion caused by nights of interrupted sleep. For the first time in what seems like forever, I have the house to myself, and the quiet peacefulness settles over me, lulling my eyelids closed.

The creak of a floorboard breaks through my half-asleep state, and I jerk awake only to find my husband's handsome face smiling down at me. Chase dips his hand in the water, and it instantly begins to warm back up.

"Mind if I join you, love?" He asks, skimming his fingertips along my thigh under the water, leaving a trail of goosebumps in their wake, and I instantly perk up. Well, all right then, date night has begun.

"I'd be disappointed if you didn't."

I watch as Chase unbuckles the leather holster and removes it, sword and all, from around his hips. His sword clangs when it hits the tile floor. Next, he pulls his shirt over his head, foregoing the buttons, and I watch as he slowly reveals inch after inch of toned, golden skin. His abs clench when he bends over to remove his socks. Then he's wearing nothing except a charcoal gray kilt, and I just stare up in awe at the golden god standing before me. We did have descendants of gods in Havenwood Falls and attending the Sun & Moon Academy, but Chase isn't one of them, although he looks the part. No, Chase is Seelie fae, like me. He radiates light and has a subtle glow that always appears brighter whenever he returns from Faerie, like he is a battery and being in his homeland recharges him.

He's a liaison for the Seelie Courts now, and a professor at the Sun and Moon Academy Halvard Campus, but spent his earlier years as a warrior with the Seelie Guard, and he has maintained the muscular physique, although he is leaner than his brother Seamus, who is still a member of the Guard. Chase's blond hair is pulled back into a man bun, which only draws attention to the sharp planes of his face—a strong jawline and cheekbones. My man still manages to take my breath away.

Chase smirks, and his blue eyes sparkle with mischief as he reaches for the button securing his kilt. With a pop, he releases it, and his last item of clothing drops to the floor with a whisper. Once he is completely nude, I can tell he is…very *excited* to see me. I'm tempted to make a joke about his "sword," but I'm suddenly desperate to be closer to him. The bathtub walls feel like a barrier keeping us apart, so I raise a hand toward him, bathwater and suds dripping down the length of my arm, and he grabs a hold, climbing into the tub. I scoot forward, and Chase eases in behind me, his long legs stretching out beside mine. With a sigh, I relax against his chest, and he nuzzles my neck.

"Happy Anniversary, my love," he says, placing gentle kisses along my steam dampened skin.

"Mmmm…Happy Anniversary." My words sound almost slurred, I'm so relaxed.

"Do you hear that?" Chase whispers in my ear. I strain to listen, extending my enhanced hearing. I hear the clock ticking downstairs in the kitchen. I hear water running through the pipes and the slight hum of electricity. Outside someone is mowing their lawn, and farther down the street a dog barks.

"What am I supposed to be hearing?" I ask as nothing unusual jumps out at me.

"Nothing. We have the house to ourselves. No children for the next twenty-four hours. These…" he cups my breasts with his big hands. "These are mine," he breathes against my neck before placing another kiss there.

Holy faeries, when he goes all possessive like this, I melt even more. I turn my head, and he meets me halfway, his lips pressing over mine.

We stay like that in the slowly cooling bathwater—kissing, touching, and reconnecting. Any heaviness from the constant worries of being a mom, wife, and business owner lift away as we focus on each other. When we finally emerge from the bath, the sun has begun to set, and my stomach rumbles, reminding me we're long past our usual dinner time. After our bath, I'm too blissed out and relaxed to think about putting clothes back on. The idea of getting dressed to go out for a dinner date and having to maintain my shields, to prevent reading people's emotions when we're in public, exhausts me.

Chase isn't empathic like me, but we've been together long enough he knows how to read me. He hands me my favorite silk robe. It's a beautiful lavender color, and the soft fabric feels great against my bare skin.

"Relax, love. I'll order dinner from Napoli's to be delivered." He kisses my forehead before leaving me in the bedroom to just be.

If we aren't going out, then I don't need to get dressed, so I leave the room in just my robe and head downstairs. Chase is in the kitchen wearing only a pair of mesh basketball shorts. I am stunned stupid, taking in his warrior's body. The brand on his left shoulder, a mark indicating he's a member of the Seelie Court, stands out. He is on the phone with Napoli's when he glances over at me, and I am caught ogling. He grins and winks before turning his attention back to our dinner order. I busy myself getting drinks, a glass of pinot grigio for me and two fingers worth of scotch for Chase. The dish rack next to the sink is full of clean baby bottles and Arabella's favorite sippy cup. Seeing them makes my heart pang. I miss my babies. This is Chanell's first night away, and up until now, I've been distracted by my gorgeous husband.

"I miss them, too," Chase says, kissing my temple before sitting down on the stool next to me. We sit at the island in the kitchen, which has a counter that serves as a bar. The light gray granite is cool against my arms. "Although, I am enjoying not having to share you right now because I missed us, love." He reaches for my hand and links our fingers together.

Yes, we needed this reconnection. Life only got busier with Chanell's arrival. Chase's position with the Seelie fae in Faerie requires him to be gone for some extended periods, so most of the daily household stuff falls to me to handle. Not that I am upset over it, but it feels like I hit the ground running after Chanell was born two months ago and haven't had a chance to stop and catch my breath. This, right now, is Chase recognizing that and giving me a chance to just breathe. I let out a deep sigh and sip some more wine, taking in the peacefulness. Here I don't have to shield myself from the barrage of emotions I am usually assaulted with when in town. Running a popular coffee shop means I am constantly exposed.

We relocate to the front porch, and I curl up next to Chase on the wicker loveseat. He tucks me against his side, and we settle in to watch the sunset, admiring the few clouds clinging to the mountain that are painted a lush combination of orange and pink. We talk about everything and nothing.

"Hi, cuz, hey Chase!" a deep voice says, and I grin at my cousin, Dalton as he walks up the front steps, carrying a bag of food. The aroma of garlic and fresh tomato sauce fills the air around us.

He just graduated from Havenwood Falls High School, and I'm still not used to his deeper voice. He has transitioned from boy to man, seemingly overnight, and I am curious to see how much more he will grow when he starts at the Academy in the fall. Since his awakening, he's been using the manipulation of air to help him with his skateboarding and snowboarding. The jumps and lifts he is capable of performing are jaw dropping, and when he applies himself, I expect him to be capable of great feats. His summer job is as a delivery driver for Napoli's, so I'm not surprised to see him.

Chase and I get up, and Dalton follows us into the house. He sets the paper bag on the island and leans against the counter. His white-blonde hair, which is longer on top and buzzed short on the sides, falls in front of his navy blue eyes, which are practically identical to his dad's. "Mom wanted me to tell you not to worry about the girls. She's going to be helping your mom out in the morning."

Dalton's mom and my mom were not only sisters, but they were co-owners of Fairy Tale Florists.

"That's awesome of her. I'll have to thank her later."

Chase hands Dalton a twenty-dollar bill for a tip, which makes my cousin smile. He claps Chase on the back, and that's when I realize they're almost the same height. A lump forms in my throat at the awareness of how quickly kids grow up.

"Enjoy your date night and make sure you have safe words!" Dalton calls out with a laugh as he leaves the kitchen.

"What do you know about safe words, Dalton!" I shout after him, and a cackle is his only response before the front door clicks shut. Shaking my head at his antics, I laugh and meet Chase's eyes. He's laughing, too, as he pulls out containers of food from the paper bags.

"That kid cracks me up," he says and pops a garlic knot in his mouth.

We settle on the sofa in the living room, food and drinks on the coffee table in front of us, next to a stack of children's books, and Chase queues up *Game of Thrones* for us to watch. Harlow and her man, Ryker, had convinced us to watch the show, and we've been hooked ever since, but having two little ones in the house makes it almost impossible to watch. Napoli's and an adult show with my love—this is just what I needed. We don't have to go out for a date. Having one at home is perfect.

Chase's warmth seeps into me, and I wind up dozing. The next thing I know, Chase is scooping me up in his arms. I nuzzle against his chest as he carries me upstairs to our bedroom. We get ready for bed, and I sink into the comfort of the mattress with Chase curled up behind me, an arm draped over my hips.

CHAPTER 2

*T*he next morning, I wake on my own. The alarm didn't need to be set, and the house is eerily quiet without the girls. As I lay there listening to the water running in the bathroom, where Chase is taking a shower, I chill for a moment to stretch out and relax. I'm not in any hurry to get up. I don't have to go to Coffee Haven, and my mom will have the girls until later in the afternoon. I've forgotten what it's like to just be and not be pulled in a million different directions.

Chase emerges from the bathroom, a cloud of steam billowing out behind him, with a green towel wrapped around his waist. He catches me admiring him and proceeds to strut over to the bed to crawl on top of me. I giggle, falling back against the pillows, and wrap my arms around his neck, pulling him down to meet my lips. He practically melts into me, and I revel in his solid weight. Only when I lower a hand to the towel and try to tug it free, does he break the kiss and place a hand on top of mine to still my movements.

"Not yet, love. We still have a date to finish," he says, before placing a quick kiss on my lips and hoisting himself off of me. I'm temporarily distracted by his muscles and whine in disappointment when he stands up.

"What do you mean? Last night was our date, wasn't it?" I lick my lips as he enters the walk-in closet and proceeds to drop the towel. *Sweet faeries, I'm a lucky woman*, I think to myself and let out a soft sigh.

He pulls on a pair of dark blue jeans that hang on his hips and then a light blue button-down shirt. He immediately rolls the sleeves up to his elbows, exposing his muscular forearms. I sigh again. "We're going to brunch. You're always serving people breakfast. You must be tired of blueberry scones by now."

"That's a blasphemous statement around these parts, mister," I tease, and press a palm against my chest in mock disconcertment. The award-winning blueberry scones we serve at Coffee Haven are a beloved food staple in Havenwood Falls. With a groan, I climb out of bed, my body pleasantly sore, and make my way into the bathroom to get ready. "Where are we going anyway?" I ask while running a comb through my long, silvery white-blonde hair.

"Whisper Falls Inn. I made reservations in advance since the place is usually packed for brunch."

I perk up at the idea of seeing Michaela Petran, owner of the inn. My stomach growls at the thought of the strawberry crepes that are part of the brunch menu. While I am enjoying our little bubble, the last time Chase and I went out as a couple, I was pregnant. I am definitely ordering a mimosa to have with the crepes. Motivated by the prospect of food, I pull a blue and green sundress on. It's form-fitting at the top with an empire waist. The skirt of the dress is a flowy cotton and is longer than what I usually wear. The soft material brushes the tops of my feet when I slide my sandals on. I grab a light blue cardigan that matches the dress and put it on right before leaving the house.

Chase holds the car door open for me, and I lower myself onto the passenger seat. When we first moved in together, we lived in an apartment in Havenwood Village, which is closer to downtown, and we usually walked to the local bars and restaurants. Since having Arabella, we bought a house in Creekwood Estates a few blocks over from where I grew up. Having my parents in the same subdivision is convenient.

The parking lot for the inn is full but after going around the square, we find a parking spot near Coffee Haven. Chase has to tug on my hand to keep me from heading in the direction of my business. Even though I know George has things under control, it's almost like auto-pilot to want to pop in and check on things.

"No work today, love," Chase reminds me, dropping a kiss on my temple. "I even told the queen no summons today. We earned this time together."

My eyebrows lift in surprise, for he rarely puts boundaries in place with the Seelie Queen. She is someone who demands full allegiance and attention.

"How did you manage that?" I ask.

He looks down at me with a smug grin on his beautiful face. "Well, she still feels a wee bit guilty about crashing Chanell's baby shower, so I used that to our advantage."

The reminder of the queen's vague premonition about Chanell's future and how she has a crucial part to play in something big sends a shudder of fear down my spine. The queen wouldn't outright say, but the ambiguity of what our daughter might face let my worry run rampant.

"Relax, love," Chase whispers and squeezes my hand, making me realize I was gripping his too tightly. "There's nothing we can do except raise Chanell to be strong and make good decisions—steer her away from dark influences. The light within her is powerful. Your uncle Jasper noticed it the moment she was born."

Of course, Chase is right, and his reminder makes me loosen the hold I have on his hand. Chanell's delivery went much smoother than her older sister's. My uncle Jasper is a healer and doctor at the Havenwood Falls Medical Center. He oversaw my pregnancy and delivery. Once Chanell was born and cleaned up, Uncle Jasper had scanned her with his powers to check for any abnormalities. Fortunately, she was a healthy and normal Seelie fae infant, pointed ears and all. Uncle Jasper did note that her very core, where her full powers would eventually develop upon her Awakening, emitted a strong pulse of positive light and energy. His initial assessment had eased our worries after the queen's spontaneous appearance at the baby shower.

We approach the corner of Main and Eleventh Streets, and Tristan Mills is sweeping the sidewalk out front of Simple Treasures Pawn Shop, his family's business. From his crisp, pleated khakis to his wrinkle-free dress shirt, Tristan exudes order and cleanliness. I think he has the cleanest sidewalk of all the businesses on the square.

"Good morning!" he calls out with a wave as we walk past.

"Morning, Tristan," I reply. "How've you been?" While our businesses are on the same street and both of us have relatives on the Court of the Sun and the Moon, we rarely get to see each other.

"Can't complain. Dad has finally, and not without a lot of complaining, allowed me to take the business online. We actually have a website and EBay store now."

"Whoa! The modern age, huh? I bet Lawrence hates that."

"You know he does, but he likes the revenue. He still grumbles about the invention of telephones and reminisces about the good old days of calling cards," Tristan says with a laugh that makes his blue eyes sparkle. I nod in understanding. My grandfather Elsmed, who is somewhere close to eight hundred years old, or older, fae knows how old he really is, struggles with technology, too. The wards that protect our town often prevent technology from working all of the time, which just adds to the frustration.

"Good seeing you. Pop in for a coffee sometime."

He promises to do so and continues sweeping as Chase and I move on. Tristan is emitting positivity and happiness, which I soak up, helping to settle my emotions. It's a warm summer day, and I tilt my head up toward the sun, enjoying the warmth that kisses my cheeks and shoulders as we wait for traffic to clear in order to cross the street. After a few moments, Chase leads us to the other side, where the wrap-around porch of Whisper Falls Inn is visible beyond a blooming hedge of azaleas. The inn itself takes up almost the entire block and sits diagonal, providing a view of the gazebo in the town square from the porch.

There's a long brick walkway leading to the front steps. As we get closer, I notice all of the bistro tables on the porch are occupied. Dining on the porch during the summer months is a recent addition Michaela Petran has made since she took over ownership of the inn that has been in her family since the town was founded. As the dining room is usually at capacity, this was an easy solution. I, too, have a small outdoor seating area on the sidewalk in front of Coffee Haven, and it's a popular spot, especially in the summer.

We climb the front steps, and I see some familiar faces, but some I don't recognize among the diners. The ski resort draws a lot of tourists in the winter, but hiking, fishing, and the majestic mountain scenery brings people in year-round. It's not surprising to see the inn is bustling with activity.

Sherry and Rusty are at a table near the entrance, and Sherry smiles at me. I wave at her before walking through the front door Chase is holding open. Sherry has been in Havenwood Falls for about five years now, and we have gotten close since she became a regular at Coffee Haven. Rusty fell hard for her the moment she set foot in town. I absorb the love and lust the two of them emit into the air, and it results in a heady rush.

Leaning into Chase, I tell him about it, which makes him grin. "I bet we give off the same vibe, love."

"You're probably right." This makes me wonder what Sedona Matthews picks up. She's a fellow empath, and her bookstore is directly next door to Coffee Haven. There have been a few times Chase and I got hot and heavy after hours in the back office. My cheeks heat at the idea, but then I shake off the embarrassment. There's nothing embarrassing about love.

Michaela isn't working at the front desk in the lobby, but her sister is. Aurelia has gone from an angsty and angry teenager to a friendly and beautiful young woman. When her older sister first returned to Havenwood Falls, the animosity Aurelia felt toward Michaela was downright toxic. One didn't need to be an empath to detect it. Over the years, especially since Aurelia graduated high school and has spent more time working at the inn, their sisterly bonds have grown, which makes my heart happy.

Aurelia greets us with a genuine smile that reaches her greenish-gray eyes, so similar to her sister's and a trait all moroi vampire share, and checks us off the reservation list before picking up two menus and leading us back to the dining room. A cacophony of voices mingles with the scrape of silverware against porcelain when we enter the room. The entire back wall that faces the lawn and gardens is made of glass doors, and they're wide open. A gentle breeze carries in the scent from the floral and herb gardens that punctuate the sweet and savory scents from the variety of food being served.

"Willow, Chase, hi!" a familiar redhead calls out and jumps up from her chair.

"Aster, I didn't know you were in town," I say when she pulls me into a hug.

"I was planning on being here next weekend, but we have a meeting with the Denver supes, so I had to come this weekend in order to renew the memory spell." She whispers this to me, aware of the human ears around us. I nod in understanding. Once a resident is outside of the protective wards for longer than a lunar cycle, their memories of Havenwood Falls disappear. It's one of the measures in place to protect the supernatural community that has been thriving here, unbeknownst to humans, save for a select few, since the 1800s. "Reeve will be here next weekend, though. She mentioned something about setting up a playdate. Speaking of…" Aster peers around us, her green eyes seeking out something. "Where are the girls?"

"It's just us grownups today. Official first date since Chanell was born."

"Good for you, guys!" Aster says with a smile. "The grandkids are at home with my dad. We're just finishing up." She gestures to their table where her mom and sister-in-law are sitting. "Enjoy your date and take advantage. If you know what I mean." She wiggles her eyebrows, making us laugh.

I'm so pleased at how settled Aster has become. When she worked for me as manager of Coffee Haven, I sensed a restless spirit within. Havenwood Falls didn't fill her cup, and she was seeking more. Turns out her mate had been in Denver the whole time, and a series of events led him right to Aster's door. Funny how fate works that way. I look up at Chase and smile. He's from a completely different realm, and we still found each other.

As we're heading to the table, I see the sign for the restroom, which immediately puts my bladder on notice. I tell Chase I'll catch up with him and veer off down the hallway. I near the bathroom, and before I even reach the door, I can sense the distress that waits for me on the other side. The emotions being emitted are raw and strong, crashing into me like waves lashing against a rocky shoreline during a hurricane.

CHAPTER 3

I take a deep breath and bolster my shields before slowly pushing the wooden door open. The source of the emotional overload isn't hard to find. I hear heaving sobs coming from the first stall.

"Are you oaky?" I call out, knowing full well the woman is not okay.

The sobbing stops and a wave of embarrassment rolls over me.

"I've done my share of crying in bathrooms. There's nothing to be ashamed of. Are you okay—do you need me to get someone for you?"

"I'm fine."

I hold back a snort. As a woman, I know that when a woman says she's fine, chances are she isn't.

"Want to talk about it?" I ask, sensing a need for connection.

"Do you have kids?" the woman asks.

A smile skates across my lips when I think of my babies. "I do. Two girls. Actually, this is my first date out since the youngest was born two months ago."

Suddenly the emotions clouding the air shift, and I feel a strong sense of relief, which lowers the tension, making it easier to breathe.

The lock on the stall door clicks, and the door swings open, revealing a woman who appears to be in her late twenties. I don't recognize her and assume she's a tourist staying at the inn. She has thick, wavy brown hair that brushes the tops of her shoulders. Her heart shaped face is blotchy from crying, which has made her eyes bloodshot and puffy. Then I notice the dark circles on her shirt. The pastel green is darker around her breasts, and the damp material is sticking to her body.

"Oh," I say understanding the problem immediately. The woman's cheeks blush, making the blotchiness more sever. "You're lactating."

"Y-yeah," she responds, and it sounds like a hiccup. "This was supposed to be a romantic overnight getaway at a quaint bed and breakfast, and I'm leaking all over the place!"

"Is your partner out there? I can go get them for you."

"God no! I'm such a mess. This is not romantic." She gestures at her stained shirt. "I can't go out there like this, and I don't want John to think I'm falling apart. He was so excited about planning this weekend, and I'm ruining it."

"Trust me, I understand. Here." I pull my cardigan off and hold it out for the woman, who looks at me with surprise. "Use it to cover yourself so you can go to your room to freshen up. Your weekend isn't over."

"Thank you! I'm Sasha, by the way." She takes my cardigan and puts it on. I sense more relief once her stains are covered.

"I'm Willow. How old is your baby?"

"Three months and two days. Jeremiah is our first, and he just got over colic. That was brutal. I was exhausted, so when John planned this getaway, I couldn't wait for some time alone, but I didn't think I'd miss my baby so much. Plus my body's just...ugh!"

"Right?" I agree with a laugh. "The leaking is the worst." And it really is. The changes your body goes through are remarkable, and I feel bad for humans—they can't rely on magic or glamours to hide the marks pregnancy leaves behind.

"The worst," Sasha agrees, letting out a soft chuckle. I get a sense she's alone in the world of new motherhood as if she's the only one of her friends experiencing being a new parent, and she doesn't have a mom or maternal figure to talk to about it. That's part of my gift, I'm able to dig deeper, beyond the emotions, to the root.

Reacting on instinct, I step forward and pull Sasha into a hug. She latches on like I'm a lifeline. I absorb her fears, uncertainty, anxiety, embarrassment, and homesickness into me. I feel her relax in my arms as I ease her burdens. Moments later she steps away, and I notice her eyes are brighter and she gives me a smile.

"Thank you, Willow. I feel much better now—no longer teetering on the edge," she says with a shaky laugh.

"It helps to have someone to talk to—someone who's been through it and understands." Sasha has no idea I'm not human and that I absorbed her emotions like a sponge and released them deep into the ground below the inn. "Go on—enjoy the rest of your weekend."

Sasha says goodbye, and I quickly freshen up, ready to take my own advice and enjoy the rest of my brunch date. On my way back to the dining room, I think about Sasha and how glad I am that my mom is around as a sounding board. In fact, it wasn't that long ago we had our conversation in a bathroom—the night I met Chase.

I can't believe it's been over six years since we first met. Chase had just taken on his diplomatic role for the Seelie Queen after his dad, who had held the ambassador position before, retired. My great-grandfather, Elsmed Fairchild, had all of the Seelie fae in town over for a welcoming reception. As soon as I walked into Elsmed's house, a warm wave washed over my entire body, leaving me flushed and aroused. Intrigued and wanting more, I followed the emotional signature, and it led me across the living room to a fae male I'd never seen before. He stood ramrod straight with his right hand pressed against his abdomen as if he was preparing to bow. I later learned his posture was from his warrior training and the pose a sign of respect for royalty. His thick blond hair was pulled back into a ponytail, allowing me full access to his face, and I stared at his beautiful features unabashedly. He was captivating, gorgeous, and a primal part of me, a part I'd never sensed before, urged me to claim him in front of everyone. I'd heard from my shifter friends that finding their mate is instinctual, the soul knows and calls out "mine." From that moment, I understood.

Chase's blue eyes had been locked on mine, and he tracked my progress as I crossed the room. Usually, I'd wait for Elsmed to make introductions, but I couldn't wait.

"Hi, I'm Willow Fairchild," I said and extended my hand for him to shake, licking my lips in anticipation of the contact. As soon as we touched, what I sensed was confirmed. When his large hand engulfed my smaller one, our energies called out to each other and immediately began to merge. His eyes widened, but he didn't try to pull away.

"Chase MacElvoy, love," he said, his voice husky like he spent his nights sipping bourbon around a campfire. I detected a brogue, and I later learned he spent a lot of his youth in Scotland. Considering he was close to three hundred years old, that youth was some time ago, yet the accent remained. When he added the term of endearment 'love', a shiver ran up my arm from our connection. He had just claimed me as his.

From that moment on, I didn't leave Chase's side, and my entire family, who was in attendance, noticed. The one time I stepped away to use the bathroom, my mom followed me with a knowing look on her face.

"Willow, what's going on with you and Ambassador MacElvoy? You've been inseparable all night." I sighed, a whimsical, dreamy sigh, and that caused my mom to chuckle. "I thought so. You've just met your match. Oh, honey!" She pulled me into a hug, and when we parted, her eyes were shiny with tears, but she wasn't sad. No, she exuded so much joy.

At the end of the night, Chase had to return to Faerie, and I accompanied him to the basement of City Hall, where the Court held their meetings and where a portal to his realm was located. The very thought of him leaving caused me to hold onto his hand tighter.

"I don't want you to go," I admitted, my throat tight with emotion. Sweet faeries, I probably sounded like a total clinger.

Chase pulled me close, and I was surrounded by his scent. His fair skin was cast in a purplish light from the portal.

"I don't want to leave, love," he whispered right before kissing me for the first time. If I thought the connection from just holding hands was a lot, the kiss was so much more. His hands skimmed down my back, coming to a stop just above my ass. What felt like tiny electrical sparks danced across my skin where we touched. I ran my hands through his hair, pulling it free from the ponytail. Our tongues swept against each other, and I groaned when he deepened the kiss. I practically melted into him, and we completely forgot Elsmed was standing nearby. I can only imagine how awkward it was for him to watch his great-granddaughter make out, but he thankfully didn't say anything. Since he could read minds, he probably already knew that Chase and I were quickly becoming a couple.

From the moment we met, we never looked back, and three months later, we were engaged. We didn't get married until two years later, after Arabella was born.

"What are you thinking about, beautiful?" Chase asks when I reach our table, and he pulls the chair out for me to sit down—always the gentleman.

"Just remembering the first time we met." I smile up at him.

"Aye, also known as the best day of my life." He leans down and gives me a kiss before sitting across from me. Aurelia hands us our menus and makes a hasty retreat as there are people waiting at the front desk.

"Here we are six years later, married with children and a mortgage. Are you happy?" I ask him, and he gives me a stern look.

"You're the empath. What do you think?" He reaches for my hand, running his thumb over my wedding band.

I take this moment to really tune into his energy, dipping far below the surface. Our energies are entwined, and I can visualize the strands. His are dark blue and mine lighter, almost like the color of our eyes, and they're twisted together in what resembles an illuminated Celtic knot. I follow his strands to his core, the source located in the center of his chest, and all the air whooshes out of my lungs. The sincere bliss and utter contentment in his soul leaves me breathless. Love seems too simple of a word to encompass his feelings for me, which echo mine. How can so much emotion be summed up by four letters?

Chase smiles and squeezes my hand. "Did you get your answer?" he asks softly.

"Yes."

"Good. Now let's enjoy the rest of our date and go get our girls. I miss their special brand of chaos."

"I miss them, too, but we have a few hours left to take advantage of an empty house, Ambassador." I lower my voice to a suggestive purr, and the heat that flares in Chase's eyes when I say his title that way makes me want to skip brunch all together. Who needs food when my husband smolders at me like he wants to eat me up?

"And take advantage of it we shall," he agrees, gesturing for the server to come take our order since he's feeling the same urgency to leave. "Happy Anniversary, my bonnie bride. Here's to many, many more. Slainte!" Chase raises his mimosa, and I clink my glass against his.

Just as we're getting ready to leave, Sasha stops by our table. She has changed into a black shirt and my cardigan is draped over her arm. A lanky man with dark hair and glasses stands beside her.

127

"Thank you again for your help," Sasha says and hands me the cardigan. "This is my husband, John."

We shake hands, and Chase introduces himself to the couple.

"I ran into Sasha in the bathroom and helped her out of a bind," I explain to Chase.

"Your wife is a goddess," Sasha gushes, making Chase laugh.

"Aye, I know and then some. I'm a lucky man." He emits a heavy pulse of emotion, which is just pure, unadulterated love that makes my knees go soft.

Life can get crazy, and we are often separated by realms, but moments like this remind me of the bond that connects us and the importance of celebrating our love. A love which has only grown over time and will help us persevere whatever the future holds for our family.

WHISPER SWEET HEXES

SF BENSON

CHAPTER 1

Winding Roads, A Chatty Angel, & A Hot Vampire

BELLA DONNA

*S*tevie Nicks blared from the tinny speakers of my aging hot pink VW Beetle—nicknamed Betsy Boo. Despite my favorite music playing and the wind in my hair, I didn't appreciate driving up the winding road. Why couldn't my friends get married in Durango?

For starters, I wouldn't have had to travel anywhere. When I was younger, I loved road trips. I thought nothing of gassing up my car, or hopping on my broom, to destinations unknown. But those days were long behind me. Between hot flashes and mood swings, simply packing my luggage was too much exercise for my weary bones.

The second thing wrong with heading out of town? I was doing it alone. The other witches and their partners would gawk at me and criticize.

"It's a shame that Bella Donna can't find a suitable mate…"

"If she didn't spend so much time at that shop of hers, she might find someone…"

"Oh, let's be serious. What man wants someone who dresses as if it's still the seventies…"

"You know the real reason she can't find a mate. A woman her size shouldn't walk around spouting hair in every shade of the rainbow..."

If it weren't for The Feminine Spirit boutique, my days and nights would be boring. Thankfully, running the business kept me so busy I didn't think about not having a significant man in my life.

Much.

Suddenly, Betsy Boo sputtered. A red light glowed on the dashboard. That was all the warning she gave before the vehicle slowed to a stop. Thick black smoke poured from the back.

Without looking in a mirror, I knew my hair had turned fire-engine red. I pounded the steering wheel. Getting stranded wasn't part of the program. Back in the day, I would have cast a spell and fixed the problem. And that was another reason I should have turned down the invite and kept my chunky butt at home. I could no longer rely on my quirky magic. Sometimes it worked perfectly. Most times, it didn't.

I exited the car and looked around. Lush forest surrounded the two-lane highway. Thankfully, Betsy Boo broke down outside of a town. A welcome sign embedded in a stone base declared my new destination was a place called Havenwood Falls. I removed my suitcase and purse, adjusted my floppy sun hat, and set off down the road.

Two problems hit me at once—the summer heat and the uphill climb. Three miles by car wouldn't have been a problem. On foot, it would be sheer torture for a short woman carrying an extra thirty pounds—and I didn't mean the luggage.

Being a witch, I had one option, provided my powers worked the way they were supposed to. At my age, not only were my hormones fickle. My unstable magic turned princes into frogs and innocent people into insects. An unfortunate situation that happened the last time I hopped on a public bus. That poor bus driver. He had a hard time explaining to the police what happened to his passengers.

Regardless, I had to give it a try. First, I attempted to fix Betsy Boo. The thick black smoke turned rainbow-colored and the vehicle wouldn't budge. Although it had been years since I roller skated, I zapped on a pair. I'd hoped for a pair of gas-powered wheels. Instead, I had to use my own energy to do the deed.

An hour later, I reached the town's Main Street. My first stop was Havenwood Falls Garage & Tow Service. A tall, thin man greeted me.

"What can I do for you?"

"My car broke down outside of town. Could you tow it for me and do the repair?"

"Sure thing. I'll tow it in, but it won't be ready until tomorrow at the earliest. We're closing for the night."

The owner of the garage directed to me to the three-story Victorian inn just down the street. The handsome man behind the desk gave me a warm feeling. Or was that just a hot flash?

"How can I help you?" he asked with a smile.

I crossed the lobby and said, "Please tell me you have a room available."

"You're in luck." He turned to the computer. "Name?"

"Bella Donna McCuinn." I handed over my identification, picking up his aura.

As he input the information, he said, "I'm Chaz."

"That's an unusual name for an angel."

"It's short for Chazriel," he said in a lowered voice. He looked around and then handed over the room key. "Your room is on the second floor. If you need anything, don't hesitate to ask."

After the day I had, I planned a quiet evening. Nothing he could help me with. "Thank you, Chaz."

"What brings you to Havenwood Falls?"

"My car broke down."

"Sorry to hear that. Is Joshua towing it for you?"

"Yes. Hopefully, I'll be back on the road in the morning."

"So you won't be in town for long?"

"No. I'm going to a wedding in Grand Junction. If I don't head out early, I won't make it in time."

Chazriel tucked a shoulder-length blond lock behind his ear. "Would that be so bad? Havenwood Falls has plenty to offer tourists."

"I'm sure it does, but I can't stay away from my shop too long."

The man rested an arm on the counter. "A business owner. What do you sell?"

Any other time, I would have been annoyed with such a chatty stranger, but something about the angel made me want to talk. "I cater to the modern witch. Everything she might need, including clothing."

Chazriel's gaze swept over me. "I'm sure you meet some interesting people."

"I do, but…"

133

"What?"

"Nothing." I didn't want to appear rude, so I swallowed what was on the tip of my tongue.

Chazriel asked, "Will your husband be joining you?"

I blushed. Then I remembered my hair—a parody of a mood ring from a bygone era. At that moment, I was certain my locks were an unbecoming shade of yellow.

The angel's eyebrows knitted together. "Did I say something wrong?"

I shook my head. "I'm not married."

"You're joking, right? A beautiful lady like you. Tell me there's at least a boyfriend."

"No. I'm single." Since the man found it acceptable to pry into my life, I asked, "Why is an angel working in an inn?"

He frowned.

Not a good look on such a fine specimen. Too bad he wasn't coming to the wedding with me.

"Actually, I'm working to earn my wings."

"Ah." I smiled, totally understanding his predicament. Some angels were fortunate to get their wings right away. Others had to prove their worth. "Good deeds are the road to Heaven."

"Exactly." Chazriel stared at me for a moment. "Turquoise is a much better color on you."

"I prefer it." It was time to end the conversation before my hair changed colors again. "Well, Chazriel, if I can help you, let me know."

He grinned. "Oh, you've already helped me."

What did he mean by that?

I gathered my purse and bag, and then ambled toward the steps. Unfortunately, I wasn't watching where I was going.

"Oof!" said a woman.

Immediately, I apologized for being so careless.

"Not a problem. You must be our latest visitor. I'm Addie." The young lady wearing ripped jeans and a black T-shirt extended her hand. A pair of kind brown eyes blinked at me from behind a pair of black-framed glasses.

"Bella Donna." I shook her hand reluctantly, picking up on her aura. I'd never met a witch who was also a hellhound.

Addie patted an old leather satchel slung over her shoulder. "All our supernatural visitors and residents require a tattoo to remain in town."

"I'll only be here overnight."

"It doesn't matter. The design is totally temporary."

I hadn't had much experience with a large supernatural community. As I spoke with Addie, I learned Havenwood Falls had their rules and regulations. The tattoo was one of their requirements. Since it was temporary and I had no way of leaving town, I gave in.

"Could I get settled first?"

Addie smiled. "Sure thing. How about I stop by your room in say… um…fifteen minutes?"

"Perfect."

Despite everything—my car breaking down, the odd angel at the desk, and running into Addie—I was in a better mood. After she did my tattoo, I'd take a quick shower and find some place for a meal. Then I'd check on the progress with Betsy Boo. If I was lucky, the repair was an easy one. But when I opened the door to the room, my disposition changed along with my hair—going from greenish-blue to red.

The bane of my existence, the vampire known as Kristoph Vescu, lay in the middle of the bed. Only a wisp of a sheet covered his nakedness.

I looked down at the key and then checked the door. The numbers were correct. Therefore, I was justified in asking, "What are you doing in my room?"

A pair of kissable lips curled up, and I glimpsed the tips of his fangs. "I think you're mistaken, Bella. As you can see, I've already made myself at home."

I half-expected some scantily dressed woman to exit the bathroom. "Why do you need a room? Weren't you going to the wedding?"

Unfortunately, Kristoph was my next-door neighbor, and our friends were tying the knot. The groom was a wolf shifter from the vampire's hometown. The bride was my bestie.

Kristoph sat up. I was surprised the sheet stayed put. Too bad.

"My car blew a tire."

"So change it and give me my room!"

"No can do. I didn't have a spare. Joshua ordered me a replacement and a spare. They'll arrive tomorrow."

No way in Hades would I share a room with the vampire. First, Thorncrest Witches didn't spend time with bloodsuckers. At least, that was what my mother always said. Which led to the second issue. Every time Kristoph flashed his fangs, my heart skipped a beat. Not that I believed he'd use them on me. The man was handsome, even for a vampire in his prime. Dark brown hair, a mustache, broody appearance, and eyes I could get lost in. Although he was on the slim side, his suits fit him perfectly. Jeans fit his backside just right, too.

"Bella, your emotions are showing." He grinned. "I've never seen mustard yellow on you."

I tried to tug my hat lower with one hand. In my desperation, I dropped my suitcase. The valise popped open and gave the vampire an unfortunate display of my ugly unmentionables—full coverage DD bras, granny panties, and a couple of girdles.

I sank to my knees and quickly shoved everything back into the luggage. "Never mind. I'll go somewhere else."

"Good luck with that," said Kristoph.

Sitting back on my heels, I glanced up. "Why? What's wrong?"

"Didn't the angel at the desk tell you?"

"Tell me what?"

"The beer and music festival starts in a couple days. This is the last room available."

"Surely, there's another hotel."

The vampire shook his head. "Not with Independence Day right around the corner, too. Look, Bella, we're both adults. I'm sure we can share the room without a problem."

"Not happening." Between Kristoph's looks and my wayward hair, I'd spend the night too self-conscious to relax.

"Come now, Bella. Would it hurt to get to know each other better? We can go some place for dinner."

I was about to protest, but my stomach growled loudly.

"Before you turn me down, perhaps you should feed that beast of yours." He laughed and then apologized. "Give me a few minutes to get dressed."

"I'll just—"

Someone knocked at the door.

"That's probably Addie. She has to do my tattoo. Have you had yours done yet?" The words spilled from my lips. When I got nervous, I chatted without coming up for air.

Kristoph grinned and pointed to a tattoo of a single drop of blood on his forearm.

"Oh, well…" I didn't know what to say.

136

Addie knocked again.

"I'll leave you two alone while I shower." The vampire hopped out of bed wearing nothing but his birthday suit. Oh, my holy Hecate! The man was better out of his clothes than in them. I dropped my gaze and prayed my hair wouldn't turn green.

Then I remembered Addie and opened the door.

"Did I disturb something?" Her gaze went to the unmade bed.

"No, nothing at all. Come on in and let's get this design done."

Half an hour later, Addie was gone and I was ready for food. I glanced down at the miniature crystal ball with a moon and stars inside on my wrist. What was I thinking?

A question that could also be applied to the situation with Kristoph. When Addie asked me if anything was wrong, I lied. Told her the vampire and I intended to meet up.

"Ready to grab a bite?" he asked with a smile. The man looked good enough to eat in a pair of well-fitting jeans and a black pullover that emphasized his slight muscularity.

"Um…yeah…" I said.

When we reached the lobby, I realized I didn't know where we were going. Apparently, neither did Kristoph. An attractive woman with brown hair and odd gray-green eyes—the kind of lady a Vescu man would date—approached us. Right away, I picked up on her vampire aura.

"Good evening. You must be my latest guests. I'm Michaela."

"I'm Kristoph, and this is—"

"Bella Donna." I didn't need him introducing me.

"Well, I'm delighted you're staying at the Whisper Falls Inn."

"We're not together," I blurted. "There was a mix-up with our room."

Michaela's eyebrows knitted together. "Oh? What sort of mix-up?"

"The angel at the desk put us in the same one," I explained.

She folded her arms and shook her head. "There aren't any angels on staff here. Are you certain he was an angel?"

"Yes. A rather attractive one. Long blond hair—"

"I wouldn't worry about it," offered Kristoph. "The guy didn't even have his wings. My friend might have picked up on something else."

I didn't appreciate the vampire jumping to conclusions on my behalf. From Michaela's demeanor, I didn't think she bought his explanation either.

"Would you know a good place to eat around here?" I asked.

"Havenwood Falls has plenty of places. It all depends on what you need. Sanguine Elixirs might appeal to you, Mr. Vescu. If you're looking for a burger, try Burger Bar. The pizza is great at Napoli's."

"Ooo, pizza sounds wonderful," I said.

Michaela gave us the directions and told us where we could get coffee or breakfast in the morning. Thankfully, by the time we reached Napoli's, my locks turned a drab brown.

We sat in a booth near the window of the casual restaurant. Thankfully, the place was practically empty due to the late hour. The perfect atmosphere for a quiet talk. Kristoph ordered for the both of us —a pizza with all the toppings, a beer for him, and a glass of wine for me.

"So, Bella, what do you think of our friends hooking up?"

"She could do better," I admitted. Personally, the groom was a major dick. His father planned for him to become the leader of his pack and figured everyone should kiss his ring—and other places.

"So true. I had half a mind to skip the event."

"Why didn't you?"

"Because Silver Alley Cellars is catering."

"When did you branch out?" Silver Alley, a distributor of bottled blood, was Kristoph's business.

"It's a recent endeavor." He reached for his frosty mug. "To be honest, I'm only doing it to prove a point, since my family members consider my business isn't important."

Distributing bottled blood was a necessity for vampires, wasn't it?

"At least your family mentions you. I'm witch non grata with mine."

Kristoph sipped his beer and then lowered the glass. "That's a good one. I think my family might hate me more. I turned down leadership."

"Same for me. My mother wanted me to become the next coven leader. I turned it down along with their way of life. When I left home and opened my shop, that was the nail in the—

"Coffin." The vampire bobbed his head. "Same for me. If I wanted the post—"

"I didn't want the position. It came with too many caveats."

We talked for the better part of an hour. When the servers began cleaning up, Kristoph paid the bill, and we headed back to the inn. As we walked, I hated to admit I found the man charming. We had a lot in common—a desire to choose our own paths in life, overbearing families, and a love for classic rock. He loved Fleetwood Mac. I wouldn't have guessed that last one about the trendy vampire.

But there was one tremendous problem that screamed at me as we strolled.

CHAPTER 2

A Sleepless Night & the Unexpected

BELLA DONNA

*T*horncrest Witches didn't mingle with vampires, especially the Vescu clan.

Ever.

Thorncrest Witches also didn't share rooms with vampires. We didn't sleep in the same beds with the bloodsuckers, either. Although Kristoph swore he always slept in the buff, he was a gentleman and slipped on a pair of basketball shorts for my comfort.

But it was too late for comfort. I knew what lay beneath the thin fabric, and my mind wouldn't stop picturing it. Images of his anatomy haunted my mind and kept me awake. After tossing and turning for an hour and breaking into a cold sweat, I slipped from between the sheets. When I reached for my robe, I glimpsed my grayish locks.

Great! My hair was as unfocused as my thoughts.

I paced the floor, trying to sort out my random musings. My hormones wanted one thing while my brain understood what my desire would get me—a bloody one-night stand and a possible write-up on *Page 13: America's Latest Supernatural Gossip.*

"Bella."

Oh, crap! "Did I wake you?"

He gave me a wry grin. "I'm a vampire."

"Meaning?"

"We don't really sleep at night."

"Oh," I mumbled. "Well, don't mind me."

Too late. Kristoph reached for a T-shirt. "Let's go for a walk. The night air would do us both some good."

Reluctantly, I agreed and went to the bathroom to change. Seconds later, I emerged in a pair of purple leggings, an embroidered white peasant tunic top, and a pair of Birkenstocks. *Was that a purring sound coming from the vampire?*

"What was that?"

He gave me a tight smile, keeping his fangs in check. "Forgive me. Let's go."

Although it was July, the night air was chilly. I was glad I grabbed my sweater. The weather was only perfect for vampires who wanted to stroll with loved ones. Too bad I'd never experience such joy. Men didn't want to be around someone like me—fluctuating hormones, bizarre hair, and a comfort level stuck in a bygone era. We walked until we reached a park with a picnic area and a playground.

Kristoph led me over to a bench, and we sat down. "What's wrong, Bella?"

"Why do you call me that?" No one ever chopped off my name, not even my mother.

"It suits you better." He leaned back and looked up at the sky. "There's nothing poisonous about you."

I shrugged. "How would you know? It's not as if we've ever spoken over two words to each other."

The vampire gazed at me and flashed his fangs. "We may not have spoken, but I've noticed you."

My heart skipped a beat. Someone like him noticing me sparked something deep in my core. Maybe he meant nothing by it.

"I'm no one special. I've seen the model types leaving your house."

"Distractions. They're the kind of females Vescus are supposed to date and marry."

Tilting my head to the side, I asked the question that had nagged at me ever since Kristoph moved next door. "Why aren't you married?"

"One, I'm not a fan of prearranged unions. My father selected someone for me, but I wasn't interested. That's why I moved away."

Although I shouldn't have asked, I did anyway. "So, what kind of woman interests you?"

"Oh… She's a free spirit and refreshingly independent." He touched my hair and rubbed a yellow lock between his fingers. "She's not afraid to show her emotions in the most creative way. Above all, she's not obsessed with her appearance. She's comfortable in her body the way it is."

Immediately, my hair turned gray again.

I covered my mouth with my palm and shook my head. The vampire was talking about me.

Wasn't he?

"Bella, what's wrong?"

It took a moment for me to find my voice. When I did, I couldn't look at him. "I'm not the woman you want. I'm not the woman any man wants."

"I don't care about anyone else. I know what—who—I want."

My head whipped up. He had to be mistaken. "Kristoph, Thorncrest Witches don't date vampires."

"And Vescu vampires don't date witches." He moved closer, and his eyes darkened with desire. "Bella, I don't care about the so-called traditions between our families. The ideology creates division. There is enough angst in the world. Supernaturals shouldn't add to the distress."

He had a point. My best friend was a witch, and she found happiness in the arms of a trifling wolf shifter. Could I find something pleasurable with Kristoph?

Still… There was a certain order to life. Dating a vampire wasn't an option for me.

"What would people say when they see someone like me with someone like you?" I asked.

Kristoph looked at me as if I was a five-course meal, and he was starving. He cleared his throat and then said, "They'll say I'm damn lucky to find such a ravishing woman."

No, they wouldn't.

People would think he took pity on a curvy chick. Or when my hair turned gray because of my emotions, they'd believe he had an old lady fetish. Kristoph's friends would criticize his choice. They'd say terrible things about me—about him—behind his back. Eventually, they'd stop coming around. Plus, I wasn't a spring chicken. There wouldn't be children for us. When the inevitable happened, Kristoph would mourn my death but not move on because nobody would want an old vampire.

I wouldn't subject him to such a fate. Although I found the vampire ridiculously handsome and charming, I had to end whatever was happening between us. He'd be upset but would thank me later.

"Kristoph—"

He placed a chilly finger on my mouth. "Shh, Bella. Let us enjoy the moment."

The vampire cupped my head and claimed my lips. His kiss emulated a strange, magical drug. I liked it. I really, really liked it.

Parts of my anatomy woke up and made their demands. I longed for Kristoph Vescu the same way he lusted for blood. I wanted to know the bliss other women enjoyed with a man they loved. But the idea of loving the vampire was almost too painful.

Our families wouldn't approve.

Our friends would question our commitment.

Would his fangs in my neck hurt?

Would he turn me into a vampire?

In a perfect world, a vampire like Kristoph might erase my doubts and fears. He'd treasure me, and other people would be envious of our relationship. But we lived in the real world. A place where people judged. A place where people assumed curvy, middle-aged women took in a multitude of cats and resigned themselves to a lonely existence. I didn't want that.

Regrettably, I dragged my lips from his.

His brows knitted together as he gazed into my eyes. "Bella, why did you pull away?"

"Because this is wrong," I said. "A relationship between us can't happen."

"Why not? I'm attracted to you." The vampire leaned in. "I'm guessing you feel the same about me. We're two consenting adults. What's the problem?"

I shook my head, and pitch black locks fell across my face. "I'm a Thorncrest Witch. You're a Vescu Vampire."

The animosity between our families originated in the Old Country. Supposedly, Dominick Vescu, Kristoph's great-great-grand sire, snubbed my great aunt Elena Dragavei. Then he insulted her publicly. Honestly, I had no idea what truly happened, but my mother did. When our family settled in Thorncrest, she swore the Vescu family were our enemy.

Kristoph sighed heavily and ran a hand through his luscious hair.

Did it feel like silk?

"That shit again?" he asked. "I told you I don't care about my family or yours. In all honesty, Dominick is an ass who should have been ended centuries ago."

"I don't—"

For once, the words wouldn't come out. Deep down, I cared what my mother and the rest of the family thought about me and my choices. Admitting it to myself was shocking. That explained why I hadn't gone home in years. It was the reason I only called her once a month. I hated the ridicule as much as I hated the prejudice.

I was about to explain myself when my phone rang. I took out the device, peered at the screen, and saw the name of the garage. It was after hours, so I didn't expect a call so soon.

"This is Bella Donna," I said with as much cheer as I could muster, given the situation.

"Hey, it's Joshua. I know it's late, but I looked at your car already. It's going to take a few days to complete the repairs."

My heart sank. "You're sure?"

"Yeah. A part will have to be ordered, but I'll call you as soon as I get it."

"Thanks." I returned the device to my leggings pocket.

Kristoph raised his eyebrows. "Is there a problem?"

"I'm going to miss the wedding. Joshua has to order a part for Betsy Boo."

"Betsy Boo?" The vampire smiled. "You named your car?"

"Yes. Doesn't everyone?"

He laughed, and it was the most mellifluent sound ever.

After Kristoph regained his composure, he said, "As soon as my car is ready, I'll drive us to Grand Junction. We can give the mechanic an address to deliver your ride after the wedding."

I flinched slightly. "You'd do that for me?"

"Why wouldn't I?"

Good question.

A better one? Why was I being so unyielding? It was an offer of a ride. Not a romp between the sheets.

Before I could respond, my phone pinged with a text message. I removed the device and gazed at the screen.

Esadora Dragavei McCuinn: Please come see me before leaving Grand Junction. It's important.

I read my mother's message twice. If I traveled to the wedding with Kristoph, he'd have to take me to her house. No way in Hades would that happen. Even if he stayed in the car, she'd know he was there. Then she'd blast me for bringing a Vescu into her territory.

It would be better if I found another way to get to Grand Junction. There had to be a bus or maybe I could rent a vehicle.

"Bella, talk to me. Your frustration is palpable." In a lower voice, he said, "Although I see nothing wrong with it, your hair resembles an abstract painting."

"Oh, no!" Whenever I became overwrought, every shade of the rainbow sprang from my roots. I muttered, "Proof, proof, proof."

"Proof of what, Bella?"

I snapped. "Proof that we can't be!"

Kristoph placed his hand on my thigh. Instead of chilling me, his touch was a fiery brand searing my flesh. My body tingled, and I wanted so much more from the vampire.

"Calm down, my sweet Bella. What was the text message?"

I drew in a breath. How long would I allow my mother to affect me so? She wouldn't live forever, and I was letting words keep us apart. Keep me from having a relationship I'd been fantasizing about ever since Kristoph moved in next door.

But it wasn't just my mother I feared.

It was the aunts and cousins who considered me an odd bird. They concluded I'd live a life surrounded by cats. On my last birthday, my cousin sent me a gorgeous silky blue-gray Nebelung. I named the rare breed cat Covaci. The year prior, another cousin sent me an orange and white Maine Coon I christened Radu. Surprisingly, Radu and Covaci got along perfectly with my familiar—a black short-hair named Lazar.

Yikes! I was on my way to becoming a cat witch!

"Bella…"

I swallowed hard and then blurted, "It was from my mother. She wants me to pay her a visit after the wedding."

"Not a problem. I can drive you."

I shook my head vehemently. "No! Have you lost your mind?"

"Not recently," he joked. When I didn't laugh, Kristoph added, "I don't care what your mother thinks about me. I'm not Dominick. I'm not my father either."

"But you're a Vescu."

The vampire leaned forward and rested his elbows on his knees. "Here's the thing about me that you should know if we're to become a couple. It's something I want, and I always get what I want."

My gut knotted.

"Bella, if I were worried about what others thought, I wouldn't have moved away from home. I wouldn't have founded Silver Alley Cellars, either. If I gave a damn about people's opinions, I would've caved when my father began grooming a blood brother to become the next clan leader."

"Blood brother?"

"A man my father sired. He assumed his gesture would change my mind. Force me to stay home. It didn't. No one in my family, or the clan, approves of my choices. That's their problem. Not mine."

"True, but my issue belongs to me. I have a slew of relatives who will make my life a living Hades." I shot to my feet. "Forgive me, Kristoph. I just…can't."

I trotted back to the inn as fast as my plump little legs could move.

CHAPTER 3

Deals & Angels

KRISTOPH

*W*hen I entered the Haven Saloon at three in the morning, the place was fairly empty except for a few souls without something better to do, occupying a table in a corner. But it didn't surprise me to see the lowest level of celestial beings at the counter. The man resembled an extra from that Andrew Lloyd Weber movie in baggy trousers and shirt.

I slid onto the stool beside him and ordered a whiskey neat. Chazriel glanced over at me. His hang-dog expression matched my mood perfectly.

Without making eye contact, he said, "Do I dare ask how things are going with Bella Donna?"

"Not good." The bartender placed a glass in front of me, and I wasted no time knocking it back. "Another. Make it a double."

"What happened?" asked the angel-in-waiting. He drank from a glass of cola.

"You don't know?"

He swept his curly blond hair off a shoulder. "I arrange things, but I don't snoop."

"Fine. We talked. We kissed."

A radiant smile spread across his face. "So things went well, vampire. Perhaps your perspective is off?"

I held up a hand, trying to ward off the intense glow coming from the man.

"There's nothing wrong with my perspective." When the high beams dulled, I glanced at him. "Why do all the manipulating only to allow her mother to spoil the plans?"

He frowned. "I didn't manipulate. I simply made it possible for the two of you to enjoy a meaningful conversation. Would it have happened without my intervention?"

"No." I slammed down the cheap whiskey and appreciated the burn.

I'd been trying to speak with the gorgeous witch for well over a year, with no success. Then one night I did the human thing—I prayed for an opportunity. The following day, the Birkenstock-wearing angel showed up at my office, claiming to have heard my plea. He also alleged he had a solution to my dilemma. Like a fool, I listened.

When I raised my hand to order another refill, the man grabbed my wrist. "You won't find salvation in a bottle. How can I help?"

"Honestly, it's all up to Bella. She has to come to terms with her family before she can move on."

"What's the deal with her family?"

"Actually, it's a problem between both families. Bella's mother is a Dragavei."

"So?"

"Dominick Vescu, my great-great-grandfather, did something he shouldn't have centuries ago."

"He fell in love with a Dragavei witch," said Chazriel.

"Something along those lines. Supposedly, she was his soul mate."

The angel-in-waiting folded his hands on top of the counter. "But he snubbed her in public."

I squinted at the man. "I thought you didn't know what happened."

"I'm a good listener. Over the years, I've learned to pay attention to what people don't say." When I didn't respond, he said, "Okay, I guessed. One might call it the snub that was heard for centuries."

"If you don't get those wings, maybe you could see if Heaven needs a comedian."

"Not hardly. There are enough of them in the realm. Friday nights are a hoot. Music, laughter, actors recreating award-winning performances—"

"You're pushing it, Chaz."

"Right, right." He chuckled. "Back to your problem."

"Bella's mother wants her daughter to visit after the wedding."

"How is that…" His voice trailed off, and then the man smacked his palm to his forehead. "It wouldn't be an issue if Bella Donna drove Betsy Boo."

"Right. You conveniently arranged for me to drive the woman to the wedding."

"But I didn't plan for any contingencies. Sorry about that, pal."

"I'm not your pal." I glared at him and then ordered that drink. Not that I could get drunk. Alcohol was simply something to occupy my time and make me appear more human.

"Calm down, vampire. Things aren't as bad as they seem." Chazriel cocked his head as if listening to something only meant for him. Then he gave me that megawatt smile again.

"Jesus Christ!"

"Not my name, but I'll let him know you said hello." Chazriel leaned in. "I believe things will work out the way intended."

CHAPTER 4

Confessions & Wings

BELLA DONNA

*F*rankly, I didn't appreciate the way things ended with Kristoph. I enjoyed kissing him—much more than I would ever admit. His mouth was just what the shaman ordered—a pair of lips capable of healing a soul and pumping life back into a body. The memory alone ignited a flame in my core. One I wanted to surge and consume me.

I shouldn't have mentioned my mother or my family's issues. That trouble was mine and mine alone. I flopped down on the bed, took out my phone, and stared at the text message. At my age, some things shouldn't bother me anymore. So why did this?

All my life, my mother and I never saw eye to eye on anything. She disapproved of my friends. Liked none of the boys I found interesting—it didn't matter that nothing ever happened with them. I was plain Bella Donna McCuinn, fond of vintage dresses and rock bands. Mother preferred Donna Karan and classical music. She relaxed at the spa. I found peace in nature.

It was long overdue for me to pull up my big-girl panties and talk with her like an adult. Before I changed my mind, I looked up the correct number and pressed the button.

After three rings, an icy voice answered. "So you received my text, Bella Donna."

It wasn't a question. Merely a confirmation.

"Yes, Mother. What's so important?"

"Must there be a reason for me wanting my only child to visit me?"

Esadora Dragavei McCuinn was a lot of things. Manipulative. Vindictive. Nosey. Needy wasn't one of them.

"Mother, let's not do this."

"Do what?" she asked with feigned innocence. "I asked you to come see me. You call instead."

I avoided sighing. "Mother, I'm not in Grand Junction. My car broke down outside of Havenwood Falls."

"Mercy me. We must have a terrible connection. I didn't hear you clearly. Did you say someone's going to fall?"

"No, I said Havenwood Falls. Never mind."

"Dear, maybe you can text me an address. I can send a car for you."

Honestly, that would solve the immediate problem, but it wouldn't take care of the greater issue.

"Not necessary. A friend will drive me to the wedding. Then we'll stop by the house."

Mother didn't hide her exaggerated sigh. I imagined her arms crossed and her eyes narrowed. The mention of my friends would make her grimace as if she tasted rotten fruit.

"Which friend is this? Jemma with the oversized posterior, or Ursula with the hideous unibrow?"

I seethed in silence. There was nothing wrong with Jemma and Ursula. They weren't runway fabulous, but they were the kindest witches in my life.

"Um… no… He's not a witch."

"Oh?" A hint of interest popped into Mother's tone. "Maybe I know the sorcerer or his family?"

"He's not a sorcerer, Mother." When she didn't respond, I assumed the call disconnected, but I couldn't be that lucky. She was giving me space to rig up my own noose and jump. "His name is Kristoph Vescu."

"A vampire! A Vescu vampire!" A litany of unladylike swear words blasted my ear.

As I waited for the deluge to end, the room door opened, and the man of the hour entered. His brows drew together, and I held up a finger.

"Are you finished?" I asked my mother.

"You are not to bring that creature to my house."

"Mother, if you want to see me, then you must welcome the vampire."

"I'll greet him with open arms and a white oak stake," she threatened.

I glanced up at Kristoph. "That's not happening. You'll be cordial to him and not bring up ancient history."

"Oh my, will that offend him? He was there for a good part of it."

Mentioning the vampire's age was meant to upset me. It didn't.

"Mother, you'll agree to my terms if you want me to come home."

"And if I don't?"

"Then we won't be there."

The scorching hot vampire mouthed, "We?"

I nodded with a smile.

"See you after the wedding," Mother said, and the line went dead.

When I hung up, Kristoph grinned. "Did Esadora call you?"

"I called her. It was time to clear the air between us."

He sat beside me. "Did you do that? Clear the air, that is?"

"Maybe. Maybe not. She had to know I was bringing you home with me."

The vampire's cheeks pinked up slightly. "What brought about this change? Earlier, you were reluctant for me to make the trip."

"I don't want to end up becoming a cat witch."

"What?"

I waved a hand in the air. "Never mind. Just know I'd rather keep company with you instead of my cats."

"So I'll be meeting the notorious Esadora Dragavei," he said, and propped himself up on his elbows. He watched me with such intensity I felt naked.

An intoxicating male scent, like a heady musk, wafted past my nose and aroused me. Fire raced through me, and it had nothing to do with wonky hormones.

"That's totally up to you." I leaned over him and ran a finger down his chest.

A purring sound came from the vampire. "Be careful, Bella. Don't start something you can't finish."

"Oh, I plan to finish more than once."

He flashed his fangs, and his hands slid around my back, pulling me closer. Gently, he traced my ample curves, and I shuddered.

In a husky voice, Kristoph said, "I have an idea."

"W-what?" I whispered.

"Let's skip the wedding and spend a few days in Havenwood Falls. When our friends return from their honeymoon, we'll pay them a visit and drop in on dear sweet Esadora."

I moaned as he cupped my rear. "I like the sound of that."

"Oh, I prefer that sound much better. I want to wake up with you whispering sweet hexes in my ear."

Waking up beside Kristoph Vescu?

It was something I'd dreamed of. Repeatedly.

I aimed a finger at the lamp. For once, my magic worked the way it was supposed to. The lights went out, and our clothes disappeared. Kristoph flipped me so I lay beneath him. The vampire's lips ravished mine. When I opened my mouth, his tongue dipped in. For the next few minutes, we nipped and sucked and tasted each other. It had been a long time for me, and I wanted to appreciate every minute.

Those fangs that made my heart skip a beat pricked at my neck. Fear gripped my heart, but it vanished in a second. As soon as he tapped my vein, I knew he was the man I'd been waiting for.

At some point, somewhere in the distance, I swore I heard a harp playing and a trumpet blasting.

Was that my magic being cockeyed?

That night, I learned what it meant to drown in a sea of love. Honestly, I didn't know if that was where we'd end up, but I wanted to find out. I'd spent far too much time having cats for companions. I desperately wanted the vampire between my sheets every night.

Much later, as the moonlight filtered through the curtain, I lay in Kristoph's arms. He stroked my back and said, "I've wanted to do that ever since I moved in."

"Really?"

"Yes, Bella. You shouldn't be surprised. You are a very desirable woman."

"But I'm—"

He placed a chilly finger over my lips. "Don't. To me, you're beautiful. I don't care what anyone else thinks. All right?"

For once, I put aside the low opinion I had of myself. "Okay." Changing the subject, I asked, "Was it just me, or did you hear a trumpet?"

"And a harp." He hugged me closer. "If you ask me, I think a certain chatty angel got his wings tonight."

"I don't know about him, but I soared."

"Yes, you did, Bella darling." He nuzzled my neck. "Care to go on another flight?"

"Only with you."

And when our lips met, Kristoph Vescu kissed away all remaining doubts and fears.

The next few days were spent in utter bliss. We toured the town and even went to the amazing waterfall. But far too soon our impromptu vacation came to an end.

Despite the excellent job the mechanic did repairing Betsy Boo, I decided it was time for a change.

I buckled the seatbelt and leaned my head against the cushion.

Kristoph slipped behind the steering wheel and cranked the engine. "Are you sure about leaving your car behind?"

"I am. I want to leave that part of my life behind me. The witch who relied on it no longer exists." She didn't. The vampire taught me there was more to life than cats and endless days working at my shop. I wanted to have great adventures and spend endless nights with Kristoph.

He grasped my hand. "To be honest, you've changed me too."

As the sun slowly sank behind the mountains, he drove away from Havenwood Falls. Although I'd forget the moments we spent there, I looked forward to new memories with the vampire.

BEATI CANTORES

BELINDA BORING

CHAPTER 1

HOLLY

 his was not happening.
I'd heard something on TV that just because you were paranoid didn't mean they weren't out to get you, and that saying was screaming in my head right now. Sweat coated my skin, and my stomach was bunched up tightly in knots.

I was being followed.

There was no way this was a coincidence, and for a second, I contemplated using my repressed magic against the person lurking behind me. I wasn't meant to use my power at all, and I knew there would be severe repercussions, but the instant I felt the hair on the back of my neck rise at Falls Market in Millers Plaza, my magic had surged upward.

It was being called to action, overriding all the common sense I held.

It didn't matter that I lived amongst supernaturals, and there were many that I could run to and ask for help. I also knew that if I bolted now and didn't look back, that I could probably reach Shelf Indulgence safely where Sedona would help deal with the threat that kept out of my peripheral vision.

Someone was there.

I felt them watching when I studied the variety of almond milk the small grocery store offered. I could sense someone in the next aisle as I selected the packet of spaghetti and our favorite brand of marinara sauce on Sedona's grocery list.

With shaking hands, I approached the cashier, my gaze furtively sweeping back and forth. But there hadn't been anything—just fellow townspeople grabbing items off their own shopping lists. I glanced up at the security mirrors hung high on the wall that gave workers a good look at the store.

Nothing.

But I *knew* something wasn't right.

My magic practically demanded I pay attention and find the source.

It wasn't until I stepped out of Daily Knead with a freshly baked French loaf for garlic bread that I saw him—a newcomer who seemed to pop up in the same places I was throughout town. At first, I'd brushed it off as a coincidence but now I wasn't quite sure. I could go weeks without seeing family friends until I was specifically seeking them out. Everyone had busy lives, so this—seeing this stranger again and feeling like I was being followed—freaked me out.

"Take a deep breath, Holly," I murmured beneath my breath, forcing my nerves to settle. This was something Micah and I had practiced over the years—how to react when dealing with a possible threat.

First things first—get somewhere safe.

Shelf Indulgence was close by, and while I could probably find refuge in closer stores, my gut said to go straight to Sedona. My brain reminded me it was Tuesday. There was a good chance Micah was at the store helping Sedona with a honey-do list.

So somewhere safe—check.

Second, find something to protect myself with.

I held the canvas shopping bag we liked to use so we didn't have to take a paper or plastic one from the market. The weight of the glass bottle inside was perfect for hitting the person should they attack me before I reached Sedona. My fingers twisted the handles tightly so I had a better chance at swinging it hard. I dropped the bread I'd just purchased, freeing my other hand.

Weapon—check.

Third, and most importantly—keep a level head and remain alert. Micah had helped me understand that being panicked wasn't the same as alert. Picking up my pace, I made sure to keep where there were people on the street. I hurried down Main Street, headed toward town square. Whoever it was that followed me surely wouldn't be brave enough to attack when I wasn't alone.

Vigilant—check.

Adrenaline pumped hard, my heart pounding within my chest. My magic still sparked and burned through my veins as if desperate to be released.

I could see the pretty gazebo of the Town Square Park up ahead, and I felt a flicker of relief. I was almost there, and then I'd be okay. I didn't know whether to laugh or cry because both emotions were dueling, intensified by the possible danger.

Eighth Street was approaching, and I lengthened my stride, not paying attention to what is in front of me when I bumped into someone.

I scrambled to regain my footing, and a strangled scream gurgled up out of my mouth.

Her eyes. They were just like the woman's I'd seen a few weeks ago—scarred and sealed shut. But it was not the same woman. Horror caused goosebumps to prickle over my skin. How was this even possible?

Just like last time, she turned in my direction as if waiting for me to say something, but terror took over. There was no way I could keep calm like Micah had drilled into me, not when intense panic hijacked my body.

"Stay away from me," I yelled. My magic slammed against my inner wards that kept it guarded. Over and over, the power tried to break free —its attempts unleashing a pain unlike anything I'd ever felt.

"Oracle." A masculine voice approached, foreign...the accent new to my ears but somehow familiar at the same time. My thoughts swam in utter chaos as I whipped about, frantic to face the one responsible for this—my stalker.

I didn't hesitate, striking him with my makeshift weapon repeatedly. By some fluke he managed to tighten his fingers around my wrist, stopping my attack cold. His strength didn't stop me, however, as I prepared to keep beating him until he let go.

My magic had other plans and instantly stilled.

"Oracle." The gruffness in his voice felt soothing.

What the actual hell was going on?

"Does she not know who we are?" The young woman I'd bowled over finally spoke up. Even though she couldn't see, I felt as though she was peering deep into my soul. I struggled against the grip of the light brown-haired man. His hair was styled in braids the same way as the men on the TV show "Vikings." Sedona and I had devoured that series. We pretty much survived on take-out for two weeks—eating our weight in deliciously greasy burgers, pizzas, and the occasional salad when Micah mocked our poor diet choices.

"I'm nobody," I answered through gritted teeth. "You. Have. The. Wrong. Person." Each word was punctuated with a strong tug until I finally broke free from his grasp. I backed away quickly, aware that I'd drawn the attention of onlookers. I was as safe as I could be, but I wouldn't truly feel that way until I was with Micah.

Raising my finger, I pointed it at the woman first, and then the man. "Stay away from me. Do you hear me? I am not someone you want to mess with." I wasn't sure how threatening I looked at that moment—chest heaving, my arm ready to start swinging my spaghetti sauce weapon again. "Just stay away."

Something flickered over his features. Realization. Disappointment. Curiosity. He went to take a step closer to me, but his companion stopped him.

"Maybe we were wrong," she murmured, so soft that I barely made out the words.

He shook his head. "The magic doesn't lie. Something's blocking her powers."

My world tipped on its axis at his response.

My father.

They were here because of that monster.

I dropped everything and ran as though my life depended on it—which it did because now everything was in jeopardy. The life I'd claimed here in Havenwood Falls was basically over, and we'd have to go on the run again.

I knew the saying that if something was too good to be true, it probably was, but I'd fooled myself into believing that karma was on my side and that I could escape my father's evil plans.

Tears flooded my eyes, and I wiped them away angrily. I was tired of living like this—constantly looking over my shoulder, never ever able to lower my guard completely, let alone make friends and live like a regular girl.

This was never going to end.

He would never stop until he had me in his clutches and my magic was his.

I stormed into the bookstore, stopping only to whip about and peer back through the window to see if I was being pursued. I wasn't, but that didn't mean the threat was over. I snorted pessimistically. I couldn't keep deluding myself anymore. This would always be my reality, and the sooner I started packing, the sooner I could leave.

I wouldn't take Micah with me this time. That was out of the question. He'd met Sedona and fallen in love, and I couldn't stomach him having to give her up because of me. Or worse, Sedona having to give up her life to follow us. I wasn't a helpless child anymore. My guardian angel had tutored me well.

If worse came to worst, I would simply release my magic and confront my father at last. I didn't want to keep hiding and being afraid of every shadow like the boogey man lived there. If he wanted my magic, then he would need to pry it from my cold, dead body.

I knew how irrational my thoughts sounded. I could practically hear the arguments from both Micah and Sedona. Hell, I could also hear Marcus and Phineas—their pleas and promises to not be so foolish and how important I was to them.

I was tired of having other people pay for my safety.

It was my responsibility alone.

"Holly." Micah's voice caused me to jump, and I burst into tears all over again. I was so tightly wound that it took very little to unravel me.

Turning away from the window, all my plans to run and leave Havenwood Falls by myself evaporated. I needed Micah. I would always need him, and that also included Sedona. As he closed the distance between us, I wiped my face and quickly switched the bookstore's sign from *Open* to *Closed*.

"He's found me. He's here," I blurted, racing into Micah's open arms. Today's events tumbled out in a steady flow, and I pretty much didn't take a breath until I'd finally purged it all.

I braced myself for the explosion of action—the flurry of activity that followed whenever my father had drawn too close in the past and we had to make a speedy getaway. Yet, Micah held me tightly, his right hand gently rubbing up and down over my back.

"Didn't you hear me?" I repeated, bewildered. I looked over at Sedona, who hadn't budged a muscle either. Something was wrong.

"Micah?" Stepping out of his embrace, I looked up into his blue eyes, searching for answers.

Tenderly he cupped the side of my face. His thumb brushed away my remaining tears. "We need to talk, Holly." There was no hint to what he meant hidden in his tone.

Brows furrowed, I stepped even farther back until I hit the front door with my body. I shook my head with confusion as butterflies swirled in my stomach.

This was new.

"Maybe I can help with those questions, daughter."

And stepping between Micah and Sedona, someone else entered the conversation.

My mother.

CHAPTER 2

"*O*h gods, look at you," she uttered as her eyes filled with tears, her hands covering her mouth in amazement. "You're the spitting image of your grandmother."

I knew I was expected to reply, to say something, but I couldn't think of a single word despite my voracious reading and extensive vocabulary. All I could do was stand there filled with uncertainty—my gaze jumping from Micah and back to my mother. How was this even possible? The last time I'd asked about her, Micah had skirted around the answer before assuring me that he was also keeping her safe.

In his defense, he looked slightly bewildered as well, as if her appearance was also a shock to him.

"How is she here?" I finally said, ignoring the woman who still hadn't torn her gaze away from me. I struggled to feel the expected— some childlike pull toward the person who'd given birth to me—but all I felt was awkward. All I knew was I felt more like an ant under a magnifying glass than a cherished daughter.

When Micah approached and pulled me into him, I didn't resist. His warmth and comfort instantly helped ease my apprehension. That might've also been thanks to Sedona using her empathic witchy mojo. Either way, I eased into the brief relief.

"This wasn't how I wanted to reintroduce you, sweetheart," he replied, holding me close. Beneath the calm he was trying to infuse into our embrace, I could feel how rigid he stood, his muscles tense. I was right. He'd been caught by surprise as well. "This is your mother. Elizabeth."

I closed my eyes and focused on grounding myself. It was a trick Sedona had helped me with whenever I felt my emotions start spiraling out of control. Right now, my insides felt like they were being obliterated by a hurricane, making me find my center near impossible.

"What do you need, Holly?" Sedona added, her voice soothing. Goddess, I loved her. "We're here for you and understand if you'd like a few moments to gather yourself." She murmured something to Micah, and I felt him nod.

"There's no time," Elizabeth, my mother, countered. "Gods, how I wish we had all the time we needed to become reacquainted before I lay such a heavy burden back on your shoulders, but if my visions are true, the sooner I return what's rightfully yours, the easier it'll be for you to harness your magic."

My brain exploded at her admission. *My magic? What's rightfully mine? Heavy burden?*

Wait . . . what did she mean by back?

Micah interrupted before I could even draw the breaths needed to ask all my questions.

"If Holly requires time, then she will get whatever she needs." Annoyance coated his words, and there was no denying the steel edge in them as well. I didn't know how well they knew each other, but I'd heard that tone enough to understand that Micah meant business.

Elizabeth's face softened. "Do you think me so heartless that I haven't factored in how my daughter might be feeling right now, angel?" There was power in her question, however, that made it hard to look anywhere else but at her. "Do you assume that I haven't factored in the danger by me simply being here . . . that I would risk all that we've done to keep her hidden because I desire idle chitchat? After all these years, do you truly second guess my intentions?"

I'd spent my entire life with Micah, and for the very first time, he did something incredible . . . he relented, and then apologized for his gruffness.

Holy crap.

"How can I be of service, Seer?" He inclined his head in a reverential nod. I'd never seen him do that before either. Who the heck was my mother?

That's when my brain caught up with the conversation.

"Wait, what? Seer?" I was the one to step away from the security of Micah's embrace toward my mother. "Is that where I get my powers from?" I asked. I could practically taste the impending revelations on my tongue. Was I finally going to be told the truth about who I was and why I was forbidden to even access my buried powers?

Sedona intervened. "How about we take this upstairs where it's a little more private? Maybe I can make us some hot tea, and we can take the rest of the evening to get to know each other."

Elizabeth's lips tightened into a grimace, and her brow wrinkled. She must've seen something in my features because she eventually relaxed, nodding. "That would be lovely. We have a lot to discuss and not a lot of time."

There was that urgency again.

Which reminded me of why I'd come bursting into the store in the first place. "We also need to do something about the man that's following me. My gut tells me he's not going to simply give up because I'm inside the store. He seems like the relentless kind." I didn't add that if he was working for my father, I was pretty sure he wouldn't give up until he hand-delivered me personally.

Someone banged on the bookstore's door. "Hello? Open up!"

Whipping around, I gasped. It was him.

"Micah!" I exclaimed, my stomach instantly dropping to my feet. Was Neptune in retrograde or was my karma that shitty that my world was devolving into utter chaos in the blink of an eye?

The man slammed into the door, splintering the wood away from the frame—his dark eyes menacing and filled with threat.

"Step away from the oracle!"

Was that a freaking ax in his hand?

Micah growled and sprinted forward, placing his body in front me, using one of his arms to sweep me backward toward Sedona. She then grabbed me and did the same—providing an electrical barrier of her magic between us and the door. Sedona began inching us toward the bookshelves, seeking more coverage.

My gaze was rivetted to the back of my guardian, however, because he stood there in all his majestic glory—his wings extended out from his shoulder blades, the white glow from his feathers extinguishing any shadow in the room.

"I command you to leave," he barked with the full weight of his divine authority. "Or I will destroy you where you stand." An orb of energy appeared in the palm of his right hand, and I could hear its power crackling in the air. He cocked it behind him, poised to throw. "I'll only warn you once."

"You dare threaten the oracle?" The man's mouth twisted into a snarl. "I have pledged my soul to protect her. Consider *yourself* warned." He stepped through the shattered door frame and toward Micah as if he didn't feel a shred of fear. Did he realize he was facing an angel?

Two warriors eyed each other—neither submitting.

"Enough!" my mother exclaimed. I'd forgotten she'd been standing there. "Stand down, Micah." She turned to the stranger who'd followed me here, and in an almost familiar language, spoke to him. All I could understand was the word *rune*.

His name.

"She doesn't understand who she is yet, Rune. Lower your weapon and remember whose presence you're in."

Before anyone could react, my mother extended her hand, gesturing for me to come forward and around the protective barrier Sedona had created. "Daughter, I know you don't have any reason to trust me, but I ask you to do so now."

She was right. The only person I truly knew I could depend on was Micah, but something inside urged me to listen. I pleaded silently with Micah as I caught his eye to keep vigilant in case I was proven wrong. My gaze moved over to Rune and the ax that now hung in his hand by his side.

"Only if he returns back to the front of the store and promises not to move a muscle." I hardened my voice and was surprised to hear how steady it sounded. I didn't feel that way.

Rune obliged, and once I was satisfied, I walked to my mother, trusting her.

"I'm listening."

Pride shone in her face, and she nodded slightly.

"What I need you to do, daughter, is see." And with that, she blew warm breath into my eyes, and magic erupted . . . one that felt old and sacred, unlike the power I witnessed whenever Sedona and others performed rituals and spells. "*See*."

Blinking, my body obeyed.

"Mom?" I uttered.

She nodded as tears fell over her cheeks.

I looked to Micah, but it was Rune that made me gasp. "You," I softly spoke. How did I ever think this man was a menace? He felt as familiar to me as Micah was, and I found myself speaking quickly in the same language my mother had used.

Old Norse.

Shit, I was Norse descendent.

Rune dropped to a knee in veneration. "I have finally found you, oracle. I have gathered your circle. Allow me to bring them here." He rose to his feet, and with cautious steps toward Micah, who had only just withdrew his wings, his appearance, clothing and all, momentarily flashed to that of an ancient Viking warrior.

My warrior.

"Someone needs to explain this to me," Sedona chimed in.

Despite the solemnness of the occasion, I burst into laughter. While I understood I had a relationship with Rune and he was someone I could trust, I still felt utterly clueless.

"Oracle?" I echoed once my nervous response settled.

"It's time I returned what is yours, daughter."

CHAPTER 3

I couldn't escape how surreal this was and how rapidly things began to unfold. I'd dreamt of this day countless times where I'd finally understand why my life was like it was and also the mystery behind my magic.

Standing in the middle of Sedona's upstairs study, lit candles flickering from various surfaces, I wet my lips nervously. Part of me wanted to scream for everyone to slow down for a second and to give me a chance to catch my breath, but I didn't want to risk this being a dream. If I woke up and discovered this craziness wasn't real and merely a figment of my imagination, I knew my heart would be crushed.

I glanced over at Micah and Sedona for the hundredth time. I needed them to be here to witness this as though they were that security blanket a child needed whenever they had to be brave. It was tough ignoring Rune and the three females he'd brought to Shelf Indulgence to watch my mother perform her ritual. Even though I recognized two of them, my brain had a tough time wrapping itself around them being here to serve me as my singers—my circle. I was still confused by all the details.

My mother. She was the one I focused on now, listening intently as she explained each step of her preparation and what the spell would involve. Apparently, in order to further add protection and keep me hidden from my father, my mom had siphoned some of my magic into herself for safekeeping. With the blessings and help from the gods, she'd bound those powers behind a barrier that only she could release.

"Ready?"

I sat opposite her, surrounded by stones and sticks she'd quickly gathered. Between us on the floor lay an athame, candle, a bundle wrapped in twine, and one of Sedona's ceremonial ceramic bowls she used for burning herbs. Curiosity was front and center in my mind—this would be the first time I'd been part of a spell that didn't come from Sedona's Book of Shadows.

Or at least that I could remember.

Nodding, I swallowed hard and closed my eyes, taking in deep breaths until I felt all my anxiety ebb away. "Ready."

The mood in the room instantly stilled, and I could've sworn that as my mother began chanting in Norse, an invisible veil parted and ushered in spirits from beyond. The hair on my arms stiffened from the electric sensation, and I realized it wasn't just spirits attending, but our ancestors. She was seeking their aid in undoing her protection.

The candle's flame between us danced joyously, lengthening in the air. There was a soft whooshing sound, and that's when I felt it—not just our forefathers, but we were in the presence of a goddess. There was no denying the room held the same energy as when Sedona called upon Gaia during ceremony.

It was time.

Mom had told me beforehand that the only thing required from me was to be there, which was a relief because I didn't have a great track record when it came to being part of spellwork. Patiently sitting there, cross-legged and my hands in my lap, I watched as she raised the athame to her palm and without hesitation, slashed the soft flesh.

She didn't even flinch. Drops of red blood fell into the bowl beneath her hand.

Norse magic required blood sacrifice, and this was hers.

Offering my own upturned hand, I held her solemn gaze as she did the same thing to my palm, slicing the meaty part. Only this time, droplets fell onto the bundle she'd brought with her, causing a magical sizzle. Whatever spell encased the small package broke on contact.

Next, with the same athame, Mom severed the twine and slowly unwrapped the leather bundle, revealing a small twig doll. There were short strands of hair woven through the wood that held an old raven skull and shiny black feather.

The puppet represented me. This is what she'd used to bind my oracle powers.

Magic swelled in the air as she softly began to chant again—her voice growing louder with each uttered word. I still couldn't understand it, but energy didn't lie. The spell was building to a climax.

Lifting the doll up in front of her face, Mom blew her breath across it before offering it to the sky. Her words became more forceful until finally her head fell backward. I could imagine her heart pounding within her chest like mine. There'd been something almost guttural and raw about her incantation.

A moment passed before she straightened, and when she did, I gasped. Her eyes were pure white and glowing brightly in their sockets. The magic that encased her began sending tendrils of light out from her body as if they were seeking a new place to inhabit. Its rightful home.

Me.

I wanted to reach out and touch it but before I could, my mother dropped the twig doll into the bowl filled with her blood, and with one last shout, lit the puppet on fire. There was no hesitation from the flames as it quickly engulfed the figure.

I waited for the tendrils to swarm toward me.

I held my breath for that instant where I felt my magic unlock inside me and reveal the full force of my power. I'd anticipated this precise moment my entire life, always wondering what the experience would be like.

There was just one last step before the ritual was complete.

As quickly as the fire had consumed the doll, the flames extinguished, leaving behind a small mound of ash. With a steady hand, my mother gathered some on her fingers and thumb before tracing the remnants over my face in different runes.

"Unlock," she whispered in English. "Receive. Become."

An indescribable sensation ignited within my chest.

My vision clouded as my focus latched on to the one driving force that screamed for release.

A song. Many songs. Melodies from the past, present, and future all dancing about in my mind. I turned to Rune and then to the women beside him. They were here for me, and while they had been robbed of their sight, I would be their eyes in this world, just as their presence would always strengthen me.

There was only one thing left to do.

I opened my mouth and sang.

EPILOGUE

MICAH

$\mathcal{J}$ still couldn't believe the past twenty-four hours.

Shortly after Holly had received her gifts and magic in full from her mother, realized exactly who Rune was, and that she was now surrounded by three wonderful new friends as her singers, the Viking warrior informed us all that there was no time to process the insanity that had unfolded because she'd be receiving her first vision tonight. According to him, her powers would open and visions would be given to her only under the full and new moons.

Tonight's lunar event was also called the Buck Moon, symbolizing the shedding of antlers for bucks and stags. Holly had been delighted in learning that small tidbit from Sedona because she felt that same sense of shedding away her old life and embracing the fullness of her magic.

I could see in Holly's tired expression just how overwhelming today had been, but I was amazed how she accepted her new responsibilities graciously and with an eagerness I'd seen before. She'd been voracious about learning new things as a child, and it was a trait that she'd embraced into her teens. I had no doubt that she'd excel in her role as an Oracle.

Sure enough, here we were, under the full moon, out in the gorgeous forest just by the falls, my sweet girl performing her first official ceremony with her singers. Sedona had mentioned this was the site where the Luna Coven met and worked their collective magic.

It was nothing short of breathtaking. I was pretty sure at any moment I would explode with pride.

Unlike last night's private ritual in Shelf Indulgence's upstairs apartment, there were important people from town here to witness the magic being woven. Sedona had notified the Court immediately after Holly's awakening ritual, so of course they'd want to be in attendance tonight. Addie and her grandmother, Saundra Beaumont, were standing off to the side, talking quietly between themselves while also keeping an eye on Rune, who was giving last minute instructions to Holly.

A pang of . . . I couldn't quite find the word to describe it . . . something flickered through me seeing him take the role I'd spent all of Holly's life serving. Perhaps it was jealousy that I was feeling—a sadness that I wasn't the only important person in her life now. I'd known the day would come when she fell in love, but this . . . the emotion made a hard lump form in my throat.

Tonight wasn't about me and how I felt, however. It was about my beautiful Holly.

God, I was honored to watch her shine.

"It's strange seeing her so grown up, isn't it?" Holly's mom stood beside me quietly. I could see her looking at the others who were here to support her daughter.

I couldn't respond, because the emotions coursing through me still hadn't released their tight grip. I was one step away from crying—tears threatening to well in my eyes.

All this time I'd thought that Holly's father was the powerful parent, and I hadn't even considered that my assumption was wrong. I couldn't fault Elizabeth for hiding the truth from even me—in her mind, the safety of her daughter took priority.

I'd assumed I was on a mission to thwart a wayward archangel's thirst and greed for power. I hadn't hesitated in accepting a sobbing mother's pleading prayers to please move heaven and earth to raise her child, to forever ensure that her magic would never be stripped away and abused for evil.

I'd considered it a divine calling—the sole purpose for my existence —never regretting for a second the sacrifice it took to always be vigilant and ready for an attack.

Now as I watched my charge with her circle, trying to learn the extent of her birthright as quickly as possible, I couldn't help but feel an overwhelming sense of pride. Despite it all, Holly Westbrook had grown into a courageous young woman at eighteen with the power to change the world. She was no longer the fourteen-year-old girl who had spent her entire life on the run and being forbidden her magic. We'd found a community here within Havenwood Falls the past four years that had not only embraced us both, but provided the perfect environment for Holly to thrive and discover who she was.

A lump formed in my throat. What a blessing this town has been for both of us. "If I haven't already said it, Micah, thank you," Elizabeth said softly. Gone was the crazed patient of Belmont Park, the mental health facility where I'd hidden Holly's mother. There was a calmness about her now that transcended the franticness she'd displayed the last time I visited. Elizabeth's role in Holly's ascension to Oracle was complete.

In fact, the task of protecting Holly was now out of my hands and placed firmly into those of Rune, the Viking warrior. What I'd do now was still unclear, but one thing was for certain—I'd never stop looking out for Holly's best interests and I'd forever be at the ready to defend her.

I acknowledged her gratitude with a nod. "It's been my absolute pleasure and joy," I answered, meaning those words with every ounce of my being. "Although I'm not sure why you couldn't have told me the whole truth from the beginning."

Elizabeth brushed a long strand of her blonde hair over her shoulder. "Would it have made you fight even harder for her had you known? Would it have made a difference?"

I shook my head. It wouldn't have. Even if all I'd known was her name and that she was mine to protect and conceal, I'd have done it without hesitation. The request had been something I'd felt deep within my soul. "No."

Elizabeth let out of breath and turned from watching her daughter. "I knew who her father was when I met him. While I wasn't aware of how cruel he could be and how desperately he yearned for power until much later, I'd foreseen our union resulting in Holly and the greatness in her future." Her gaze got a faraway look as if she was seeing into her memories. "It was my own foolish ego who believed he wouldn't pose a threat . . . that an archangel wasn't capable of such lust, but I was wrong.

The instant he held Holly in his arms, the gods granted me a startling revelation."

"That he would use her to destroy the world and rewrite time?" I added, already knowing this was the reason. It was unfathomable to believe back then that an agent of Heaven could harbor such desires.

Elizabeth rested her hand on my arm lightly. "That was part of the vision. What I didn't ever share was what followed." She shuddered. "It was so much worse, Micah. The destruction and chaos he would unleash would ripple throughout the rest of time and across all dimensions. The threat was so catastrophic that my gods revealed his plans and dictated my course of action. You were chosen for the strength and honor you still hold. Out of all the decisions I've ever made . . . you are one I have never regretted."

The truth was so much more than I'd ever expected. There was no trace at annoyance about being kept in the dark, either. I was just relieved I'd been able to do my part successfully.

"He's still out there . . . searching for her." I didn't need a vision to know that.

Elizabeth nodded, a slow knowing smile curving her lips. "True, but his influence and ability to corrupt her diminishes every minute she spends with her circle honing her gift. The time will come when if he should come face to face with her, Holly will hold the power to destroy him completely."

The admission sent me reeling.

The ability to obliterate an archangel from existence was unheard of. "Do you think she'll show him mercy?" I asked, curiously.

Shrugging, Elizabeth squeezed my hand. "What does your own heart tell you, Micah? You raised her. What do you think your daughter will choose?"

Daughter. That's exactly how I felt about Holly. I also knew what her heart would pick.

A lump formed in my throat, making it hard to answer. Instead, I changed the subject. "What about you? Where will you go? Would you like to stay in Havenwood Falls with us?"

Sedona had mentioned the possibility the night before as we lay in bed before sleep. She'd talked about offering her grandfather's apartment above Shelf Indulgence to Holly's mom—the kindness making me love her even more.

Her brow creased above her nose. "The gods have other plans for me. I am still in their service." I waited to see if she'd expand a little more on her cryptic response, but the sounds of drums beating to a steady rhythm drew my attention away.

I couldn't have picked a better location for this special ritual.

Dressed in white, the singers all but glowed beneath the fairy lights that were strung from the tree branches above them. Someone had placed lit candles all about, the flames flickering and dancing in the subtle breeze. Shafts of moonbeams peaked through the foliage above, and it seemed as though the four young women wore halos of silvery light around their heads.

I recognized Rhian join Addie on the side of the circle, standing close to where one of the gossamer curtains hung from the tent that had been erected for tonight. The air stilled, and a feeling of reverence sent a hush through me.

As beautiful as everything looked, it paled in comparison to the energy now building.

The ritual had begun.

I would never get used to hearing how angelic Holly sounded and the way her voice wove magic in the air along with Arya, Liv, and Quin. It was like we were witnessing a symphonic masterpiece being created before us. The beauty of it stole my breath.

Each note hung above them as swirls of energetic colors danced and swayed to the music they made. The circle of women closed tighter around Holly, their hands still keeping the pulsing rhythm on the drums as though she was the heart, and they were its beat.

"Something's happening," Elizabeth murmured. "Look!"

I'd already noticed. Holly's entire body began to glow as her pupils disappeared and were replaced with white. Her body lifted slowly up from the ground, her arms floating gently by her side.

She was having a vision, and judging by the ripple of soft murmurs around us, there were other people here to witness the ritual that I hadn't seen earlier. Court members stood by the boulders just outside the tent's perimeter, and I spotted Rusty Higgins with the sheriff, their arms folded against their chests, visually affected by the magic that emanated from the singers.

No one could take their eyes away from the four young women—

their magic was absolutely palpable. It was clear to see that I wasn't the only one mesmerized by Holly.

I wanted to stepped closer and intervene, but Elizabeth grabbed my hand, stopping me. I looked at Rune, who studied Holly and his sisters intently. That was another revelation shared last night. He was their older brother and guardian.

Time seemed to stand still until slowly their song quieted, and the circle stopped singing. Holly's eyes returned to normal, and she now wore a confused expression.

"What is it, oracle?" Rune asked gently, taking a few steps closer. "What have you seen?"

She shook her head as if she was trying to make sense of something. I knew what she was doing because I'd witnessed the same quirk countless times over the years. Given a chance to think, Holly would figure it out.

"There's a woman," Holly spoke—each word measured carefully. "She's hurt. Trapped. It's dark. She's alone." Her gaze met mine. "She's afraid." She closed her eyes again as though she could reenter the vision again for more details. Disappointment crashed over her features. "Micah…it's worse than that. When she is rescued…*how* she is rescued…*everything* changes."

I could see her physically shaking, her face white as a sheet as she fidgeted with her hands. All I wanted to do was rush to her like I'd always done, gather her in my arms, and help chase away whatever distressed her. It was a bittersweet moment witnessing her grow before me into a strong young woman—despite watching her struggle under the weight of her newly released powers. She might have been shaking like a leaf, pausing to catch her breath and steady herself, but there was no denying Holly would not only conquer her emotions, but that she'd become stronger because of it.

Holly's singers encircled her again with their arms offering support. It was clear whatever their oracle had seen and felt affected her.

Rune looked toward the Court members, his gaze landing on Addie and her grandmother Saundra. "Would the leaders like to sit with the oracle and hear about the full vision?"

"Yes, she'll need to meet with the Court," Addie answered.

"Are you okay to do that now, sweetheart?" The circle had made an opening so I could approach and comfort my daughter. "Do you need something to help remember what you saw?"

Holly shook her head. "It's ingrained into my mind, Micah. I can still feel the fear coursing through my veins." She squeezed my hand. "This is who I am. I'm ready."

She'd embraced her role and magic completely, accepting her new place in the world. Gone was the quirky teenage girl who made me laugh at her silly antics and liked to tease me relentlessly.

Holly Westbrook was the oracle.

And I would follow her wherever she needed me.

RESONANCE

SUSAN BURDORF

CHAPTER 1

*S*herry pulled the door open and stepped inside Coffee Haven grateful for the wash of rich coffee smell that enveloped her. She breathed deeply. To her, coffee was the stuff of life. Nothing perked up her spirits more than a cup of Coffee Haven double shot of espresso vanilla mocha coffee.

She nodded to Harlow who was scrubbing down the counter.

"I got you," the young barista called to Sherry as she made her way toward her favorite table.

"And a scone?"

"And a scone, coming right up," Harlow answered. Her grin was infectious, and Sherry smiled back even though smiling was the last thing on her mind these days.

Pulling out the laptop from her bag, Sherry plugged it in and settled her pens, notebook, and file cards within reach on the table. She'd heard from her agent that her latest book—a romance between a witch and a wolf shifter—was up for auction, and it was time to get started on the next in her paranormal romance series set in a mysterious town of exceptional citizens loosely based on her experiences in Havenwood Falls. Of course, no one knew that, and most would certainly not believe her even if she did tell them just how much her adopted hometown was featured in the books she'd started writing several years ago.

With Rusty out on extra patrols due to some crazy stuff happening in Havenwood Falls lately, Sherry felt claustrophobic in the cabin.

Amazing how just having Rusty at her side opened up her world. She'd often heard other married friends complain about how being a couple meant losing so much of yourself, but Sherry never felt that way.

Life with Rusty made her life complete, but not in an all-consuming way, which meant she actually missed him terribly when he was gone and had to fill the emptiness with other pursuits, like drinking her favorite beverage in her favorite café.

Sighing with her first taste of the daily rejuvenator that made life worthwhile, Sherry tapped into her newest story and was soon lost between its pages. Two hours later, she leaned back just in time to see a woman walking by with her baby in a stroller.

Sherry felt the familiar twinge of regret in her abdomen that she and Rusty had still not had a child despite their desire for one. At first, she'd feared his being a supernatural was the reason, but seeing other packs with young ones had alleviated that fear. Then it was worry that she was barren, but a trip to the doctor a month ago had assured her that was not the case either.

Now, it was just a matter of waiting for the bundle of joy to arrive in their future. And in the meantime, they would just carry on as usual. At least, that's what Sherry told herself as she tore her eyes away from the smiling mother and child.

"Hey, Sherry, how are you?" Cece stood in front of her, holding a small plate with a scone and a cup of coffee. "Mind if I join you? Or are you busy?"

Sherry smiled at her dear friend. Cece owned the local music store and was an angel, in more ways than one. She was literally an angel, a mind reader of consummate skill who was known for her ability to calm people down when life took its depressive toll on them; and she was an angel in the friend arena, often showing up with great advice to assist those in need.

Sherry moved her notebook to the side and gestured for Cece to have a seat. The pretty blonde angel set her coffee and scone down while scrutinizing Sherry with deep concern etched on her face.

"What's up with you, Sherry? I haven't seen you in town for a few days."

"Been busy. Finally have the details for the last book finalized and off to the editor and hoping everything will be okay because that book was hard."

Cece took a sip of her coffee, her gaze tight on Sherry's face until Sherry turned red and lowered her eyes.

"I hate when you do that," she said with a laugh.

"Do what?" Cece asked. Her face was all innocent, but a slight tilt of her lips let Sherry know she knew very well what she'd done.

"You stare at me like you know exactly what I am thinking."

"Well, I am a mind reader, but not to worry." Cece put her cup down and leaned toward Sherry, lowering her voice. "I respect our friendship too much to actually read your mind unless you want me to."

"I know." Sherry sighed. Worrying her lower lip, she considered her next words. "I'm not happy lately, but I'm not sure exactly why I'm not happy. Does that make sense?"

Cece nodded but said nothing else.

Sherry snorted then turned to look out the window. The mother and child were across the street now.

"Ah," said Cece. "I don't need to read your mind to see what's bothering you now."

Sherry pinched her lips and shrugged. "Don't get me wrong. I am so very happy. Rusty is amazing, and I love him so much."

"But?"

"But I want to give him a child. No, I want a child. I want something else to love. Loving Rusty has opened me to being able to love so much more. I want a child."

Cece nodded in understanding. "I get it. You are a very giving person, Sherry. You deserve to be completely happy."

"I know you are an angel. Could you…?"

Cece smiled with regret. "I know what you want me to do, but I don't have that kind of power."

"I know," Sherry said with a sigh. She leaned back, closing her eyes until she could calm her breathing. Asking Cece to make that kind of magic was asking for the impossible. Sometimes life couldn't give you everything you wanted. She would have to accept that the way Rusty had.

Changing topics, Sherry looked at Cece with a very serious expression. "So, how are you doing, Cece?"

"I'm doing okay," Cece answered taking another sip of her beverage. "Sherry, be patient, okay? Everything will work itself out, it always does."

"I know, I know." Sherry shrugged. "I'm just too impatient. I want what every woman wants, I guess."

"And what's that?"

"To make her chosen mate happy. And I think a child would make Rusty and I complete."

Cece nodded. "I understand, but aren't you happy now? You and Rusty are perfect for each other, and family is more than just a mother, father, and child."

Sherry chuckled. "Yes, we are happy. I just wish…" Making a face, Sherry sipped her coffee and looked at the mother and child again.

"Ah." Cece followed Sherry's eyes and looked out the window. "They look very happy."

Sherry nodded, watching the mother and child laughing. The child looked to be about two, with her mother's blonde hair and smile. She wanted that, a little boy like Rusty, and a little girl like her.

The door opened, and in walked a group of teens, all laughing and full of life as they ordered their beverages and scones and wandered out again, taking all the air in the room with them.

"Sherry," Cece leaned across the table to squeeze Sherry's hand gently, "don't do this to yourself. You need to find peace. Perhaps focus on your writing for now and let the rest of the chips fall where they will? Yes, I know, a horrible cliché, but sometimes that is the best way to cope with things."

Sherry squeezed Cece's hand back before releasing her friend and leaning back with her coffee in hand.

"Agreed. I will say a prayer and then let it go." But the wistful glance out the window to the mother and child who were moving out of sight was anything but calm.

CHAPTER 2

*a*t home later that afternoon, Sherry was engrossed in her story edits when Rusty came home.

She heard him rustling around in the kitchen and went to greet him.

Slipping her arms around his lean waist and leaning her head onto his strong back, she squeezed him with all the love in her heart. Listening to his heart faintly beating through the thickness of his clothes, she felt her own heart responding with a slowing beat.

Rusty was the best thing that had ever happened to her, and Sherry knew without a doubt that if they were never to have a child, she would be okay with her immortal lover. The fact that she would grow old and die, and he would go on without her, was something she'd come to grips with a long time ago.

"Hey," he said, rubbing her bare arms with strong calloused hands. "What's this for?"

Sherry released him and joined him at his side where they both looked out the kitchen window into the nearby forest. She hesitated before answering.

"I was just thinking how much I wish I could make you a father." She bit her lip, avoiding looking at him when she heard him sigh.

"Sherry…"

"I know, I know. You keep saying we will be parents when it's time, but I want that time to be now. I feel a difference in the air. Don't you?"

Rusty pulled Sherry into an embrace and lowered his head to kiss the top of hers. "I wish I could tell you that we'll be parents, that what's wrong is not us, but I don't know why we aren't parents yet."

"We could go to the clinic in Denver," Sherry started to say, but pulling away slightly in his embrace, she saw him shaking his head.

"You know we can't do that. There are things about me that a doctor outside of Havenwood Falls wouldn't understand."

Sherry looked deeply into his soft brown eyes and nodded. She knew very well that his DNA would be immediately flagged as something so different that it would need to be studied. That was not acceptable.

His heartbeat was so strong, and Sherry relaxed and just let their embrace be enough.

She wasn't dissatisfied with her life with Rusty. She just wanted so much more. She wanted to give him that gift of a piece of them both so badly that not being able to do it was ripping her up inside.

Rusty stroked her hair until she calmed and then whispered, "We are okay as we are, aren't we?"

Sherry nodded. Hiding her tears in his chest, she agreed. "Yes, we are absolutely fine."

He held her for a moment more before releasing her. "I have to go. There's a meeting of the Court tonight, and they asked me to attend."

Sherry stepped away, her gaze locked on his. But instead of questioning him, she nodded and said, "I'll have dinner waiting for you when you return."

Then Rusty was gone, and Sherry was left in an empty house that lost all life the minute he left.

She wasn't giving up. She promised herself she would give him a child. She knew that when she was gone, as her mortal life would definitely end before his, that a child of theirs would be a comfort to him. That was what love did for you, made you want the impossible for the one you loved.

CHAPTER 3

*R*usty walked into the meeting room of the Court of the Sun and the Moon to find a group of very serious faces in the room.

No one was joking or cracking a smile. They all stood in small groups, whispering and gesturing with animation, but no joviality.

There were all the familiar people here—Saundra Beaumont, Mathilde Augustine, Roman Bishop, Lawrence Mills, Elsmed Fairchild, Michaela Petran, Teeny Weeny McFeeny, Lilith Blackstone, Mayor Barbie Stuart—and he caught the eye of his cousin Ric Kasun, the sheriff, who nodded but didn't move toward him to speak.

Taking a seat, Rusty waited to find out what this meeting was called for and didn't have to wait too long.

Standing behind the table on the dais at the front of the room, Saundra asked everyone to take their seats.

"Hello, everyone. Thank you for being on time. I think we're all here, so let's get started."

The rest of the Court moved to their chairs behind the table, Addie and Ric taking their usual seats on either side of the dais. At the front of the audience sat the waif-like figure of Rhian, an SMA student, and a young child not much smaller than her. Rusty was the only other person in the audience, this being a closed meeting, which meant the subject was serious and confidential.

All eyes were on Saundra, who cleared her throat before continuing.

"Rhian has brought us interesting news and other…gifts. Rhian, do you mind giving a report of what you've been up to?"

Rhian stood, turning so she could face the Court without excluding Rusty, her face wearing an unusually serious expression that raised goosebumps on Rusty's arms. Rhian was a triple moon goddess, and when she wasn't taking classes at SMA worked with Zandra, once known as the Collector, to protect Havenwood Falls. If she had the kind of news to call a meeting like this, then there was definitely something going on that bore listening to.

While Rhian explained why she was there and talked about more blind witches, Rusty's attention was drawn to the young girl who sat in the chair beside the goddess with her head bowed.

He didn't recognize her, and he felt that he should if she were a resident of Havenwood Falls. The girl was definitely magical, for he could sense magic flowing from her in heavy waves that were not uncomfortable and didn't make him think immediately of danger, but rather of something different. He knew she wouldn't be here without restraints if she was a threat to Havenwood Falls or anyone here, but he still instinctively knew she would need watching.

She looked very young, perhaps twelve in human years, and very slender. She appeared to be uncaring of her surroundings, the slump of her shoulders making him wonder what trials she'd seen or experienced as she carried an air of defeat around her.

As if aware of his scrutiny, she looked up and turned toward him. In her eyes, he saw such pain that he was left momentarily breathless. The sadness and emptiness in her eyes spoke to the journey to Havenwood Falls not having been an easy one, and he wondered if she were somehow connected to what had happened to Quin and these other witches like her.

The girl lowered her head after a moment, but he still felt gripped by the agony he saw in her expression. Glancing around, he didn't notice anyone else reacting to her pain. Everyone was watching Rhian while she explained further details of the witches she had brought to Havenwood Falls, and Rusty straightened in his chair at the mention of an Oracle.

"This child," Rhian glanced down at the small child in the dark robes who had captured Rusty's attention, "was also magic-trafficked. She's not blinded and not part of my mission, but when I rescued Liv, the third witch, I couldn't leave this one there."

"So now we have a dilemma about what to do with her," Saundra said.

Several questions were raised by others, which Rhian strove to answer as quickly and efficiently as she could.

"As far as I know, the child is not a danger to anyone, but her magic is strong. She was imprisoned in a way that makes me think there were plans to use her for some dire purpose. I couldn't leave her there in the hands of those abusers."

More questions. More answers. None of them satisfactory to Rusty, who felt compelled to interrupt. Eyes on the young girl, he stood when given permission to speak.

"Rhian, Court members." He nodded in deference to the Court members who acknowledged him, nodding in return. "I have some concerns about this child. First and foremost, what do you intend to do about her? I mean, she's here, but where will she go now?"

"That's one of the many questions of the night," Elsmed said.

"What do you know about her?" Rusty asked. "What's her name? What kind of magic does she have? What did they do to her? They didn't blind her, but she was obviously important to them or why keep her as a prisoner at all?"

Rhian shrugged. "I told you everything I know about her. She hadn't been with Liv, the other witch, long, so Liv doesn't know anything about her, either. Like I said, I couldn't fathom leaving her there in those conditions. I'm sorry for any trouble this causes, but I hope you all understand."

The girl remained silent throughout the discussion, her head lowered, and her body trembling slightly as if she feared being harmed.

Rusty felt compassion for the child welling up in his chest, and without realizing it, his thoughts became words. "If you don't know what to do with her, why not let me take her home until you figure it out? Sherry and I have a spare room in the cabin we can give her, and since Sherry is home all day anyway, the girl will not be alone."

Saundra Beaumont said, "I think it would be a good idea to have her stay with someone who can provide constant attention and supervision. She hasn't told us anything about herself. We don't know if there's been damage to her magic or possibly a memory spell or her own reluctance, but she hasn't spoken a word to any of us. And, to be honest, we have not had much time to figure it out yet."

Saundra gazed at the young girl before looking at Rusty. "If the Court has no issue with it, I see no reason why you and Sherry couldn't keep the girl for a time."

The girl in question reacted by stiffening but said nothing in protest.

"Are you sure you and Sherry are willing to do this?" Michaela asked. "I know from experience how difficult it can be."

Rusty nodded, certain Sherry would be thrilled to have a young girl in the cabin with her, especially one so obviously damaged and in need of her special skills. Michaela had been forced to take care of her younger siblings, also emotionally damaged, when she'd barely reached adulthood herself, but his and Sherry's situation was different.

In Sherry's former life, she had been a high school counselor and worked with troubled children. While someone like this might not have been her usual type of client, she would at least have the knowledge to try to coax information from the girl that might benefit the Court. Sherry also had so much love to give someone in obvious need of it, evidenced by their earlier conversation about children.

Rusty retained his seat and kept his eyes on the girl during the rest of the meeting. Once things broke up, Saundra came directly to him and asked again if he was sure he and Sherry were willing to take on the responsibility of the unknown girl.

"We don't know much about her at all. We don't know what she's capable of. We don't know why she was there in the first place," Saundra said, glancing over her shoulder at Rhian and the girl. Rhian kept her hand on the girl's upper back.

The girl had yet to raise her head since looking at him earlier in the meeting.

Rusty nodded.

"All we know is she's a witch," Rhian said. "They were draining her magic, but she seemed to replenish it quickly from what we can see. I feel her purpose didn't have anything to do with the Oracle like the other witches, but, like I told the Court, I couldn't just leave her there."

"I'll make sure Sherry knows as much of this as it is possible to tell her without disclosing the confidential information about the witches and the oracle," Rusty assured the Court members and Rhian.

Rhian looked the young witch in the eyes. "We are going to find out who you are and what we can do to help you return to your people if we can, but in the meantime, this man and his wife are opening their home to you. He is safe. I promise. His name is Rusty, and he's a wolf shifter. He will see that you come to no harm."

The girl raised her head to look from Rhian to Rusty, then lowered her eyes again, nodding her head that she understood. She didn't speak, and Rusty had a sudden worry that she *couldn't* speak.

Taking the girl's small hand, Rhian put it in Rusty's much larger one and stepped back. "She will need clothes and all the rest. We brought nothing but the clothes on her back with us."

Rusty nodded. "I'm sure Sherry would love to take her shopping tomorrow."

He knelt to the girl's eye level and said, "I'm honored to be chosen to watch over you. I promise, like Rhian said, that no harm will come to you while you are with us. Are you ready to go?"

The girl bit her lip, but after a moment's hesitation, nodded yes and squeezed his hand.

"Rusty, are you sure Sherry is okay with this?" he was asked once more.

With an assurance suddenly lacking, he nodded. "Sure. Sherry will be thrilled."

Closing the door behind them, he prayed he wasn't being over-confident in his belief that Sherry would be happy to have a young girl, with unknown trauma behind her, living in their home.

Here goes nothing, he thought. *Or something very special.*

CHAPTER 4

*S*herry was curled up on the couch with a book when Rusty entered their cabin. He'd asked the young witch to stay on the porch while he went inside.

Sherry jumped up when he walked in, a huge smile on her face. "Let me warm up dinner. That was a long meeting. Everything okay?"

Sherry started toward the kitchen. Rusty cut the distance between them in three quick strides and pulled her into an embrace.

"Hey!" Sherry said, laughing as she hugged him back, "What's that for? Did you miss me that much?"

Her laughter died out at the serious expression on his face.

"What's going on, Rusty? What's happened?"

Rusty paused then gestured to the couch where he asked her to sit while he paced in front of her for a minute. He struggled to find the words then finally muttered, "By the moon!"

Sherry chuckled. "Well, it must be serious if you're swearing before you've even told me what's going on."

The sound of a cough on the porch caused Sherry to swivel her head toward the door, and before Rusty could stop her, she was pushing open the screen.

"Well, hello. And whom do we have here?" Sherry held the door open, glancing around to see if anyone else was standing with the young girl in the dark robes who was on her porch.

"Um...let me explain," Rusty said in a shaky voice. He reached for the girl's hand, which she placed in his and stepped daintily into the room while Sherry held the door open.

Rusty led her to the couch. The girl sat, her hood over her bowed head, hiding her face completely.

Sherry stood at the door, looking from Rusty to the girl in confusion.

"What's going on, Rusty? Who is this?"

Rusty sat next to the girl. Patting the couch next to him, he motioned for Sherry to join them.

Sherry let the door slam behind her, the sound making both Rusty and the girl jump as Sherry sat. Looking curiously at the girl who shrank deeper into her cloak, Sherry waited for Rusty to explain.

"So, at the meeting tonight we were talking about...some things, and it turns out this girl has no family that anyone knows of and she needs a place to stay. I volunteered us to watch over her while the Court figures out a long-term solution."

Sherry considered his explanation, the expression on his face promising she wasn't going to let him off so easy.

"What's your name?" she asked the girl in a soft voice.

The girl shrugged, not speaking.

Sherry's eyebrow rose in question as she looked back at Rusty, who also shrugged.

"No one knows, and she doesn't speak."

"Won't speak, or can't speak?" asked Sherry.

Again, Rusty shrugged. "Not sure. She was brought to the meeting tonight to decide what to do with her, along with other topics on the agenda."

Sherry bit her lip while she considered Rusty's statement. "And what are we to do with her?"

"Take care of her?"

Sherry hesitated. Standing, she knelt down in front of the girl, and with a finger under the girl's chin, she raised her face to study the young child.

"Who are you?" she asked slowly.

The girl met her gaze squarely but didn't answer.

In her eyes, Sherry saw deep pain and something else that was not quite fear, but something close to it. She'd seen this same expression in the kids she'd counseled who had been abused, and it broke her heart.

"Okay," she said without taking her eyes from the girl's face.

"Okay?" Rusty's tone was confused then hopeful. "Does that mean she can stay?"

"Far be it from me to deny the Court something they ask of us." Sherry stood. Brushing her hands on her jeans, she looked toward the back of the living room where their guest room was.

"I'll get the room ready. Why don't you see if our guest would like something to eat? I think there is a pizza in the freezer if you want to see if she would like that. Be back in a few minutes. After dinner, I think we should consider a shower then bed."

Then she was gone. The girl watched her go then turned to Rusty.

"She has no magic." The girl's tone was derisive and cold.

Rusty stared at her in shock.

"So you can speak," he said with a tight smile. "Any reason why you didn't speak before now?"

The girl shrugged. "Nothing to say," she said in that same cold voice.

She moved past him to the kitchen. Opening the refrigerator door, she took out the meal Sherry had put on a plate and covered with foil to be reheated when Rusty returned home. It was a steak, potato, and vegetables.

"This will do," she said. She sat on a tall stool at the breakfast bar, legs swinging while she waited for him to fix her meal.

"That's…" He started to say, "that's mine," but stopped himself before the words came out and put the foil back over the cooled food, popping it in the oven and setting the temperature to reheat it.

Pulling the pizza from the freezer, he set it on the pan and put it in the oven with the now claimed steak. Pizza was fine, he convinced himself.

Later, while he and Sherry shared some pizza and wine and watched the young witch devour his meal, Rusty pondered if that was what parenthood was always like—sacrificing for the ones you loved even if you didn't really know them yet.

Sherry was quiet throughout the meal, her gaze on the girl, who had taken off the robe during the meal. She was very slender, her bony shoulders poking through the thin cloth of the non-descript brown shift she wore, making her look like a little girl playing dress up in someone else's clothes.

She wore black boots with no socks on her feet. Her arms and lower half of her legs were bare, and on her arms Sherry noted scratches and other marks that looked remarkably like bruises that had healed and been bruised again. The purplish red was turning yellow. Some of the bruises resembled fingers, and she wondered what torture this girl had gone through.

Exchanging glances with Rusty while the girl finished her meal, she promised him without words that they would be discussing this after the girl was settled in bed.

The girl had not spoken again, all questions asked by Sherry going unacknowledged until Sherry realized that pressing the girl would be a mistake, and she let the questions go. Rusty tried, but couldn't get her to speak, either. With an exasperated sigh, he left the conversation to Sherry and stepped outside for a minute.

Sherry tried a few more techniques she'd learned as a counselor, but the girl was adamantly not responding to her at all, and she gave up. There would be time tomorrow to find out who this girl was and what had happened to her.

After her shower, Sherry found a nightgown that while too big for the girl, would at least cover her nakedness. At first the girl had refused to take a shower, but finally relented when Rusty asked her to do it.

She was in and out so quickly, Sherry wasn't sure the girl had actually gotten any water on her, but she did smell more like the lavender soap and jasmine shampoo than the crusty, dirty clothes and matted hair she'd been sporting earlier.

Sherry tucked the girl in, offering her a nightlight, which the girl refused with a gesture before turning her back to Sherry and pulling the covers over her head, effectively shutting off all further communication.

Sherry stood in the doorway a moment before turning out the room's light and closing the door.

Striding quickly into the kitchen where Rusty was putting their dishes in the dishwasher and cleaning up the remains of their meal, she leaned against the counter and pierced him with a look that caused him to sigh.

"I know." He closed and locked the back kitchen door and followed Sherry into the living room. Grabbing the wine and their glasses from dinner, he sat on the couch next to her.

"You know what?" Sherry accepted the wine from him and settled back on the couch, knees drawn up and facing him. He braced his back against the other end of the couch and sighed.

"She had nowhere else to go," he said by way of explanation.

"A little warning…"

"I know I should have called you, but it all happened pretty quickly. The Court has a lot going on, and I couldn't just leave her there. Someone else probably would have stepped up, but I felt like we are just as capable as anyone else, if not more. Plus, we have the space in our home—and in our hearts—to help her…right?"

Sherry sipped her wine. Closing her eyes, she couldn't get the pain in the girl's face out of her head. "She's damaged."

Rusty nodded. "I know."

"She's really damaged. I'm not sure I can help her. And she's magic, isn't she?"

Rusty nodded again. "We think—no, I guess we *know* she's a witch."

"She was in a very bad place, wasn't she?" Sherry asked, her voice softening. She turned toward the door where the girl was sleeping.

"Yes," was all Rusty said. He took a long swallow of the wine, emptying his glass. He poured more and offered the bottle to Sherry, who declined.

"I don't know if I can help her. But maybe Cece can?"

"That's what I thought, too. Between the two of you, maybe you can get some information from her."

"What's her name?"

Rusty shrugged. "No one knows. She won't say. Maybe she doesn't remember?"

"Maybe," Sherry said. "What happened to her clothes and her things?"

Rusty shrugged again. "She had nothing when she came to us."

"Well, first thing we do then is take her shopping." Sherry smiled. "Nothing bonds us women more than a shopping trip to buy clothes. Hope your credit card can stand the dent we are about to put in it tomorrow," Sherry said with a giggle as she held her glass toward Rusty who tapped his against hers.

"If it means we can help her, I think I can stand the damage." Then Rusty's smile faded at the memory of the girl's derisive comment about Sherry not possessing magic, and he hoped he wasn't wrong about bringing the girl into their home.

CHAPTER 5

*T*he next morning dawned bright and clear.

Sherry groaned and rolled out of bed, memory of the girl in their guest bedroom foremost in her mind. She wasn't sure what the girl even liked to eat but figured no one could pass up sausages and eggs, so that's what she would start with. While they were in town today, she'd see about picking up some food the girl would like.

Rusty was already gone, had probably left during the night to do his nightly patrols like usual, and Sherry hummed as she brushed her teeth and washed her face to start the day. Heading into the kitchen, she was surprised to see the girl was already up, her hair damp and a towel wrapped around her as she sat at the breakfast bar on the same stool as last night, waiting for her.

Sherry slapped her forehead in disgust at herself. How silly of her. The girl had nothing to wear. How could they go shopping?

Just then there was a knock on the door.

Sherry nodded to the girl in apology and opened the door to see Cece standing on the porch with a bag and a pair of shoes in her hand.

"Hello. I understand you have a houseguest who might be in need of some clothes?"

"How did you...?" Sherry asked in surprise then grinned. "Rusty called you, didn't he? Come on in. Where did you get these?"

"Oh, I got the sheriff to have his kids open Backwoods a little early, and voila, here you are. Jeans, shoes, socks, undergarments, T-shirts, and a jacket. I think that is everything she will need to get started. I just hope everything fits. She is a tiny one, isn't she?"

Sherry took the clothes to the couch and motioned the girl to come over and check it out. The little witch stared at Cece with big eyes but didn't say anything. Looking at the clothes, the girl picked out a few items and retreated to the bedroom to change.

"Quiet one, isn't she?" Cece said to Sherry once the door closed behind the girl.

"She hasn't spoken a word to me yet," Sherry agreed. "I was just about to fix some breakfast. Would you like to join us?"

"I can't stay. Just wanted to be sure you had the clothes first thing. Gotta get back to the music shop."

Although she was an angel and didn't need to eat, Cece would sometimes do so with her friends. Usually, she would enjoy a cup of coffee with Sherry, who was a known coffee-holic, and one of Coffee Haven's magnificent blueberry scones.

"So, what are your plans for today?" Cece asked. She was reluctant to leave and not sure why.

"I might need your help later. Okay if we stop by?" Sherry nodded toward the girl. "Did you get anything from her yet?" Sherry tapped her temple, indicating Cece's ability to probe minds.

Cece shook her head. "Rusty mentioned that you might need me to see if I could help her remember things about her past. I think Elsmed would have already tried that, and he is much more skilled than me. I am just getting a general impression of pain, and hurt, and not just physical. But there is a dark barrier that won't allow me to penetrate too deeply into her mind. Sorry. I can try again, and maybe with more time I can discern something."

Cece frowned, her beautiful eyes troubled, before continuing. "I do not feel danger from her, but I don't feel anything else right now. She seems to be very good at blocking intrusions into her mind for someone so young. Or perhaps those barriers were put there by whoever held her prisoner."

Sherry nodded and sighed. She hadn't expected this to be easy. She could tell the child's torture had been very severe just by the girl's demeanor, but she'd hoped Cece could point her in the right direction.

"Thanks for trying."

Sherry closed the door behind Cece and turned back toward the girl who'd just come out of the room in the clothes Cece had brought.

"Ready for some breakfast?" she asked with a too-bright smile.

CHAPTER 6

*a*n hour later, eggs and sausages and bacon under their belts, the two headed into town. Sherry parked the car in front of Coffee Haven and stepped inside with the girl close behind.

"Hello," Sherry said to the barista. "We'll have two blueberry scones and a tall coffee for me and a hot chocolate as well."

"Coming right up," said Harlow. Taking two cups from behind her, she said, "Name for the second one?"

Sherry glanced at the girl with her, who refused to say anything. Turning back to the barista she said, "Just put Sherry on both of them, please."

"Sherry 1 and Sherry 2, it is," Harlow said without missing a beat. "Coffee is number 1."

"Great, thanks." Sherry started walking toward one of the small tables near the large picture window. She didn't look to see if the girl was following her but was relieved when she joined her at the table within a few seconds.

"Now, my plan for today is to get you some decent clothes and maybe see what we can get you to eat. What do you like to eat?" Sherry looked at the child with a friendly expression, which was unreciprocated.

As a matter of fact, all the girl did was shrug then turn to look out the window.

In profile, she looked even younger and thinner than Sherry had first thought.

"Sherry 1 and Sherry 2," Harlow called out.

Sherry excused herself and retrieved their drinks.

Handing the girl her hot chocolate, which was declined, Sherry set it down on the table. The scones were brought to their table a minute later, still warm and oozing blueberry goodness onto the plate.

"Sorry for the delay," Harlow apologized. "There was a rush order we had to take care of first."

The girl smiled at the barista and then returned to the blank expression when she caught Sherry looking at her. Carefully lowering her head, she took a long sniff of the scone before breaking off a piece to eat.

Sherry watched the girl's reaction to the buttery, flaky pastry. She hid a smile behind her coffee cup when the girl's eyes widened in pleasure. The minute she realized Sherry was watching her, she pushed the plate away and refused to eat any more of the pastry. The hot chocolate remained untouched as well.

Sherry frowned. Watching the girl, she was struck anew by how frail she appeared, and yet marveled that she'd managed to survive whatever had happened to her. A small part of Sherry wanted to pull the girl into an embrace and reassure her that all would be better now, but she knew instinctively that the girl would hate that.

Even though she was a witch, she was so young that Sherry wondered how she'd coped with all that had been done to her. So many questions raced through her mind, but the girl held herself so tightly wound that Sherry knew she'd have to step lightly or risk the girl retreating so far inside herself that she would never be able to heal from the trauma she'd suffered.

"Hey there, how are you two doing?"

Sherry jumped at the sound of Rusty's voice and embraced him. "We're fine. Just enjoying a scone. Coffee for me, with hot chocolate for our young friend." Sherry answered in a too happy voice that sounded fake even to her ears.

"Oh?" Rusty looked at Sherry's empty plate and then the full one by the girl. "Seems like one of you is enjoying those delicious scones, but maybe that one was meant for me?" He pretended to reach for the scone, and both Sherry and Rusty jumped when the girl snatched it before his hand could get near it. She began to eat it, looking at him with a much sweeter expression than she had given Sherry a moment earlier.

She finished the scone quickly and drained her hot chocolate without stopping for a breath.

"Guess you liked it after all," Rusty said with a soft chuckle.

The girl smiled at him like she had with Harlow before pressing past him toward the exit. She stood there, waiting for Sherry with an impatiently tapping foot.

"Well, I guess we're off," Sherry said, gathering her purse. One more quick kiss and she followed the girl out with a wave in Rusty's direction.

As they passed the window on their way to the clothes store, Sherry looked over her shoulder to see Rusty watching them with a frown that he quickly changed to a smile and a wave when he saw her looking.

When they arrived home, the girl took their purchases to her room while Sherry brought the groceries into the kitchen. Once they were put away, she knocked on the girl's door.

"Would you like a snack?"

The only answer to her question was a *click* as the girl locked the door.

Four hours later, Sherry was fixing dinner when Rusty came in looking tired and dirty from his time in the woods. Lately, he was out there practically every day and night for hours at a time and wouldn't tell Sherry why.

CHAPTER 7

$\mathcal{T}$he girl had still not said anything to anyone since her last conversation with Rusty several days ago, and Sherry feared the damage was so great the girl just couldn't talk about it.

Using all the tools she'd learned in her training as a counselor, Sherry worked to get the girl to open up. The house seemed even more silent with the girl in it when Rusty was gone than it had before her arrival.

Sherry began to notice little things about the girl that she found curious. She was tidy and very particular about where her things were kept. She never looked Sherry in the eyes, kept her head lowered and subservient, but Sherry didn't feel the girl respected her at all—it was more like she was waiting for something but only she knew what. Sherry also noted the girl reacted more positively to anyone with magic, but not even Rusty could get her to talk, although he did confess that the first night she had said a few words to him.

But he wouldn't tell her what was said between them, saying it was just a few words and nothing important.

Sherry pondered what to do next. They'd been to the music shop a few times to see if Cece could help, but the angel couldn't get past the barrier, and the girl didn't seem to care.

Not having a name for the girl really bothered Sherry so she started calling her Mary, just to have a name for her. Mary didn't seem to mind. She answered when Sherry called her that.

Sherry walked to Mary's room but hesitated when she got to the door. Without knocking, she turned back to the kitchen. Rusty had a meeting tonight with the Court, so it was just Mary and her for dinner.

Sherry pulled a bag of lettuce from the fridge along with carrots and cucumbers. "Mary," she called to the girl, "would you like to help me fix dinner?"

Silence was her only answer.

Sherry pulled a bowl from the cupboard and grabbed a knife from the drawer. She was so absorbed in cutting that she missed seeing Mary arrive. Looking up and seeing the girl surprised her, and she felt the knife slide along the side of her finger before she realized it.

Swearing in surprise, she rushed to the sink to wash out the cut. Wrapping a paper towel tightly around the wound, she hurried to the bathroom where her bandages were stored.

When she returned with a reddening bandage on the wound, she found Mary with the knife spinning in the air in front of her. Sherry gasped. Mary spun around, the knife whizzing past Sherry's ear to embed itself in the wooden post separating the kitchen from the living room, where it wiggled with the force of its momentum.

Mary didn't look sorry, and Sherry's eyes narrowed.

Was the girl startled by Sherry's entrance, or had it been an intentional attempt to harm her? Sherry dismissed that momentary question as ridiculous. With some difficulty, she pulled the knife from the wood and returned to cutting up the vegetables for the salad, using a different knife. She didn't take her eyes off Mary the rest of the night.

When Rusty returned an hour later, he looked upset, but wouldn't talk to her about it, and Sherry put thoughts of what had happened earlier aside.

Mary went to bed without being asked to that night, and Sherry settled in for a quick read before bed. Forgetting already about the wound, she was reading when she felt Rusty holding her hand.

"Hey," he said, rubbing her finger that had finally stopped bleeding. "What happened here?"

Sherry shrugged off his concern. "Nothing. Just cut myself making the salad tonight."

"Oh?" Rusty looked confused. "When did lettuce become so violent?"

Sherry laughed. Leaning forward, she kissed Rusty on the lips before leaning back and pulling him with her, book falling to the floor and sliced finger forgotten as she lost herself in his kisses.

Arms around him, she slid her hands up his shirt to feel his bare skin against her spread palms. Sighing with contentment when he kissed her neck and returned the favor of a hand up her shirt, she remembered the look on Mary's face when the knife nearly struck her, and her ardor cooled.

Feeling her change of mood, Rusty sat up, pulling her with him and asked, "What's wrong?"

"Not a thing," Sherry assured him. "The couch is just not as comfortable as our bed."

"That's true," Rusty agreed, and with a quick flip, he stood up and carried her in his arms to their bedroom where knives were the last thing on either of their minds for the next several hours.

CHAPTER 8

"*D*o you have to go out again? These patrols are becoming very worrisome to me," Sherry said, trying to pull Rusty back into bed.

He slipped on his shirt and slid on his shoes. Turning to give her a last kiss, he said, "I have to go. Nothing I can talk about but know that it is necessary."

Sherry flopped back onto her pillows, a pouty expression creasing her face. "I know. I get it, but I still miss you when you're gone."

Rusty leaned down and tweaked her nose, a smile on his face as he backed out of the room, blowing her kisses until he was out of sight.

Sherry rolled over and gripped a pillow around her middle. A sudden movement caught her eye, and she looked up to see Mary standing in her doorway. The girl was just staring at her.

"Mary?" she asked, sitting upright. "Are you okay? Do you need anything?"

The girl stared at her with a small twist of her lips, the only expression on her face as she slowly turned and walked back to her room.

Sherry shivered. Sinking back under her covers, she had a sudden urge to get up and lock the bedroom door and couldn't explain why.

"Ouch!" she said when her finger began throbbing in pain unexpectedly.

Going into the bathroom, Sherry removed the bandaging and stared at the fresh blood oozing from the wound that had looked to be healing earlier. Quickly washing the cut, she dried the area then wrapped a new bandage around it. The cut hadn't appeared deep enough to need stitches, but maybe she should go to the clinic tomorrow and have it checked out anyway.

Climbing back into bed, she turned her face to the door. She half expected to see Mary standing there again, but there was no one there.

"You have a great imagination," Sherry whispered into the darkness. "How about you save it for the next novel."

Shaking her head at the foolishness she thought her worries were, she closed her eyes and was soon asleep.

CHAPTER 9

*S*he slipped from her bed, careful not to step on any of the boards that creaked and made her way to the bedroom of the sleeping woman.

She had no magic, but she did somehow control the man who did have magic. The witch found that interesting.

She also found it interesting that her magic was returning. Being here was making things she'd thought lost return to her.

She liked this.

She didn't like the name Mary but tolerated it while she waited for the sign.

She knew there was something she was supposed to do; she just couldn't remember what it was. But being here in this town had awakened in her the desire for her magic again.

She was one of them.

She belonged here.

This woman with no magic was not one of them.

She didn't belong here.

She would have to be careful.

But she knew what she was meant to do.

She would wait for the right time.

She could feel it would be soon.

The spinning knife, its silver calling to her, singing to her.

That was the first test.

CHAPTER 10

*T*ime was flying so fast, and the summer was dwindling. Sherry didn't mind summer. She liked the way the woods smelled at this time of year—earthy and damp and cool in the mornings and warm and sun-soaked in the afternoons.

She was humming while she packed a picnic for her and Mary. They were going to go up to the woods and hike and have a lunch at her favorite place. Maybe a change of scenery would open Mary up and she would say something instead of just staring at her with that questioning expression all the time.

"Mary," she called to the girl. "Ready?"

Mary appeared in the kitchen before Sherry had even closed the lid of the picnic basket, and Sherry gasped in surprise.

Laughing nervously, she said, "I hate when you do that."

The girl didn't answer, just stared at her with those eyes that Sherry felt were reading her and finding her wanting.

"Okay, let's go."

Rusty was out in the woods today on another patrol. They might even run into him while they were up there, as she'd told him where she was taking Mary and he said he'd try to swing by.

Once they arrived at the entrance to the trail Sherry liked to walk, they took the picnic basket and blanket and entered the woods.

Sherry glanced at Mary and smiled with pleasure. The girl's face looked more animated than she'd seen her in the short time they'd been together. Here it was mid-July and they'd only had her for a few weeks, yet Sherry was finding the company of the strange girl to be a lot better in recent days than before.

The girl was still creeping about the house in her usual silent way, but she'd seemed to warm up to Sherry slightly in the last few days, which had warmed her heart. Sherry hoped this trip would be the change they needed to finally get the girl to open up.

"I love the woods, don't you?" Sherry said hoping to start a conversation.

Mary didn't respond but was looking around them with increasing interest.

"The sounds in a forest aren't like any other. There's a magic in the air here that is so serene. Almost like the trees are hugging you," Sherry continued. She knew she was babbling, but she couldn't stop herself.

They walked farther into the woods, going so deep in that the trees towering overhead created a canopy that blocked the sunshine, bringing the temperature down about ten degrees. Sherry shivered, goosebumps rising on her bare arms.

Mary walked silently beside her.

Sherry finally reached the small open area she thought would be perfect for their picnic. Ahead of them was a path that led to an old, abandoned mine, a place Sherry thought they might like to explore once they were done eating.

Spreading out the blanket, she set the picnic basket down and began pulling out the food. Mary was watching and finally reached out to help. Sherry thanked her. Handing Mary a peanut butter and jelly sandwich, she took one for herself and began to eat.

Studying the girl, she said between mouthfuls of the bread and gooey sugary sweetness of the peanut butter and jelly, "Mary, I want you to know that you can talk to me. You can tell me anything, and I won't judge you."

Mary ignored her. Slowly eating the sandwich, the girl was too curious about the area they were in to pay Sherry any attention. Pointing down the trail, she glanced over at Sherry with a questioning look.

"Oh, yes. Down that path is an old mine I thought we might explore once we're done eating."

Mary stood up, handing Sherry the sandwich, and pointed to the trail.

"You want to go now?" she asked. Standing up, she set their meal inside the picnic basket and followed the girl, who'd already left her side and was wandering out of sight.

Hurrying to catch up, Sherry was surprised to see how quickly the girl was moving. It was like she was on a mission, and for a minute, Sherry slowed her steps. Something about the way the girl was single-mindedly focused on the mine worried her, but then she dismissed it as foolishness. This was what she wanted, wasn't it? She wanted the girl to want to be there with her.

When they reached the entrance to the mine, Sherry started to give a brief history lesson on the mining industry, but Mary was inside before Sherry could get more than a sentence or two into her speech.

"Mary, wait for me, please. It's dangerous to go inside too far."

Sherry stepped inside in time to see the girl disappearing around a bend. "Mary, wait."

But the girl was gone. Sherry turned the corner as the girl rounded another one ahead and was lost to sight.

Sherry, now worried the girl might become lost, turned on the flashlight feature of her phone to guide her steps as they were in so far now, no light reached them after the first bend. *How could the girl see anything?* she wondered.

"Mary?" she said. A sudden release of dirt from overhead reminded her of how dangerous the mine was, and she felt a sudden urge to get Mary and leave.

Thoughts of cave-ins and dead miners raced through her mind, sending her feet forward quickly.

She rounded another turn to find herself in a wide area that looked to be a staging area at one time, as old mine cars were lined up against the wall and unused timbers were stacked nearby.

Mary was in the center of the room. She turned to face Sherry when she entered, her expression more animated than Sherry had seen in a while.

"Mary, you shouldn't have raced ahead like that. This mine is still dangerous."

"My name's not Mary," the girl said into the darkness, and Sherry nearly dropped her phone in shock.

Mary/not Mary was talking.

Sherry gasped. "Mary…I mean, what is your name then?"

"Accad. And I am here to…"

Sherry was now beside Mary, or Accad, and started to pull her out of the room. A sudden shift from above caused dirt and stones to rattle down, and Sherry realized the roof might be caving in. Her first instinct was to get the girl and herself out of the room.

Pulling the reluctant girl toward the entrance, Sherry said, "Accad, we have to go. Now. This mine was a bad idea. I think it's going to cave in."

Without waiting for the girl to answer her, Sherry hurried them out of the room, crashing rocks and dust flying at them as they ran toward the entrance. Sherry held her phone in one hand, the flashlight feature lighting their way as they ran around bend after bend, and she prayed they were actually heading toward the entrance and not deeper into the mine.

Accad gasped out, "You are not magic. You will steal my magic. You will make me use my magic for your own evil intentions."

Sherry stared at the girl in shock. They were running for their lives from a ton of earth that had decided that today was the day to fall in, and this child was worried about her magic?

"What makes you think I want your magic?"

"You don't have any," the girl said between gasps of air.

"I don't need magic," Sherry said. She stopped running. Gasping and coughing at the dust filled air, Sherry took the girl by the shoulders and said, "I don't want your magic. I want you to be safe. That's all I've ever wanted."

Accad stared at her with wide eyes, and feral screams came from her, great sobs shaking her body. "You all want me! You all want my magic. You can't have it!"

Sherry glanced around them, suddenly unsure which way to go. The rumbling overhead was increasing, and she knew they didn't have long before the whole mine collapsed around them.

Pulling the girl again, she headed toward the entrance, relieved when they rounded the last bend to find the light from the entrance dimming the darkness.

Suddenly a large rock tumbled free behind them, and the sound of timbers snapping had Sherry panicking. Picking up Accad, she ran toward the light, panting and concentrating on making sure her feet found solid earth as she grew closer to the daylight.

Just when she thought her chest would burst from the exertion of their flight, she sighed in relief. Just a hundred feet more. Suddenly the sound of timbers snapping was so close, she knew they were still in danger. Before she could think about it, she threw Accad through the doorway.

Timbers cracked, stones rained down, and the entrance to the mine was black with rocks and dirt.

Sherry was trapped, and just as she realized that, a large rock loosed itself from overhead and smashed her phone before bouncing and trapping her underneath it.

Blackness overtook her as she realized Accad was safe.

CHAPTER 11

*A*ccad stared at the mine entrance over her shoulder from where she'd landed when Sherry had thrown her free. Rolling over onto her back, she stared up at the blue sky in amazement.

The human had saved her.

The woman with no magic had saved her.

How had that even been possible?

Why would the woman save her?

This wasn't what she'd been told would happen.

She'd been told that people without magic would always try to steal hers. That she would need to kill them first.

Accad cried. Shocked at the wetness on her face, she touched the moisture. Bringing the salty tears to her mouth, she drank the drink of regret and cried more and more, great sobs shaking her tiny body until she feared her bones would break apart.

A sound behind her startled her, and she whirled around to find Rusty standing there, out of breath and scared. She could smell the fear and worry on him.

Accad scrambled to her feet.

Running to Rusty, she launched herself into his chest.

"She saved me. The woman with no magic saved me."

Rusty pulled the crying girl free and said, "Her name's Sherry. That woman may not have magic like you or me, but she is my everything. Where is she?"

Accad pointed to the mine entrance, blocked with rocks and dirt.

"I'm sorry. I'm sorry." Accad sobbed. "She…she threw me out of the cave, and she's still in there."

Rusty ran to the stones, frantic with worry. "Sherry! Sherry, are you in there? Answer me if you can. Please, Sherry, please be okay."

Rusty started pulling the rocks out of the way, tossing them like they weighed ounces instead of tons.

Accad touched him on the arm when he stopped his panicked attempts to clear the entrance.

"Let me help. If you keep tossing stones like that, you will just bring more of the ceiling down and maybe hurt her."

Rusty stepped back, seeing the logic of the small witch's words.

Accad closed her eyes and reached out with magic that she pulled from the earth. Rusty watched as the small girl moved rocks to the side, making sure to keep the walls upright, rebuilding broken timbers for support.

The rumbling of the cave-in receded as the stones and timber anchored the cave entrance.

Inside, Rusty raced to pull Sherry from the darkness of the mine into the sunshine.

Straining to hold the magic, Accad slowly let the stones and timber fall once more, sealing the mine's entrance so no more unsuspecting explorers would be harmed.

Sherry had a bloody gash on her head that was oozing blood.

Accad, still holding the earth's magic, put her hands on Sherry's head and healed the wound. With a green fire leaking from her fingers, she ran her hands over Sherry's body, healing broken bones and blood vessels as she went.

Rusty let her do it, aware that Accad was not only healing Sherry, but herself as well.

The girl oozed magic, and Rusty knew the Court would need to know this as soon as possible, but Sherry was his priority at the moment.

When Accad finished, leaning exhaustedly against Rusty, she whispered, "I've done all I can do with my magic. Now it is up to Sherry's magic to do the rest."

Rusty pulled the small girl into a quick embrace before releasing her with his thanks.

Sitting next to Sherry, he gently put her head in his lap while he waited for the love of his life to awaken like Sleeping Beauty or one of those fantasy heroines she so loved to write about.

Rusty couldn't believe what had just happened. The details were uncannily similar to what the new oracle had predicted a few nights ago. The Court hadn't been sure Holly Westbrook had the powers her new family claimed she had, but now there was no doubt. He just didn't want to think about what else Holly had said about this moment, what would come after these events. He couldn't worry about that now. Sherry's well-being consumed his focus. He caressed her forehead, willing her to waken.

Sherry opened her eyes a few minutes later to find both Accad and Rusty staring at her with worried expressions that quickly changed to excited smiles and hugs.

"Hey, you two," she said with a smile as she sat up and leaned against Rusty, his strong heartbeat a match to her own. "What's with all the worried expressions?"

Accad smiled tiredly. Yawning, she said, "Can we go home now?"

Rusty and Sherry exchanged a glance then smiled at the small girl.

"Absolutely!" they both said at once as all three stood, walking down the path toward home.

EPILOGUE

*S*itting on the porch, the three watched the sun setting through the leaves of the trees, sunlight bright then dulling as it slipped into night.

"Not too dramatic," Rusty said, holding Sherry's hand. His face was turned away, but she noted the way his jaw clenched.

She squeezed his hand then took Accad's hand into her other and laced her fingers with the young witch's. Accad smiled and raised her glass of grape juice against Sherry's wine glass.

"We are done with dramatic. Life will be so much better now. I am so happy to spend it with the two people in this world I love the most." Sherry tried and failed to keep the tears from welling in her eyes.

Rusty reached out and tenderly wiped away a tear.

"No regrets?" he asked. He held her hand to his lips.

"None at all," Sherry said holding his gaze for a moment longer than necessary to reassure him of her decision.

Accad leaned against Sherry's shoulder as the night descended on them, a family in more ways than one, their love a beacon to the future.

MAGIC, MISCHIEF & MAYHEM

KRISTIE COOK

CHAPTER 1

*C*atching myself before I face-planted, I reached for the nearest arm to regain my balance. Quin's hand grabbed mine, steadying me with a rock-solid strength that was one benefit to her recently acquired vampirism. I knew she was on my right, and her sister, Liv, walked on my left, her hand grasping my other one as they guided me down the sidewalk toward their surprise for me. With a blindfold across my eyes that they insisted on, we were literally the blind leading the blind. Only, the newcomer witches had adjusted extraordinarily well with their loss of sight. Me, not so much. At least mine was temporary.

"Okay, Addie," Quin said as we stopped and they turned me. I had a pretty good idea of where we were. My other senses might not have been quite as developed as theirs since I hadn't lost one of them, but I was a witch hybrid, too—and I'd lived in this town all my life. Besides, the delicious scents of fresh-brewed coffee mingling with garlic bread gave everything away: We were standing in front of the once vacant storefront between Broastful Brew and Napoli's on Stuart Street, across from the fire station.

"The blindfold wasn't necessary, you know," I told them. "You can't open a new business in Havenwood Falls without me knowing about it."

"No shit," Liv, witch-turned-bear-shifter, said. "The shop isn't the surprise."

Quin stepped behind me and untied the blindfold. "You can open your eyes."

The bright, late July sun truly blinded me for a moment, and I blinked against the sudden light. And then I burst into laughter. The girls giggled with me.

"Oh, my goddess. I love it!" The front was fabulous, with an image of Ganesha, the elephant-headed Hindu god of luck and fortune, painted on the window. I'd known about their business, but not the name. They must have made a last-minute change, and that's what had me laughing.

The shop's door opened, and Arya stepped out, her blonde locks catching the morning sun. "Addie Beaumont, you wanna Get Stoned?"

"Absolutely!" I was so incredibly happy for the three witches, who had been through so much hell. Ripped from their homes, used and abused in a magic-trafficking ring, turned into vampires, a wolf shifter, and a bear shifter against their will, and their sight violently taken from each of them, it was a wonder they functioned at all. Not that they didn't have severe emotional trauma still to work through, but coming here to Havenwood Falls and then to be reunited with each other, their brother Rune, and their oracle, Holly Westbrook, had done wonders.

Arya stepped aside so I could enter the shop, the sisters following me in. Holly stood by the cash register at the back, a huge smile on her face as she bounced on the balls of her feet.

"Isn't it perfect?" she squealed as I took it all in. "So many beautiful crystals!"

And there really were. Glass shelves lined the walls and more stood in the center of the room, almost all of them displaying rocks in all shapes and colors. Some in their rough, raw forms. Others tumbled and polished. There were spheres of various sizes, carved flames, pillars, generators, wands, palm stones, carved skulls, and other figurines. From amethyst to zoisite and seemingly everything between. The few shelves that didn't show off crystals and gemstones in all their glory displayed crystal singing bowls and jewelry.

On the walls were beautiful paintings of goddesses and nature, as well as posters about crystal magic, chakras, and sound healing.

"The energy in here is insane," Holly added.

"It really is," I agreed. It didn't surprise me.

The shop had been Quin's idea before she'd ever known about her sisters and their purpose, sprouted from an off-handed comment I'd made about her abilities. She was an earth elemental witch, deeply connected with nature and all that came out of the earth, including crystals and minerals. She was also more attuned to energetic bodies than anyone I'd ever met, including other witches and psychics in town. It was so strong, she could easily move around as though she had perfect eyesight, able to innately sense everything in her surroundings, including people's energy bodies. So I'd said one evening as we sat in my living room, when she still lived with me, that she'd be an amazing energy healer.

We'd discussed whether her gift was heightened by the loss of sight or by the vampirism, which would normally rob a witch of all her magic, but not in this case. Then we found out she was a singer for the oracle, which made her a seer in a different way. Her sisters had that same remarkable energy-sensing ability, and they loved the idea of joining in on the shop.

"Our official grand opening is tomorrow," Quin said, beaming, her dark tan skin glowing, whether from the sun filtering through the front window or the energy of the crystals or excitement, I didn't know.

"We figured tomorrow's new moon energy would be the perfect time," Liv added, twirling a lock of dark auburn hair around her finger. Like Arya, she'd already put some meat back on her bones since their rescues last month.

"Because new moons are for setting intentions, new beginnings, and starting a new cycle," Holly recited, always eager to share the knowledge and wisdom she'd gained.

I browsed the store, inspecting the shelves more carefully. "Your collection is incredible."

"It's all because of Marcus," Quin said. "He's been wonderful, so supportive of everything we wanted to do."

"That still blows my mind," I admitted, inspecting a carnelian sphere.

"He's really an awesome guy when you get past his curmudgeon self," Holly said, and I could hear her love for him—as well as that bit of pride in her voice as she rattled off another new word she'd learned. I glanced over at her to see her lips curving in a faint smile.

To be honest, I would have never guessed this about Marcus St. James. Although he'd lived here since almost the beginning of Havenwood Falls, I didn't know the vampire well. At least, not until he started taking an interest in Quin and her sisters once Holly told him about them. Who knew the recluse had such a soft spot? Once Quin told me his full story, my heart had stuttered, and I understood what drew him to her and her sisters.

I had just reached for a big chunk of black tourmaline when a loud pop came from outside, followed by the sound of glass shattering against the pavement. Holly and I froze. The sisters dropped to their knees, each with an arm over their head as they reached for each other. We were all on edge these days, especially after part of Holly's first prediction had come true a couple of days ago with Sherry Higgins, Rusty's wife. We'd been waiting for the other shoe to drop. Was this it?

Another pop and shattering glass sounded, now from farther down the street. I ran out of the store and turned to the left just as it happened a third time. A male runner jogged down the street in a smooth pace, and after several more steps, a bolt of lightning shot out of his body and shattered a streetlamp. I immediately recognized the culprit—Dingane, one of the SMA students who stuck around over summer break, who was also an Impundulu lightning bird.

"What the hell," I muttered as I took off in a sprint down Stuart Street, away from town square and into the residential area. "Dingane!" I shouted. "Stop!"

He kept going, ignoring me. Fortunately, he was only jogging, and using a touch of hellhound speed, I quickly caught up to him, tackling him to the ground—and hoping I didn't get electrocuted.

"What the f—" he shouted, rolling over to face me. Reddish lightning sparked across his eyes for a brief moment before he recognized me, cutting off the expletive. He jerked the ear buds out of his ears. "Addie? Er, I mean, Professor Beaumont? Why...what...?" He seemed at a loss for words.

Realizing we were sprawled out on Biddie Half-Moon's lawn, I jumped to my feet and gestured down the street. "Did you not even realize what you did? Dude! You're lucky it was me who saw you and not a cranky Court member."

He stood and looked back at the mess of glass on the streets. "I don't understand."

"You were shooting lightning bolts out of your ass as you ran, D!" I ground out between clenched teeth, trying not to shout so any nearby humans wouldn't overhear. I couldn't believe nobody had seen him. Thank the goddess for small favors.

He laughed. "You're joking, right?"

"Right. I felt like tackling you for the hell of it."

His expression sobered, and his hand went to his ass, his eyes widening when he felt the telling hole singed in his shorts. "Oh, shit. Sorry, teach. That's, uh—" he looked around, a bit dazed "—that's honestly never happened before."

"Are you okay?" I demanded.

He took a moment to self-assess and shrugged. "Body—yes. Pride—no."

I gave him a quick once-over. I didn't see any injuries or sense any kind of magic on him, such as a spell, perhaps casted as a joke. Frowning, I ordered him to run a few paces. No more lightning shot out of him as he did.

"You're sure nothing's wrong?" I persisted.

"Nothing. I feel fine."

Shoving a hand into my hair, I blew out a sigh, not knowing what to do. He'd be in big trouble with the Court if I took him in, and it appeared as though it had been some kind of fluke. Or the spell had worn off. Either way, he wasn't a bad kid, even with all of his history that would have sent others down a road ending at the state prison. Instead, he'd ended up at SMA and had a promising future. Sensing his honesty regarding his innocence, I glanced down the street once more, just to be sure nobody else had witnessed anything.

Dropping my hands to my hips, I gave him my best stern professor look. "Walk home. Stay off the energy drinks. And you call me A.S.A.P. if it happens again."

He nodded vehemently. "Yes, ma'am. Thank you, ma'am."

I narrowed my eyes and pointed a finger at his chest. "Don't call me ma'am. I'm not old."

D pursed his lips. "Uh, sorry, ma—er, Professor Beaumont."

Rolling my eyes, I dismissed him with a wave, and when he turned around, I whispered a quick spell to fix the hole in his shorts, before turning to head back to the shop. I still couldn't believe nobody had seen him or even seemed to have heard what had sounded like gunshots or fireworks when the 4th of July had come and gone a few weeks ago. I couldn't remember off the top of my head which SMA witches had stuck around town besides our own residents, who certainly knew better than to try this. I'd have to check my list when I got home because this kind of prank was so not cool, and the guilty parties needed reprimanding.

Damn. When did I become such a curmudgeon? Maybe I *was* getting old. Soon I'd be yelling at them to get off my lawn.

My phone rang as I walked back toward Get Stoned, and I pulled it out of my back pocket. Grandmother Saundra's name flashed on the screen. *Shit.* Maybe Dingane wasn't going to get off so easily.

"Good morning, Grandmother," I answered with false cheerfulness.

"Adelaide," she said, her voice tight. Yep. Poor D was in trouble.

"I took care of everything," I said before she got too riled up.

"And what good explanation does your new dragon-shifter friend have for breaking the rules?"

My brows pinched together, my eyes squinting. "Wait—what? Do you mean Rune?"

"Yes, Rune. I thought you said you took care of everything."

"Um…what does Rune have to do with it?"

"Melissa Lewis just called the sheriff's office, reporting that she saw a dragon flying over Miles Mountain."

CHAPTER 2

en minutes later, after a quick stop at Get Stoned to let the girls know I'd been called away on Court business, avoiding the full truth so they wouldn't worry about their brother, I hopped the fence of my backyard and stomped into the forest beyond. If Rune had been flying, which he often did as reconnaissance to ensure his sisters were safe, he'd come this way to return to the home they now shared two doors down from mine. I fumed as I waited.

The real Rune was not quite as arrogant as the personas Rhian had given him when she'd brought him from the Viking era and into our timeline. Because we kept sending him away as a potential threat to our town, she'd had to drop him in a couple of times before she herself could arrive to explain. Regardless of the aliases she'd given him, he'd been Dimples McCocky Pants to me. But Rune…Rune was cocky, yes, but not in the way that was only based on sexual attractiveness.

Yes, he was still sexy af, even more in his true form, but he was cocky in the way that a dragon-shifting, Viking warrior, Asgardian protector of the seeress and her singers had every right to be. He was strong. He was powerful. We hadn't seen him fight yet, but he bested our locals in all the sparring matches he did for training. And did I mention he was hot as fuck?

So his cockiness was well deserved and didn't annoy me as much as it had before. However, he was a true Viking with a total disregard for the rules. Always questioning and testing and basically doing whatever the hell he wanted. I didn't exactly mind that either—after all, I'd been engaged to Tase Roca, oldest sibling of the most rebellious family in town. I apparently had a thing for the bad boys. I did draw the line, though, at breaking this very basic, number one rule (after no harming the humans): keep the secret.

"Where the hell are you?" I muttered, tapping my fingers on my hip bone while carving a groove into the forest floor with my pacing. It'd been at least thirty minutes since the report to the sheriff's office. Rune didn't usually take this long to make his rounds in the sky.

As I turned, I noticed movement through the trees, in my own backyard. A moment later came a knocking sound, followed by Skywalker's caws, my raven familiar serving the role as doorbell. With a sigh, I tromped back through the forest to see who'd come to visit via my backyard. To my shock, Rune stood on the steps, and my mouth went dry. He wore only leather pants and boots, no shirt, his ponytail of thick, sandy brown hair and braids hanging past his muscular shoulders, pointing down to the perfect curve of his godlike ass. His biceps bunched as he lifted his fist again to bang on my door.

"Avoiding me much?" I asked once I reached the fence.

He spun, and if my mouth had been dry before, now it was the Sahara Desert. Viking-esque tattoos spanned over his broad, well-defined chest and down the washboard abs. He wore a simple black leather necklace with a pendant of Thor's hammer. When he'd first arrived, his beard had been cut close along the jawline but hung long from the chin, pulled into a chintail—what I had dubbed it—but that stood out a bit too much for the locals. It had taken some persuasion, but he'd finally given in to trimming it to match the length of the rest of the facial hair. The sides of his head were still shaved, because, damn, it was sexy as hell. More than once I'd been tempted to run my hands over the stubble to know what it felt like. The scars scattered over his body, even the one that slashed across his forehead and curved around his right eye, were not imperfections but added to the sexy warrior visage.

When my gaze drifted down to the V that disappeared under his waistband, my dry mouth was suddenly flooded. My tongue slipped out to wet my lips as I forced my eyes upward to meet his. The dark, midnight blues sparked as one side of his mouth turned up, popping the dimple just above the beard.

"I'm standing at your door," he pointed out, even his voice full of the promise of sex.

Hopping the fence, I strode across the yard. "I see that."

"So I believe that's a sign that I'm not avoiding you."

"And how did you get here?"

He glanced to his left, toward his own backyard. "I walked." He pointed to his boots. "You move one foot in front of the other until you get to where you're going." Now he gestured at me. "Like you're doing now."

I stopped in my tracks and folded my arms over my chest, trying to ignore my body's response to the smirk on his face. "I mean, you didn't take your usual route home. As though you're avoiding me."

His brows pinched together, and he rubbed at his beard. "Did I go somewhere?"

Now it was my turn to be confused. My head tilted to the side. "Were you not flying just a bit ago?"

"Not since dawn."

"Oh." I frowned. If Melissa Lewis hadn't seen Rune flying over Miles Mountain, who *had* she seen? All dragons, as far as we knew, had cloaking magic. All of our local dragons certainly did, and they knew the consequences of not using it. In fact, even if it hadn't been a rule, they didn't *like* to be seen. They didn't like to be gawked at, as humans would do, the infatuation with the myths and magic of dragons never ending since the medieval ages.

I needed to call Grandmother.

"When I was out, though," Rune continued, "I saw something you should know about. Maybe take it to your lords."

"Court," I immediately corrected, having grown used to his choice of words. Goddess help us if Roman Bishop ever heard himself referred to as lord or earl—we'd never hear the end of it. Then Rune's tone registered in my brain, and worry shot through my gut. "What?"

"The trees in one part of the forest appear to be dying. I believe it is a sign."

"A sign of what?"

He shrugged. "I do not know. Maybe the oracle can tell us tomorrow."

"What do you mean dying?"

"The tops are brown. I do not believe that is normal for this climate at this time of year?"

I turned to survey the forest behind my house. The trees looked normal to me. "Where?"

Rune's voice came low from behind me. "A perfect circle around the mine where that woman had been buried."

Shit. He meant Sherry. The subject of Holly's first vision. The vision that had concluded with the promise that everything would change when she was rescued.

I thought I heard a thud of the other shoe dropping.

"I need to see it for myself," I said, but at that moment, another thud sounded to my right, and it wasn't a shoe. When I looked over, my heart stopped for a second as I stared in horror. "*Skywalker?*"

I ran for the dead black bird, but as I came closer, I realized it was a crow, not a raven. A third thump was followed by a fourth and then a fifth. I looked up to see dozens, if not hundreds, of crows falling from the sky, already dead before they hit the earth.

Ducking my head, I ran for the house with Rune on my heels, slamming the screen door behind us. We both spun to look out as lifeless crows continued to rain down.

"What the *fuck* is going on?" I shouted.

CHAPTER 3

𝒶n emergency Court meeting was called that evening for obvious reasons, but when Rune and I turned the corner to the back of City Hall, my steps faltered.

"What's everyone doing out here?" I wondered aloud, though my companion would have no idea, considering he'd only been in town for about a month. On the other hand, this was his third or fourth Court meeting already; probably eighty percent of the supes who'd lived here their entire lives had never been to even one.

Elsmed, Teeny Weeny McFeeney Wu, Mayor Barbie, and my grandmother had arrived for the meeting and stood outside the metal door that led to the basement stairs and the Court's meeting room. The fact that they hadn't gone inside yet was bizarre, but even weirder was that as we approached, their voices drifted over to us, discussing a topic they would have disciplined others for even mentioning in public. Why didn't they at least have a muffling spell in place?

"We have to get on top of this," Elmsed was grumbling. "Too many of the supernatural population are exposing themselves in public. I don't know if this is one of those dumb human social media challenges or what, but we must put a stop to it! Every single one of them should spend time in jail!"

"Um, Elsmed," Mayor Barbie cut in, patting a hand over her pink cotton-candy hair, her voice a near whisper, "your glamour is slipping."

I strode up just in time to see the old fae's chin elongate to reach his chest and the points of his ears extend from the cover of his hair. His icy blue eyes widened at the same time the rest of his face seemed to age backward by half a century. He clapped his hands over his face, his fingers dancing over his features as if to ensure this was really happening.

"I don't think it's a social media challenge," I muttered as I pushed through them and opened the door. They all looked down at the handle and up at me, frowning. "What?"

"We couldn't open it two minutes ago," Teeny Weeny said as she walked through.

"Not even you, Grandmother?" I asked Saundra.

She passed me and replied over her shoulder, "Not even me."

That was worrisome. If our Court members and not even one of the High Priestesses of the Luna Coven couldn't pass through the wards around the Court room, we had serious issues.

But why could I?

The rest of the Court joined us, making their way to their seats on the dais.

"Any idea what's going on?" Michaela whispered, pausing by my side before going to her own seat.

"Only that something's happening with the wards," I replied under my breath. I hadn't been able to figure out anything more than that in the last few hours since the crows fell from the heavens.

The meeting was heated, started by Sheriff Ric Kasun storming in, smoke practically pouring from his ears.

"Do you know what kinds of calls we've been getting all day?" he demanded as he stood at the front of the audience section of the Court room, although the seats were empty aside from Rune. Until we figured things out, this remained a confidential matter. "Streetlights shot out by hooligans, as the neighbors seem to think but my guess is something else. Amanda George thought her neighbors had a meth lab after an explosion, only it was Patty Parker who had blown up her kitchen with a spell that she does every week with no problems. Not to mention the dead birds."

"Or the shifters," Elsmed said, eyeing Lawrence Mills at his side, then the sheriff.

"Tristan had no idea," Old Man Mills growled. *Huh.* So his son, Jetta's brother, had been the dragon that was seen over Miles Mountain. That was unexpected. Not like Tristan at all.

"Or the fae," Mayor Barbie added, giving Elsmed a pointed look.

"Tell me you have an explanation!" the sheriff cut in, nearly yelling. "Deputy Conall—my own *son*—grew a snout and claws while trying to write a speeding ticket—to humans!"

Michaela's eyes met mine, and we both sucked in our lips, trying to stifle inappropriate laughter. My body began to shake, and I had to look away from her before I burst. This was definitely not the time or the place, but the vision of Mr. Stick-Up-His-Ass Conall with a wolf's snout—

"Adelaide," my grandmother snapped, her tone sounding like it wasn't the first time she'd said my name. "Tell us what Rune found and what you discovered with the wards."

Composing myself, I stood but gestured at Rune to speak first. He told them about the trees, then I took my turn.

"Before the meeting, I was able to check on the wards," I started.

"Oh, good," Mathilde Augustine said. "I was experiencing troubles with my own magic and unable to connect with the wards myself."

"Me, as well," Saundra said. "I couldn't even open the door upstairs to enter tonight. So what did you find, Adelaide?"

My muscles tightened, though I tried not to show my apprehension on the outside. I hated having to say this, but with a quiet exhale, I blurted it out. "Our wards have been weakened."

"What!" Lawrence Mills banged his fist on the table. "How could this happen? Who's not doing their job?"

I suppressed a growl at the accusation. "It's not a matter of someone not doing their job. The wards were fine, until…well, it seems until the child witch used her magic to save Sherry Higgins the other day."

"So the child caused this?" Elsmed demanded. "Where's Rusty? We need to bring that girl in immediately!"

"Rusty's doing his job," Kasun said. "Making sure nothing else goes wrong out there."

"The girl didn't do anything wrong," I said. "Not intentionally anyway. We've learned that she channels energy from the earth and feeds the magic to others, to boost theirs. It's probably why they'd trafficked her. Unfortunately, when she did it here, she also channeled from our wards, which draw energy from the earth. And as we all know, magic affects individuals differently, which is why some have been affected by this but not most. And in strange and unexpected ways."

"It certainly sounds like the child did something wrong to me," Old Man Mills said. "We can't have someone with this power just running around, especially a kid with no self-control!"

I shook my head. "Actually, it says more about our wards. They've served us well thus far, but if a child can unknowingly do this, then what can an attacker intent on destroying us do?"

"An attacker like Hermod," Rhian's voice came from behind me. I hadn't known she'd been invited to the meeting. Or perhaps she hadn't. The goddess had a way of just showing up to things. She strode up the aisle until she stood next to me in front of the dais. She glanced around me to Rune on my other side before looking at the Court again. "This is why we need the singers and the oracle. I still believe they have the answers we seek to stave off Hermod."

"The new oracle?" Lawrence asked with doubt in his voice. "How do we even know she's real?"

Rune tensed for a moment next to me, but Saundra spoke up before he could.

"She was spot on with her first prediction," she pointed out, and Rune relaxed. "All the way down to the rescue of Sherry igniting a new type of problem—this problem with the wards. If you could sense magic like the witches can, you would know she's the real thing."

"When will they sing again?" Elsmed asked, those icy eyes piercing into Rune.

The Viking remained non-plussed, standing at his full, enormous height but still relaxed, in that cocky demeanor he had. "They sing under the new and the full moons. So tomorrow night. There is no guarantee they will deliver your answers, though. They see what they see, not what anyone else demands."

"What about our other seers?" Teeny Weeny asked. "I can look in my Tell-All Ball, but it also tells me what it wants me to know, not the other way around."

"The Oracle of Delphi might be able to help," I said, "but Lana has a century-long list of petitioners."

"Weren't we given a permanent place on that list when we need it?" Mathilde asked. "I believe that was our agreement."

Saundra nodded. "It was. Sheriff, please check with Ms. Velis about getting us in." After he nodded, she continued, "Hopefully tomorrow night our newest oracle, Ms. Westbrook, can provide answers as well. In the meantime, we apparently need to fortify our wards. I will call a Luna Coven meeting straight away."

Straight away meant that night, so after the Court made more plans then adjourned, the Luna Coven gathered on the grounds of Falls Campus, the lower school of the Sun and Moon Academy, on the edge of town. We met in the high school's library, each of us ordered to research a different aspect of warding until we found the right combination that would strengthen our already heavy-duty wards. Heavy-duty until now, anyway.

It was nearly dawn by the time we came up with a new option. We'd cast the spell at midnight, under the new moon, right after Holly's ceremony.

CHAPTER 4

*T*he following night, members of the Court, Rhian, Rune, and I, and Micah and Sedona, Holly's parents for all intents and purposes, gathered in a clearing of the forest near the falls. With no light from the moon, we'd strung faerie lights between trees, casting a soft glow on the scene. In the middle was the same set-up as before, a teepee-like tent made of white gossamer that fluttered in the slight breeze. The tent was only a visual marker to separate the singers and oracle from the audience because we could see them perfectly and it provided no protection. The singers sat cross-legged on cushions with frame drums in their hands, and Holly sat in their center.

As it did last time, their song started out slow, a luscious, mesmerizing melody as they beat a steady rhythm. I could feel the energies settling around them and the entire space as they sank into a world only the four of them could see. My own body relaxed, my tense muscles softening as I began to slip into a meditative state.

I snapped myself out of it. This was for them. My job right now was to stay aware and ready to act if anything went wrong.

Feeling his gaze on me, I looked sideways and up to Rune next to me. His full lips curved into that sexy smirk, his midnight-blue eyes full of knowing. He'd told me once how easy it was for observers to fall into the singers' spell and end up missing crucial details about what the oracle saw—details that cost lives. Before I fell under *his* spell, I turned my attention back to the ritual.

Holly's eyes rolled back and became opaque, and the song's pace suddenly quickened, the singers' voices growing louder and sharper. The drumbeat hastened, sounding like footsteps running through the forest. Although their words flowed in a language known only to them, the notes were full of urgency and anguish. A swirl of tense energy built around them, strong enough to stir the air...to lift their hair and whip at their gowns and the gossamer fabric of the tent around them.

Her eyes still glowing and white, Holly rose to her feet...and higher...lifting off the ground until she hovered a foot or so in the air. Her arms rose out to her sides. Her face twisted into an expression of fear, her mouth yawning wide open as she let out a piercing, pain-filled wail.

Micah lurched forward, but Rune grabbed him in a stronghold and held him back.

"She's not in real pain," Rune reminded her guardian.

"Her heart is," Micah growled, twisting his body to break free. As built as the dragon shifter Viking warrior was, I was surprised Rune could contain the angel. Micah was holding back.

"I would never let anything harm her," Rune swore. "But you'll do them harm if you interrupt. They must finish."

At that moment, Holly and her singers all let out a guttural scream, the kind that seemed to be ripped from the darkest depths of their inner beings. Then they all collapsed to the ground, falling silent.

Everyone remained perfectly still, not a muscle twitch or even a blink of an eye as we all watched the pile of young women. When they didn't move, Micah broke from Rune's hold and rushed toward Holly. She lifted her head, blinking as her eyes returned to normal, although she seemed to not see at first. At least, not see her immediate surroundings.

"Micah!" she sobbed, reaching her arms out, searching for him. "Oh, god, Micah!"

"I'm here. I'm here." He dropped to his knees between Arya and Liv and swallowed Holly in his arms. "It's okay. I'm here."

"You...you were dead," she cried, and even from here I could see her trembling in his arms. "And Sedona...everyone. The whole town..."

He rocked her back and forth, soothing a hand down her back. "No. I'm okay. We're all okay right now."

Shaking her head, she inhaled a stuttering breath. "But we won't be."

The Court members began closing in on her, but Rune was suddenly between them and his sisters. "Not. Yet."

Lawrence Mills jabbed a finger at the Viking. "If there's a threat to our town—"

"She will tell you," Rune cut in, his eyes challenging the old man to fuck around and find out. Although Lawrence was old, he was still a supe, a dragon. But Rune was even older—and his superior. "Give her the time she needs to return to the present."

"How much time?" Saundra asked. "Do we need to reconvene tomorrow? The coven is meeting soon to fortify the wards—"

"No!" Holly shouted, and we all turned back to her. She stood on wobbly legs, her sisters and Micah surrounding her. She leaned into Micah's support but shushed him when he started to tell her this could wait. "It *can't* wait. What you're doing with the wards—it will be the end of Havenwood Falls." Her breath hitched. "Of the world."

"How?" Elsmed demanded.

"The magic will be too strong. It will be like a spotlight illuminating our world as one full of magic…and also like a…" She paused, searching for the right words. "Like a lighthouse for Hermod, a big, bright signal that we're here. He'll turn his attention our way and destroy…*everything*. I…I saw it all." She blinked rapidly but couldn't hold back the tears. Rivers flowed down her cheeks. "It was…*horrible*."

"It's okay, Holly," Micah soothed. "It won't happen now. We'll be okay, thanks to you."

She shook her head, pushing off of him and finding her strength again. "I don't know if we will be. We have to do more. If we do nothing…we also die."

"What does that mean, girl?" Lawrence growled.

"Exactly as she said," Elsmed murmured, his face pale, his normally ice-blue eyes wide and glassed over, as though what he'd read in her mind would haunt him until the end of his days.

Rhian slipped between Lawrence and Elsmed. "Holly, did you see what we can do? Did you see how we can protect Havenwood Falls and this world from Hermod?"

Holly swallowed then nodded at Rhian. "I did. There is a way." Her gaze swept over the Court members and then for some reason landed on me. "We have to make our town go dark. Make it disappear completely. As in, gone from the world."

CHAPTER 5

*L*eaning my elbows on my thighs, I rubbed circles into my temples and massaged my gritty eyeballs while the Court continued their discussion at the front of the room. They'd been at it for nearly thirty-six hours, since Holly's big revelation two nights ago. Each of us had left and returned at different times to try to get some rest, but it was damn hard to sleep knowing what we did.

At first, they'd brought Holly and the singers to the Court room to give a more detailed accounting of what she'd seen. She'd been so shaken up, though, Micah had swept her in his arms and carried her out of the room to take her home, ignoring the Court's protests and leaving Elsmed to fill in the gaps from what he'd seen in the young girl's mind: the threat of Hermod that had been hanging over our heads for years becoming very real. Very deadly. In fact, downright apocalyptic.

Entire cities destroyed. Fires blazing across the lands. Earthquakes splitting nations in half, and tsunamis flooding more. Billions dead from Hermod's pummeling. He didn't discriminate between the magical and the mundane—he wanted to destroy our world.

Of course, we'd held off on fortifying the wards, which put us at risk already, and the Court members had discussed that for most of the first night. But according to Holly, explained more by Elsmed, it was already too late. We had to do more to protect Havenwood Falls and this world from Hermod. She'd seen the solution: to remove Havenwood Falls' existence from this world.

To hide.

I hated the idea. But I also hated the idea that our town could be putting the entire world at risk. I wasn't the only one torn. The discussion had become heated at times as we debated how, exactly, to make Havenwood Falls—our fucking *home*—disappear.

"We could say there's a gas leak or a sink hole or even create some kind of disaster and force everyone to move away," Michaela had suggested, her voice thick and heavy. Being her best friend since we were five years old, I knew not one ounce of her being liked that idea.

"Would there be enough scattering of the magic for that to even work?" Lilith Blackstone asked. "I know my family would stick together, and Macy's engaged to an Augustine. We're all linked too closely to truly go our separate ways."

"Sacrifices will have to be made, no matter what we do," Elsmed replied, and there had been grumbling that escalated for a while into a debate of what anyone would be willing to sacrifice.

"Can the wards be fortified enough to completely hide us?" Mayor Barbie had asked, turning the conversation's focus back on solutions sometime early yesterday morning. "Similar to what protects the college?"

"SMA's protection partly comes from the mountain it's hidden under," Saundra said.

"But also by Zandra's goddess magic," I reminded her. "If we had strong enough magic, like hers and Rhian's—"

"That takes us back to the initial problem," Roman interrupted, still somehow sounding like he was bored out of his mind. "That much power only serves as a beacon to Hermod. Personally, I say we take our chances. I believe we can defeat him. We have that weapon Zandra gave us when she attacked our town last time, that the Guardians put together."

"But at what cost?" Odette Alverson countered. The siren rarely attended meetings, but as soon as she'd been notified of what was going on, she'd come straight here.

"The weapon was used in the scenario Ms. Westbrook saw," Elsmed said quietly. "It appeared it would destroy Hermod...but took our town and much of the world with him. That would be the cost."

As more discussion and debate ensued, I watched something pass between Mathilde and Saundra, an unspoken exchange. Mathilde glanced at Roman, who was arguing with Michaela, then back at Saundra, lifting her brows. Something flickered in my grandmother's eyes, and rubbing her chin, she nodded slowly.

Standing, she raised her voice over everyone's and declared, "We seal ourselves, the entire town, into a pocket realm."

Everyone fell silent.

"Just like we did with the Hungarian Hunters," Saundra had continued, referring to a band of supernatural hunters that had attacked the people of our box canyon twice, in 1849, before they'd arrived in Colorado, and again in 1876. She'd been one of the survivors. Her parents had not.

"You want to entrap us in a dagger?" Old Man Mills asked in disbelief, referring to the Blue Dragon Dagger that had been used as the portal for the Hungarian Hunters.

"It doesn't have to be a dagger," Mathilde murmured, and everyone's tired minds became sidetracked on what kind of object our town should be hidden away within.

"Hold on," Michaela said, slapping her hand on the table to silence everyone. "Are we seriously considering this? How would it even work?"

Being one of the members who had cast the spell on the Hungarian Hunters, Roman replied, "We would be sealing the town away in its own realm, hidden from this world, and, if we're lucky, from Hermod."

Saundra, who had helped with the spell on the hunters in 1876, continued with the explanation. "We could use our current wards to set the boundaries—everything within would become part of this secret realm. Life in Havenwood Falls could continue much as it does now, but with no coming and going. Nobody could leave town to venture out into the rest of the world, like we do now. Nobody can come in, either. No more visitors. No more people needing a safe haven like ours finding their way here. We would be on complete and thorough lockdown."

"So no tourists," Michaela said.

Grandmother pursed her lips and nodded. Dropping her gaze to the table, Michaela frowned. Her family's very livelihood—Whisper Falls Inn—relied on tourists. As did many businesses and the families they supported.

Sacrifices, Elsmed had said. How great would they be?

The discussion carried on. More solutions were proposed, discussed, and hotly debated. But they kept coming back to the idea of the pocket realm. At some point, Mathilde, Grandmother, and a couple of others broke away for their appointment with the Oracle of Delphi.

"Lana Velis not only corroborated everything Holly saw, but she's already packing up to leave town," Mathilde had announced when they returned earlier this evening, or last night, I supposed it was.

"She's running away?" Lawrence scoffed.

Saundra gave him a pointed look. "She confirmed that a pocket realm is the best solution for the town and the rest of the world, and the Oracle of Delphi can't very well meet with her petitioners if she's locked away in another realm, can she?"

"We have yet to make a decision, though," Mayor Barbie said.

"She's already seen it happen," Elsmed replied.

Not everyone was ready to accept that fact. Me included.

I'd thought about my family and loved ones...my friends...my community. My town. A town I would do *anything* for to protect it and the people who called it home.

I'd thought about Michaela's family and Whisper Falls Inn, then all the other families that relied on tourists to make a living. What would they do if there were no newcomers? How would they survive?

I'd thought about all of our locals who had family spread around the globe. The McCabes. The Alversons, since Serena had left town so long ago, her sisters coming and going once they graduated high school. The Bishops, including my good friend Callie and her bestie, Graysin and then Everett, who we would never see again. Gabriel Doyle's wife Alina and her family. Hunter James's wife Izzie's siblings. Circe Alexander who was now part of the Luna Coven but the coven she'd been raised by, her family, lived in Arizona. The Rocas... My breath had hitched at that one. What would these families do if cut off from their loved ones?

I'd thought about the students of SMA, too, how our inaugural class was supposed to graduate next May. What would we do with the college? Would we force the students to be cut off from their families? The whole point of the school was to train an army to protect supernaturals around the world. How could they do that if they were locked away in another realm? But there was no way SMA could remain out of the pocket realm. Could it? And would that be good? There was a lot of damn magic under that mountain. What if something happened that exposed it to Hermod, attracting him to this world after all? The sacrifices the town would be making would be for naught.

I'd thought about all of the supernaturals who had found refuge in our town over the years. So many young people who'd been new to their abilities or struggling to control them, being called by the magic of the town, stumbling across our borders and eventually finding a home here. How many more were out there who would no longer have this option if we were locked down?

I'd thought about the singers, the witches who had been taken from their homes to be sold as magic slaves, into a trafficking ring that made them commit all kinds of horrors. If they hadn't been rescued by Rhian and brought to Havenwood Falls, where would they be now? Of course, this was exactly why she'd brought them. Exactly why Holly had awakened to her gifts. Exactly what we had hoped to learn: a solution to Hermod's threat.

I'd thought about how Holly and Micah had come to town in the first place. *Why*. Why they had stayed, not only because of Sedona but because Micah knew this was a safe place to give Holly a settled home.

Of course, that had been after we'd fought the Collector, a/k/a Zandra, nearly losing Holly, Harper Sinclair, and others to her just so the goddess could teach us a lesson. So she could prepare us to face Hermod. It'd taken everything our town had to defeat her—and we really hadn't. Then it'd taken more than half the student body of SMA College of Supernatural Guardians. And that hadn't been a real fight, either. Zandra had held back both times and still had nearly destroyed our town. How the hell could we defeat Hermod, a more powerful god with vengeance in his heart and psychotic anger issues, when Zandra, Rhian, and other deities together hadn't been able to? Elsmed had already laid out the cost of even trying.

And I'd thought about Tase and Carter. The sacrifices we had made to protect them as well as this town. Had that been for nothing? Had the last ten months of feeling like my heart would never be whole again been a waste? *Would* it be whole again, with them permanently gone? I'd thought I'd accepted it. I'd thought I had pretty much healed. But maybe there had always been a tiny spark of hope that we'd be reunited because now with the realization that I may truly never see Tase again…

I'd stood, ignoring the looks from the Court members who'd bothered to even notice I was still in the room.

Yes, I would do anything to protect my family, my friends, my community, my people. My town. *Anything.*

Then I'd left.

I went home to shower and put on clean clothes and feed the beasts. Then I'd gone to the library on the SMA campus to join the Luna Coven in their research. Like the Court, they'd been working on solutions nonstop since Holly's revelation. Like the Court, they kept coming back to the same one.

"There has to be another way," I insisted when they told me that upon my arrival.

I went to work with them, poring over books others had already pored over multiple times, hoping to find something they missed. We brainstormed as a larger group, as smaller groups, and one-on-one. We researched our brainstormed ideas. I slipped off to the restricted section of the library there, then the one on the college Halvard Campus, then to the most tightly protected restricted library off the Court room, where we kept the oldest of grimoires and ancient tomes.

"Adelaide." My grandmother's voice cut into my thoughts of the past thirty-six hours, of desperately trying to find the perfect solution. And we had.

Removing my hands from my face and blinking tired eyes, I looked up toward the dais to see all eyes on me.

"What are your thoughts, Addie?" Mathilde asked.

I blinked again. "You want my opinion?"

"Of course," Saundra said. "I don't think I'm speaking for only myself when I say that I have full faith that you will do exactly what needs to be done to protect us all. We want to know what you would do." She gestured toward the front of the dais. "You have the floor."

I looked over at Rhian, who had rejoined us sometime in the past hour or so. She gave me a nod of encouragement. She knew, too.

Swiping my hands on my jean-clad thighs, I exhaled a long breath before standing. I strode to the center aisle and stood in front of them all. If Grandmother had her way, I'd be sitting on the other side of the table before too long. Perhaps by the end of this year.

If we survived that long.

"You're right," I finally conceded, lifting my arms in the air in surrender. "The pocket realm is the best solution." I took another deep breath before diving into the details. "Actually, two pocket realms—one for the town and a separate one for the college. Together they still harbor way too much magic, even for a hidden realm. Besides, it does no good to train an army that can't do its job. The two realms will be connected but on a limited basis, the portals between them opening only for school breaks. The SMA realm will be connected to the Earth realm, as well, but only twice a year—at the beginning of the school year and at the end —unless they are needed. The Havenwood Falls realm will be completely cut off from the Earth realm for an unknown length of time. Until Hermod is no longer a threat or we come up with a better solution."

It could be a year. Could be ten. Could be forever.

I began to pace in front of them as I continued, all of them listening with full attention. "The Luna Coven is now focused on researching the spell to make this happen. Entrapping a couple hundred hunters in a limited area of the Infernum isn't exactly the same as sending an entire town and a few thousand people into its own realm. We will need every type of magic at our disposal—witches, fae, deities, angels, everything. It will be extremely dangerous. We just witnessed how differently magic affects individuals. Shit could go wrong. Some could be seriously hurt. There's a chance some won't survive the kind of power needed to create the spell."

Stopping my pacing, I turned to face them, looking them each in the eye. "In fact, there's a risk that this kind of power could destroy the whole town. Wipe us completely off the map...which would serve our intent in the end."

Their expressions were grave, and I knew they understood. But none of them protested or stopped me from continuing. They really did trust that I would bring them the best solution. Or I should say the least shitty one.

"We need to be upfront with all residents and let them know what's going on and what the plan is. It's only fair. We need to give them time to process and decide what to do. If they want to leave, they should be allowed to do that. If they want to call family members back to town, they should be allowed to do so. This includes the humans."

I paused again, letting that sink in.

"You want to tell the humans about what's going on?" Lawrence demanded. "That means telling them about us!"

"I know. But they have the right to know, to choose. We can't force them to stay. We also can't force them to leave the only home many of them know. They have the right to choose just as much as our supernatural residents."

"You seem to have a plan all worked out," Roman said, his ocean-blue eyes studying me as his fingers templed over his chest. "When do you propose this all to happen? You know many humans will panic. Even some supernaturals."

I nodded. "We tell the supes first. Call a mandatory Court meeting and explain, the sooner the better. I think we should give the humans only a couple of weeks so if anyone freaks out, there's not enough time to expose us or plan some kind of attack they'd never win. The City Council can call a meeting and some of you can be there to explain."

Mayor Barbie, who also worked with the human council, nodded. "I will handle that."

"How much time does the Coven need to create this spell?" Elsmed asked.

I swallowed, about to make this all very real. "Our deadline is the Autumn Equinox, when the atmospheric energy will be strong, hopefully helping us. So about six weeks from now."

"Autumn Equinox—that's Founders Day," Mayor Barbie murmured.

"How poetic," Roman drawled, and if I wasn't mistaken, I thought he appreciated it as much as I did.

Just as the clock tower a few stories above chimed twelve noon, Saundra banged the gavel on the table, ending the ridiculously long meeting. "We have a plan," she said. "Let's get to work."

To be continued...

A FINAL GOODBYE

ROSE GARCIA

CHAPTER 1

I dug my short, pink painted nails into the palms of my hands as I struggled to make sense of the words coming out of Addie Beaumont's mouth. I mean, I knew the top-secret meeting with the town supernaturals was going to be something important, but I wasn't expecting a doomsday scenario.

With my gut twisted in a knot, her explanation of what was going to happen to the town flew over my head. But somehow, I managed to latch on to the most important points…the town was in danger and going into a pocket realm on September 22nd, SMA would be going into a separate realm, the magic to make it all happen might kill everyone, and anyone who wanted to leave could do so.

My gaze swept the room as I took in the faces of everyone around me. Most of them held steady and serious expressions, some had stitched brows, but a few had parted mouths, as if they had been literally stunned.

I felt the stun too.

Shifting in my seat, I eyed my best friend, Taylor, sitting next to me. I shot her a look of surprise mixed with disbelief and a dash of panic.

"Is this for real?" I whispered.

Taylor swallowed. "Yeah, it's totally real."

"Holy shit," I muttered, my heart beating out of control as I continued clenching my hands, the indentions in the skin of my palms becoming deeper by the second.

"It's going to be okay," Taylor reassured. "Everything is always okay in Havenwood Falls."

Even though her words were meant to be reassuring, I heard the doubt in her tone and saw the worry crease between her eyes.

This was different.

With Taylor's attention back on Addie, my thoughts zipped to Joe. He wasn't at the meeting because he and his pack had been called away for a work thing he couldn't tell me about. With the serious vibe in the room, I was sure that whatever he was doing had to do with the threat to town.

My heart raced as I fished my phone out of my jeans pocket and stared at the screen. If I texted Joe and he was in wolf form, he wouldn't get the message until he shifted back. I thought of not bothering him, but quickly pushed that idea aside. I needed to talk to him as soon as possible.

Babe, big news at the supe meeting. Text as soon as you can. Love you

I chewed my bottom lip as I stared at my sent message, then added another.

Actually call. Need to hear your voice. Love you

I shoved my phone back in place, my stomach clenched so tight I thought I might actually hurl. I had survived so much already—a car crash that had left me bloodied and near death, a deadly house fire back in Houston where I lost *everything*. I had even dodged a kill order from Death himself.

Or had I?

Fear prickled the back of my neck as a fresh wave of fear consumed me. Was this whole thing Death's way of coming for me again? Was my number finally up? My eyes darted around the room, searching for the snarky reaper named Shade. Instead of finding him, my eyes met Lyra Beaumont's. The powerful and wise witch had her short brown hair pulled behind her ears, and her head tilted slightly in my direction.

Even from across the room, Lyra had been able to sense my freak out. Which was no surprise. She was like family and had taken me in when I first arrived in Havenwood Falls and had nowhere to go. We cooked together, laughed together, and spent holidays together. Her home was like my own. And when Jan Kelly, my neighbor from Houston who was like a grandmother, arrived in Havenwood Falls, Lyra had been just as welcoming with her. In fact, the three of us lived together for a few weeks until Jan bought her own house and I moved in.

With my thoughts now on Jan, and Lyra turning her attention back to her daughter Addie who was still going over the plan for the town, a horrible thought sprang to mind. What would happen to Jan when the town slipped into the pocket realm? Had Addie mentioned humans and I had missed it?

I leaned toward Taylor.

"Has she said anything about humans?" I asked in a not so quiet voice.

A smattering of shushing rang out. When it died down, Taylor spoke so softly I had to lean in even more to hear her.

"They can stay with the town or leave. Now pay attention. This is important."

"Okay, yeah. Pay attention."

As much as I wanted to focus on everything Addie was saying, I couldn't. My mind darted all over the place, wondering what Joe and I should do. Jan too. Should we take our chances with the town, even though we could all end up dead? Or should we leave for a guarantee at life? I didn't want to die. Not at all. I was young and had my whole life with Joe ahead of me. Plus, it had taken Jan such a long time to find me. Didn't she deserve long and happy golden years?

Everything inside of me screamed to take the safe way out and leave Havenwood Falls.

But would Joe feel the same?

CHAPTER 2

When the meeting ended, no one spoke. No one even moved. But then, a soft chatter trickled through the room as everyone started talking about the seriousness of Addie's news and the dangerous plan for Havenwood Falls. I wondered how many of them would stay, and how many would go. No doubt, that's what many of them were discussing.

Taylor's chair scraped across the floor, jarring me from my thoughts. "I'll be right back."

She wove her way through the crowd and to her sister Harlow. As she moved, I eyed the other SMA students in the room. Besides residents, only those who stayed in town for the summer were here. The rest of the students would have their own meeting on campus.

"I can't believe this is happening," Dingane said. The tall lightning bird wore a confused expression as he and my once frenemy, Cat Vega, came over to me. Cat flipped her long dark hair behind her shoulder, as if announcing her presence.

"Well, I can believe it," she said in her thick Spanish accent. "This town has too many problems. And so does SMA."

I crossed my arms. "You're right about that. There always seems to be some sort of danger or craziness looming around here." I blinked, suddenly thinking about what had happened to D with his lightning misfire. "Oh, shit, D. I bet this whole threat caused your lighting to come out of your butt when you were jogging."

"Dang," he uttered, scratching his head. "That's right. Whatever is happening had to have caused that."

Cat huffed. "Exactly, and I am done with it. ¡*Ya no más!*"

D released her hand and faced her with stitched brows. "What do you mean, done with it?"

"What I mean is I am out of here. Gone. Leaving. I would rather take my chances out in the real world than be trapped in a town with a target on its back. ¿*Comprendes*?"

Uh-oh, this could get crazy. I scooted back from the tall, beautiful, and sometimes overly explosive couple, knowing full well how heated their conversations could get. Especially when Cat got worked up.

D rubbed the back of his neck, staring down at the ground. After a few long seconds, he stepped closer to her and took her hand. "Cat, I know this is scary, but this place is the first home I've ever had. Even with the dangers, and with us not being able to leave, I'd rather be here than anywhere else."

Whoa, she wanted to go, and he wanted to stay. I gulped, as I watched the couple, wondering if that was going to be me and Joe. At first, I was thinking Joe would do whatever I wanted. Now, seeing the emotion on D's face, I realized how naive that was of me. D was willing to risk everything to stay here, and he wasn't even from here. Joe, on the other hand, was born and raised in Havenwood Falls. His family and his entire pack were here. Watching D and Cat in a face-off made me realize Joe would never leave.

"Come on," D said, tugging her forward. "Let's talk about this in private."

At first, she didn't move, as if signaling her resistance. But finally, she gave in. Without a second glance at me, they left the room and disappeared through the crowd. With them gone, my attention went back to Taylor. She and Harlow huddled together with the rest of the Augustine family. I waited for her to look my way so I could tell her I was leaving. When she did, I rose to my feet, pointed at the door, then gave her a wave. She waved back, mouthing that she'd text me later.

Once outside, I knew exactly what I needed to do: go home right away and talk to Jan. Before stepping away from the building, a hand touched my arm.

"Infiniti?"

I turned to see Lyra. "Hey, Lyra."

Compassion filled her brown eyes. "I wanted to check on you before you left. Are you okay?"

"Well, I'm a little freaked out, but otherwise okay. I'm heading home to talk to Jan."

She nodded slightly. "There always seems to be something with Havenwood Falls. But like we always do, we will get through this."

Her positive outlook was meant to calm me but fell short.

"Yeah, of course we will," I said with a weak laugh, trying my best to believe she was right.

Not missing a beat, and knowing me all too well, she moved in close and squeezed my arm. "My door is always open should you want to chat about the meeting. Or anything else for that matter."

Night had fallen, completely erasing the daylight, and cold air swept over me. "Thanks, I appreciate that."

"Of course, Infiniti. Anytime."

We parted ways, and I continued to the nearby neighborhood where Jan's house was. With my hands shoved in my pockets, my stride increased the closer I got. When the quaint two-story house with green siding and white trim came into view, I paused. Soft light from inside gave the house a warm glow, and I didn't even have to guess that despite the late hour, a delicious dinner was simmering inside.

Eager to talk to her, I swept in through the door and called out, "I'm home!"

The savory aroma of beef stew and vegetables wafted through the air while soft jazz music played. "I'm in the kitchen, dear! I've kept dinner simmering until you got back!"

I joined her and found her stirring a large pot with a big wooden spoon. Her short, thick white hair was pulled back with a blue headband, and a red apron donned her tall frame.

"How was the big meeting?"

I thought of how to tell her the news while being calm, but my mind wasn't cooperating. "We're all gonna die."

Her stirring stopped. "I beg your pardon?"

I plunked down on the stool by the kitchen island across from her and let out a heavy sigh. "Remember how I told you about our trials at school? How they're training us to be an army against that god Hermod and other threats? Well, they found a way to protect the town, and the world from him…except the solution might kill us all."

"Oh," she said. She took the spoon out of the pot, turned off the heat, and sat next to me. "That must've been some meeting."

"It was. Addie said we have to slip into another realm because Hermod wants to destroy magic and our world. The town will go into one realm, and SMA will go into another. She also said if anyone wants to leave, human or supe, they can. But they have to choose within the next month because after that, they can't leave at all."

"Oh," she said again, but this time in a different pitch with the word drawn out and hanging in the air for a bit. "What would life be like for those staying? Assuming, we are not destroyed that is."

I focused on the stuff I remembered. "If we survive the magic, the town will continue to be like it is, just no coming and going. So, for most people, life won't really change. But there's no telling how long we'll be removed from the outer world."

The light and easy tune playing from a speaker on the kitchen counter switched to an upbeat one with annoying horns.

"Alexa, off!" I called out.

Silence took over, and a long pause hovered in the room for a while before Jan spoke again. "When is this going to happen?"

"September 22nd."

"That's just about a month and a half," she muttered, looking up and away, as if studying an invisible calendar in her mind. She brought her gaze back to me. "What do you think we should do?"

I rubbed my forehead. "Part of me wants to stay, but another part of me wants to leave because I don't know if I can take another life-or-death disaster."

She drew in a deep breath. "Well, first off, I'm with you, my dear. Whatever you want to do is fine with me. Beyond that...my initial thought is for us to take our chances and stay here in Havenwood Falls. I really like it here. Also, if we stay, you can continue your studies at SMA. There's also the matter of Joe. He is your betrothed and from here. What does he think?"

"He's out with the pack patrolling the town, so I haven't talked to him yet. But I'm scared we might want to do different things."

She reached out and took my hand. "You have time to think on things, and I trust you will make the right decision. Talking with Joe might give you some clarity. But at the end of the day, you need to do what is best for you."

Jan was right, but the idea of Joe and I wanting different things had me feeling awful.

"I know!" Jan suggested in a perky tone, pulling me from my heavy thoughts. "Let's enjoy a good meal. I always find that good meals make everything better."

The flavorful broth with tender meat and perfectly cooked potatoes and carrots hit the spot. And when I finished my second serving, I was feeling way better. Until later, when I was alone in my room. I spent the rest of the evening texting Taylor while waiting to hear from Joe. But he didn't call or text. Drifting off into a sleep, I said a silent prayer for him to be okay, fresh fear over the fate of the town settling deep inside me.

CHAPTER 3

A whisper tickled my mind, drifting around me as I dreamed about being with Joe at a white sand beach with crystal clear waters. We were sitting on blue canvas chairs with a big blue umbrella between us, sipping on yummy rum drinks with orange wedges.

"Babe," the whisper prodded. "It's me."

My eyes fluttered open, my night light illuminating the room enough for me to see Joe sitting on the edge of my bed and looking down on me. I didn't have to ask him how he'd gotten into my room in the middle of the night because this wasn't the first time he had slipped in through my window. I threw my arms around his neck, holding him close to me as I breathed in his soothing scent of fresh soap laced with sandalwood and cedar.

"Oh, Joe. It's awful."

"I know," he said. "I wanted to tell you what the meeting was going to be about, but I was sworn to secrecy so the Court could tell the supes at the same time. The pack and I were only told early so we could patrol the town while everyone gathered."

We stayed holding each other for a while before he pulled back and brushed my long wavy hair out of my face. "Are you okay?"

"I've been worried sick," I said, sitting up all the way.

He kissed me with his soft lips then scooted back. "I thought you might be, which is why I came over here as soon as I could."

I took his hands and held them close. "What are we going to do?"

He tilted his head. "What do you mean?"

"I mean, are we going to stay and risk being killed, or are we going to leave?"

He pulled his chin in and studied me with confusion in his green eyes. "Is that a real question?"

I pulled my hands away and folded them on my lap, not appreciating his tone at all. I had real fears with legitimate concerns. "Yes, it's real," I snapped. "You of all people should know that I'd actually like to avoid death—the entity and the state. So, excuse me if I'm asking what we should do."

"Hey, now," he said, taking my hands back. "I didn't mean anything by it. I'm just surprised you'd wonder what we should do."

I shrugged, my eyes watering over with tears. "I don't want to die, Joe. I want to live, and get married to you, and have babies, and do all the things. Is that so wrong?"

He smiled and pulled me in for a hug. "No, it's not. I want the same things. But this town is our home, and these people are our family. And I believe, really and truly, that we will survive this like everything else we've survived."

My tears had morphed into sobs as I buried my face into his chest, wanting nothing more than to live happily ever after with him in Havenwood Falls. "You really think so?"

He rubbed my back, holding me close. "Yes, I really think so."

When my tears emptied, my fears calmed enough for other emotions to rise to the surface. Mainly, tender wanting for my sexy wolf shifter. In perfect tune with me, his body sensed my longing. He pulled back, wiped the tears from my face, and stared into my eyes.

"You are so beautiful," he said, trailing his fingers down my neck. "So very beautiful."

My body called out to him as I took his hand and slipped it under my shirt. "I want you, Joe. Right now."

He licked his lips as his wolf desire came through. "I am always ready to give you what you want."

He climbed off my bed, made sure the door was locked, then turned to face me. He slowly stripped off his clothes, and I did the same, my body pulsing with desire as I admired every muscle and curve of his perfect form.

"Oh, Joe," I moaned, writhing with desire as he kissed every inch of my body while slowly working his way up to my mouth.

"I love you, Infiniti," he breathed, pausing to gaze at me with pure yearning. "No matter what happens, I will never leave you. Not ever."

There was something different about our intimacy that night—something deep, desperate, and emotion-filled. It was almost as if we were the last people alive, in a dying world, up against insurmountable odds.

And maybe we were…

CHAPTER 4

*J*oe and I had spent all night in the throes of passion and somewhere between pure bliss and exhaustion, I had fallen asleep. Sitting up, I looked around for him. Sunlight trickled through my window, and he was gone. I took my phone from my nightstand and checked my messages. Sure enough, he had texted at six in the morning.

Babe, Jan is stirring so I'm leaving. Text me when you wake up

He texted again two hours later.

The pack has been called away. All is fine, don't worry. I'll text you when I can

Setting the phone aside, I lay back and stared at the ceiling. When my phone chimed, I took it with a swipe, anxious to hear from Joe again. But the text was from Taylor.

Taylor: Hey, checking on you. You ok?

Me: I'm fine. But that meeting has me freaking out

Taylor: Same. Want to meet at Coffee Haven?

Me: Sounds good. Meet in an hour?

Taylor: Perfect. See you then

I tossed off my covers and made my way to the bathroom. When I stripped off my clothes, and before I hopped in the shower, I glanced at myself in the mirror. To my horror, I saw red splotches across my neck and chest.

"Oh, shit," I muttered. Joe hadn't given me a hickey in a while, and had always asked first if he could, but I guessed we were so caught up in each other he had lost all control. I'd have to cover them up for sure.

After a quick shower and getting dressed, I rifled through my things and found a gauzy lightweight scarf to cover up the evidence of my passionate night with Joe. After a quick goodbye with Jan, I left to meet Taylor.

Coffee Haven buzzed with activity. The aroma of coffee, vanilla, cinnamon, and hazelnut tickled my taste buds, making me feel warm and fuzzy inside. Craning my neck, I spotted Taylor right away. She was sitting at our regular booth in the back with two coffees and a couple of plates of the oh-so-delicious, award-winning blueberry scones.

"Mmm," I said, sliding in across from her. "Thanks for getting this. Let me know how much I owe you."

"Girl, you don't owe me anything. I got here before the rush and decided to order for us before the line got too long."

I sipped my warm vanilla-flavored latte, then said, "I'll pay next time."

"Deal," she said, sipping her own drink.

After a few more sips, and a bite of the perfectly baked scone, she leaned forward a bit and asked in a low voice, "How are you taking the news from the meeting?"

I swallowed my bite. "I was really upset last night, and I thought I was better, but sitting here knowing most if not all of these humans might be gone has me freaked all over again."

Taylor eyed the table next to us with a slight frown. "Yeah, I'm freaked too. And honestly, I think there are lots of others who feel the same."

I nodded. "I know Cat and D do."

Taylor's small eyes went wide. "Really?"

"Yeah. Cat told D she didn't want to stay trapped in a town with a target on its back. Then D said he wanted to stay because this place is the only home he's ever had."

"Wow, that's heavy," Taylor said. "I wonder what they're gonna do."

"I don't know. But I can relate to Cat." I pushed my plate aside, suddenly losing my appetite. "I'd like to avoid the whole target on the back thing too. Especially after everything I've been through."

"I can see that. You've been through a lot, Fin."

"Yeah," I said, my voice drifting off. "And Joe is like D. He doesn't want to leave. But he also said last night that he'd do whatever I wanted."

"He said that?"

"He did," I said, feeling guilty about asking him to leave his home.

"He's mated to you and all, so I guess that makes sense. But you're not serious about leaving, are you?"

I shrugged. "I don't know. What about you and your family? Y'all are staying, right?'

"We're totally staying. Clay is, too. He wants to tell his family in Maine, but Addie said he has to do it with one of the school's Regents to help explain things without freaking people out. So they're making the arrangements. It's all so intense. But back to you. Do you really want to leave?"

"Well, I'm madly in love with Joe, and I never want to leave him, not ever. But I guess, with everything I've been through, I'm just, I don't know, afraid of dying."

"Everyone is afraid of dying in some way or another," she offered. "I just think some are better at accepting it than others."

I took my fork and stabbed at a blueberry on my plate. "Well, if you can help me accept it, then I'm all ears because I'd really like to not feel this way."

She sat up straight in her seat, her eyes suddenly filled with hope. "I have an idea."

I matched her posture and straightened my back. "You do?"

"I read this book in my high school Psychology class about conquering fears and stuff, and one of the things it said was to make peace with the things that are bothering you. Kinda like eliminating regrets. So…what's *really* bothering you?"

"Besides the town slipping into another realm with magic that might kill us all?"

"Yes, besides that. What is the root of your fears? Or think about it this way: assuming we all survive, which I truly think we will, what is so bad about slipping into another realm?"

"Oh," I said. I pressed my back against the cushioned booth, my mind immediately taking me to my neighborhood where I grew up. "I don't have family in Houston anymore, but I kinda thought I'd go back there one day to see everything. My neighborhood, my street, my lake… all those places mean something to me. And even though my house burned down, part of me wants to see how it was rebuilt. If we survive the magic of slipping into another realm, I won't be able to go back home to Houston."

Taylor was nodding her head, listening to me intently. When I finished, she cleared her throat, then moved in close again. "I have an idea. What if you went there now and saw everything and kinda said an emotional goodbye?"

I blinked. "Go there for a final goodbye? As in hop on a plane? I don't think we really have the time for that...do we?"

"I wasn't actually thinking of a plane, but more of a portal."

"A portal?" I asked in a voice a lot louder than I intended.

"Shhhh," she said, waving a hand at me, looking around our booth to make sure no one was paying attention to us. "I've been working on my portal skills, not just at SMA but on the side with Harlow, and I'm actually pretty good. So, if you want to go home and say goodbye to all the special places, I can get you there."

My heart swelled with excitement, and suddenly I realized how important it was to see the place where I grew up before Havenwood Falls went dark.

With wide eyes, I said, "Let's do it."

And then, at the same time, we both said, "But we can't tell anyone."

CHAPTER 5

*T*aylor and I strategized when and where to do the portal. Thinking the town and even the mountains and caves would have an unusual amount of preparation activity going on, we agreed to do it at my house. Jan worked most days as a volunteer at the library and would be there all day the next day. So that was our target.

When the next day rolled around, Jan left for the library like she always did. Then Joe texted that he would be busy with pack business all day. With the coast clear, I texted Taylor to hurry and come over. She showed up a few minutes later.

When I swung open the door, her mouth fell open before she laughed. "Hickeys? Really?"

My hands went up to my neck. I thought I had covered the red marks with makeup, but apparently, I hadn't done a good enough job. "Joe and I got carried away the other night."

"I can see that," she laughed.

She came in, then looked around as if to make sure we were alone. "Jan's gone right?" she asked in a low voice.

"Yep. And Joe's busy."

"Perfect. That should give us plenty of time."

Nervous excitement budded inside of me as I thought of going to my old neighborhood to say goodbye.

"So where do you want to do the portal?" I asked her.

She scrunched up her face while she thought. "Let's go to your room.

And you should probably cover up your love marks, in case you interact with someone in Houston."

My heart skipped a beat. "You think I'll see someone I know?"

She shrugged. "I know you had the whole time jump thing when you came here, but there's always that chance you'll see someone you know. Like an old neighbor or friend."

"I hadn't thought of that, but I guess you're right."

We went upstairs straight away. Taylor waved her hands around the corners of the room while I rummaged through my drawers for a scarf. "What are you doing?"

"I'm placing a barrier around the room so no one can pick up on what I'm doing."

"Good idea," I said, tying a thin black scarf around my neck. "We definitely don't want to get in trouble."

"Definitely not," she added. "Now, stand here with me in the middle of the room."

I stood in front of her, and she placed her hands on my shoulders. "Stay perfectly still and do exactly what I say."

I swallowed. "Okay."

"Now," she said, her voice lowering in that witchy serious tone of hers. "Focus on your old neighborhood—see it in your mind as if you are there. Think of a spot that's private. Somewhere where the portal won't be seen."

I cleared my mind and did as she asked, envisioning the homes, the sidewalks, and the yards. I even focused on the sound of birds chirping and the smell of dirt and grass. My mind eventually fixed on the path around the lake across from my street where there was a cluster of trees and a spot in the middle where I used to hide when I was little. It was the perfect place for the portal.

"I've got the spot."

"Excellent. Keep your mind on it while I begin."

She began chanting under her breath. With each word, the light in my room seemed to dim. The force even lifted the dark hair from her shoulders. With a gulp, I fought to steady my nerves when the ground vibrated. I yelped, stepping closer to my best friend.

"Focus on your destination," she whisper-shouted before resuming her chant.

I closed my eyes to avoid being distracted but opened them when the temperature dropped. My heart skipped a beat as the area in front of Taylor began to shimmer and then parted.

I blinked, not once or twice, but several times in complete awe that Taylor had really and truly done it.

"Whoa, you really are powerful," I muttered, eyeing the black hole that was the size and shape of a door in the middle of my room.

She smiled, almost puffing up her chest a little, but she didn't admire her handiwork for long. "Thanks, but my skills are still new. So whatever you're gonna do, do it now. Oh, and hurry back before it collapses."

Fear raced down my back. "Collapses?"

"I mean, yeah, but don't worry. The portal should last about an hour because that's how long my portals have been lasting. But to be on the safe side, do whatever you need to do as fast as you can."

Even though a healthy dose of fear coursed through my body, my excitement won over. I wanted to see my neighborhood that I loved so much, just in case I never had the chance again.

"Got it," I said, inching forward. "Here goes nothing."

With my eyes closed, I held my breath and walked through. A cold sensation wrapped around me but didn't last long as heat and humidity took over, covering me like a wetsuit. Recognizing the feeling of a Houston summer, I opened my eyes with a smile.

Tree trunks circled all around me, and leaves and dirt piled around my Converse. The smell of grass and dirt filled my nose, and three rapid sneezes burst out of me.

"Ah, hot and humid Houston," I said with delight, rubbing my nose. "How I have missed you."

CHAPTER 6

*M*y once large hiding spot was smaller than I had remembered, and I had to wedge myself between thick tree trunks to exit the woodsy space. After a quick glance over my shoulder at my portal back to Havenwood Falls, making sure it was still there, I brushed off my jeans.

To my right sprawled the large lake with the spraying water feature in the middle. And to the left was the winding gravel trail that led to my street.

"I can't believe I'm here," I muttered to myself as I started making my way down the trail.

With my shoes crunching on the gravel, it dawned on me that I hadn't seen anyone on the usually busy trail. I slowed my pace, thinking not even a weed eater or a lawn mower could be heard, when droplets of rain sprinkled down on me. I shielded my eyes and look up to see darkening clouds in the sky.

"Great," I said, remembering it was August in Houston and usually very rainy.

I shoved my hands in my pockets and curled my shoulders in as I continued at a quicker pace. I passed my favorite bench where I had my first kiss with a kid named Billy Weber, followed the lake trail to the sidewalk, crossed the street where I had fallen off my bike and broken my arm, then made my way down Woodway Drive.

With droplets of rain coming down even faster, I hurried my pace, my mind remembering all the good times I'd had here. Countless sleepovers with friends, bike races, pie fights, lemonade stands, and so much more.

This was also where Death came for me and my mom and burned my house down and took her away from me forever. And Joe had saved me. A rush of tears flooded my eyes at all the joy and loss I had experienced on this street, and how now I was saying goodbye, possibly forever.

Without bothering to wipe my eyes, I continued forward, keeping my stare cast down and focused on the sidewalk as I moved even closer to my house. What would it look like? Who lived there now? Seeing the painted number on the street curb, I stopped. I slowly raised my stare and saw something I wasn't at all expecting.

Every window was boarded with plywood.

My brow furrowed as I struggled to make sense of what I was seeing when I noticed the house next door was boarded too. So was the one beyond that. I spun around toward the house where Jan lived, which was now occupied by her church friend, and it too was boarded.

A crackling burst of lightning exploded overhead, followed by massive gusts of wind. I crouched to the ground, remembering August was the peak of hurricane season, and I was apparently standing on my street amid one!

"Shit!" I hollered.

My mind frantically processed my situation. I could use my supernatural abilities to freeze the weather or book it back to the portal. Peering at the ever-darkening sky, I shot up to my feet and started hauling back to the lake. With my eyes squinted against the rain, I pumped my arms and wove my way around the gravel path. When I spotted the opening between the trees, I squeezed myself through.

But the portal was gone.

My heart stopped, panic seized me, and I couldn't believe my eyes. "No, no, no!" I kicked at the leaves, I pounded against the tree trunks, I shook the nearby branches. "Taylor!"

Thunder rumbled as the rain continued falling and the wind gusted even harder. I sank to my knees, forcing myself to stay calm even though I was literally coming unglued with thoughts of being stuck in Houston and not being able to get back to Havenwood Falls before the realm jump because hurricanes could immobilize a city for weeks.

I slowed my breathing and calmed myself with self-talk. "Okay, Taylor somehow lost her connection, which is no big deal. All I need to do is call out to her and she can pick up my signal, or whatever, and then she can re-do her portal."

Standing upright, I placed my hands out in front of me with my palms up and focused on my petite best friend who was like a sister to me. "Taylor, I need you to come get me. Please, please, please. Lock on to me like Scotty and Kirk and beam me up. Or out. You know what I mean. Just get me out of here." Another blast of thunder sounded. This time it rocked the earth beneath my feet and pierced my eardrums. "Right the hell now!"

A hand stuck through the branches, followed by a pant leg, until a tall guy with dark hair and piercing green eyes who looked like a cross between an actor and a biker entered my hideout.

I blinked. "Fleet?"

It didn't take me long to recognize the guy who had helped me the first time I had ended up in Havenwood Falls. He had even helped me and Joe when I was back in Houston and almost killed by Death himself. Though because of the wards around Havenwood Falls, I knew he only remembered the stuff that had happened in Houston.

"Hey, kid," he said. "I heard you calling for help."

I threw my arms around his waist and held on tight. "Fleet," I mumbled against his leather jacket. "Thank goodness."

He wrapped his arms around me and patted my back. "I can't wait to hear why you're back in Houston and why now, but first let's get out of this storm. I have a place not far from here where we can stay until this passes."

I jerked away from him, thinking that if I left, Taylor would never find me. And if Taylor never found me, I'd never see Joe again. Fresh tears flooded my eyes. "I can't. I need to stay here so my friend can find me."

He tilted his head and raised a brow at me, keeping his cool as rain and wind whipped through the branches and doused us. "And you think your friend will find you here?"

"Yes, because this is where she left me."

"She left you?"

"Not left as in *left* me; but left as in she brought me here through her portal."

He ran a hand through his wet hair. "All right. I get it. This is one of those supernatural things about that town where you and that guy named Joe went."

"Yes," I said. "It is. Will you just wait here with me?"

"Sure. But this rain is just the outer bands of the hurricane, so we can't stay too long."

"Okay, not too long," I said, my teeth gritted together in panic.

Fleet eyed the trees that offered little protection from the blasting wind and pelting rain. He swept his dark wet hair back from his forehead, then held his hands out in front of him. With a flick of his fingers, everything within our small space stilled as if a weather on/off switch had been flipped.

"That's right," I muttered, gazing at the effects of the hurricane that swirled on the other side of the trees. "We have the same power."

He cocked a brow. "You figured out how to use the energy power within you?"

"Yes. But I'm not as good as you. I'm still learning."

"Good for you, kid," he said, crossing his arms and leaning back against one of the larger tree trunks. He kept his attention narrowed on me. "Last time I saw you, you and Joe were heading to that supernatural town. I guess you found it."

"We did, and I've been there ever since." I glanced down at my soaking wet shoes. "I only came back to see my neighborhood before I disappear from this realm possibly forever."

"Say what?"

I didn't think I should tell him what was going on in Havenwood Falls, but I didn't have to worry about it because he stopped me with a shake of his head. "You know what? Don't tell me. The less I know the better. But what if your friend doesn't show up? Then what?"

The fear of being left behind and never seeing Joe again boiled to the surface. With my tears spilling out of me, I blubbered. "Then I'll be stuck here forever, and everything I knew about Joe and Havenwood Falls will slowly fade from memory."

The pain of forgetting Joe tore through me, forcing me to close the gap between us so I could sob into his wet shirt. I had cried like that with him before. I had also been rescued by him before, but I didn't think this time would be the same.

"Desperate situations seem to be a thing with you," he said. "And crying."

I shrugged my shoulders. "I guess."

When my tears finally emptied, I moved back and wiped my face, feeling lower than low and completely regretting coming here.

"If your friend doesn't come, you can always stay with me."

"Thanks," I said, hating that he had said that because I didn't want that notion released into the universe. But there it was, floating around in my possibilities. Doing my best to counter it, I added, "But I'm sure Taylor will come for me."

I imagined Taylor in my room, freaking out because her portal had glitched. I wondered who she'd go to for help. Hoping it was Harlow and not Addie.

Trying to keep my cool, I studied Fleet. "What are you up to these days anyway?"

He kept his back against the tree trunk, maintaining his cool demeanor. "The usual. Helping people with their dire situations."

"Well, thanks Fleet. I guess I owe you. Again."

"We're not out of this yet."

The storm increased in strength. And even though we were protected from the rain and wind by Fleet's supernatural powers, the trees swayed back and forth and the ground shook with each thunderous rumble.

As the minutes passed, my stomach sank as I began to wonder if the hurricane was preventing Taylor from making the portal. Was this my destiny? To leave Havenwood Falls forever? To never see Joe again? I didn't want to believe it, couldn't even fathom that possibility. But something inside of me said I had made the biggest mistake of my life coming here.

CHAPTER 7

*T*he relentless barrage from Mother Nature continued its onslaught. The rain and wind pounded us, the lightning and thunder crashed all around. I stayed close to Fleet, grateful that he was with me while I continued focusing on Taylor as best as I could.

"Son of a bitch," Fleet mumbled, looking around. "The lake is overflowing."

I spun around to see water gushing into our space and creeping up over the top of my shoes. "Oh, no."

Fleet shook his head. "I'm afraid I can't hold this storm anymore. It's way too big. So we gotta go."

A cold rush of panic doused me. I bit my bottom lip, my mind racing, my body shivering. I clutched the top of my shirt and twisted the fabric into a ball. Leaving this spot meant saying goodbye to Havenwood Falls and Joe forever. There was no way I could survive that kind of loss. Not in a million years.

Joe was my one true love.

"I can't leave," I managed to squeak out through my tear strangled throat. "I can't."

Splotches covered my vision as my heart broke into a hundred thousand pieces. I couldn't see. Couldn't breathe. Could barely even think. All I knew was that I'd rather drown waiting for Joe than give up on getting back to him.

"I'm sorry, Infiniti. But we can't stay here."

My body lost all feeling as unimaginable pain ripped through me. I didn't even realize I was sinking to the ground until Fleet scooped me up and held me to him.

I covered my face with my hands as the horror of never seeing Joe again gutted me, sending out a cry somewhere between a yell and a moan that I hardly even recognized was coming from me.

I was ruined. Forever. And I would never be the same.

Fleet started working his way out of our hiding spot. But then, he stopped. "I'll be damned."

I jerked my head up and wiped my eyes, seeing a shimmer in the air. It grew long and wide, revealing the same black hole I had seen earlier.

"Taylor!"

Fleet lowered me to the ground but held on until he knew I could stand. "You got it?"

"I think so," I said, waiting a few seconds to make sure my legs were really working, every fiber of my being filled with desperation to see Joe.

"That Joe is lucky to have you."

I flung my arms around him and squeezed. "I am lucky to have him." Then I squeezed again. "I'm also lucky to have you as a friend."

"Yeah, yeah," he said, with a chuckle. Then he released me, adding, "You better get going."

Glancing around at the storm, I asked, "Are you gonna be okay?"

He lips pulled up into a smile. "I'm always okay."

I flashed him a goodbye grin then turned and hurried through the darkness before it disappeared. The air transformed from stormy and wet, to dry and cold, and then, finally, to room temperature. Snapping my eyes open, I found myself in my room with Taylor and Harlow.

Taylor rushed me and hugged me so tight she squeezed the air right out of my lungs. "Oh, my goddess! I'm so sorry! Something happened to my magic, and I lost my connection to the portal! And why are you wet?"

I held on to her for a while, waiting for my catapulting heart to return to normal, relieved to be back in Havenwood Falls. And that's when I realized, without a doubt, that Havenwood Falls with Joe was my home. Not anywhere else.

"It's okay," I muttered. "You got me back."

She pulled away and motioned toward her sister. "Well, Harlow did."

"You're welcome," Harlow said with a wink.

My door flung open, and Joe rushed in. "What's going on?" he asked in a panic-filled voice. He eyed me up and down. "What happened? You're soaking wet!"

Taylor stepped away from me, taking Harlow's hand, and headed for the door. "Um, we'll let you two talk," she said.

Without giving them a second glance, Joe cupped my face in his strong hands. "Are you okay? I felt that you were in danger and raced over here as fast as I could."

"Yes, I'm soaking wet. And yes, I was in danger, but I'm okay now. I'll explain everything, but I need to tell you something I figured out."

He swallowed, almost as if afraid of what I had to say. "What is it?"

I pulled him to me. "That this place, Havenwood Falls, is my home. I belong here with you. Forever. No matter the danger, and no matter what we may face."

He blew out and buried his face in the crook of my neck. "Oh, babe. I am so relieved to hear that."

We stayed locked in our embrace for a long time, holding each other close, our lips connecting over and over and over as my heart burst with love for him and for Havenwood Falls. Thinking that no matter what, everything would turn out okay for us.

SUNSET HORIZONS

T.V. HAHN

A TEENY WEENY WU TALE

"*W*hat are all these things laying out on the table?" Tang asked when he walked into the kitchen after his return from studying at the library.

I fixed my wonderful husband a cup of Dragon's Well Green Tea, his favorite, then beckoned him to sit down with me.

"We had a very interesting day today," I replied. "You could say these items are sort of mementoes."

"It's an odd assortment of mementoes. Well, except for the tin of tea. So tell me about your interesting day," Tang responded.

I proceeded to explain to him that since our darling daughter Ting, or as the Pixie Sisters like to call her, Ting-a-ling, had been growing like a weed, Nina, my nephew Mat's new wife, had made her a little dress that was patterned after my petal dresses, large pockets and all. She also tie-dyed it because she said it was fitting since Ting is our flower child. She had also made it just a little large since as a faerie, she was growing up faster than human children did.

Tang chuckled over the pun that Ting, who literally blossomed from a plant, was growing like a weed. I didn't intend it to be a pun, but it was kind of funny. He also wasn't sure what the tie-dyed dress had to do with a flower child, so I filled him on the background of the sixties—hippies, peace movement, and all. I guessed he had not watched *Forest Gump* yet.

"Well, back to our day. After Ting finished watching *Raya and the Last Dragon* for the umpteenth time, I took her upstairs and helped her get dressed, so we could go down to Shear Magic to have Charlotte do something with her hair."

Nina had also made Ting a matching bandanna, which was a good thing, since Ting was born with a little blue bell hanging from her forehead. The bandanna was supposed to keep it under wraps, so to speak, but the little flower just kept popping out. I was hoping Charlotte would be able to come up with something to work with it.

Shear Magic had samples of multi-colored strands of hair that Ting was mesmerized by, and she kept saying, "Pudry Dwagon." Ting's little tyke tongue sounded something akin to Gaelic, I though, so I guessed she was saying "Pretty Dragon" or it meant something else completely.

I explained to Charlotte about the movie, and fortunately it was one of her faves too. Charlotte took one of the colored strands that had a mix of blue, violet, pink, and white, showed it to Ting, who bobbed her head and the little blue bell up and down in agreement to Charlotte's selection. Thanks to her, Ting's little bell now looked more like a curl right in the middle of her forehead. After she colored Ting's hair, she snipped the dead ends off with a very exquisite pair of scissors, the kind my ancestors used. It was shaped somewhat like a butterfly, with an intense amount of filigree but it appeared more like a dragon. Ting was fascinated with the scissors and now was saying "Pudry Dwagon" and pointing at the scissors that Charlotte slipped back into her pocket.

As I was telling Tang about our visit to Shear Magic and the dragon styled scissors, he picked up the small pair of snippers that lay on the table amongst the other various objects, and just said, "Hmmm."

I continued to tell Tang how we crossed through town square, and on such a wonderfully sunny late summer day as this was, the gold encrusted fountain in the center of the square shimmered more radiantly than I could ever remember. Ting was practically glowing with the sight and blabbering whatever language or nonsense could escape her lips, and still repeating over and over "Pudry Dwagon." It was still fairly early in the day, but I intended to meet Mayor Barbie at the Broastful Brew later, so I gave her a little heads up by dialing 911 on my cell phone. That was my speed-dial number for my dearest and oldest friend Barbie Stuart, the mayor of Havenwood Falls, and soon to be Ting's Goddess Mother.

"Hold on!" Tang piped in at this point. "What is a Goddess Mother anyway?"

"You understand your Spirit Crane. In my world, Goddess Brid is my guiding goddess, similar to your Spirit Crane. When a new Child of the Goddesses is brought into this world, you hope to find the right person who will help coach her understanding. Were you always in touch with your Spirit Crane, or did you have help along the way?" I asked him in return.

"One does not live for centuries without having help along the way. Whether you have magical, mystical, alchemical, or otherwise talents. Yes, I understand, and you so graciously bring me to this acknowledgement. Thank you. However, I am still struggling to understand so many objects that that are spread out on our kitchen table. Forgive me for asking?"

I patted Tang on the hand, signaling to be patient, while I continued to tell him about our interesting day.

I dried little Ting's hands with her colorful bandanna, which we had tucked into her pocket so she could show off her new hairstyle, because she had put her hands in the fountain to play with the shining water. Then I took her hand, and we walked back over to Eleventh Street to go to Gretchen's Toy Shoppe.

Gretchen's had a fascinating array of toys, including many collectibles, from Barbie dolls to antique china dolls, and even Ty Beanie Babies. I thought maybe I could get an idea of what to give Ting for a Founders Day present, since only the Goddesses would know what she would like by the time she reached her first birthday at the rate she was maturing. Ting was impressed with a beautiful china doll dressed in a kabuki that was adorned with embroidered dragons.

Tang asked me how much that cost us? I told him that it cost nothing, although that doll had an $800 price tag on it, but it was a Ty Beanie Baby that really caught her eye. To the extent that her violet eyes began to glow and turn bright blue. Gretchen had an original Magic the Dragon Beanie Baby that was retired from the market, including what collectors claim are tag errors that made it rare. It really didn't make any difference. While Hattie Hartwood, owner of the store, was trying to explain the numerous errors, including wording of the poem, addresses and even the stitching on the wings that didn't match the original poem, Ting just lit up brighter and brighter. She was hopping up and down on one foot then the other, saying…

"Pudry Dwagon?" Tang interjected as I told the story to him. "How much did that cost us?"

Again, I explained that it did not cost us anything, because that rare Ty Beanie Baby was selling on e-Bay for $25,000. Tang raised an eyebrow as he toyed with the stuffed dragon that was also in the mix of things on the table. In fact, I told him that I hastily moved Ting out of the store, before she got keen on any other expensive toys.

I thought I would take her over to Hey-Nice Glass! Maybe one of Hannah's blown glass figures would entice little Ting, and surely that would be far more affordable. Sure enough, Ting was bedazzled by all the sun-catching glass baubles and shiny figurines, but she fixed her gaze on one small ornament. It was, naturally, a dragon. I began thinking maybe she shouldn't watch *Raya*, anymore. It seemed that she was totally consumed with dragons, and of course she was chanting "Pudry Dwagon" as her eyes glowed with a fiery orange then cooled to a more iridescent turquoise and she hopped up and down on one foot then the other in excitement.

"Well, like mother like daughter," Ting said. "That little hopping thing you do must be a family trait. The eye-color change is rather unusual. I know she has those violet hazel eyes, but I am sure I've only seen them change from violet to blue and back again." Then he picked up the small glass dragon, which had a little loop on the top and a gold thread, to hang it as an ornament, from the table. "Was it this color turquoise?"

I nodded and told him that I couldn't buy it because Hannah had only made that one to celebrate the Havenwood Falls High School Dragons' long-awaited division victory last year. I wasn't exactly sure what division that was. Anyway, she said she could make another for Ting in any color she would like. I wondered if she could make it like a prism, to match Ting's new vibrant hair colors, not to mention her ever-changing eye colors. In any case, Hannah gave me a ballpark figure that was definitely more in our price range, so I let her know I'd get back to her on the color if she could do it by Founders Day.

We went back to Town Square Park, and I sat down in the gazebo to call Barbie and let her know we were now heading to the Broastful Brew and would be there in a few minutes. Ting was blissfully bobbing around the gazebo and stopped at one of the posts opposite from where I sat. She was eyeing a little mosaic that hung there and was doing her little hip-hop and singing her Purdry Dwagon song. This time her eyes glowed a kind of red, but with a silver tint to them almost. The mosaic was crafted by one of the love-sick art students at the high school, then nailed to the gazebo post. It was heart shaped, with a dragon figure pieced in with varying pieces of glass and tile, giving it a silver dragon feel—the football team's mascot.

I had to pull the little one away from the hanging heart, so that we could get to the Broastful Brew and not keep Barbie waiting.

Sure enough, Barbie was already at our customary table, as we walked in with the shopkeeper's bell ringing behind us as we closed the door. Anytime I heard a little bell like that I always thought of Mabel, the owner of the Broastful Brew. She was also one of my nephew Mat's employers. I waved to Mat, who was behind the counter. Ting ran over to her Aunt Barbie and hopped right on her lap, which made Barbie squeal with delight, and began playing with the dragon pendant that Barbie always wore. It was a charmed charm that gave Barbie her own supernatural powers, one being not to age.

I asked Ting to go over and visit with her cousin for a little bit, as Aunt Barbie and I had some business to discuss. Ting had stuck out her tongue and said, "Bidness, blecch!" and we both laughed at that as she gleefully skipped over to the counter, where Mat lifted her up and sat her right on it.

"I don't know, Barbie, how I'm going to be able to help the Court with our plans for this pocket realm. I don't really have anything to offer," I started our conversation.

"Nonsense, Siobhan! You have some very important talents that we will need to utilize," she replied.

"Such as what?" I asked.

"Well let's see, you can shimmer just about anywhere, fly faster than most flying supes, create portals, use your tell-all ball, and apparently do a little time-traveling in between. And let's not forget you came into some extraordinary powers when you found your father's wand, so much so that you were able to trap the Wu! Ha, in more ways than one. Now, if you don't think those are abilities we need, you are sadly mistaken." She corrected me.

I guess I just never really saw myself that way.

"Not only that," the mayor added, "we will need Tang to help with the spell weaving. Remember, Addie said we will need *all* the magic."

I noticed Tang was fiddling with the dragon pendant that lay on the table top up while I told him about my meetup with Barbie. When I told him the part about her saying they were going to need his talents, he became illuminated, and he set the pendant back down on the table.

Mat and Ting had been hitting it off when I got up to leave. He asked if we would like a tin of Dragon's Well tea, and he brought over the little green metal box painted with a glorious golden dragon on it. Ting's eyes brightened to an emerald green color while reciting her now well-known chorus.

"Thanks, Mat, but I think we have plenty for the time being. Maybe in a few weeks." I lifted Ting off the counter and planted her tiny Ting feet on the ground. She skipped over to Barbie to kiss her goodbye, and Barbie kissed, hugged, squeezed, kissed again, squeezed again, our tiny Ting, before we departed and she headed back to City Hall.

Barbie's mention of Addie made me think of the blind witch sisters who had recently opened a healing crystals store around the corner from the Brew (Mat's pet name for the coffee joint). They had named it Get Stoned, and Tang thought that was hilarious. It really was such a good name for the shop.

It was starting to get late, and Ting would be needing a nap soon, but we had enough time to stop into Get Stoned and check on Quin, Arya, and Liv. These three sisters were witches but had befallen a cruel fate, and we were not sure who had abducted them and wrought such evil upon them. Their eyes had been gouged out, and each had been turned into something other than their witch self, a vampire, wolf shifter, and bear shifter. Although this turning would have normally stripped them of their witch powers, apparently those were stronger than what ever villain caused this mayhem was aware of.

Quin immediately felt our presence when we entered. In spite of the traumatic loss of eyesight that she and her sisters suffered, they seemed to have found some peace with it, and I actually believe it was because they had the base healing nature of witches and the ability to find the right elements to do what needed to be done to help.

Ting was glowing over a magnificent pale pink crystal centered on a stand in the middle of the shop. There was a strange aura surrounding the stand, almost as if it was a security system of sorts. This time, her hazel eyes were glowing pink! Naturally, she was murmuring her never-ending mantra 'Pudry Dwagon' as she set her total focus on this stone. No matter how many times I tried to get her to pronounce *pretty* properly, it seemed to be useless.

Quin said, "I feel your daughter has an extremely good sense of our stones. This one is amongst the rarest in the world! Only five that are over three carats have ever been found in the world. This one is about 4.2. The largest happens to be in the Smithsonian at 9.41 carats."

Quin lifted the stone off the stand and at the same time the force field toned down.

She continued, "It is called Poudrettetite—kind of pronounced like Pudry-tite. So, the little one is already on the correct path to enlightenment. It's not its real name as it has been around for centuries. It is known in Burma to have extreme healing powers over mind, soul, and body. That also means that in the wrong hands, it can be extremely dangerous to a mind, soul, or body."

Ting said "Pudry Dwagon" one more time, and at this point, as a mother, I felt the need to correct her. I explained this was not a dragon, it was a rock, stone, or call it a crystal, but it was not a dragon.

"Good for you!" Tang complimented me. "Ting is cute and charming and all, but we have to teach her the nature of things, and what they are called. That's why I know you are the perfect mother for our little flower."

Arya explained that like most minerals, Poudrettetites are not really new. Just like many elements, they had yet to be discovered by those who deemed it important to label them. In this case, they were named after Poudrette. Meanwhile, our sisters had been aware of the energy of the stones as well as every other elemental thing on this planet. Liv piped up to give a little background on the crystals that were normally found in small if not tiny segments, including, oddly, in Quebec. She explained that in ancient Asia, it was believed that the fragments of this powerful crystal were the remains of the scales of the last dragon ever seen there. Quin filled us in more on the legend. It did not surprise any shaman or witch that fragments of possibly the last dragon's scales were found in Canada. The last dragon was on the brink of extinction and was trying to find any refuge for survival.

Tang agreed about the last dragon legend and in fact said that he knew first-hand that it was no myth, but a fact. His attention was now drawn to the crystal that shone in the midst of the other items before him. When he touched the stone, he seemed to fall into a trance. This was one of my husband's unique talents, and it was obvious the crystal was familiar to him. Well, at least his eyes didn't glow pink. Soon after, he shook his nearly bald head, his white and gray braided queue swinging back and forth, and came out of the trance.

"Did the sisters give you this rare crystal?" he queried, with a bit of delight at having this beautiful specimen in our possession.

"Well, that's just it. None of these things were given to us or bought!" I said then hesitated.

"Well, the tea tin here, I know is ours, right?"

I grimaced and pointed to our Dragon's Well tea tin on the shelf above the stove, shaking my head no.

"When we left Get Stoned, I brought Ting home and took her upstairs to change and take her nap. I helped her out of her dress and gave her a pair of pajamas to wear. As I started to put the dress away in the closet, I noticed her big pockets appeared to be bulging. I emptied them to find all these objects." I gestured to the collection on the table. "I wasn't sure what to do. It appeared that our daughter had picked up some bad habits from the Pixie Sisters, like how they take someone's loose button, or that sock that everyone thought had been eaten by their dryer, or a lost earring that someone blamed on their house's blackhole."

"Siobhan, are you telling me we created a klepto-pixie instead a fairy baby?" Tang worriedly asked me.

"My dearest," I answered, "I don't think that's the case." I didn't want to blame Ting for anything until I found out the truth. "At first, I thought that maybe she was given these things without my knowing it, though I couldn't see how that was, since she was with me almost every second."

I continued to explain that after Ting's nap, I set her up in the parlor with Cyllene, my other dearest, oldest friend and Oreiad, a tree nymph, and part-time Nanny to Ting. I also instructed Cyllene that Ting was not to watch *Raya and the Last Dragon* under any circumstance. Then I went to make a few phone calls to get to the bottom of this possible thievery.

"I started making my phone calls and soon came to realize there was something else awry. My first call was to Charlotte to apologize about the pair of scissors. But she told me that her pair was still in her pocket. I tried to tell her these looked exactly like hers, and then took a picture of them and texted it to her."

"Madame Tahini, those are exactly like mine. These were my grandmother's and crafted especially for her by an admirer. I was under the impression that this was one of a kind. I guess her admirer might have had an eye for other ladies also." Charlotte had replied with a bit of sadness in her voice.

"Charlotte," I consoled, "I doubt that is the case. I feel in my fae blood that your grandmother was a one and only, like your scissors. I am not exactly sure how this pair came about it, but I will figure it out."

Next call was to Hattie Hartwood, again to apologize about the Beanie Baby dragon and let her know we would return it tomorrow. However, Hattie refused the apology because she still had her rare dragon, in fact she was holding it as we spoke. The one on the table was downright identical, including all the errors that Hattie had pointed out.

Tang stroked his goatee and just said, "Hmmmm," knowing I wasn't finished.

A similar call was made to Hannah, and she too said that she was still in possession of the glass dragon that Ting fell head over heels in love with. She also told me that any glass she made she microprinted her initials on them, and since she only made one of these, then some fraud had copied her work.

I checked out the bauble myself, and with my fae eyesight, I could make out the microprinted initials. I took a big gulp then called Mat at the Broastful Brew but this time just asked him if he still had any Dragon's Well tea left.

"Aunt Siobhan, we keep two tins in stock at a time. One for the Brew, and of course, one for Tang. We still have both. Do you need one? I can bring it over tonight if you would like," Mat had replied.

"I just told him I would let him know later after I spoke with you, since it was a bit pricey," I said to Tang. "I really started wondering what all this could mean. I knew Barbie's pendant very well, and I could tell this was hers, but when I dialed 911, the voice on the other end assured me her dragon pendant was safely dangling from the necklace she was wearing, and was so glad that Ting took such an interest in it."

"And the crystal?" Tang asked.

"Sweetheart, I couldn't very well call the sisters and text them a photo. I was about to go over there when you came home. Would you go with me to find out what they think about it?" I implored.

He was immediately on his feet and had the crystal in his hand in response.

I let Cyllene know we were going out for a few minutes but should be back shortly. Ting and the Pixies were on the floor rumbling and took no interest in our departure.

Tang and I walked across the park, stopping at the gazebo to ensure the mosaic original was still on the post, which it was. Then we crossed by the fountain, where I caught a glimpse of the glittering gold dragonhead coin, whose twin was on our table.

It seemed like a much longer walk this time than the entire stroll Ting and I took earlier today. I dreaded going to Get Stoned, in case the rare pale pink Poudrettetite that was in Tang's hand was theirs.

Quin once again greeted us as we walked through the door, "Ah, Madame Tahini, good to sense you again! You brought the Wu with you too. Wonderful! I believe the professor will find our crystals very useful in his crafts."

We both caught sight of the spectacular pale pink crystal that sat on the center table with that sensational aura-forcefield hovering around it.

I took Quin's hands and had Tang place the crystal in her palms while explaining our dilemma.

"Madame Tahini, Doctor Wu, this stone has the exact same weight as ours, and it has the same identical energetic resonance as ours, as if it were an identical twin right down to the DNA. I guess there are now six crystals over three carats. Please take care to handle this stone with caution. But it is a good thing that Havenwood Falls has two of these, as they most likely will be useful considering what we are all up against."

We knew she was referring to Hermod's plans to destroy Havenwood Falls and our entire world. Tang placed the precious piece into his pocket, put his arms around my shoulder, and we headed back home.

He tried to comfort me and assure me that apparently Ting had a twinning talent. He also suggested we take this information to the Court as soon as possible.

"Maybe Ting and I should go see Addie first. We still have some time before Ting needs to eat dinner and go to bed," I said, hoping and actually feeling he was probably right about this being Ting's magical ability. There was very little other explanation for it.

"I'll text Addie and let her know I'm coming over with Ting."

When we got home, I went into the parlor, where Ting was happily dancing and wrestling with the Pixie Sisters. Cyllene fluttered above their hub-bub ensuring that no one was getting hurt.

I took Ting by the hand and told her we were going to visit her Aunt

Adelaide. Addie was not really her Aunt, of course, and neither was Barbie, but they were all like family to me, so we had always referred to them as aunt around Ting. Ting jumped up, took my hand, and started pulling me to the front door.

"Sweetie, I think we will take the backway this time," I said, hoping that we would not run into any Purdry Dragons along the way. Addie had texted me back to come to the greenhouse in her backyard, where she was working.

On our way out through the kitchen door, I gathered up the twinnings and put them back in my satchel and took it with us.

When we got to her greenhouse, we found her four familiars, Skywalker, Kylo Ren, Princess Leia, and Chewie all standing watch in their respective corners, with Adelaide in the center standing over her worktable.

"So, Teeny, let me see what you have here." she said, not even looking up from whatever spell she was in the midst of concocting, but scooting over some mixing bowls to make room for the bag of tricks we brought her.

I explained to her quickly how we had determined that each of these items were not just copies, but exact replicas and according to the witch sisters, right down to the DNA. Addie nodded, telling me that the sisters, who were residing right down the street from her, had already stopped by and told her of this mystery.

Ting went over to take a closer look at Princess Leia, the dragon familiar, and began to hop up and down saying, "Pudry Dwagon."

"Ting! Don't even think about it! Come over here!" I ordered her.

She turned around to head back then pointed to the back of the room and said again, "Pudry Dwagon."

Both Addie and I looked up to see Rune, the all too handsome hunk of a Viking dragon warrior, the focus of Ting's announcement.

Now Addie was the one to say, "Ting! Don't even think about it!"

We all laughed as I took Ting's hand and brought her over to the table.

"She has a remarkable ability. There's a chance this could be very important to us and to our plans. If anything, it would be helpful to be able to reproduce things since we won't exactly be able to order anything online." Addie continued in a more serious tone, "We will definitely have to inform the Court, but I'd like to bring this to the coven first. May I take these things with me?"

"Of course, Adelaide!" and with that we left the future of Havenwood Falls in her hands.

As Ting and I walked back to my townhome, this time taking the more expedient path, since I decided I shouldn't be so worried about Ting wanting to twin any Pudry Dwagons, we caught the most stunning sunset imaginable. A vibrant mixture of violet, pink, turquoise, orange, red, and yellow, so much like the spectrum that had flashed into Ting's eyes each time she saw a Pudry Dwagon.

Ting pointed to Miles Mountain and sang Pudry Dwagon, and sure enough, along that skyline was a striation of clouds that appeared as the image of a dragon. I prayed to the goddesses that this was a good sign for the fate of Havenwood Falls, as well as for my little family.

A TALE OF TWO CLUBHOUSES

E.J. FECHENDA

COUNTRY CLUB

*A*s I smooth the sleeveless red satin dress and study my reflection, I take a moment to peep on my fiancé who is finishing getting dressed behind me. He's not facing me, yet even his profile makes my knees weak. Ryker's long blond mane is tamed, pulled back into a man bun. His jawline is strong and coated with stubble. At first glance, he looks like a relaxed CEO with the crisp white button-down shirt that's tucked into black dress pants, but then I observe the other details, making his look uniquely his. The sleeves are rolled up, revealing his muscular, tattooed forearms, and his wallet with biker chain is in place. I know he'll put on his black leather boots before we leave. They've become a fixture by the front door ever since he moved in with me.

His attire is a compromise for the first part of tonight, when he and several of his MC brothers will be integrating with the Havenwood Falls elite at the country club. My grandmother, one of the coven leaders and member of the Court of the Sun and the Moon, insisted upon hosting our engagement party at the Creekwood Estates Country Club, which means Ryker and his brothers will be leaving their cuts behind for the first part of the evening. When we move on to the after-party at the MC's clubhouse, the cuts will be back on and the fancy clothes off. And I mean *off*, as nudity at an MC party is a given. In fact, I think it might be a requirement.

Ryker looks over and catches me spying on him, meeting my gaze in the mirror. He flashes a devastating, panty-melting grin right before he crosses our bedroom toward me, stalking me like the lion that he is. His golden eyes trace my body from head to toe, and he lets out a rumble of a purr in approval.

"Oh, no," I say, backing away from him. "Save it for later, lion king. If we're late and I show up with sex hair, I'll never hear the end of it from my grandmother." Not to mention my parents, and my sister Taylor will never let me live it down.

Ryker backs me up against the wall and brushes my long, dark hair to the side, exposing my neck. He trails his nose from the soft skin behind my ear to my shoulder, inhaling deeply and leaving a trail of goosebumps in his wake. His chest rumbles, the thin material of my dress a non-existent barrier to the vibration that sets my body on fire. I place my hands on his shoulders in an attempt to move him back, but instead I curl them around his neck and pull him in for a kiss. Oh, my goddess, he renders me helpless, and I turn into a puddle of hormonal goo in an instant. Ryker takes over the kiss, dominating my mouth will little nips and a thrust of his tongue. All of my protests and reasons for not doing this fly out the window. It's our engagement party, and we can show up whenever we want, right?

We arrive fifteen minutes late, which isn't terrible. We're not the only ones late either, as there are three cars in front of my Mini Cooper waiting for valet. I glance over at Ryker and can't help but giggle. He always looks ridiculous behind the wheel of my car. He basically has to become a contortionist to fit his six-foot-five, muscular frame inside. Normally we'd take his Harley or his Bronco, but I didn't want to risk injury climbing in, out, on, or off in my four-inch stilettos.

"Don't start, Country Club. We could have taken the Bronco, and I'd have carried you everywhere."

"Yeah, and flash the guests my goods?" I smooth down the short skirt of my dress over my thighs. Just the suggestion of my naughty bits being on display for others triggers Ryker's possessiveness, and he growls, placing a giant hand on my thigh.

"Mine," he says with another growl. The claim never gets old and sends a wave of arousal through my body. I'm half tempted to have him haul me off to a shadowy corner of the golf course and have my way with him again. His nostrils flare, and I know he's sensing my need. At this rate, we're never making it to the party.

"Yes, babe, I am yours, but we can't." The last part comes out with more of a whine than I intend. I lift his hand from my leg and place it back on the steering wheel in time for him to pull up. Before he can protest, my door is being opened by the valet. I step out and wait for Ryker.

He unfolds his giant body from the Mini, and the valet attendant takes a step back, staring up and up with his mouth hanging open when Ryker stands at his full height. Ryker grins at me as he tucks the paper ticket stub in his pocket. I shake my head at his amusement. He loves that his very presence intimidates people. My big, bad sexy lion shifter biker. Not only is he Ryker, my hot as hell fiancé, but he's Crusher, an enforcer for the SIN MC, and damn good at it, too.

Ryker reaches for my hand, lacing our fingers together, and we walk to the main entrance of the country club. The sun is beginning to set, making the stone walls glow rose gold in the fading sunlight.

Orion, Ryker's younger brother, is waiting for us inside. He's leaning against the wooden concierge desk, wearing an almost identical outfit as his brother, except his shirt is black. His hair is a shade lighter than Ryker's and long, but not long enough to pull back. The waves are wild and untamed, much like Orion. He smirks when he sees us, causing his dimples to appear.

"About time you showed up." His nostrils flare when he detects the reason why we're late. It's hard to keep secrets from shifters. They literally smell everything. I feel my cheeks heat with embarrassment but shake it off. I might as well get used to it since this is my life now. "Really, bro? You couldn't keep it in your pants until later?" he teases, and Ryker cuffs him on the back of his head.

"Look at my woman. Do you blame me?"

Orion scans the red dress that hugs my curves and lets out a low whistle. "Nope. Looking good there, 'Low. There's still time to upgrade to the better Pride brother." He winks.

Of course, this causes another possessive growl to rumble deep in Ryker's chest.

"Stop riling your brother up." I smack my hand holding my clutch against Orion's chest. He deftly bounces away with a laugh before I can smack him a second time.

"Harlow!" My sister's voice echoes off the high ceilings, and I turn in her direction to see her rushing at me from the dining room, which is reserved for the engagement party. Her dark hair is pulled up into an elegant twist, and she's wearing a gorgeous emerald green dress that hugs her curves. "Thank goddess you're here. Grandmother is driving me crazy. Didn't you get my texts?"

"What texts?" I pull my phone out of the clutch to see I have over six missed texts and two missed calls. "I didn't hear my phone."

Taylor takes one look at my hair and the dewy after sex glow coating my skin and rolls her eyes. "Clearly, you were distracted."

Orion throws an arm across Taylor's shoulders and starts guiding her back toward the dining room. She shrugs off his arm and nails him with a glare. "Knock it off, pussy cat, or my boyfriend will neuter you with a spell."

This causes Orion to jerk away and cup his junk. I can't help but snicker. Clay is a powerful witch, like me and Taylor, and he's also madly in love with my sister. Orion just can't help himself. I swear sometimes he's part trickster demon. One of the country club members coming out of the restroom turns her nose up in disdain at Orion's antics. His personality is such a stark contrast from when we first met. I've seen Orion void of life and haunted by darkness, a darkness I helped rescue him from. I much prefer this lighter version.

The doors to the wide entrance are propped open, and we enter the dining room as a group. The usual sounds of a party greet us, the buzz of multiple conversations, the clink of glassware, and soft jazz playing in the background, piped in from the sound system. I pause for a moment, Ryker at my side, as I take in the room. Like a middle school dance, there's a clear divide. Not between boys and girls, but on one side, surrounding the bar, are several members of the SIN MC and several of my friends. On the other side, the clusters of high-top tables are being used by my family's acquaintances. The middle of the room is jarringly empty.

My family, the Augustines, is one of our town's founding families. If I had been born during the era of debutantes, then most assuredly, my sister and I would have been part of the socialite scene. I certainly wouldn't be permitted to marry a biker who is basically an orphan. My grandmother did make a shady attempt at an arranged marriage with my friend Curtis, and that was as well received as using magic in front of humans.

Speaking of Curtis, I spy him by the bar with his arm around his boyfriend's waist. They're chatting with our friend Shayna, one of the few humans in the room. Shayna has her eye on one of the bikers, hungrily staring at Oscar Vega's ass. She's always been a thirsty girl.

As I scan the room again and look at everyone in attendance, a pang of sadness tugs at my heart. Our town is on the cusp of a pivotal change. We're not safe anymore, and drastic measures are being put in place to protect the haven my family and the other Old Families established over two hundred years ago. We're basically going to seal the town off into its own pocket realm. The lockdown is looming, and our town will never be the same. Some of these people might decide to leave, and while they're here celebrating our engagement, they won't be here for the wedding.

Once the humans are told about their supernatural neighbors and are given the choice to stay or leave and never return, will Shayna decide to go? She's one of my bridesmaids and one of my closest friends, except she has no idea I'm a witch. Will our friendship survive once she knows the big secret I've been keeping from her?

At the other end of the bar, George Davis, the manager of Coffee Haven, and his wife Amanda, who is a kindergarten teacher, are enjoying glasses of wine. They're humans and have a young son to consider. Will they decide to leave too?

I watch as Taylor meets up with her boyfriend, Clay. He's not from around here, his family is in Maine, but I already know he's decided to stay. He'll finish up his last year at the Sun & Moon Academy and graduate with my sister. They've already made plans to rent a place in town together after graduation. Paisley and her boyfriend, Timber, laugh at something Clay says as he points at their friends, Fin and Joe, who are wrapped up in a heated kiss. I chuckle when I see the young couple as they are usually caught up in each other.

Movement out of the corner of my eye captures my attention, and Ryker squeezes my hand. I turn to see my grandmother, Mathilde Augustine, heading toward us. Her long skirt covers her feet, giving the appearance that she is gliding across the floor. My parents aren't too far behind her, hopefully to run interference. I love my grandmother, I really do, but her role in the community often forces her to put the town first, before family, so we aren't seen as receiving favoritism.

"Did you get lost on the way here, dear?" she whispers in my ear when we hug.

"Sorry, grandmother." I don't bother to give her an excuse. It's easier to just apologize and move forward.

"Ryker, Orion, you look...presentable," she says after surveying them from head to toe. "Your guests have been waiting." Without hesitation, my grandmother tugs on my arm and leads me to the table where several members of the Court have gathered.

I notice Elsmed has a glass full of bright green liquid that is emitting smoke. I think it's absinthe. Perhaps it is with a fae twist. He congratulates Ryker and me on our engagement before handing us a thick envelope. The paper is course, and our names are scrawled across the front in a slash of dark ink.

Ryker and I thank him, and Lawrence Mills, the grouchy dragon shifter and patriarch of his clan, begrudgingly congratulates us next, but he surprises me when he hands me a small, wrapped box.

"The saying is something old, something new, something borrowed, something blue, correct?" I nod, unsure where this is going. "Well, open it," he orders gruffly.

I glance up at Ryker, and he shrugs. I hand him my clutch and the envelope from Elsmed, so I can unwrap the present. Once I peel away the paper, I pull the lid off and gasp. Nestled on a bed of black velvet is a narrow, white gold cuff with three diamonds inlaid at the top. The cuff is engraved with a filigree design. It's an antique, that much I can tell. The gift itself is beautiful, but the fact that Lawrence is giving away a piece of his treasure, something dragon shifters are dangerously protective of, renders me speechless.

"That's something old," he says. "From one of the survivors of the Titanic. It brought them good luck."

"Thank you," I say sincerely. The thoughtfulness of the gift makes me soften toward the old man. Whether it's the impending lockdown and the potential consequences, or perhaps his growing family has changed him, but this is a kinder, more sentimental version than the one I'm used to. I glance over to the bar where Lawrence's daughter, Jetta, and her mate Conrad are sitting, enjoying a night out free of their twin babies. Willow and Chase are chatting with them. Probably swapping diaper changing horror stories. I don't plan on joining the parenting club anytime soon. Survive the lockdown first, get married second.

My grandmother stays at the table to talk with the elders, so Ryker and I head across the room to the bar.

"Crusher!" Kai shouts out in greeting when he sees us approach. The vampire is a fully patched SIN brother now, after he and Orion prospected together. A chorus of cheers follows Kai's greeting, and Monte, another SIN brother, immediately barks out an order for tequila shots.

"Girl, it's going to be a long night!" Reyna says and pulls me next to her and Shayna, where shot glasses are already lined up. Reyna and I have become friends since our men are in the MC together, and being that she's a kelpie unicorn, she finds the Unicorn Farts coffee drink we serve at Coffee Haven hilarious. Ever since I asked these two to be my bridesmaids, they've been hanging out more, and I hope their growing friendship will give Shayna another reason to stay in Havenwood Falls once she finds out about the lockdown and is given the ultimatum. Once again, the guilt at keeping the secret eats at me, and I grab a shot glass.

"Oh, you're brave!" Sherry says when she joins us. Her mate, Rusty, is right behind her, fist-bumping Ryker. "I rarely have anything stronger than the dark roast at Coffee Haven."

"Sherry, how goes the family life?" I smile when my friend's face lights up at the question. She and Rusty have recently taken in a pre-teen witch.

"We had a rocky beginning, but it's been amazing since then. Thank you for your help with all of my witch questions."

"Of course, anytime."

I notice my grandmother making her way through the crowd and heading in my direction. I quickly slam another shot back.

"I have to go mingle, but I'll be back," I tell the girls and snag Ryker's hand, pulling him away from the bar. "Let's get this over with, big guy."

We head off my grandmother before she reaches the bar. She takes us around the room, and we say hello to the guests, who are more her friends than ours. I stare longingly at the crowd around the bar, which is growing increasingly more boisterous as the night wears on, much to my grandmother's annoyance.

"Mom, leave Harlow and Ryker be. This is their party after all." My dad comes in to rescue us about an hour after we were hijacked. "Come on, have you seen Gallad and Macy, yet?" he asks, leading us away from my scowling grandmother. My cousin, Gallad, and his fiancé, Macy, are standing at a high-top table eating some hors d'oerves. When I see the bacon-wrapped scallops, my stomach growls, and so does Ryker's.

"Come on. You guys relax. I'll have one of the servers swing by with food and drinks."

I smile gratefully ay my dad. He's one of the managers at the country club, and he quickly falls into his role, sending one of the servers off to the kitchen. I pull Macy into a hug. She and Gallad have been engaged a lot longer than I have and haven't even set a date yet. I envy them and have thought about eloping to Las Vegas just to avoid dealing with the stress.

"Hey, cousin, how are you holding up? Is grandmother driving you crazy yet?" Gallad asks with a teasing tone.

"When is she not?" I fire back, and he laughs.

I honestly feel bad for Gallad, as he's been working closely with our grandmother in preparation for when she steps down from the coven. He'll be taking over her role one of these days. It's nice to hear him laugh as I know he is balancing a lot. I'm sure their wedding is far from his thoughts. Willow confided in me earlier, after seeing my cousin at Coffee Haven this morning, that the anxiety Gallad was emitting had her worried. If he and Macy had to plan a wedding on top of everything else, it would be too much.

Grandmother Mathilde has been in her controlling matriarchal glory with two of her grandchildren getting married. At least Gallad is marrying Macy, who is a Blackstone, and a member of one of the founding families. His match was met with much more approval and favoritism than mine, despite the fact that the Blackstones are witch hunters and our family are witches. Outside of our town, such a coupling would be a disaster and forbidden.

"Are you guys ready for your last year of school?" I ask Macy, stealing one of the scallops off of her plate and popping it in my mouth. "You look amazing, by the way." I admire her vintage dress. It's a deep blue and straight out of the fifties with a flattering scooped neckline. Her white-blonde hair is pulled up in a messy bun.

"Thanks!" She smooths the skirt of her dress, and the motion causes her engagement ring to glint in the soft light. "I grabbed this at Callie's Consignments. As far as SMA goes, I just want to graduate already. It doesn't seem appropriate to be going to school when there are much bigger concerns we should be focused on. I feel selfish and guilty in a way."

"You're not alone as I feel the same way. Who knows what it will be like after the lockdown? Perhaps we'll end up in a bunker far underground somewhere, just existing and not worrying about getting married. Makes this engagement party seem kind of ostentatious and pointless in the grand scheme of things."

"Whoa, hey, easy there, Debbie Downer," Gallad says, placing a comforting hand on my shoulder. "You went a little dark there for a moment." He smiles, but it doesn't reach his green eyes. I'm not an empath like Willow, but I can tell he's trying to force positivity.

"You okay, Country Club?" Ryker asks, pulling me against him, so my back is flush with his chest. I let out a deep exhale and melt into him when he wraps an arm around my waist.

"Yeah," I say breathily. "I am now. Sorry, sometimes the reality of our short timeline just kind of hits me, and I think of all the things that could go wrong. It's a lot."

"I know. We'll get through this together. You and me are just getting started, and we're forever, baby." Ryker nuzzles my neck, scenting me.

Gallad pulls Macy into his arms and drops a kiss on her cheek. Macy leans into his touch like she's starved for his attention. "There will be changes. Some people are leaving, and I'm sure more will decide to leave town. Those of us that choose to stay? We'll all get through this. We have so many powerful beings in our town that our chances of successfully evading Hermod are extremely high," Gallad says with a confidence that once again seems forced. Forced or not, it's a confidence I wish I shared.

"See that's what concerns me. A collective of powerful beings will make us a stronger beacon for Hermod, right? Wouldn't that make us more of a target? Maybe we should all leave. Spread out and disappear into the landscape of cities and towns all over the world." I grip onto Ryker's arm that's holding me against him and tilt my head to look up at him. "Should we leave?"

It's a conversation we've had almost daily. Something will come up to trigger my anxiety. Being a member of the Luna Coven, I'm tasked with helping to create the pocket realm where Havenwood Falls will be locked away for the unforeseeable future—perhaps only a year or two but just as likely forever—or at least for my lifetime. What if we fail? What if we're making ourselves a bigger target? The weight of that responsibility is heavy more days than not.

"If you want to leave, I'll follow, you know that, but I think we should stay." His golden eyes are intense as if they're peering right into my soul. His deep voice helps to soothe my insecurities. I nod and relax my hold on his arm.

I think about what that would mean, leaving my friends and family behind. Looking over at the bar, I see Aster and her sister Reeve. They're moving back from Denver with their families. I was thrilled when they told me their plans. We had more to lose than gain if we left. "No, we'll stay. I'm just freaking out. Ignore me."

"I could never ignore you. Especially in that dress," Ryker purrs in my ear only for me to hear. "Let's move this party to the SIN clubhouse. The sooner the parties are over, the sooner I can get you out of this dress."

After seeing the last of the guests out, Ryker leaves to have the valet bring our car around, and I stay behind to wait with my parents. My mom sways in place, all the champagne having gone right to her head. I'm in a similar state. I lost count of how many drinks I had and how many toasts were made.

"What a wonderful night," my mom sighs happily and leans back against my dad, who doesn't hesitate to wrap his arms around her waist.

"You two are kind of disgustingly cute, you know that?" I say with a grin. It's true. Ever since they became empty nesters, I've noticed they've become more affectionate with each other. "I hope Ryker and I are like you when we're old and decrepit." *If we live that long*, the anxiety I've tried to bury all night whispers in my head.

"Hey, I resemble that remark," my dad says with a laugh.

"Are you heading home or braving the SIN clubhouse for the after party?" I ask them even though I know the answer will be no. While they have grown to love Ryker and Orion, they're still not a fan of the MC. My mom's face scrunches up in distaste.

"That's all you, sweetpea," my dad responds just as Ryker joins us. "You'll keep my girls safe?"

"Always," Ryker says. I hug my parents goodbye and take Ryker's hand.

"See, that party wasn't so bad. Grandmother was surprisingly chill."

He chuckles at that and shakes his head. "She still managed to stare daggers at me, but the old witch is growing on me. Who knows, she might even like me one day."

"Well, we're all going to be stuck in a pocket realm soon without access to the outside world, so we're all going to have to get used to each other."

"At least we'll still have our own place. We can lock the door and hide whenever we want," he suggests. I marvel at his optimism that everything will work out. I've experienced magic going bad and know the risks involved in creating a pocket realm. I don't say anything, though, determined to keep the night positive. We are celebrating our engagement after all.

SIN CLUBHOUSE

*R*yker pulls away from the front entrance of the country club clubhouse and navigates the quiet streets of Creekwood Estates. There are a few street lights, dimly lit along the sidewalks, but for the most part, the moon and stars provide the most light. Burger Bar is busy when we pass it, the parking lot full of mostly teenagers enjoying the last days of summer break. As we turn south at Eight Street, a few revelers are out front of Haven Saloon on the corner, smoking. We enter the industrial part of town and can hear the MC clubhouse from a block away. Heavy bass rattles the windows as we pull up and park next to a row of motorcycles. One of the prospects stands guard, which I have come to learn is a standard security measure to make sure the bikes aren't tampered with. The prospect exhales a plume of skunk scented smoke.

"Crusher," he says almost reverently and dips his head when we walk by. He holds the door open for us, and the music becomes almost deafening. Where the party at the country club was all refined, the atmosphere here is the exact opposite.

I am reminded of the first time Ryker brought me here as it was just as chaotic. The loud music, the smell of sex, sweat, smoke, and booze saturating the air, and the extreme public displays of affection. I have seen more than one club member receive a blow job from one of the club bunnies. A few of my friends, plus Taylor and her friends, who were at the earlier party are here, but for the most part, this party is for Ryker. Not quite a bachelor party, but with a similar vibe, most likely enhanced by the lingering effects of the recent full moon. We have left behind the refinement of the country club set.

The main room of the clubhouse is an open area with a long bar that stretches the length of the back wall. Neon signs for various beer and liquor brands decorate the other walls. A pool table is set up in the middle of the room, surrounded by leather sofas that look just as weathered and worn as some of the cuts the club members wear.

Kai sits on one of the sofas with Miranda straddling his lap. I spot my sister and Clay by the bar next to Paisley and Timber. They have full shot glasses lined up in front of them, and I can't help but smile. This is their last weekend before returning to campus, and they deserve to have all of the fun possible. Who knows what will happen when we create the pocket realm for Havenwood Falls and then a separate realm for the college campus? That means double the risk for shit to go wrong. Now that I think about it, doing shots is a great idea and will hopefully stifle the negativity that has taken up residence in my head. I leave Ryker to his conversation with Liam Peters, the club's president, and move through the crowded room to join my sister at the bar.

"Is this Warded Whiskey?" I ask, lifting a shot glass that's full to the brim with amber liquid to my mouth. "This is the good stuff."

"Nothing but the best for my sister. Dad sent a bottle over."

"He's a good man," Ryker says from behind me, making me jump. For being such a big guy, he can be stealthy as fuck. He reaches for another shot glass. "To us, babe." He taps his glass against mine in a mini toast, and we both toss the whiskey down our throats. It hits my stomach and warms me up from the inside out.

"We should elope," I blurt out and immediately slap my hand over my mouth. I never could handle the whiskey, and it acted more like a truth serum.

"You can't elope. Grandmother will murder you." Taylor gives me the side eye before pouring another round of shots.

"Well, Grandmother isn't the one getting married."

"Where is this coming from, Country Club?" Ryker places his hands on my hips and pulls me back against him. "We can elope. Shit, we can go to City Hall tomorrow and get married. I thought you wanted a big wedding?"

"What if things go horribly wrong on Founders Day? There are huge risks with the spell. What we're going to attempt—all the magic we're going to use—it could backfire. I want to cram a whole lot of living in now, just in case. We could go to Vegas. One last trip outside of the town's wards before we all die or are sealed away forever."

"Okay, and you're now cut off." Taylor removes the second shot of whiskey from my hand.

"Yeah, way to kill the mood, 'Low," Curtis says, appearing next to my sister. He passes my shot of whiskey to his boyfriend, Seamus.

"Hey!" I try to grab it back, but Ryker distracts me by kissing my neck. He's an expert at distractions.

"If we go to Vegas, Seamus can try his luck at the slots." Seamus is part leprechaun and has the nickname "Lucky Day" for a reason.

"No. Enough of this eloping talk. You're getting married here." Taylor pours us all another round.

"Awww man, so we're not going to Vegas?" Orion pouts before draining a shot glass. "That would have been epic!" Where did he come from? He had been playing pool when we arrived. Perhaps Taylor is right, and I should be cut off as I clearly can't keep up with my surroundings.

"Where's Gallad and Macy? We could have a double wedding in Vegas. I'll portal us there right now." At the mention of creating a portal, I notice Taylor grimace, and she shares a look with Fin, who is leaning back against Joe. He has his arms wrapped around Fin's waist, much like how Ryker is holding me. Our sweet possessive shifters are so tactile. I peer around the clubhouse and can't find my cousin or his fiancé. That's when I remember they were heading home after the party at the country club.

"Yes! So, we *are* going?" Orion pumps his fist in the air.

"Where are we going?" Shayna asks, joining the conversation late.

The presence of my human friend is sobering. She will suspect something is up if I mention going to Las Vegas as she knows how important a family wedding is for me. I hate that I can't tell her what is going on yet. I hate that I've had to keep my witch identity hidden from her, too. There have been too many secrets in our friendship. It isn't fair that the human residents of our town will be given less time to make arrangements. I argued this point during our last coven meeting, but the leaders, including my grandmother, weren't swayed.

Before anyone can stop me, I snag another shot of whiskey from the bar and quickly down it. The liquid courage bolsters what I've just decided to do. With a whisper of a spell and a flick of my wrist, I stop time. Everything goes silent and still. The only people who aren't frozen are me and Shayna, who is taking in the scene with wide eyes, and her mouth is gaping open like a fish out of water.

"Did someone spike my drink with acid because what the fuck is going on?" She starts to pant as if she can't take a deep breath. I'm afraid she's going to hyperventilate, so I reach out and place my hands on her shoulders.

"Shayna, look at me." I force her to focus on me and my steady breathing, not the people frozen in place around us. I only have a few minutes before the spell wears off and need her to really hear what I have to say. She takes a few deep breaths, and I feel it when the tension in her shoulders fades away. "I'm probably going to get in trouble for telling you this, but you're going to find out in a couple of weeks anyway. I'm a witch. My entire family are witches. Ryker and Orion are lion shifters. In fact, you're one of the few humans in this room."

She immediately tenses up again as she processes my truth bomb. She blinks a few times and then she swallows hard as she looks around the clubhouse. I try to see what she does. Kai, who is smiling, exposing his canines that are slightly longer than normal. Ryker and Orion who are large, muscular, and have golden manes of hair, plus a feline slant to their eyes. Paisley, with her hair that is always a different color without ever visiting a salon. Today her hair is a blend of greens and blues.

"Are you fucking with me?" she asks, meeting my eyes.

"No. I'm sorry I haven't told you sooner, but there are rules in place for those of us who are supernatural. We've had to keep our identities a secret."

"Okay…" Her dark eyebrows draw together when she frowns. "I believe you, and it actually explains a lot."

"What do you mean?"

"I work at the medical center, and I've seen some pretty bizarre things. Also, I remember that night at the bar when you tossed that guy who got handsy with me. I mean, you tossed him like he weighed ten pounds."

"I wish I could have done more," I mumble, which makes Shayna laugh.

"I thought you were a badass, but a witch? That's incredible. And you're doing this?" She waves her hand around the room at everything frozen in place.

"You're not mad that I never told you?"

Shayna shakes her head and pulls me into a hug. "Never. I know you, 'Low, and I bet your grandmother is one of the reasons why you could never tell me."

I laugh and nod. "Yeah, she's one the leaders of my coven, and she's strict about the rules."

"A coven? Bad ass!" Her expression is a mixture of awe and wonder, but that quickly changes to one of concern. "Wait, why are you telling me now? What's going on, and how much trouble are you going to be in?"

"I don't care anymore. It might not matter a month from now anyway." With the few minutes left before my spell wears off, I tell Shayna a condensed version of the impending lockdown and what it means for the future of Havenwood Falls.

"Holy shit." Shayna sinks down onto an empty bar stool next to where Orion is standing, as if the knowledge I just imparted upon her is physically, not just emotionally, heavy. She's still sitting there in shock when my spell wears off and the party resumes around her in an eruption of noise that makes her squeak like a startled mouse. Orion gives her a look, but then shrugs his shoulders. No one is aware that I stopped time except for Ryker as I had moved out of his arms.

He seeks me out in seconds, not that I moved very far from where we had been standing. He takes in Shayna's stunned silence. "You told her."

"I had to."

"I agree. It was the right thing to do. I didn't like keeping her in the dark either." Relief floods my system, and I sink against my fiancé, my mate. He wraps his arms around me and holds me close. Just being able to tell Shayna the truth has lifted a weight, and even more is lifted when Shayna tells me what I hoped to hear.

"I'm going to stay. Havenwood Falls is my home, and besides, I already committed to be in a wedding." Shayna winks and then turns to Orion.

She doesn't act weird or ask him to shift into his lion form or anything. Instead, she demands he keeps the drinks coming. And just like that, I feel better about the future. Everything will be okay.

"Do you still want to elope?" Ryker asks.

"Nope. We're getting married here as planned, and it's going to be the best day."

"You bet your sweet ass it will be," he growls in my ear, sending a shot of arousal straight down my spine to my panties. "Our life is going to be a series of best days, babe. You just wait and see."

REMEMBRANCE

MORGAN WYLIE

CHAPTER 1

"*A*s much as I love all of Havenwood Falls and everywhere within the magical mountain where we attend SMA...this is my favorite place to be," Macy said, lying on her stomach, reaching her hand toward the residual splashes of water escaping the rushing falls before they plummeted down into the pools at the base of the mountain. Her fingers played with the drops that landed upon her hand as her body stretched almost over the edge of the small patch of grass-covered mountain ledge. "I can see all of our town from here. I can't imagine not being able to see it whenever we want and only on school breaks."

From their vantage point, the town square and the businesses, the cemetery and the church on the outskirts, and Macy's family vineyard and inn were all visible. She took it all in and soberly committed it to memory.

"Be careful, Mace, or you'll end up one with the falls," Gallad said, attempting to lighten the mood, and tugging her waist back toward him where he sat deceptively casual, though he watched her every move. Though it was still a summer day in early August, high in the mountains the warmth of the day diminished earlier and earlier.

She turned her head back toward him with a playful look that dared him to say more, taunting him to see just how far she might lean over that dangerous edge before he would react. Not far.

He yanked her back even closer to him and tickled her mercilessly.

While she laughed uncontrollably, he playfully reprimanded her, "You asked for it."

Macy rolled over and pulled him down for a kiss, effectively and purposefully ending the tickling torture. The kiss ended all too soon in her opinion, but the sun was just setting, which was part of their plan and reason for being near the top of the falls: to watch some of the last sunsets of summer before they went back to school. Would the sun still set in their protected pocket realm? Would they experience the seasons as they did now?

The end of summer quickly approached, and so did their last year at Sun & Moon Academy College for Supernatural Guardians. The last several years had been a whirlwind of classes, activity, magical threats, training, etc. So much had changed in just the last weeks, making this year potentially the most challenging and the most intense one thus far —depending on the threat with Hermod.

"I'm not ready for summer to end yet," Macy said wistfully, looking out over the town of Havenwood Falls, "but I am excited to get back to our dorm towers and friends who will be back!"

"This summer went by way too fast," Gallad agreed. "We only have one year left of SMA though. Plus we'll be busy and focused on training. The year should go by pretty fast when you look back and realize that three years have already flown by."

"And we have so much to look forward to after graduation," Macy added with a twinkle in her eyes. They had gotten engaged the spring after they had graduated high school with no other prospects of school on the horizon, when the town opened the secret college for supernaturals from all over to train and learn how to protect their communities and ways of life. However, with the excitement of a new school and new supernaturals to meet, Macy and Gallad had mutually decided to postpone their wedding until after they graduated. What was four years to young eighteen year olds anyway? Plus they had each grown a lot as people and gained an immeasurable amount of knowledge and skills for their future.

"We do, it's true," Galled answered with a knowing smirk that heated Macy's blood and sent the butterflies in her stomach soaring. After a moment of passion-filled tension, Macy got up and sat on a nearby boulder.

"So much has changed. High school seems so long ago, doesn't it?"

she said, more somber, a sudden change in tone, staring in the direction of the public school Havenwood Falls High. "Remember when life seemed simple and easy when all we had to worry about was homework, maybe an after-school job, and if you were going to get asked to prom? Well, and you know, coming into our powers."

Gallad laughed. "I don't think we thought about the same things. I always knew you would go to prom with me."

Gallad's eyes grew distant with the memory of the short season of time when he actually wasn't sure that was true. Macy had left Havenwood Falls because she didn't think she could control her witch hunter urges, and because she was tired of being in the dark about said powers until she turned eighteen. She had only missed the beginning of their senior year, but Gallad did question if she would be able to get back to Havenwood Falls. With the memory charm beginning to take effect and her sadistic relative Dante Blackstone trying to recruit her, she nearly hadn't been able to get back to him at all. But she did; they had found a way together.

He smiled then, remembering her seeing him when she crossed the boundary back into town. "Yeah, I knew you would always find your way back to me."

"Oh, you did, did you?" she teased, but seeing that haunted look in his eyes from the time she was gone broke her heart. She never wanted to be the cause of that pain again. She sighed and contemplated. "We've gone through a lot since then. The town and her people have gone through a lot in the last five years with more to come."

"Too many to name or count—although I'm sure someone in the archive department knows for certain," he said with a chuckle. "We have weathered it all well for the most part, I think. And we will weather this new storm just as well," he added with confidence.

"I agree, but I still can't believe what we are all about to face. I mean, the entire town is at risk of destruction, and we're trying to create a world within a pocket realm. It sounds crazy, but what else is new in our world. I can't imagine what the humans will do or think when they learn the truth of our town." Macy paused. "There's nowhere else I'd rather be though. I wouldn't dream of leaving. Our supernatural Court has overseen and handled unexpected things well in the past and will continue to do so," Macy said with pride. Her mom, Lilith Blackstone, held a seat on the Court and her grandmother before her. Someday the seat would pass to her as future leader of an Old Family—one of the founding families of the town.

"Speaking of Court, I have potential news," Gallad began, his eyes filled with withheld anticipation. Then he stood and paced in the small space next to Macy's boulder but careful not to get too close to the edge, the roar of the rushing water his only competition to be heard. "Nothing is official and it's not to be shared yet, but Grandma spoke with me about her seat. She plans to step down in the near future. With all the new changes coming, she feels it's time, and my dad is next in line. However, he has been dealing with some health issues and is not sure he wants it. Truth be told, he's never really wanted it as long as I can remember. It seems like a lot with everything going on, but it's still a ways out..."

Macy sat forward. "Spit it out, Gallad. What are you saying?"

He stopped and gazed into Macy's awaiting face. "Grandmother Mathilde is offering her seat to me. It's early. I don't know if I'm ready or if the Court will see it as the right time. But she's offered it to me." Gallad seemed uncharacteristically nervous. Nervous about the position? Nervous about telling her?

Macy was quiet for a moment then lunged into his arms. "That's amazing! We knew it would come someday, just not this early. Of course, the Court will want you—you're a badass asset to the future of this town! I'm happy for you, Gallad."

He kissed her fast but hard on the lips, leaving her dizzy when he pulled away. "Your support means everything, Macy. I wasn't sure how you would feel about it since we had talked about it one day being us both taking our families' seats closer to the same time. Probably a much later time, but time doesn't seem to wait for us."

"Wait," Macy perked up with a thought. "What about SMA? How can you do both: learning Court responsibilities and finish school?" Macy's eyes went wide, thinking he might choose to leave school early.

"I think that's a little premature as it's not happening yet, but Grandma said she would stay on until I graduate then we'd go from there. Plus there's too much happening right now, and she needs to stay in her position. She's not in a hurry but wanted me to begin thinking more seriously about my responsibilities with the family and the coven as well," he added.

"That makes sense," Macy said casually even though internally she felt a huge relief that he would not be leaving school. "It will be strange to go to school and not be able to come into town whenever we want but have to wait for holiday breaks. I guess that's pretty common for students at college, right?"

"It will go fast, Mace, don't worry. It will be over before you know it, I'm sure of it," he said optimistically with a wink. Wound up, Gallad continued to pace in thought.

After a moment, Macy had another question, one she'd thought of often but figured they'd have more time in the future to bring it up. Time seemed to be catching up to them.

"Gallad?"

"Hmm," he replied absently.

"I was curious about our names."

He stopped and looked at her with a puzzled expression. "What do you mean?"

"Our names. Our last names. We each are in line for our family places on the Court: the Augustine and Blackstone seats. We are getting married someday," she stated plainly so not to get stressed out by the mere thought. "In my family, traditionally the non-Blackstone spouse took our name. And as a seat-holder we bear the family name. You are an Augustine and expected to be one; also with family history of spouses taking the Augustine name, such as in the case of your Grandma Mathilde's husband taking her married name. Would we each keep our last names? Would we hyphenate one or the other? I know it seems small, but I can't help but wonder what we might do. Our names are part of not only our future but also our identities. Have you even thought about this detail?"

"No, I hadn't thought of it. I assumed you would just take my name and use Blackstone for court business, but now that I've said that out loud, it sounds selfish and presumptive of me," he admitted sheepishly. He shrugged then offered, "We could each keep our individual last names, I guess."

"How would anyone know we were married then? Hasn't anyone had to deal with this before that we could ask?" Macy's tone rose in pitch, laced with a hint of panic. She stood from her boulder and tried to pace as well, but the lack of space where they stood by the falls prohibited it.

"We shouldn't let this little thing get in the way of the important things going on in our town right now, Macy. We can talk more about it as the time gets closer," Gallad said softly.

Macy looked him in the eyes and nodded. "You're right. We can talk about it later. Something such as our names and our identities means nothing," she said sarcastically and began to walk back along the path down the mountain.

"Macy, that's not what I meant and you know it. I think the stress of the potential changes is adding weight to this. We have time to figure it out." He reached for her hand, which she gave, but the building moisture in her eyes suggested she wanted to be alone.

She inhaled slowly, adding calm to her demeanor. "You're right. I don't do well with big changes that I don't know how to process the unknowns. I just need a little time, Gallad. I have a family meeting about the changes affecting our businesses tomorrow, but then let's go out. And don't forget about Harlow and Ryker's engagement party on the thirteenth. It's good to still have fun and celebrate important milestones even in the midst of all the uncertainties."

"Sure, Mace, let's do that," Gallad said, eyeing her as they continued to walk back into town, releasing her when they passed the road to her family home.

"Goodnight, Gallad. Love you," Macy said with a small wave.

CHAPTER 2

*T*he next day, Macy strolled down Blackstone Road from her parents' home in Havenwood Heights. She loved everything about Havenwood Falls in all seasons, but with all the changes coming, Macy sighed with weighted nostalgia—the kind when the future state of everything becomes uncertain. Macy breathed deeply, inhaling the crisp morning air of fall that arrived early in the mountains, the scents of pine, flowers, and grapes tickling her nose. The distant sound of the rushing water cascading down Mount Alexa was a soothing balm to her ears.

Her entire family, immediate and extended, were to meet at NamaStays Inn—also the original home ancestors Marie and Judson Blackstone built when they arrived in Havenwood Falls in 1854. They intended to see how everyone felt with the upcoming changes to their world. Being one of the founding families and with her mom, Lilith, on the Court of the Sun and the Moon, her family had been informed early of what was coming to their little town. Macy had had a little more time to process everything since the town meeting with all the supernatural residents, but not much, and she still struggled with the thought of things changing too much around town.

Still, the human population hadn't been told yet, and they needed to stay very hush-hush about it all so as not to induce a mass panic amongst the town. But it was serious, and she wondered who would stay and who would go. Thankfully, she didn't need to worry about any of her family leaving, since they were all members in one way or another to the supernatural world and had deep ties to Havenwood Falls. They would all stay, no question.

Arriving at the inn located next to the Stone Falls Winery and vineyard, she absorbed everything with pride. The rows and rows of grapes next to the rented bungalow cabins, the winery, and Soothing Sips tasting room in the town square, and most recently, her brothers' venture with their microbrew business—her family had built everything. She loved being a Blackstone.

The thought gave her pause as she thought of her conversation with Gallad. He had to feel the same way about his family, the Augustines. They, too, were an Old Family with deep roots, and she knew he held a lot of pride at being connected so strongly with them. She couldn't take that away from him no more than he would from her. She knew that. Perhaps she overreacted…a bit.

Pulling her platinum blonde hair up in a bun on the top of her head, she lunged up the few steps to the wraparound porch of NamaStays Inn and let herself inside.

"Welcome, Macy, to the *End of Times* family meeting," Brock said with a loud and menacing voice as if he was an announcer for a haunted house. He even added a creepy "Mwuah-ha-ha" at the end. Brice snickered next to him, but then flung an arm into Brock's stomach after seeing the serious and not amused look on their mother's and grandmother's faces.

"Wow, it even got a name." Macy chuckled. Though after seeing the melancholy looks on her mother's and grandmother's faces, she, too, quieted herself. She hung her jacket in the closet then took a seat in the main area, looking around at each face she loved so much: her immediate family, Grandma Eva, Aunt Letti and Uncle Tranner, Brock's new girlfriend Chalise, Hollis and Ryne, and Sunny. "Am I the last one here?"

"I think so, honey," her dad, Reggie said. "Now that we are all here, let's chat about the most recent news from the Court meeting. We can keep it casual, but we want to know how you all are first, then let's go through how it could impact our businesses—especially the tourism side —and way of life."

"You want to know how we feel about the end of the town?" Brice asked with sarcasm but also a hint of anger.

"Yes."

"Brice!" Macy said with shock.

"What? It could be the end. Didn't they say it could backfire and obliterate the town?" he retorted. Sunny, next to him, reached over and grabbed his hand.

"I don't think it will come to that, Brice," Lilith stated, but the worry etched in her eyes said she was worried. "The covens are doing everything they can to ensure the spell will work properly to keep us all safe."

A moment of heavy silence fell before Brock brought up business. "I think we are all still processing things personally. Maybe it would be better to start with business questions."

Reggie nodded for Brock to proceed. Even though Lilith was the matriarch of the family, Reggie ran most of the day-to-day business dealings.

"If the town is closed to anyone coming or going after Founders Day... how does our business even work? We are founded on tourism with the inn and the bungalows. The tasting room and the winery can service the town still but to what extent?" Brock continued.

"Although with the town not able to get out, alcohol sales might shoot through the roof!" Brice shouted with the revelation then laughed.

"Nice, little bro," Macy chided and smacked his arm, to which he pretended to recoil in pain.

"But seriously, we won't be able to do online sales anymore. That part of our business for both wine and micros was just beginning to pick up," Brock stated.

"If everyone is so certain this new boundary is temporary, Brock and I could set up a base in Durango and service the towns outside of Havenwood Falls then come back when it's all over," Brice suggested, somewhat serious.

Macy shot a look at him. "You've already contemplated that, haven't you? The memory wards would take effect immediately. Didn't you hear that part? You might not remember us even if we came to get you later. We don't even know if it would wear off. Temporary hasn't been defined. It could be a year or a decade or longer!"

"Macy, it was just a suggestion," Brice said with a soft tone. "Plus, you'll be in the mountain at school most of the year anyway. You won't be able to come and go as you please anymore."

She stood, suddenly unable to breathe evenly in the small space. "I didn't think anyone would actually consider leaving. I thought everyone would be here when I came back. Plus I'd still remember you!"

Macy stormed out of the inn, gasping for much needed air.

CHAPTER 3

*G*allad stood at the entrance to the same portal he had entered on numerous occasions for the last several years. However, this time instead of a large group of students anticipating a new year, he was alone in the dark. He could have turned on the lights, but with the large windows throughout the school, enough light spilled in from the bright full moon outside. Plus he didn't want to draw unnecessary attention to his purpose. Hidden within one of the large classrooms of the private high school, Sun and Moon Academy, several gothic arches contained what appeared to be mirrors. These were the portals—when officially opened—that would enter him into the secret campus within the mountain, home to the Sun & Moon Academy College of Supernatural Guardians, also known as Halvard Campus. However, the portal would not open to students for another week.

Gallad pinched his forehead as he thought of his options. Sunny Blackstone had called him with something she had seen. She was young, but the things she saw were accurate. Even though Sunny was a witch hunter, they had learned she was also part seer. Sunny's vision was clear: he was to find a book that held some kind of information they would need for what was coming. He wasn't clear on what the information might be or whether it would actually be helpful.

Gallad had already taken most of the day and searched the town library, the private high school library, and even the secret stacks beneath the original library within the Tomb of The Order of Castors—which he had access to as an alum member of the secret society. Thankfully inside the same building, this was his last attempt. He hadn't found anything similar to what Sunny had seen in her vision from that morning thus far. He'd had a feeling the other options were wrong, but he wanted to rule them out first. Which was what led him to where he stood presently, debating if what the young seer/witch hunter saw was worth pursuing the trouble he was about to stir up. Something worked at the back of his skull, his own magic responding to the power of the moon, and a sense of rightness flowed through him. His town and all the people he loved was worth it. He picked up his phone and dialed the one person who he had complete faith would believe what he was about to say without question and as a High Priestess of the Luna Coven would give him guidance.

"Grandma, it's Gallad. Sunny Blackstone had a vision. I want to run it by you," he said.

"I'm listening," Mathilde Augustine replied, ready for business.

"In her vision, she saw a cavernous library. It was dark and shadowy, filled with strange noises and glowing orbs inside an endless dark tower. In it she saw me receive an ancient looking tome that held within it explosive secrets... Well, actually she used the words 'magical booms' but it was given with a grave tone filled with weight and urgency. I've been in all the town libraries—including your own just to be certain—and haven't found such a book or a library that fits the description she gave," he explained.

"Except one." His grandma had quickly caught on.

"Except one. Since I'm not living on campus for the summer, the portal to Halvard Campus won't open for me until next week. Is there any way to get permission for early access? Should I go ahead and call Addie? She could come with me, if so. This is important for Havenwood Falls, Grandma, I feel it in my soul," Gallad pleaded, the truth of his words growing stronger with each passing second.

The line was silent longer than a heartbeat.

"I'll call you right back. Stay where you are. I'll call Addie so she knows it is coven sanctioned."

Mathilde hung up the phone. Gallad stood still as his heart pounded within his chest, knowing time grew short but also that this was the answer. He could feel it. The extra power of the full moon reverberated through his veins; not to mention the blood of some of the most powerful witches he knew ran through him. He let the knowledge of that ground him and give him peace. He would find what he was meant to find. His phone rang, startling him out of his communion with the moon.

"Grandmother, did you find anything out?" Gallad asked quickly, staring at where the portal would open.

"Listen carefully, Gallad. You will have only a short window of time. The portal can be temporarily opened for you, but only for one hour's time. Be in and out quickly. If you do not get out in time, the portal will close and you will be stuck in there until it reopens next week. Addie will be there to activate your tattoo so you can enter the portal. Tread carefully."

"Thank you, Grandma. I know some of the professors and summer students as well as the caretakers will be inside. I'll stay focused."

"There are always mysterious things and beings hidden in places of magic. Be on guard and do not linger on anything not your mission. Do you have my ring I lent you this morning?"

Gallad looked down at his hand, which held his grandmother's opal moon ring. It had been in her family for generations. "I do."

"Absorb as much of the moon's power within it before you enter the tunnel into the library. You may need the extra light in the depths of the library's dark spaces."

"I will. And thank you for believing in me, in what Sunny saw," Gallad said, filled with emotion.

"We need all the information we can get right now. Let me know when you're back in Havenwood Falls. Remember, one hour. And watch out for rogue books," Mathilde said with a chuckle then hung up.

Gallad inhaled slowly, and when he looked back toward the portal his cousin Addie Beaumont was already approaching it to meet him.

They spoke briefly to each other while Addie enchanted the school tattoo on his wrist. Once she was finished, she magically produced a small hourglass in her palm. "You have one hour. Be quick, cuz. And good luck. Meet you back here in an hour."

Magic swirled in colorful streaks within one of the frames, creating the portal. Gallad strode through the portal, and Addie followed him, saying she had her own work to do on campus. They walked down the path and across the bridge in silence, both of them weighed down with heavy thoughts. Once they reached the courtyard, they went their own ways, Addie toward Halstein Hall where her office was and Gallad toward the library. He straightened his shoulders, then strode inside. He'd been in the creepy library before, but this time he was alone, a strong sense of foreboding dread his only companion.

At fifty-seven minutes, Gallad met Addie back at the portal on the Falls Campus side.

"I made it," he panted as he bent over with an ancient leather book cradled in his hands. Addie smiled and nodded her approval as she looked at the last falling grains of sand in the timepiece.

"I trust you found whatever you went looking for," she said, pointing at the book in his arms.

Gallad nodded. "I did. Thank you. I also think I found some creature no longer resting in the depth of the library. It may have gotten out if you need to tell anyone about that."

Addie rolled her eyes but chuckled. "Thanks for that."

He laughed but took in a deep breath and refocused. "Now I need to get this book where it belongs, for the sake of the town."

"Yes, that book should have been in the restricted library off the Court room. And somehow I missed it when I searched the Halvard Campus library. You were meant to find it. I know you'll find the information the town needs, Gallad. I have to go, but I'm sure we'll be seeing each other soon," Addie said and took off back toward her office. Gallad pulled out his phone as he stepped through the magical swirling portal just before it closed and crossed back into Havenwood Falls.

"Grandmother, I found it. I'm bringing it to you, but...if this book contains the information that I think it does, just based on the few pages I had time to look through, you'll need to call another coven meeting." Gallad hung up and swiftly strode toward his grandparents' house. The weight of the world—or at least their little part of it—literally weighed on his heart.

CHAPTER 4

*M*acy's mom, Lilith, her grandmother, Eva, and Aunt Letti found her leaning against one of the fences, staring at the vast rows of grapes within the vineyard. They didn't say anything, but simply joined her. The sun had just begun to set on another day, one day less of normal and one day closer to the biggest change their quaint town in the mountains had experienced to date. Their last family meeting had ended so emotionally a couple days before, the Blackstones had called another and waited on everyone to gather.

"I didn't take into account all the little things that would change once our town disappears from the rest of the world. I know it might be temporary, but it might not. I saw all the Augustines at the engagement party last night celebrating together, and I wondered if the Blackstones would be together when the time comes for my wedding." Tears slowly streamed down her face. "The thought that Brice and Sunny, Brock and Chalise might actually leave…it hit me hard. I know their business is important, and I wouldn't want to take that away from them, but I don't want them to leave." Macy inhaled, and her breath hitched with emotion. "I know that's selfish because I won't even be here much this year as I'll be sequestered within the mountain at SMA, but at least I know I can come back at breaks. They might not be able to come back… ever." Tears fell down Macy's face.

"Change is never easy, Macy," her mom said, placing her hand lovingly on Macy's shoulder. "We don't want them to leave either."

"When our ancestors, Marie and Judson, came to Havenwood Falls back in 1854, they left everything they knew behind them and traveled from the east coast by wagon train. They had no idea what they would face or if they would even find what they sought. But they were brave because they believed in the possibilities of a new life, of a world for them and their families to be free to be themselves and free to start over if they wished. This could be our new beginning," Grandma Eva encouraged.

"Your Uncle Tranner left his entire clan to be with me and come to Havenwood Falls when we got married," Aunt Letti chimed in. "It was a difficult change for him, but he believed in what we had built here. We are each other's home, no matter the small details or the big. He continues to remind me our love superseded any challenges and outweighed anything he had to leave behind—I don't know if I believe him, but he's still here," she added with a wink and a squeeze of Macy's wrist.

Her family was coming along her side, lending their love and support. Taking a deep breath to steady her emotions, she relished in the family bond they had, which had grown even deeper in the last several years.

"There you all are," Hollis shouted from the porch at NamaStay's Inn. She headed toward them, her black hair flowing with the wind. Instead of her usual black jeans and leather jacket, she sported gray jeans and a light-weight green sweater. Hollis being a coexisting member of Havenwood Falls instead of a rogue witch hunter out hunting witches was another testament to the sheltering benefits of the small mountain town.

Macy waved her toward them. Following Hollis came bright and bubbly Sunny and their newest addition, Chalise. Their family had grown much in the last several years. And it broke Macy's heart to think of any of them not being there any longer.

The three ladies joined them. The contrast in each couldn't have been starker. Most noticeable was their hair: Hollis with black, Chalise with bright red, and Sunny with her light blonde.

"What are you doing out here?" Chalise asked, looking closely at each of the women then scanning the rows of grapes.

"Discussing the challenge change brings," Eva answered. "When it was my turn to step down from my seat on the Court of the Sun and the

Moon, I knew it was time, but the transition from something I had grown comfortable with to the unknown of my future was challenging. But I knew the benefit that Lilith would add, and I loved her enough to give her that opportunity to grow."

Lilith watched her mother speak with a softness in her eyes. "I didn't know that was how you felt, Mom." She reached over and squeezed Eva's hand. Macy's heart filled with love watching her own family evolve even before her eyes. It struck her that one should never stop growing and evolving. And neither should she.

"You know I am not yet ready to step down from my seat, Macy. I feel my place is still there while I have something to offer, but one day it will be yours if you want it," Lilith added.

Macy nodded. "I know, Mom. Gallad's time may be coming sooner than later. We were discussing all the changes, and we seemed to come to a hitch. We both are in line for our families' seats. It seems so trivial now, but we couldn't figure out how our last names would work since both families keep their names. Do I give up Blackstone? Or could I ask him to give up Augustine?" Macy rambled more to herself at that point while the others simply let her. "But it shouldn't matter. Like you said, Aunt Letti, he is my home, and I wouldn't not be with him for any reason. The name thing doesn't matter, especially now in light of so much changing."

Brock and Brice sauntered toward them. Brice waved as they were noticed.

"We were looking for you all. It's nice having everyone around these past couple days," Brock said, reaching for Chalise's hand.

"We're reminiscing of all the changes in our history," Macy jumped in, "and brothers, I owe you an apology. Of course, I don't want you to leave town, but I also understand if you need to. I'll support you no matter what, and we'll figure it out one way or another."

Brock then looked from Brice and Sunny over to Macy with a big cheesy grin on their faces. "Well, it's a good thing we decided we need to be with family for this season, because we'll be here when you come back from breaks," Brock said, and he and Brice smothered Macy in a sibling hug.

"Unless we all die then you know…" Brice said nonchalantly, earning him smacks from multiple people around him.

"Not cool, Brice," Macy said through her tears of joy.

They remained silent for a moment, each lost in their thoughts and their gazes fixed on something beyond the beauty of the vineyard. Abruptly, Macy backed away from the fence and looked at each of them with a smile. "I think it's time for my own big change. I need to find Gallad! We barely spoke the last couple days except for at Harlow and Ryker's engagement party last night, but he was so distracted and tense, it felt forced. I got a quick peck on the cheek, then he left right after it was over. He's either been so busy with coven stuff or he's avoiding me."

"Not avoiding you, but seeking an answer," Sunny said lightly with a smile as if she knew something.

Macy swung her head in Sunny's direction, her gaze narrowed on her face. "Sunny? What do you know?"

"I saw a vision. He's been seeking a book with information for the town. All I know is there were magical booms," she said with her hands spread wide in the air as if she could see fireworks or explosions of some kind in front of her. "But he found it now, so he'll be at the school library tonight," Sunny said matter-of-factly, as if what she knew wasn't odd. And for Sunny it wasn't. She was part seer, and her visions had been accurate so far, but they were unpredictable and didn't always make sense to anyone else.

"The high school? Like Sun and Moon Academy?"

Sunny nodded.

"Then that's where I need to go." Macy paused, hesitant.

"Go!" they all shouted at her, startling her into action. Macy ran. She could've borrowed one of several of their parked cars in the lot, but instead she ran down Blackstone Road toward the turn off for the private high school, Sun and Moon Academy.

CHAPTER 5

*A*s she ran through the gates and the courtyard toward the old gothic school building, Macy couldn't help but wonder what the book was Gallad had found and how it would help Havenwood Falls. So much was happening, her head was practically spinning with it, but one thing she knew beyond a shadow of a doubt: she loved Gallad and they would weather whatever came next together. These thoughts carried her through the giant double doors, a mix of thick wood and metal grommets and handles, into the school.

She had attended Havenwood Falls High, the public high school, but knew her way around from attending extra classes on the history of Havenwood Falls and other important supernatural courses she was required to take in preparation for taking her future seat on the Court. Climbing the staircase to the two-story library, she began to experience that familiar itch at the back of her neck when witch magic was near.

Her steps slowed, and she steadied her breath, focusing her mind to control the witch hunter side of her nature. She had grown in her control much over the years since the hunter urges awakened at eighteen, but being a witch hunter, she still experienced the sensations. It was her will and decision to continue to keep it in check that assisted her in overriding that part of her. The buzz created tingles that shot down her arms like electrical currents. Judging by the strength of these sensations, she was about to walk in on a number of witches.

Her mind focused on an image of Gallad smirking at her in the way he did, the way that made her heart flutter, and she pushed the other feelings to the back of her mind. Macy inhaled slowly through her nose, centering herself, then breathed out through her mouth. She opened the door and entered the library.

Something had happened. The energy was strong but frazzled and chaotic. The witches, especially those of the Luna Coven, were present in large number. Some wore expressions of concern, others panic. She had walked in on a meeting of some kind. One thing was certain: something big was going on, more than helpful information for a boundary spell. She didn't need to be magical to feel it.

Macy was about to step out of the room and leave the witches to their business. She could find Gallad tomorrow. He needed to be there at that moment. But then she caught his eye from across the room. He looked a little pale, but confident, and when their gazes locked, his shoulders relaxed and he looked relieved to see her. Macy stood rooted in her spot, awaiting him as he made his way to her.

"I'm so glad to see you." He kissed her on the lips quickly then pulled away, and his eyes bore into hers. "What are you doing here?"

"I was coming to find you. Sunny said you'd be here, but I thought you might be alone," she said sheepishly, glancing at the others beyond them who went about their business as if they existed in their own world. "What's going on?"

"I found something. That's why I've been so distant, trying to understand what it means. It's big, Mace, and we're trying to figure out how to handle it. It's another piece to the puzzle." Gallad's words held weight, and his tone was somber. Apparently what he found hadn't been a good thing.

"Gather 'round, everyone. Let's discuss this as one so we are all on the same page," Mathilde Augustine spoke from behind a podium used for lectures.

"I should go, Gallad. Find me tomorrow," Macy whispered and began to slip out behind him. She spotted Saundra Beaumont standing with Addie, other members of the Augustine family, Roman Bishop, and many more.

"No, stay with me, Macy. I need you close," he replied and grabbed her hand and held it tight.

Mathilde glanced their direction, waiting for all eyes on her. Macy wanted to hide in a hole, but Gallad stood tall and with his expression, silently made a request of his grandmother—now acting in official capacity as a High Priestess of the Luna Coven—who nodded, giving permission for Macy to stay.

"See, you stay," Gallad whispered with a knowing smirk on his face. Macy stepped up next to him then and stood beside him. She would stay.

"Coven, two days ago with the assistance of our goddesses through the vision of a young seer, Gallad was led to an ancient tome hidden from sight until this appointed time. There is more at stake with constructing the pocket realm around the town than we originally knew. More and more information seems to continue to come to light through our oracles and seers. Information to assist us, and also to challenge us. There are big risks, which we already knew. If you choose to stay in town, everyone will be called upon to offer their magic to join the spell. Not just witches, but all who have magic to give," Mathilde exhorted. "We've been researching to find ways to best create the pocket realms for our town and for the college in order to keep everyone safe."

"What did Gallad find?" one of the witches in the back asked out of turn.

Mathilde shot him a glare for disrespecting the forum, but in light of the situation and the fear, which could be tangibly felt, she let his outburst slide. She held up the ancient, leather-bound tome.

"The book *Uncommon Mixing of Magic and Repercussions* explained several times in ancient history where magic was conducted similar to the way we are planning to do. However, because of the magnitude required for its success, the spell has the potential to backfire, causing a magical boom—as Sunny Blackstone called it—that could destroy everything. This we already knew. But according to new information, conversely it could short-circuit our magic, leaving us in the dark, effectively creating a temporary magical void in our wards. We would be vulnerable. Additionally, the magical force could do the opposite of our ultimate goal and attract Hermod immediately, leading him to us right when we're most vulnerable. We already knew that some of us may not survive the magical surge. This is but one more hurdle to overcome."

Unease and small chatter broke out around the room. Confusion stirred in the air, and Mathilde raised her hands in supplication to her people. "We knew this was not going to be easy. We knew we were attempting something uncertain. But now we have more details to help us prepare. Witches of Havenwood Falls, now is the time to ban together, not to allow dissension to grow out of fear. Please listen and help us prepare our town. This is our responsibility. We must come up with contingencies and create back-up plans to keep our people safe. That is our charge tonight. Break into groups and find our solutions!" Mathilde charged the coven with authority and confidence. She glanced back at Gallad, who gave her a supportive nod. Individually and in groups, the witches poured over open books spread across multiple tables, seeking answers once more.

Macy felt faint. Suddenly, her issues with a name change seemed even more trivial. He held her hand tightly and pulled her around the room with him as they listened in on various plans being devised, and unfortunately more questions being raised. The people were afraid, but they had a focus, and they were determined to save their town.

She squeezed Gallad's hand and brought his ear close to her face. "You have a lot going on here. I need to go, but walk me out?"

Gallad walked quietly with Macy down the stairs and out the front doors of the school into the private courtyard. It was late, and the moon was still large, though waning in the sky. Small decorative lights graced the property and designated the stone paths. "Macy, I don't know what will happen, but I know I love you, and I want to spend whatever time we have left together."

Macy smiled, her expression filled with love as tears flowed from her eyes and blurted out the thing most on her mind. "Gallad, I want to marry you. Not in the future, but now, in the place we love as we know it, where everything we know and love is just as it is. We don't know who will leave and who we'll never see again. We don't know if this magic will work or who will even survive it. We don't know if Hermod will find us," Macy rambled out in a rush. "Everything is uncertain except…I know I love you, and we'll look to the future together and face it as a team."

Macy wiped the tears off her face and impulsively got down on her knees. She gazed lovingly up at him. "Gallad, will you marry me before the end of the world comes?"

They'd already drawn out their engagement, waiting for graduation. But when time seemed to be of the essence, why wait?

He burst with emotion and fell to his knees in front of her and kissed her. "Yes, I will marry you, Macy Blackstone. Anytime. Anyplace."

CHAPTER 6

*D*ays turned into weeks as Macy and her family busily prepared for a somewhat impromptu wedding. The distraction was nice from the worries and concerns of their final "normal" days in Havenwood Falls. Gallad had been busy with coven work and preparations for the boundary spell that would be performed on Founders Day. Not to mention they had both started classes again at the end of August and had been even busier since then.

The idea of being married while in their last year of college was still surreal and something Macy couldn't quite wrap her brain around yet, but she decided to take one day at a time. Some things—most things at this point—were out of her control, and she would take them as they came. Even things such as finding a dress on such short notice. They couldn't really get anything shipped into town so quick, and Nina at Dress Perfect could custom tailor a dress, but the choices of fabric hadn't stuck out to her.

"Macy?" Aunt Letti asked. Apparently, her aunt had entered NamaStays Inn and Macy hadn't even noticed. SMA students were still able to come and go into town until Founders Day, and when Macy had time, she continued to learn her family's business as she would one day be the matriarch of the Blackstone family. One day far off in the future, she hoped.

"Sorry, got lost in my thoughts," Macy replied, sliding off the stool she had perched on behind the front desk.

"Which thoughts this time?" Letti asked with a knowing chuckle.

"The dress. I can't seem to find the right one. I know this was fast, but I still want to have the perfect dress, you know?"

"Stay here. I'll be right back," Aunt Letti said with a grin filled with conspiracy.

"What are you up to?" Macy asked, humoring her great aunt.

"Just stay there." Aunt Letti shuffled to a back room. She was only gone a minute or two when Macy heard something crash.

"Letti? You okay?"

Aunt Letti came back through the door she had disappeared behind, waving Macy off. "Yes, yes, I'm fine. Just knocked over a pile of old hat boxes. There's too much junk back there."

She cradled in her arms a long rectangular box. Macy figured it had been white at one point in time, but the box had taken on a yellowish hue.

"What is that?"

"This," Aunt Letti said as she placed the box on the front desk counter, sweeping some pens and random items to the side. "This belonged to your great great—however many greats there are— grandmother Marie Blackstone. She wore it when she and Judson got married. See if it's anything you could work with," Aunt Letti said sheepishly as she removed the lid from the box.

Macy gasped as Letti pulled the dress out. "Oh, Aunt Letti! It's practically perfect." Macy beamed as her fingers gently traced over beads and lace. "I could take it up a little here as I think I'm shorter. And maybe in a little here," she said pinching fabric at the waist and bust-line. "Are you sure it would be all right if I wore it and made a few alterations? I'm not sure about the blue color but maybe I can work with that."

"I think it would be the most fitting for you to wear it. You were young when she died, but I know she held a special connection to you, Macy Marie Blackstone—you are middle-named after her. Marie would have loved to have you wear it."

"Thank you!" Macy said, clutching the dress to her chest, tears of joy falling from her cheeks. "Can I take it home and try it on?"

"Yes, yes, go! The inn is slow right now. I've got it. Actually, I wonder if it will ever be used again, once the boundary is up and guests no longer arrive," Letti said, suddenly solemn with the realization of yet another change. She inhaled and steeled her shoulders. "Never you mind. We'll come up with something. We always do. We're Blackstones. You go try on your dress. You're running out of time before the big day." She shooed Macy out the door.

Macy placed the box in her car and drove the short way into town to pick up a couple things. She ducked into Coffee Haven to grab an iced coffee. A new tension she had never felt before rested over the town. Macy glanced around the room and waved at a couple friends she saw, but also took note of several she recognized as human watching everyone else with suspicion.

The human city council had a meeting the night before, revealing the truth of the little town they thought they knew, the town they called home. The humans learned supernatural beings with power and magic coexisted amongst them. Expressions ranged from curious to hesitant to straight up fear. Not only did they just find out they'd been living amongst magical creatures, but they had two weeks to decide if they would continue to live with them in full knowledge, or if they would leave their home and move away.

Macy thought if she were in their place, she'd feel uncertain and a little trepidation as she interacted with people, unsure if her own neighbor might be a supe and what kind they were. Could they be dangerous? Should they be concerned? Even though they had lived there for possibly years without that knowledge, suddenly everything was different.

Some people interacted as if nothing had changed, fully embracing the truth. Others seemed to be mentally connecting the dots of things they had seen or heard now that the truth was revealed. Macy wondered how different their town would look in a couple weeks.

Until then, she had her wedding to finish preparing for and homework to complete.

The day had finally arrived: September 10th, a full moon for the most powerful and magical connection with their bond—at least that was what Gallad had said. Macy didn't care what day it was, but if the witch she was about to marry cared, then so did she. A marriage union between a witch and a witch hunter was rare. Marie Blackstone had married Judson, who later had discovered he was a witch all along. There was proof it could be done. Macy and Gallad planned to be further proof love truly did overcome all things.

Macy walked down the steps from within NamaStays Inn—the original home Marie and Judson built when they sojourned to Havenwood Falls all those years ago. Adorned in Marie's dress, though altered by Macy herself, she was a vision. Her long blonde hair was done up in a high knot on her head with black and pink sparkly clips and accessories. She had bleached the fabric white and sewn thin layers of sparkling pink fabric into the skirt and train of the dress. She even left one of the layers the original blue in honor of Marie. It wasn't so traditional, but it was her. And to complete the look, she wore sparkling black converse high tops she had been saving for a special occasion such as this.

At the bottom of the steps waiting for her stood her parents with big smiles on their faces. Her dad, Reggie, held unshed tears in his eyes as he held out his hand for her. The sun was setting, and the moon in its fullness was beginning to rise. They escorted her out to the vineyard and to a path lit with little sparks of magic and floored with pink, black, and white flower petals. Their path wound through rows of grapes leading toward the mountain. The walk was lengthy, but it was time with her parents she cherished.

At intervals along the way stood another member of her family who joined the procession behind her. She could have chosen to have bridesmaids but her heart wanted her family to stand with her—with the exception of her best friend since kindergarten, Ruby Jean. She also joined the processional as they neared the clearing within the forest at the base of Mount Alexa near Bels Creek. Macy almost wished she could be one of the attendees and watch as her family entered the clearing—a sight they had to be, for certain.

But as soon as Macy saw Gallad standing at the end of the path of petals, her breath hitched. He stood dressed in an all black tuxedo, short in the front with longer tails at the back. But what pierced her heart was the expression of adoration and complete acceptance on his face. He was her home, her other half, her soulmate. She practically floated to him, her family filing into their seats as she went.

What seemed like half the town showed in attendance: the Augustines of course took up the opposite front rows from her own large family, but also friends from school old and new came. Sheriff Kasun and his family attended, Lyra and Addie Beaumont, the Bishops who were still undecided if they would stay in town, Davis George who managed Coffee Haven along with his wife—who were humans and would be leaving—smiled and waved. The Howes, Michaela Petran along with her husband Xandru, the Underwoods and Fairchilds sat off to the side along with so many more.

Macy's heart was full as she took in everything and everyone who had come to support them. They were all a part of her story in Havenwood Falls. But then her gaze got lost in the eyes of her future husband. Time stood still as she willed him to feel how much she loved him. Saundra Beaumont officiated the wedding and walked them through the traditional vows then the time came for them to add in something they had both felt to do.

"Friends and family, Macy and Gallad have something they want to present to each other, to you, and before you as their witnesses," Saundra announced then stepped back, giving them the lead.

Macy and Gallad turned toward the audience and smiled.

"We would like to do something a little different, but join with us as we do," Gallad invited. "On this day, in this time, we would like to honor our past, present, and future. We both come from founding families, families who sought to be free to be who they were meant to be, families who sought to start something new, families who crossed the divide of not only land but challenges unknown to them. Many of you come from families who did the same. Many of you benefit because of those families—what they endured, what they conquered, what they discovered about themselves and who they could be together. This is the ground they tilled and sowed," Gallad said, his hands gesturing out toward the town they had a clear view of.

Ms. Ruby Howe of Howe's Herbal Shoppe, also a local witch, stepped toward them as she had been instructed, handing each of them a handful of seeds. A young woman, Jasmine, a moon fae with an affinity to grow night blooms, stepped up next to Ms. Howe, holding pots of dirt. Jasmine had not been in town long but had become friends with both Gallad and Macy.

"With these seeds, we recognize what our ancestors have done for us, but also we symbolize our future and the growth we will continue to have because we will continue to sow into our world, we will continue to grow despite our challenges and uncertain times. This is what we have to hold onto. This is our remembrance," Macy said, as they each took the seeds and planted them into the two pots Jasmine brought up with her. When they were finished, Jasmine and Ruby Jean placed them on either side of Macy and Gallad then sat back down.

"This is a time for new beginnings now and after our world changes. It's our turn to create the new beginnings, even if it all comes to an end," Macy encouraged.

"Because that is who we are. We are creators, we are founders, we are conquerors! And we can do it together," Gallad added as the audience clapped and cheered, encouraged. He and Macy turned toward each other. The Augustine family and the Blackstone family all rose from their seats, circled around the couple, and held hands, uniting the families as one. Mathilde next to Eva, Lilith next to Ronya, Gallad's mom, and so they went, Augustines mixing in with Blackstones.

Saundra's words rang out from where she stood off to the side, "I pronounce you husband and wife. Everyone else raise a glass and toast to the couple…and to our hopeful future! And Gallad, you may kiss your bride!"

Everyone cheered and stood. Fireworks went off somewhere in the distance above them. Thanks to Jasmine's power, flowers magically burst from the seeds in the pots and rose high above them all with blooms the size of plates, reflecting the radiant white glow from the full moon. The vines and leaves joined over their heads, creating a beautiful canopy of night flowers.

With the remembrance of the past as their anchor and their unity binding their present, they would face the uncertainty of what was to come with hope and room for something new.

FESTIVITIES, FAREWELLS & FOUNDERS DAY FINALE

KRISTIE COOK

CHAPTER 1

There were two types of people when the world was about to end:

Those who hunkered down, locked in tightly at home, possibly reciting prayers and spells of protection, their stomachs knotted up to the point they would hurl, except they haven't been able to eat in days, so there was nothing there to expunge.

And then there were the rest of us who figured there were no more fucks to give. Come tomorrow, we'd either live or we'd die. Nothing more we could do about it now. But tonight...tonight we chose to *live*.

The bars had filled beyond capacity hours ago, the crowds spilling into the streets from the Dirty Knuckle near the ski resort all the way to Haven Saloon and Soothing Sips on town square to the tasting area of Stone Falls Winery to the northeast and even up the side of Mt. Alexa to Fallsview Tavern and out to Miles Mountain to Silk Nightclub in the west. Trust me—I'd been to them all just today. Havenwood Falls had become one big party, bigger than any Founders Day, Samhain, and New Year's Eve combined.

And nothing like *any*thing this town had seen in the past.

Because as of this afternoon, unless there were any last-second, panic-induced fleers tomorrow, everyone who was going to leave Havenwood Falls before lockdown had already left. Which meant everyone who was still here knew exactly who their neighbors were and *chose* to still live among us.

Fangs were out, though only for show—we had to keep some rules in place and no harming humans against their will was one.

Glamours were turned down…or, contrarily, all the way up in full-fantasy mode as some fae loved to show off.

Wolves and lions ran the streets only to shift back to human form to take another shot or do a keg stand.

Charms, enchantments, and spells flew, refilling drinks, playing tricks on drunk friends, and adding atmosphere with dancing colors and phantom music playing REM's "End of the World" on repeat. Tempest, Natalie, and some of the other SMA students were in competition for who could produce the biggest and most colorful magical fireworks over Town Square Park.

Lawrence Mills had come down from his lair in Havenwood Heights several hours ago to admonish everyone for not taking tomorrow seriously enough. It was my grandmother—Saundra Beaumont—of all people, who told him to stop being such a stuffy old man, silencing the entire outdoor party for a long drawn-out moment as Old Man Mills gaped at her. Then, to everyone's awe, he shifted. Lawrence fucking Mills shifted into a frost dragon in the middle of Main Street, right in front of Coffee Haven and Callie's Consignments. He, his family, and a couple of other dragons had been flying over town all night.

Although there was still a lot of tension threading through the air, in a weird way, everyone was also more relaxed than they'd ever been before. Being able to be their true, authentic selves without having to be vigilant about control and hide from the humans seemed to have brought everyone closer rather than tearing us apart as had been feared. It made me wonder if we should have come out to the humans a long time ago.

Of course, we'd all been bonding over this shared threat ahead of us. I wondered if we'd still be coexisting so well after being trapped together for a year or a decade or more. It hadn't been easy holding a town like ours together when everything had been a secret. What would it be like now? Would Havenwood Falls still even exist when it was safe to come out of the pocket realm? Or will we have all destroyed each other?

"Bratty Addie Beaumont!" Michaela slur-shouted from right next to me, jerking me out of my drunken stupor as she threw her arm around my shoulders and squeezed with all her vampire strength. "You are my bestest friend in the whole wide world. Djid you know that? Ever since kindy-garten!"

I laughed and took the shot she was about to spill out of her hand, tossing it back myself. The liquid burned all the way down and warmed my stomach. Though it was technically still summer until tomorrow, the chill of autumn nights in the mountains had begun weeks ago, so the liquid heat felt good.

"If tomorrow ends us all, I am sooooo thankful we'll be together," she continued, leaning into me and nearly taking us both down. She smacked a wet kiss on my cheek.

"And I thank fuck you came home five years ago," I said, wiping my cheek before planting a kiss on hers. I leaned in too hard, though, losing my balance, and this time we did fall to the ground in a heap. Michaela howled in laughter, and I joined her until we were both rolling on the sidewalk in hysterics.

Two looming figures walked up, silencing us…for a brief moment. We looked up into the male faces, each giving us a look that tried to be stern but the amused exasperation shone in their eyes, and we burst out in laughter again.

"All right, I think it's time to get you home," Xandru said, leaning over and slipping his hands around Michaela's waist to lift her to her feet. She wobbled and nearly fell again, so he swung her around onto his back.

"See you tomorrow, Bratty Addie! I lurve youuuuu," Michaela called over her shoulder as Xandru carried her down the street toward Whisper Falls Inn.

I blinked up at Rune, wondering why there were two huge neon hamburgers behind him. No, wait, just one now. How the hell did we get this far down Main Street anyway? Oh, right—burgers and fries and shakes. We'd come to Burger Bar for midnight snacks. Rune held his hands out for me, spreading his fingers wider as though asking if I was going to accept his offer of help.

"Are you going to give me a ride, too?" I asked as I grabbed his hands and let him pull me to my feet, his touch like an electric zing through my nerves.

"I believe you'll be riding me tomorrow," he said, his accent thick and such a damn turn-on. Everything about him was. I could no longer deny it. I nearly fell over again with another fit of giggles at his words, though.

Steadying me by slipping his arm around my waist, he began guiding me down the street toward the one where we both lived.

"You know, in my time, 'riding you' has a whole different meaning," I teased the Viking warrior.

"Oh, it means the same in my time," he said, his voice full of promise. I looked up at him with wide eyes to be greeted with that sexy-ass smirk. "In fact, I am certain the Vikings defined that meaning."

I swallowed, not for the first time wondering what it would be like to ride him in that way.

We'd grown...close the last couple of months. With Holly and his sisters staying in Havenwood Falls, he never considered doing anything different. He'd made himself a permanent fixture in our town and by my side. He shared ancient Asgardian and Nordic wisdom and magic for the spell, claiming he wanted to ensure this was done right for the protection of his family and the oracle. But that didn't explain why he fed my familiars when I was too tied up with the Court or SMA to get home to them, or ensured a Napoli's pizza greeted me when I finally stumbled through the door after a long day of preparations, or mowed my lawn, fixed my dripping faucet, or stood guard outside between our houses, protecting me as much as his sisters when some of the townspeople had been riled up about the lockdown.

Or why, when Dr. Frazer and I finally had that dinner he'd promised at the beginning of summer, Rune's figure had been looming in the window of Fallsview Tavern the entire time.

He'd claimed he wanted to admire the view of the great falls and the town below from the outdoor patio, but I knew better. He was a dragon, for goddess's sake. He admired the view from the sky every chance he got. Besides, he tended to forget how similar I was to his sisters—part witch and part something else. My senses weren't quite as strong as theirs, but my inner hellhound could smell his jealousy from inside the restaurant.

That wasn't the only reason that Dr. Frazer and I had agreed to remain platonic—we were both dealing with a lot right now—but I had to admit, Rune was a big part of it for me. Not his jealousy, but the fact that I couldn't stop thinking about him. Not even when the sexy Scotsman was weaving an exciting and colorful tale about his time travels, his bare leg brushing against mine under the table.

I was probably a dumbass for choosing the edgy, Viking warrior over any chance with the blue-eyed, kilt-donning PhD and academic. But what can I say? I'd always had a thing for the bad boys over the pretty ones.

The thing was, though...Rune was also really damn beautiful.

"I have been told that before," he said, reminding me he was still by my side as we walked up to my house. "By a Saxon princess who probably should not have been saying such things to me, a pagan."

"Saying what?" I asked, confused.

His dimples popped when he smiled. "That I'm beautiful."

Shit. Had I said that out loud?

He winked before turning. "Go inside and get some rest, Addie Beaumont. You have a big day tomorrow."

As if.

CHAPTER 2

$\mathcal{T}$he sun rose at 6:59 a.m. In exactly twelve hours, it would set, and that was how long we had to put everything into place and do the spell that would lock Havenwood Falls and SMA away into their own little realms.

The day started with a giant-sized potion of hangover cure that had been distributed throughout the town. Some residents were still drunk and had to be sobered up first. Magic did not mix well with alcohol, and we had massive magic to do today.

For the sake of the younger children and in an attempt to maintain a level of normalcy, some Founders Day activities went on as usual, including the games and the Burger Bar-sponsored picnic in Town Square Park. The scent of grilling meat wafted through the air, and families gathered on blankets to share a meal, acting as though this wasn't possibly their last meal ever, even when that had to be weighing down everyone's private thoughts.

It certainly was mine, which was why I only picked at my food as I sat on the wraparound porch of Whisper Falls Inn. I preferred to do magic on an empty stomach anyway to keep my energy field light. As light as possible under the circumstances anyway.

I glanced over at Michaela across from me. She looked to be lost in thought as she stared through the bay window at the beautiful parlor inside. She'd put so much love into this inn when she'd restored it. Her family had built it the first year the Old Families settled in the canyon, but after her parents' deaths, it had fallen into disrepair. Aunt Luiza hadn't been able to keep up with it *and* take care of Aurelia and Gabe, especially as she'd been aging rapidly and approaching death's door herself. Five years ago, right around Spring Equinox, Michaela had returned to town, just in time, and the rest was history.

"Are you sure you're going to be okay?" I asked her, tilting my head toward the inn.

She tore her eyes from whatever she'd been staring at and turned them on me. "Of course. Why?"

"An inn with no guests…"

"Didn't I tell you? We have plans for that. First of all, when SMA portals open for breaks, there are going to be hundreds of students wanting out of that mountain for a few days or a few weeks at Christmastime, and unless they're from here, they can't go home. We have a place for them to stay. Plus, we've been brainstorming ideas with the Blackstones, and Gabe and Brice came up with a killer idea they got from some sci-fi show." Her eyes lit up. "You probably know it. You're a big *Star Wars* geek. Something called a Holly Deck?"

I rolled my eyes. "A holodeck, and that's from *Star Trek*."

"Right. That's what I said."

"You said *Star Wars*."

Her brows pinched together. "There's a difference?"

My mouth fell open. "How the hell have we been friends since *kindy-garten* and you don't know the difference between *Star Trek* and *Star Wars*!"

She pulled back, throwing her hands in the air. "Whoa! Sorry! Dude, you're really on edge over this big spell, aren't you?"

I gaped at her, speechless. She wasn't wrong, but neither was I.

She started laughing. "I'm just jerking your chain. I know the difference. Spock is Luke's father and all that." My brows shot up, and she laughed again. "Okay, okay. I'll stop before you curse me to watch all ninety movies again."

I snorted, shaking my head. "Just tell me about their idea."

"Okay, so some of us are perfectly happy with our lovely little town and rarely have a desire to leave it, but others like to travel and might go a little stir crazy, right? They need that change of scenery. So Brice and Gabe came up with the idea to glamour or enchant the rooms as different travel locations around the world. Guests can choose where they want to 'go,' and we can have a fae or witch create the illusion for them. They can go to Paris or Tokyo or sit on the beach in Maui or wherever their heart desires."

"Wow," I said. "That's really ingenious."

"Right? Their generation is so creative and resourceful."

"You're making us sound old." I wrinkled my nose, and she shrugged. "Do you think that will really keep you and Sindi busy enough to make you happy, though?"

Now she gave me a small smile and leaned in closer, dropping her voice. "It should for Sindi. I hope to be busy with…other things."

"Other things?" I whispered conspiratorially.

"We're finally going to fix up the Petran estate home in the Heights and then…" She paused for dramatic effect, and I pinched her leg. Smiling, she continued, "Xan and I think this might be a great time to bring the next generation of moroi into Havenwood Falls."

I pulled back to study her, my brows lifting. "Really?"

"Why not? If we survive tonight, we have to create hope for the future."

Dancing in my seat, I clapped my hands together. "I'm going to be an auntie!"

She snorted. "Not yet. But we're going to start trying soon."

"I hope not yet, considering how much you drank last night," I teased. "But trying is the fun part."

Her bright eyes twinkled as they slid over to the other end of the porch, where Rune sat with Sindi and Adrian, Xandru's younger brother. "And what about *your* fun? Did you finally decide to give in to the distraction?"

I shrugged but couldn't help my smile. "Maybe."

Rune polished off his last bite of burger at that moment and stood, his eyes scanning over the park across the street before he turned them on me. "Are you ready for your ride?"

I bit my lip, feeling a bit of heat creep up my neck as Michaela stifled a giggle that had her body shaking. Rune gave me that lopsided, cocky grin, knowing exactly what he'd done, before striding down the steps and across the lawn. He stopped at the gate to wait for me.

Xandru came out of the inn just as I was standing and wrapping up the remainder of the burger I'd shredded for the trash. He'd been on the phone with his sister Alina the whole time we'd been eating, which might have been the reason for Michaela's faraway look earlier—she'd been eavesdropping. I looked up at him expectantly, my eyes locking with his gray-green ones that were so much like his brother's. All the morois shared the color, but Xandru and Tase had the exact same shape, too. Xan only shook his dark head at my unspoken question.

"I'm sorry," Michaela said, taking my hands in hers and giving them a squeeze. "I know it's not what you were hoping to hear."

I exhaled a heavy breath.

"I'm fine," I said, pulling my hands free from Michaela's hold and waving a dismissive gesture in the air.

"Are you sure?" she asked.

"I pretty much knew that would be his decision. It's the right one."

"It's best for everyone," Xandru agreed. "Alina's going to stay in Chicago with him, so he won't be completely without family."

"That's definitely best for everyone," Michaela muttered. She wasn't exactly best friends with either Roca sister, but especially not Alina. Xandru didn't even like her much, but Alina and Tase had a decent relationship.

Glad he wouldn't be completely on his own, I nodded, although that one little crack in my heart that had yet to heal deepened a bit more. I wondered if it would ever heal now.

Tase's decision was final: he had chosen to stay out of Havenwood Falls. Xandru and his siblings had gone looking for him a couple of weeks ago, given permission to lift the memory spell so Tase could remember them and his home again, if only temporarily. So he'd been told everything. Remembered everything. Including me. Including his family. Yet, he wouldn't be coming home.

But it really was best for him, for his son, and for our town, especially now.

A little over a year ago, Rhian had learned from Zandra that my twin sister, Rachelle, hadn't died in the first Collector battle as we had all believed. Out of spite and jealousy and who knew what else after that fight, she'd cursed her own son, Carter, then sent him to live and bond with his father, Tase. As half moroi, a quarter witch, and a quarter hellhound, Carter's blood was a potentially deadly combination as it was, but she had to make it worse. She cast a spell that would trigger his vampire gene on his tenth birthday, and as long as he lived in Havenwood Falls, he'd kill and kill and kill until he became strigoi, an unstoppable monster—or the Court ended him first. But if he left Havenwood Falls, all would be fine. As long as Tase and Carter weren't with me, in this town, Rachelle would leave them alone. She didn't give a shit about her son. She just wanted to hurt us. And she'd won.

Carter turned ten this year.

So right after last Samhain, Tase and Carter left Havenwood Falls. Nobody, not even the Court, knew the full story. They might see Carter as too much of a threat, wherever he lived. Tase had promised me he would find Rachelle and force her to break the curse so they could return. Of course, once they were safe, the memory spell kicked in, and he didn't remember that promise or me or the rest of his family.

He'd met someone new, even bought a house with her. They would all be fine away from Havenwood Falls.

It *was* all for the best. I knew it deep down, but still part of me had hung on to a little bit of hope.

"Are you ready?" Rune's voice carried across the front lawn of the inn. He'd turned to look at me expectantly, the sun glinting on his light brown braids. He knew my story, most of it anyway, told over a few too many bottles of wine. He'd likely just heard Xandru's news, having dragon hearing and all. The cocky twinkle in his midnight blue eyes was gone, and now they regarded me with warmth and compassion…and something else that made my insides soften.

Maybe my heart would fully heal again after all, I thought as I hugged Michaela and Xandru and headed toward Rune. Toward a potential future.

Assuming we had one after tonight…

CHAPTER 3

*O*ur first stop was our individual homes for each of us to gather last-minute items to take to campus. I'd convinced Saundra to maintain her seat on the Court and as a High Priestess of the coven until next summer so I could see through the final year and graduation of our inaugural SMA class. With the sealed realms, that meant living on campus full-time now. Rune had agreed to temporarily fill in for one of our combat instructors who had decided not to return to SMA. His sisters insisted he take the position permanently—he could be a little overbearing, especially with not much else to do with his time—but he agreed only once he was sure the pocket realms were stable and they would be safe in his absence.

Quin would be moving back into my guest room to keep my house going and care for my plants. With her and Rune both gone, Arya and Liv could spread out a little more in the cramped two-bedroom cottage the four of them had been sharing. I'd been a little concerned about leaving the three blind witches to live on their own, but of course, they wouldn't be alone. They had Holly, and Holly had Sedona and Micah, who'd ensure they were all okay. And no doubt Marcus would provide anything they needed. There were many others around town who'd also look after them. That was the kind of town we had, especially now.

"Don't worry—I'm not leaving you four here," I assured Skywalker, who'd landed on my shoulder as soon as I entered the house and cawed in my ear the whole time I packed my last-minute items. "I need you to help with the spell, then we'll all go to campus together tonight." Princess Leia snuffed a plume of smoke out of her nostrils from her perch on my headboard. "I promise!"

Chewie carried in a package of bones with a Pyntz Butcher Shoppe label on it and dropped it in the box I was about to close up. The beasts were excited to go to campus with me. They'd never been before, always protecting the house in my absence. Only Kylo Ren seemed a little put-off by the whole idea, but he was a cat and would be put-off by anything that wasn't his idea. He also knew Quin was moving back in, and he adored her. But in the end, he'd stick with his siblings and me.

"I'll be back to get you. We're doing big magic tonight so rest up for now," I told them as I headed for the door.

Rune was already standing next to my jeep when I came out, but he rushed toward me to take the boxes I was carrying. We drove to the Falls Campus of the lower academy and the portals in silence. Nerves were starting to set in, and tension was growing. I could feel it in the streets as we drove, in the car, in the pit of my stomach.

"Are you afraid?" Rune asked after I parked in front of the gothic building of the lower school.

I'd started to reach to release my seatbelt, but my hand fell into my lap as I stared out the window and nodded. "A bit," I admitted. "Guess I'm not Viking material, am I?"

"I believe you would be a formidable shield maiden, Addie Beaumont. There is nothing wrong with fear. It's what you do with it that determines whether you're a Viking who fights...or a coward who sacrifices others for himself—or herself. You would die for this town."

I nodded again. "Absolutely."

"Why?"

I turned to look at him, my brows pinching together. "Why?" I asked stupidly. "What kind of question is that?"

He twisted in his seat, studying my face. "What is it that makes you love this town so much that you're willing to give up everything for it?"

"Um...all of it?" I looked back out the windshield, my gaze scanning over the lower school's campus and all the people coming and going with last-minute preparations. "It's my home. It's where everyone I love lives. Well, almost everyone. These people are more than my neighbors, co-workers, and friends. They're my family. Even the ones I don't like so much, like Roman Bishop. He's like the distant uncle who's an asshole but I know would have my back when it came down to it. And there's the newcomers who have never felt like they belonged anywhere until they came here. Who knows what would have happened to them if they didn't discover Havenwood Falls? If they never found home. People like Holly and your sisters."

I thought about Dingane, too, the Impundulu who'd been shooting lightning out of his ass when this all started and was one of our students. I was glad he and Cat Vega had decided to stay. I hadn't been so sure after their quite vocal blow-up right after the public Court meeting last month. Neither had a true home before coming here. I hoped they'd found one now.

There were so many others like them, students at SMA and residents in town.

"But it's not just the people," I continued. "It's the businesses I've been going to since I was born, their sameness comforting, and also the new ones that awaken the senses with fresh offerings. It's the schools I went to, the streets I learned to drive on, the parks we'd play in when we were little and sneak off to drink or make-out when we got older. It's the snow and the skiing in the winter, and the wildflowers in the summer, and the beautiful colors of fall, even the messy mud of snowmelt in the spring. It's all of the festivals and celebrations, even the weird and quirky ones...*especially* the weird and quirky ones."

My gaze lifted to Mt. Alexa behind the school, and I gestured at it. "I've painted those peaks so many times over the years that every jag and drop is committed to memory. The slopes around us are just as much home to me as the walls of my house or my mom's place. When I leave town and return, I feel like the mountains themselves welcome me home as I drive through them, the trees waving at me as I pass by. Our little box canyon surrounded by some of the tallest peaks in the state feels like we're nestled in Mother Gaia's arms, embraced with love and fiercely protected. I feel so safe here, like the mountains would never let true harm come to us. I guess I've always felt like we already live in our own little pocket realm." I shrugged and looked back at him. "It's my home. It's where my heart is."

I wondered if he regretted asking the question after that monologue, but when I looked back at him, his eyes gleamed with understanding and appreciation. "It is your reason for fighting. Until the death."

My lips tilted up as I nodded. "Whatever it takes."

"You would make a good Viking," he said before opening his door and climbing out of the jeep.

Students were starting to return to Halvard Campus from Founders Day activities and after saying farewells to their families. Some were staying back to help us with the town's spell, and the portals would remain open for us to return until midnight, then they'd be sealed until fall break at Samhain. Most students, though, would be on campus to help with the creation of the SMA realm. Since I couldn't be in two places at once, my cousin Gallad was taking point here with Rhian by his side.

After Rune and I dropped our things in our apartments, we left the faculty tower to find Gallad and Rhian, who walked us back to the portals.

"You're all set?" I asked them as we gathered in front of the Valkyrie statue in the center of the vestibule where the portals were. She would serve as the host for the school's pocket realm. If all went well, the campus would be embodied within her stone protection in a few short hours.

"We'll be fine, cuz," Gallad promised me, full confidence in his voice. "And if we aren't, well, Rhian here can bring us all back from the dead."

He said it as a joke, but our collective breaths caught as the three of us stared at each other with renewed fear. Memories of zombies attacking the campus the first year flashed in my mind—zombies accidentally created by Rhian's necromancy magic when she'd lost control. She was a goddess of the moon, but also of night and of death. It had been Hermod himself who, in the hopes of eliminating her magic, had twisted her power over death into a dark, ugly thing.

"Fuck," I breathed. "Didn't think of that. Rhian…if this magic is too big and people die and you can't control yourself…"

"I will do everything I can to not start the zombie apocalypse," she promised, forcing a smile that didn't reach her big blue eyes. "But if you don't want me here…"

Pushing a hand through my hair, I blew out a heavy breath and shook my head. "We need your magic. I guess if shit goes wrong, it will at least be contained under the mountain."

"Unless zombies can cross through the portals?" Gallad wondered out loud, rubbing at his jaw. His brow creased. "Will their tattoos still work?"

The hell if I knew.

"Gallad Augustine," I barked at him, "stop with the doomsday shit! This is bad enough as it is."

He let out a nervous chuckle, throwing his hands in the air. "Okay, okay. Like I said—we'll be fine. And if not, we won't know because we'll all be dead and hungering for brains."

Scowling at him, I threw my arms around him in a hug, then gave one to Rhian. Then with a prayer, I went back through the portals with Rune, pleading with the goddess that this wasn't the last time I'd see them.

"What are zombies?" Rune asked as we drove toward town square.

"Just one more thing to worry about," I muttered before giving him the quick and dirty explanation from pop culture as well as our personal experience with Rhian's version. "When I was young, I'd sometimes wonder what would happen if zombies invaded a town like ours. Like, if a vampire fought a zombie, could they turn each other? Would they become a new kind of nightmarish creature? Or could they give each other a final death? And would there be zombie wolves or mountain lions…or dragons?"

"You were a strange little girl."

"Tell me about it." I sighed. "Trust me, now I'm regretting ever sending those thoughts out into the universe."

The risks were piling up: The magic of the spell could be too powerful, harming or even killing some of our people or, worst case, destroying the entire town. The immense energy could light us up like a Christmas tree, practically screaming at Hermod across space, time, and dimensions to come get us. There would be a period of time where our wards will be weak and possibly altogether gone, making us more vulnerable than ever, right at the time that we were attracting Hermod's attention. If Hermod attacked when the wards and weapon were down, he'd not only destroy us but the rest of the world. But if we all died from the magic itself first, the zombie apocalypse could become reality, starting in a small town in Colorado and spreading to who knew where from here.

"Good times," I murmured as I pulled into a parking space behind City Hall.

The Court was gathered in their room in the basement, standing around a large snow globe. Inside was a duplicate of Teeny Weeny's 3D map of the town, an exact miniature replica of the town itself with every building, street, park, and body of water. The duplicate had been created by Teeny's daughter, and Hannah blew the glass globe around it. This was our talisman—the object that would hold our pocket realm.

"It's hard to wrap my mind around," Sheriff Kasun was saying when Rune and I walked in. "How our whole town will fit—in there."

"That's why it's called magic," Mathilde quipped. "You don't need to understand it. You only need to believe in it, just like you do in the moon."

"It's three-thirty," I said, striding up to them, trying to sound confident, though the knot in my stomach was growing. "Almost time. One more rundown before we begin?"

Michaela moved a little to the side to make room for me to join them. Rune stood right behind me, close enough that I could feel the heat of his body against my back. We were all gathered in closely, but his was the energy that could distract me. I forced myself to focus on making sure everyone knew their places and their roles.

Fifteen minutes later, we headed up the stairs as a group, united in spirit to do what it took to protect our town and this world and in faith that it could be done. Despite that pile of risks that seemed to rise higher than Mount Sousa.

"Ready for that ride?" Rune asked me with a teasing smile after the others had gone their ways.

Rubbing my hands on my jeans, I nodded. "Just one thing—how do I hold on?"

His grin widened. "Squeeze with your thighs. The harder the better."

And before I could respond, he shifted.

CHAPTER 4

I climbed onto Rune's dragon back, and despite his double-entendre laced suggestion, I searched for a way to hold on. There really wasn't anything but layers of scales along his back and neck, no convenient horns or anything in reach. When his large wings lifted and we began to rise into the air, I decided magic and my legs were my best bet.

Phase One began, which encompassed ensuring the weapon Zandra had given us was locked into place just in case Hermod attacked. Its magic would also help fortify the boundaries of the new realm. The SMA students had put it together at the end of the second semester of their first year, but once we knew it worked, the pieces had been re-collected and put away until needed. We'd hoped that time would never come, but here we were.

Rune first flew toward the top of Mt. Alexa, straight north of the fountain in Town Square Park to where the weapon piece that represented the element of Spirit had been placed once again. A small crowd of witches, fae, and others were gathered, signaling me that they were ready. Rune then banked left, doing a near U-turn in the sky as we headed south to the point where the weapon piece that channeled Fire had been placed. Another group gathered around it gave me the signal that they were ready, too. Next we flew to the east, then across town to the far west, then down to the southeast, then back to Mt. Alexa, each group's elemental piece in place and ready. Finally, we flew a full circle around the outskirts of town, completing the pentagram of energy that the weapon pieces created.

The final piece was at the fountain itself, which had once again been moved aside to access the boulder beneath it. Rune hovered over Town Square Park as Natalie Putnam stood with my grandmother holding the staff fist over fist. The clock tower on City Hall donged the first of four times, and with a nod to each other, they thrust the staff downward, into the boulder that held it.

On to Phase Two.

The fourth dong was the signal to everyone across town to begin, and I shot a blast of energy into the air that sprayed out like a firework, confirming that we were ready. With another flick of magic, I opened the doors to my house below us and to the north, and my familiars charged out and raced to meet us in town square. Then Rune dropped to the ground in front of City Hall, and I climbed off and hurried to join my mother and grandmother, members of the Court, and others around the boulder with the staff and the snow globe right next to it. We closed our eyes to focus, and together we chanted the spell. Others all over town, filling the streets, scattered in the forests, and gathered around the weapon pieces joined in.

Fae, deities, and mages of all kinds leant their magic. Shifters, vampires, and other supes allowed us to channel them, boosting our power. Familiars joined us, sharing their magic, too. Every single supernatural being who'd stayed behind contributed in any way they could.

The energy built quickly, zinging over my skin and through my flesh. What felt like the flutter of hundreds of butterflies erupted in my gut and spread outward into the collective field.

Getting the energy started was the easy part. Growing it to the level we needed and then keeping it there until the spell was complete were the challenges.

We pulled from the Earth, from the Water, from the Air, from the Fire of the sun. We continued chanting, weaving the energy together to surround our town and the mountains and forests beyond to the edge of the wards, creating a shell around us.

We built and we built and we built.

The energy became harder to hold, difficult to contain. I could hear grunts and moans from around me, but kept my eyes closed, focusing.

The crown of my head began to pulse, the beginnings of a headache forming from the energy's pressure.

The clock let out five gongs. Two hours until sunset.

We continued chanting, weaving the spell, building the power. My head felt like it was going to implode from the pressure. Sobs, moans, and wails filled the air as the magic began to fight against us.

Six gongs.

One more hour.

A scream tore through the air, and my eyes popped open to see Patty Parker collapse to the ground on the far side of the circle from me, her hands gripped around her head. Glancing around the circle, I noticed blood seeping from noses and eyes and ears.

Then Michaela cried out, and my heart stopped as she dropped to the ground, still as death.

"Keep going!" I shouted through sobs at seeing my best friend's still form as other bodies fell.

I lost track of time. The sun was low to the west. Sunset was almost here. Were we going to make it?

Just as I dared to think that, Phase Three began.

All of the magical energy in the town, in the falls, in the people, and the ground below was gathered into the spell. The staff began to shake in the boulder. The ground itself quaked under our feet, causing many to lose balance.

Then I physically felt the whoosh when the wards dropped.

It felt like someone had whipped off our collective coat in the middle of winter, and we stood naked in the midst of a blizzard, completely bare to the elements. I'd never felt more vulnerable in my life.

More screams rent the air. More of our people began dropping, unconscious or dead, I didn't know.

Out of the corner of my eye, I saw a flash of light soar over the top of Mount Sousa. I looked up to see what looked like comets or fireballs shooting toward our town.

"Hold it!" I yelled again as panic began rippling through those of us still standing. I could feel it building in my own chest, and I forced it down, even as I felt thick wetness leak from my nose and eyes. A tickle from my ears. I could smell the iron of blood.

"Hold it!" Grandmother echoed me as those fireballs grew in the sky above us, approaching quickly.

What were they? Had we summoned a meteor storm and sentenced the world to an immediate end? Or were they something from Hermod as he turned his attention on us?

"Hold it!" Roman's voice now boomed across town square and through the streets as though he'd used an amplifying spell.

The chanting grew louder as we gave everything we had to hold the power. A thrum pulsed through the town, as though the Earth's heart beat to the rhythm and cadence of our words. The ground shook again, harder this time. Something hot hit my arm, making my skin sizzle, and I wasn't the only one who yelped. Sparks from the sky were landing on us, the fireballs growing ever closer.

Then the clock struck the first gong of seven.

Phase Four.

"NOW!" I shouted.

At once, our words changed. I could barely breathe as I drew on the energy we'd built, my chant coming out in pants as we weaved the spell to create the pocket realm. The magic expanded as the volume built, the words echoing off the mountains.

And just as the first fireball was about to hit the clock tower before the final gong, there was a huge WHOOSH followed by a big BANG.

It felt like an explosion rocked our world, and I fell to the ground, hitting my head on the side of the misaligned fountain.

Everything went dark.

And silent.

When I'd been young and training, Grandmother had sent me to Bali to learn sensory deprivation. I'd done the float tanks before, but she'd wanted me to learn how to create it myself, because the loss of our physical world senses allowed our inner world senses—our psychic abilities and connection to the spirit realm—to open up.

I felt like I'd just done that.

No light. No sound. No smells. No feeling. Nothing.

As though everything had ceased to exist at all.

But only for a moment.

Light returned first, followed by sounds. Then the whole world crashed over me as I opened my eyes and took it all in.

No, not the *whole* world.

Just Havenwood Falls.

I wasn't sure *how* I knew, but I knew we had done it.

I glanced over to where the snow globe had been when we started. It was gone—but not gone. It surrounded us.

Then I saw Michaela, and on my hands and knees, I lurched toward her.

"Kales!" I shrieked, grabbing her body and turning her over. My heart flew into my throat when I took in her gray complexion, dried blood crusted under her closed eyes. Her life force had been drained. "Oh, goddess, no. Kales, no."

Xandru dropped next to me, gathering her into his arms and rocking as he held her against his chest.

"Michaela," he whispered, a plea in his voice, "you can't go yet. You promised you'd never leave me again!"

I glanced around as people rushed to other bodies scattered around the park, my head shaking back and forth in denial. We knew there were risks. We knew there would be consequences. But knowing didn't make it any easier to accept.

A groan came from beside me, and my head swiveled to see Xandru's shoulders drop. A breath of relief whooshed out of him. "Kales."

"Xan?" she whispered, and I couldn't help the cry that escaped me. "Bratty Addie?" My best friend's eyelids fluttered before opening, the strange yet beautiful eyes staring up at her husband first and then cutting over to me. She pushed herself up and looked at me in shock. "Is Addie Beaumont fucking crying?"

Laughing, I threw myself at her, snatching her out of Xandru's arms and into my own.

"Just allergies," I said as I squeezed her tightly.

My watery eyes lifted upward, and I mouthed a thank-you to the goddess, the Universe, whoever was there. As though in reply, the sky seemed to brighten a little with streaks of orange, peach, and pink, and the clouds were gilded in gold as the top of the sun sank behind Miles Mountain. It was possibly the most gorgeous sunset over my beautiful little town that I'd ever seen.

CHAPTER 5

*L*ast night's party was little more than a child's birthday compared to the one going on now.

As soon as we realized we'd accomplished our goal, Natalie had sprinted for SMA and the portals, with other students right on her heels. Even while inspecting the bodies that had fallen during the spell, I hadn't been able to release my breath fully until their return. We hadn't lost anyone, and only a few had sustained injuries, none of them lasting. The last bit of light in the west disappeared and the stars shone in the night sky by the time the students returned, and it wasn't just them. They brought the entire student body back—we could hear their jovial cheers long before we saw the first of the crowd rushing down Stuart Street.

"It took a bit longer than usual for the portals to activate," Natalie had explained once she found me. "I was about to lose my shit at first. But then one by one, they opened and let us through. It's definitely... different going through them. It's definitely changed."

"So it worked. Both realms worked," I said with a relieved grin. I turned to Rune, and without thinking, I threw my arms around his neck. "Because of you. None of this would have happened if not for you and your sisters finding Holly. If you hadn't come into our lives..."

He returned my smile, and my panties just might have melted when those dimples came out. He began to lean in, and I braced myself for our first kiss when we heard the clearing of a throat next to us.

"What am I? Chopped zombie brains?" Rhian asked, her arms crossed over her chest and one eyebrow cocked.

Releasing Rune, I spun and swallowed her tiny body in a tight hold. "Thank you, thank you, thank you!"

Then remembering who I was hugging, I immediately let go and stepped back, dropping my head in respect. She'd become such a good friend, sometimes it was easy to forget she was a goddess.

"Oh, stop that," she said, throwing her thin arms around me. "When Addie Beaumont hugs someone, I know it means something."

True. I hadn't cried, embraced others, or even grinned this much in a long time, possibly since middle school.

Someone passed me a drink, and the rest of the night became a blur.

Unlike last night, though, we weren't able to party all night long. At least, those of us returning to SMA weren't. Life was back to normal and classes in full swing tomorrow morning. It was hard to say another round of goodbyes, although at least this time we knew we'd see each other again.

"You have my full faith that you'll take good care of those students," Saundra said as she hugged me. "I know I've always had high expectations for you, Adelaide, but only because I've always known your potential." She pulled back and gripped my chin like she used to do when I was a child trying to learn her complicated spells. "And not once have you ever disappointed me. In fact, you have turned out even greater than I ever imagined. You are so much more than a beautiful young lady. You are a true leader, a talented witch, and an inspiration to us all. When you are ready, my seat is yours."

I swiped at the tears spilling down my cheeks. "Thank you, Grandmother. That means so much, but—"

"I know. Not yet, but that is *your* choice. You are definitely ready for the position in every way possible. The town will be blessed to have someone like you on the Court."

Choked up on tears, I gave her another hug, then I said goodbye to my mom, to the witch-sisters, and to Michaela and Xandru, Sindi and Aidan, and Gabe. Aurelia had already headed back to campus. I limited my farewells to them, though, otherwise I'd miss the closing of the portals because it'd take too long to get to everyone. As I'd told Rune, the whole town was family to me.

"Have fun with your baby-making," I whispered to Michaela with one last hug.

"Have fun with your own distraction," she said, glancing at Rune before winking at me.

He and I headed toward campus, and I hadn't realized how close we were to midnight until we reached the portals and everyone else had already gone through. Only my familiars were there, waiting on us.

"You ready to start this new life?" I asked the gorgeous Viking warrior next to me.

He gave me a curt nod, and after inhaling a deep breath, I was about to step through the swirling energy of the portal.

"No, not yet." His large hand wrapped around my wrist, and he tugged me into him. His free hand lifted to my face and slid over my jaw until his fingers cupped the side of my head. He leaned in, tilting me back, and our eyes locked for a long moment. His searched mine, asking permission, and my only answer was a flick of my tongue to wet my lips. Then his mouth crashed against mine.

The kiss was everything I'd imagined it to be and so much more. He really was going to be one hell of a distraction this year. And maybe many more beyond.

The first chime of midnight had us jumping apart, then laughing together.

"We better go," I said. "We can finish this over there."

Grinning with all those dimples on full display, he nodded. "I'm ready now for this new life...with you, Addie Beaumont."

EPILOGUE

The goddess kicked off one half-burnt boot and then the other, pushing them to the side of the doorway. She held tightly to the bundle in her arms, her leather jacket wrapped around a precious object inside, and took a moment to appreciate the Valkyrie statue and the new energy within it. Then she limped barefoot down the path, across the bridge, and into the courtyard. The large cavern under the mountain was deadly silent, which she welcomed after the day she'd had. She'd made it home, to one of her safest places across the multiverse, the one she'd made eons ago before humans ever found this private corner of their world. The one Hermod had yet to find.

Though he'd come too damn close today.

Every part of her body hurt with blisters and bruises, every injury taking its time to heal. She didn't have to look in a mirror to know half her hair was singed to the scalp and the blonde locks that remained were black with soot. She'd take care of all that later.

First, she had something precious to tend to.

As she entered the largest structure, she turned to the right and strode for the artifact room. Shelves upon shelves of strange objects from near and far greeted her. Her collection. She glanced down at the leather bundle she held.

"No, this won't do. This one is special."

She climbed the steps up three levels, then made her way to her private office. Placing the ball of leather on her desk, she plopped into her chair with a sigh. She thought she could fall into a deep sleep right then and there. But first things first.

Unwrapping the leather jacket, she lifted the glass orb out and carefully set it on the desk, leaning to stare into it. She'd found it in the middle of the box canyon outside the mountain, resting in a field of wildflowers. Although civilization or any sign of human life was more than sixty miles away, she knew exactly what it was, how it had come to be.

"What I have done for you," she murmured, peering in as though she expected to see the miniature town inside come to life.

The battle had been brutal. But she'd survived. Unfortunately, so had Hermod.

She'd been so damn tempted to let the town's spell fail, allow him to attack, and force the town to use the weapon against him. The weapon she'd given them precisely for that purpose. After all, they'd drawn his attention to them, to this world, to one of her last safe havens left across all realms and dimensions. Part of her thought they deserved to have to finish the fight they'd unknowingly started. And finish that spiteful, hateful bastard once and for all. She couldn't do it by herself or even with several of her Vanir sisters.

That little town, though—they could have made the difference. They had the heart and the love for each other and their world that was necessary to power the weapon. She knew, because she'd once been a part of that town, when they'd known her as Kialah.

But it was that heart and love that had kept her from making them use it.

Rhiannon had been the one to convince her. If not her, Elsmed probably would have, if given the chance. Rhian, as she preferred to be called these days, had fallen for the school and the town as soon as she'd arrived. She'd been so angry when she'd learned what Zandra had done to them.

"They need to learn to stand together and fight him!" Zandra had said. "They have what it takes to end him! You want it just as much as I do."

Rhian shook her head. "But at what cost? They've already lost too many to your antics. Don't make them do this."

She'd reminded Zandra of why she herself had fallen in love with the people of the town. Why she'd made a new home for herself on the mountainside so she could eventually give the estate under the mountain to them for their school. Why they didn't deserve the destruction Hermod would bring to them and their world, even if they did eventually kill him.

So when the power of the spell built and Hermod turned his attention on this world, Zandra had gone after him all on her own. She couldn't finish him, but she could distract him and send him off in another direction in a completely different dimension. He'd nearly killed her, but she'd accomplished her mission and made it back alive.

"You'll need to give me time to make sure he's truly turned away from here for good. The world I sent him to is also equipped to end him, but I just don't know if they have the heart for it. Not like you. Only time will tell." She picked up the snow globe, peering inside it again. Then she turned around and placed it on the highest shelf. "For now, you will sit up here, Havenwood Falls."

Perhaps someday in the future, she thought, she could take it down and bring the town and its people into this world again.

Perhaps...